The Curate's Wife

E. H. YOUNG

With a New Introduction by Sally Beauman

Virago

Published by VIRAGO PRESS Limited 1985
41 William IV Street, London WC2N 4DB

First published in Great Britain by Jonathan Cape 1934
Virago edition offset from Cape 1950 edition

Copyright © E. H. Young 1934

Introduction copyright © Sally Beauman 1985

British Library Cataloguing in Publication Data
Young, E. H.
     The curate's wife.—(Virago modern classics)
     I. Title
     823'.912[F]   PR6047.046/
     ISBN 0-86068-446-6

Printed in Finland by Werner Söderström Oy,
a member of Finnprint

All the characters and events
in this book are imaginary

THE CURATE'S WIFE is, as its title suggests, a study of marriage. It begins on a note of happiness: it is early days in this marriage, in fact the couple's first morning in their new house. The scene is of cheerful domesticity. The cistern has been gurgling all night; Dahlia awakes to discover that her curate husband, Cecil Sproat, has slipped out of bed and gone downstairs to make her tea. She listens anxiously for the sound of breaking china; she gets out of bed to look out of the window and then quickly back into it when she hears Cecil returning with the tray. She has known him for eight months only, been married to him for three weeks, she still wanders 'round him in circles, like a tethered dog exploring its new ground, liking it well, and anxious to respond to its owner's complete satisfaction'. But she knows him well enough already to understand that this moment is important to him, that he has planned a surprise, and so—in bed once more—accepts the tea with suitable surprise and pleasure.

It is a moment of the gentlest and most understandable duplicity—husband and wife are in happy accord. But it will not continue so, as the image of the tethered dog suggests. This marriage has a long testing ahead of it, Dahlia's duplicity will not continue so amiable, and Cecil's devotion will not always be the simple and straightforward affair it is now. For Dahlia has become the curate's wife, her own identity superseded, taken over, by his; she has to come to terms with what it means to be a wife. And Cecil—who has given considerable and earnest thought to what it means to be a curate, has to ponder—somewhat to his surprise—what it means to be a husband. Particularly since—and this is even more surprising—he discovers that his marital and his ecclesiastic roles overlap.

We are, in short, on territory familiar to readers of E. H. Young's earlier novels, particularly *Miss Mole*, at that nexus where questions of love, religion and morality intersect. We will concentrate on a man for whom religion is a matter of faith, but above all of clearly defined codes and creeds, and a woman, without faith, who trusts in the instincts of a generous heart, love between human beings being the only ethic to which she attaches much importance. It is the cerebral versus the instinctual approach; the masculine versus the feminine. It recurs, again and again, in E. H. Young's work, but never more forcefully than here, where we move to that traditional prop and mainstay of the Christian church—the Christian marriage.

The Curate's Wife stands as an independent novel, and can be read as such, but in fact it is a sequel, so closely interwoven as to be almost a second volume, of a novel E. H. Young wrote some two years earlier, *Jenny Wren*. Dahlia, then unmarried, appears in that novel, although it concentrates its main attention on her sister Jenny, re-introduced some halfway through this book. Both novels share roughly the same location—the Clifton area of the city of Bristol, here referred to as Radstowe—but in *The Curate's Wife*, the territory of the action has been shifted slightly but tellingly. In *Jenny Wren* both sisters lived with their mother, Louisa Rendall, in her recently acquired boarding house overlooking the Avon Gorge. By the time this novel begins, their circumstances have changed. Louisa, a simple and warm-hearted countrywoman, who married out of her class when she wed Jenny and Dahlia's gentleman father, has married again. Her new husband was once her lover, and now farms land the other side of the river. Her marriage, prompted by a muddled attempt to make herself respectable, and so to better the marital prospects of Jenny, has proved, unexpectedly, to bring her contentment.

So, in a novel that will investigate the nature of marriage, we begin with glimpses of two other marriages: Louisa's first marriage to Sidney Rendall, which had been a deeply unhappy one, its memories scarring both of her daughters. And her new marriage, in which, discovering she can get along with Thomas Grimshaw, and that her old farming expertise has returned and is now useful, Louisa is happy because she can at last be herself.

But, if we are to examine marriage, we are also to examine the equally perplexing nature of romance. In their former lives, in the attic bedroom of their mother's boarding house, both Jenny and Dahlia dreamed—they were very young—of romance, of (as Dahlia remembers) 'dark rapture under the heavy trees, and of a lover quite different from the curate who had stopped to speak to her and walked soberly with her round the hill above the river'.

vii

Jenny, in the previous novel, has pursued romance inexorably, in the desirable shape of Cyril Merriman, heir to the Merriman estates, and has made the bitter discovery that the shallow Mr Merriman, unlike her own father, is horrified by the idea of marrying outside his class, and has no intention of having a woman like Louisa for his mother-in-law.

Dahlia has taken a very different course. She has married her rather plain curate (both sisters are usually over-susceptible to good looks) in spite of the fact that she is not in love. It is a discovery that has deeply shocked the more romantic Jenny, and their conversation on the subject at the end of *Jenny Wren*, has reverberations that continue throughout this novel:

> 'Do you love him?'
> 'No,' Dahlia said coolly, 'but I'm going to. I think it's best to be friends first.'
> 'It isn't romantic.'
> 'It will be romantic afterwards.'
> 'After what?'
> 'When I've married him,' Dahlia said.

She then sounds, and is, quite confident. But, in this novel, her confidence is to falter. When she meets the dramatic Simon Tothill, and for the first time in her cramped life spends time with people her own age, going for drives, going to parties—'having fun', as she defends it to her irritated and somewhat jealous husband—she discovers that the idea of romantic love is less easily shaken off than she had supposed. It still tugs at her. Simon Tothill is handsome and dashing and her husband is not; she herself is twenty-one and has never been 'in love'. The fact that she has ridiculed that sensation to her sister does not, she discovers, make herself immune to it.

And so, very carefully and delicately E. H. Young begins to weave the strands together: parental devotion; sisterly affection; friendship; marital accord; Christian charity; romance: all these emotions are, at different times, described by that one useful all purpose word 'love'. 'Love' is used as an excuse for emotional blackmail; it is adopted as a term to describe monstrous and stifling possessiveness; it is, above all, used as a weapon in a constant series of power games played out in the novel between husbands and wives, and between parents and children. It is also, and very movingly, seen as a free and regenerative force: but those moments of insight and clarity come to the characters here, as in life, only infrequently.

The novel focuses on the marriage of Cecil and Dahlia, over a period in which quiet but multitudinous changes take place in their relationship and in their characters. Yet its timespan is very short. It begins in September; it closes just after Christmas, a season that has chiefly been remarkable for its absence of good will. Perhaps because she was aware that the passage of just three months confined her somewhat when her subject was a union for life, E. H. Young balances her portrait of the curate's marriage with a portrait also of his vicar's, the redoubtable, lazy, and very engaging Mr Doubleday. Her plot, which is slight, weaves back and forth between the two households, enabling her to contrast two marriages, one newly embarked upon, the other having settled into a pattern of domination and surrender established over thirty years. It also gives her free rein with her considerable satiric gifts, and the portraits of both Mr Doubleday and his horrendous wife, are masterly.

In the Doubleday's marriage the peace Mr Doubleday devoutly seeks has been achieved by reversing the stereotypic husband-and-wife roles. Mrs Doubleday, in her tall ugly hats, is a rude, interfering, and unkind woman, proud of her position in the parish, snobbish about her descent, and unwaveringly certain of her essential rightness in all matters. She has always confused bourgeois respectablity of the stuffiest kind with Christian morality, and her husband, whose own views on the matter are a great deal more liberal, not to say Christian, has avoided confrontation, on that issue and on every other. Mrs Doubleday rules the roost; her husband skulks in his study before a warm fire, pretending to busy himself with parish affairs, but in fact consoling himself with detective novels which he hides under his armchair cushions. Both Dahlia and Cecil are fond of Mr Doubleday, and both dislike Mrs Doubleday cordially. Indeed, we first see that Cecil has mettle when he risks confrontation with Mrs Doubleday over her appalling rudeness to his wife.

The Doubledays have a son, Reginald, who has been working abroad and is about to return home. Reginald is the great and secret passion of his mother's life, and it is here, in her treatment of this theme, that E. H. Young's insight deepens, so that Mrs Doubleday is rescued from caricature; she becomes at once a comic and a tragic figure. Her obsession with her son, it is clear, stems from a monstrous and bitter egotism. She cannot bear to share him in any way with her husband, and deludes herself into believing that Reginald has no contact with his father. It is Reginald's imminent arrival, and Mrs Doubleday's unconscious fears of all attractive young women—one of whom might one day take him away from her—that provokes her first, and as it happens, her last major quarrel with her husband. In that quarrel she goes too far, and says too much: in a stroke, her domination of her husband is broken. Quite quietly, not very dramatically, but nonethe less unmistakably, Mr Doubleday begins to assert himself, and his wife, suddenly deprived of the role she has assumed for thirty years, begins slowly and pathetically to crumble. The arrival of her son, the cue for some of the most economic and telling scenes in the novel, completes her bitter and belated education.

This sad, and also very funny, story of the Doubledays in which marriage, devoid of all physical love, has declined into a domestic *détente*, is used throughout the novel in counterpoint to the story of Dahlia and Cecil. To this end they too could come, as they both gradually realise; to avoid that fate it is neccessary for them both to change.

It would have been easy, of course, for E. H. Young to have taken authorial sides, and to have weighted her case, as a lesser novelist might have done. But she does not. It is one of the quiet triumphs of the book that both the man's case and the woman's is presented with equal sympathy and with equal insight. Dahlia's virtues—her generosity of spirit, her honesty and freedom from cant, are balanced by Cecil's intellectual rigour, capacity for self-criticism and sense of duty. Her vices—of which frivolity and insensitivity are the worst—are balanced by his earnestness, his tendency, which he himself admits, to be a prig.

E. H. Young once confessed to an interviewer that she had a taste for melodrama in the theatre, which is interesting, because melodrama is almost entirely absent from her own writing. The process of adjustment, of alienation, reconciliation and alienation again which takes place within the curate's marriage, is conveyed with the most delicate of touches, and repays close reading. There are no screaming marital rows; no violent fights. At one point Dahlia removes her wedding ring, and lies on the extreme edge of the marital bed, seething with rage that she has to suffer Cecil's physical proximity, but this is exceptional. There is a scene, later in the novel, where Cecil finally rounds on his wife and upbraids her; significantly, we learn of it, but do not witness it. What we are shown, rather, is the minutiae of misunderstandings, the single sentences and the silences that, in a marriage, have such destructive accumulative force.

The central area of contention, for Dahlia and Cecil as well as for the vicar and his wife, is power. Compared to Mrs Doubleday, Cecil is the gentlest of tyrants, but he has tyrannical leanings, nonetheless. In marrying Dahlia he has given her a role in life; she is his wife, and he feels obscurely betrayed when she reveals an independence of mind. Dahlia bitterly resents this:

Life would be much simpler with her will, her thoughts, and her footsteps following Cecil's, but how very dull this docility would be, how bad for both of them! She was as little willing to face a future of constant sparring, and, to her common sense, it seemed ridiculous that they could not agree to differ and find, perhaps, that they could love each other with a lasting excitement because parts of each other were just out of reach. That was what she had expected of marriage, it was what happened during her short engagement, what ought to continue, in spite of a wedding ring, and in a little burst of temper, she removed that ring, with a vicious pull, and sent it spinning across the floor.

This issue, common to so many marriages, continues to perplex both curate and wife for most of the novel—it is helped neither by Dahlia's impatience nor Cecil's pride. On this occasion, however, it is provoked by the misfortunes of one of his parishioners—over which (the girl is unmarried and pregnant) Cecil has behaved with a singularly callow and punitive righteousness. He is roundly taken to task by the girl's mother; to his horror he discovers that Dahlia too takes her side. It is one of the key scenes in the novel, and is but one example (there are many more), of the skill with which E. H. Young interweaves her themes. At issue is not simply a difference of viewpoints, as Dahlia later argues to herself before discarding her ring, but something much deeper. Cecil is a prude in sexual matters; sexual indulgence, except within the sanctity of marriage, is the sin he finds it most impossible to understand or to forgive. Dahlia, aware of that censure, which applies, of course, to her own mother's past conduct, feels none of his repugnance. When she pleads on behalf of the girl in question, she is also pleading on behalf of herself, and her argument is a compound one: it is a plea for understanding, for moral largesse and for compassion. Cecil's answer—it is not immediate—will affect his standing not just as a man and a husband, but also as a man of the church. Here, as in *Miss Mole*, another Young novel with a strongly religious background, roles are reversed: it is the Minister, not the sinner, that needs help, and instruction.

This question, of the nature of true morality and its obfuscation by rigid creeds and conventions, is one that has also been posed in *Jenny Wren*; it recurs in all E. H. Young's novels. Since she herself defied convention, living with a married man from the age of thirty-eight until her death in 1949, it was obviously an issue which affected her daily, and was central to her thinking.* This novel, published in 1934, written when she was in her early fifties, is her most complex and most honest exploration of the subject. It is rivalled most closely by *Miss Mole*, a technically more experimental and innovative novel than this. But *The Curate's Wife*, although totally traditional in form, can take the exploration further, mainly because the courtship element of the narrative has been relegated to the subplot, and so, at a stroke, Young has freed herself from the speculative problems that bedevil any novel ending with a proposal.

She has freed herself, in fact, to do fully what she does best—to examine moral issues within the context of a wittily and acidly observed provincial society. Though that society has changed in the years since 1934, the fundamental questions she raises are as relevant today as when Young wrote. She was a feminist, of course; it is implicit in everything she wrote. And she was a feminist in what is,

*A fuller account of E. H. Young's life is given in the introduction to the Virago editions of *Miss Mole* and *Jenny Wren*.

perhaps, its purest sense: she believed in and celebrated the virtues of women—especially those virtues that made them different from men.

So, even at the end of this novel, which is graceful, she has the honesty to leave one central question unanswered, still in the air despite all apparent resolution. It is a question that has recurred throughout the book. Not—will this man and this woman stay together? But—should they?

Sally Beauman, London, 1984

ON a morning in September, the first morning in the house he was to share with Dahlia, the Rev. Cecil Sproat woke early and, resisting the temptation to stay in bed and consider the happy future, to watch Dahlia in her pretty sleeping posture, her bright hair ruffled on the pillow, he rose and went quietly from the room, determined to begin the day with an act of service and wake Dahlia with a pleasant tinkling of teacups. Dahlia, however, was awake already, though her eyes were shut. She had been awake for a long time, planning her work of putting the house to rights and waiting patiently for the moment when Cecil would wake and steal out to make the tea. She had been prepared, the night before, for this kindness, when he made unnatural, though apparently careless inquiries about the tea-caddy, and she would not disappoint him by obeying her feminine impulse to follow him and hasten a simple process which, unaided, would be complicated and slow. She would wake in grateful surprise at the right moment, for she was a wise young woman and though she was an honest one she set no value on a painful truthfulness in small matters, so she kept her eyes shut and listened a little anxiously for sounds of breaking crockery. It would grieve her to have one of her new cups and saucers broken, for these were part of her mother's wedding gift, chosen with earnestness and the desire to find, in china, some likeness to her view of Dahlia, and the breakfast service was gay with birds and flowers. 'I'll like to think of you, using these of a morning when the sun's shining,' she had said.

Dahlia remembered those words and, forgetting her semblance of sleep, she went to the window and parted the curtains. There was no sunshine yet, though there was the promise of it in a blue mist on The Green. It was like water that had risen silently in the night and the branches of the old trees seemed to be looking down at it in a grave hope of seeing themselves reflected there.

The scene was familiar to Dahlia, for her marriage had not taken her many yards from her late home and she could see the curving upper end of Beulah Mount on the other side of The Green. On her left hand, the church spire topped the trees and, when all the leaves had fallen, the chimneys of the Vicarage would be in sight. At the prospect of this privilege, Dahlia smiled. The last thing she had expected was to marry a curate but, having done so, there was some compensation in a vicar who amused her and a vicar's wife who could not be amused, but she only gave the pair a passing thought. She was wondering if her mother, no doubt already astir in the farm on the other side of the bridge, remembered that this was Dahlia's first morning in her new home, and then, further south and west, there was her sister Jenny, no doubt still in her bed and most unlikely, if she were awake, to be thinking of anything but her own day. And now Dahlia sighed in contrition for having given these two so little of her attention during the last weeks. But here was The Green with the intersecting paths on which the three of them had walked so often; there was the church where she had gone to establish the family's respectability and had found Cecil Sproat; hidden by rising ground was the bridge across which Jenny had passed in happiness and grief, towards which she had looked for the lover who did not come; beyond it was the country of her mother's voluntary banishment, and Dahlia was assailed by a sense of her responsibilities and the lasting, indissoluble nature of affection rooted in common interests and memories and blood. She had known Cecil Sproat for eight months or

8

less, she had been married to him for three weeks and guiltily but frankly, she faced the fact that, at present, Jenny's discontent or her mother's sense of exile were harder for her to bear than any possible sorrow he might suffer. She knew Jenny's mind, she knew her mother's and, not uncritically, her being seemed to be intertwined with each of theirs, but it was a long cord that attached her to Cecil Sproat; she wandered round him in circles, like a young tethered dog exploring its new ground, liking it very well and anxious to respond to its owner's complete satisfaction, but always a little watchful, a little shy of approach, behind an honest happiness. She thought it was a good thing to begin cautiously, to expect some disillusionments. There was always the chance that the future would be even better than she hoped and Cecil seemed to her a little pathetic in his certainty of enduring bliss. He was a good deal older and less naturally sanguine than she was, but she had passed her early days in the shadow of an unhappy marriage and she had too much imagination to believe that she and Cecil were sure to avoid disenchantment, too much sense not to return to bed when she heard him on the stairs. She had a gift for preserving the good moment without hampering it with the past or spoiling it with doubts of the future, and this was a very good moment. His manner was satisfactory. If he was pleased with himself, he concealed his state; but she knew he was pleased with her and secretly she applauded his gravity and restraint as he put down the tray.

'Just what I wanted,' she sighed, smiling at him over the pretty cup, but she was not referring to the tea.

'I think there's something wrong with the cistern,' he said.

'I know there is. It's been twittering all night, but we'll get used to it.'

'There are such things as plumbers.'

'And bills,' Dahlia said. 'Besides, we must leave the

9

cistern until Mrs. Doubleday has inspected the house. She would like to tell me it needs attention. It's a very shabby house,' Dahlia said, looking at the faded wallpaper, 'and that will please her, but she doesn't really want to be pleased, she wants to disapprove, so we'll let her tell us about the cistern.'

'You're determined not to like Mrs. Doubleday.'

'I'm determined to laugh at her, but I'm afraid I may get fond of her, it's so hard not to get fond of people, and then I shan't have nearly so much fun. I know life isn't fun,' she said, forestalling him. 'I know that very well. That's why we have to make it for ourselves.'

'But not, perhaps, out of other people.'

With her head on one side, Dahlia studied him. 'If you hadn't been so kind about the tea and if you didn't look so nice in your pyjamas — I do wish you could wear them in church — I might be rather cross with you,' she said. 'I don't see how one can get fun in any other way. Oh dear! What would have happened to you if you'd married a good earnest girl? I do believe I'm your salvation. Under God, of course,' she added hastily.

'So do I,' said Mr. Sproat solemnly, wisely ignoring the flippancy which, indeed, did not trouble him. It was easy to pay lip service to charitableness and reverent speech; it was a habit out of which he was willing to be shaken, and his thoughts went back to a night when, desiring Dahlia, he had seen her gay sanity as the thing he needed. 'So do I,' he repeated.

'And you're mine,' she said lightly.

He shook his head, but she was remembering another night in summer, when she sat on the doorstep in Beulah Mount and dreamt of dark rapture under the heavy trees and of a lover quite different from the curate who had stopped to speak to her and walked soberly with her round the hill above the river.

'All the same,' she said, 'I'm going to be a little awkward for you in a worldly sense. I know that.'

'Not awkward at all,' he said stoutly.

'Oh yes, I am, but I'm rather reckoning on Mrs. Doubleday for getting rid of us. She has a lot of influential relatives, at least she says so, and if she disapproves enough she'll send us where we can worry some of them, because she probably disapproves of them, too. Then, perhaps, you'll get your vicarage in the country.'

'And then I shall think I oughtn't to have it.'

'Oh,' she reassured him, 'there's heaps of wickedness in the country. There'll be plenty to do.'

He had been looking down but now he looked up, and showed her the eyes which Jenny had once said were the colour of mud with the sun shining on it. 'I wish I knew what wickedness is,' he said in a puzzled tone.

She had the confidence of her years. 'I'll tell you one thing that it isn't,' she said. 'It isn't being happy and doing what you like — not necessarily. Jenny and I used to wonder why you didn't live with lepers and we decided it must be because you'd enjoy it. But you'll have a real cross with a wife whose mother used to take in lodgers.'

'Absurd!' said Mr. Sproat and he went downstairs at the sound of the postman's knock.

It was absurd, but it might be absurdly serious in Upper Radstowe where social distinctions were still marked, where the wholesale dealer was respected and the retailer scorned, and Dahlia's mother, married to a working farmer across the river, was possessed of a full-blown beauty which was like an affirmation of her suspected history and of a country accent most embarrassing to the Rev. Cecil Sproat, delightfully shocking to Mrs. Doubleday. Dahlia could laugh at the situation as it concerned herself; she felt no shame for her mother; Cecil had promised to feel none and he would try to keep that

11

promise, but frankness had always been Dahlia's chief weapon: it could disarm opponents, it could break down cankering reserves, and her mother, with her faults and her nobility was a fact to be faced if she was not to become an unmentionable shadow.

'Why do you talk like that?' Cecil complained when he returned.

'Just to get it over. Just to know where we are. And because I thought there might be a letter for me this morning and I see there is one.' She held out her hand for it. 'I didn't want you to be considerate and pretend you didn't know the handwriting. There's not the slightest need to feel sensitive for me.'

'I don't believe there's a speck of meanness in your character,' he said. 'I'm going to have my bath. You're far too good for me.'

'Oh, don't!' Dahlia begged, but she laughed. 'Just wait and see what being a parson's wife does for me!'

She opened the flimsy envelope. She could imagine her mother at the unaccustomed task of writing, her elbows well spread, her head, with hair of Dahlia's own dark red, close to the paper, not frowning over her difficulties, for she seldom frowned, but going doggedly to work and getting it done while Thomas Grimshaw was not in the house.

'I want for you to have a letter in the morning, wishing you happiness,' Louisa wrote. 'You'll be busy getting straight and don't think about me, not for a bit and then we'll see. It's been a good harvest. We've had a cow died. I never liked those Herefords. Too much white about the face for me. I want us to have Jerseys instead. The birds are looking good for Christmas. I get Jenny's letter every Tuesday. Writes it on the Sunday when the shop's shut, I suppose. Doesn't seem right to me, her being there, but says she likes it and nothing about young Cummings. Well, Dahlia, no more now from your loving mother, L.

12

Grimshaw. I've seen that Merriman but didn't look. Better not, but I wished I could have slapped him. I'll send in some eggs when the man's going into town.'

The last words were scratched out with characteristic carelessness and they were easily legible. 'But I'm not Jen. I shouldn't mind taking the eggs. She might have known that,' Dahlia thought, and this revelation of her mother's second thoughts and her uncertainties in connection with her children made Dahlia want to run across the bridge as soon as she was dressed. Thomas Grimshaw on that side of the water, no more than Mrs. Doubleday on this, should hamper freedom of intercourse, yet the truth was that spontaneity had been checked long ago; it had never really begun until the few weeks between Louisa's secret marriage to Grimshaw and Dàhlia's engagement to Cecil Sproat. It was only then that Jenny and Dahlia had been taught, by their own emotional experiences and her simplicity, to see clearly beyond the manner, the accent, the points of view that worried them and discern a woman with a big heart and a humble love for them. It was her simplicity that had persuaded Louisa to marry the man who, long ago, had been her lover, believing that so she would remove the only possible objection to Jenny's union with young Merriman, for she and Dahlia were the daughters of a man who had thought little enough of this landed gentry of no more than three generations standing and with a mother respectably married, the past atoned for, what obstacle remained? The failure of her effort was perhaps still puzzling her a little but she would feel no bitterness of regret. She would shrug her broad shoulders, tell herself she had done her best and decide that, with Dahlia married to the curate, it was just as well to be out of Upper Radstowe, her natural place was on a farm, and Dahlia, so her letter indicated, need have no fear of awkward intrusions.

13

THE house was rented very cheaply by the Sproats because it was old-fashioned and in bad repair and had not been inhabited for some time. Too narrow for its height, it had a forlorn, bereft appearance and with one windowless side wall, it looked as though it had been clearly sliced from some broader building. It was, in fact, the original creation of some one without an eye for form, but it had its place in the medley of houses round The Green. Its face was morose, its figure ungainly, its arrangement was inconvenient and its stairs were many: a low rent, a narrow, unkempt garden at the back and an individuality of its own were its attractions for Dahlia, who had a contriving mind and preferred grappling with this oddity in houses to enduring the draughts of a bright little laboursaving villa without a single cupboard. Moreover, there were no such villas in Upper Radstowe and Mrs. Doubleday's recommendation of furnished rooms or a flat admitting every sound made by the neighbours, had settled the matter for Dahlia.

'It's nice to be so near the church,' she told Cecil blandly.

This produced a rather grim smile from him. He hardly knew how to deal with Dahlia's attitude towards his calling. It seemed to have a slightly comic element for her and she was indulgent towards it, as though it were a game she did not understand but tolerated for his sake, and considering her youth and his years of earnest service, he felt a natural irritation, but when her kind candour made her add, 'Because we can always see the clock,' the momentary sting was eased. Her little shafts had no venom in them; she drew them at everything she saw and if they happened to touch a spot where he was sensitive, she could not be blamed for that, or, at least, he could not blame her yet. She was beautiful and gay and independent, she was like light in a dark place to Cecil Sproat and his fear of what she might ultimately make him see was at present submerged in his desire for her.

'If you think you'll be happy in that house, nothing else matters,' he said.

'I'm always happy,' was her not quite satisfactory reply. He was used to remarks from women with a more personal application and, from this woman, they were his due. Marriage had not made her more lavish of them, she did not seek them from him and, somewhere at the back of his mind, was the idea that her admirable independence could be a little excessive at times. The content she should have owed to him seemed to be derived from life itself and this morning, when they breakfasted in picnic fashion, in the room opening on to the untidy garden, he wished her eyes would rest more often on him, less often on that challenge to her industry.

'There'll still be flowers in the Cummings's garden,' she said. 'That will be nice for Jenny. And I expect she likes the old furniture. You can't imagine her where things are ugly.'

'No,' said Cecil, a little coldly, 'but you can imagine that they might be good for her.'

'Why?' Dahlia asked in a tone of intelligent interest.

He hesitated for a moment. Her question made him suspect a too easy moral inclination in his remarks, and he said, rather lamely, 'It might make her think less about herself.'

'How?' Dahlia was still intelligent and interested.

'Oh!' he exclaimed, 'I suppose I'm a prig.'

'Not really,' Dahlia said gently.

'And before I've lived with you much longer you'll make me think I'm a fraud.'

'But I shan't mean to.'

'No, that's the worst of it.'

'We're not quarrelling, are we? It seems a little bit like quarrelling.'

He was on the point of saying he hoped they would never do that, but he stopped in time, gave her a sensible sort of kiss and helped her to gather up the breakfast things. 'I must go and see Doubleday,' he said.

'And he'll say, "Well, Sproat, well Sproat! Here you are, here you are!" But she'll be shopping, with her toes turned out. You know, she puts her feet down as though she wants to keep the pavement in its place. Do you think he and she ever had a nice morning like this, with everything in a muddle, but happy because they were together, because they were starting something new, though the cistern was out of order and the wallpapers were dirty? I've a good mind,' she said in parenthesis, 'to pull some of these off myself. No, I'm sure she had some managing sisters who got the house tidy before she came back from her honeymoon — and what a honeymoon, with Norman saying everything twice — and nothing worth saying at all — and then they settled down neatly and that's how they've gone on.'

'It's difficult to see how it could have been romantic,' Cecil conceded, putting a vision of Mrs. Doubleday against Dahlia's vivid face, 'but you never know and I suppose they must have had some feeling for each other. Perhaps they still have. And anyhow, they have a son.'

'Well, I haven't had time to have one and I can't believe their's wasn't another of those miracles you believe in. Don't look shocked. It's much more delicate to think of it like that. And what kind of son is he?'

'I don't know. He's doing something abroad, I believe.'

16

'Perhaps he's a black sheep,' Dahlai said hopefully.

'I don't think so. Doubleday seems proud of him.'

'But if Mrs. Doubleday was, she'd talk about him.'

Here Dahlia's shrewdness was at fault. There are gods whom their worshippers do not name unless they must and such a god was her son to Mrs. Doubleday. Speaking of him was sharing him; worse still, it was acknowledging Mr. Doubleday's part in the production of the perfect being and she was not willing to give him any of the credit. The mental processes of years had, for practical purposes, effected Dahlia's miracle. Reginald Doubleday was really Reginald Crawley, the son of his mother, with the conventional use of his father's name. Outside the Vicarage she rarely mentioned him; only the arrival of a letter, or some necessary reference, induced her to speak of him to his father, and in this restraint Mrs. Doubleday probably had her only aesthetic satisfaction. Mr. Doubleday was puzzled by it and therefore he refused to think about it. Life, fairly faced, is full of puzzles and Mr. Doubleday did not like them. Some of them were to be found and ignored in the religious articles to which he had subscribed, some of them in the difference between an act of sin and the startling goodness of the sinner and, another puzzle was his wife's unnatural reticence about their son. Occasionally he horrified himself with the suspicion that she was withholding some discreditable information, but generally, he accepted her attitude as he accepted other mysteries and pushed them aside as disturbers of the peace which was so dear to him and which, in some ways, Mrs. Doubleday helped to give him. She protected the dignity of his office against his own good nature; she knew that the attractive path of least resistance frequently leads to difficulties as yet out of sight and it may have been in an instinctive craving for guidance that Mr. Doubleday wooed her. He had never tried to examine his motives in turning from the temptation of mating with pretty amiability in favour of an already rather gaunt Miss Crawley, one of the three active daughters of his first vicar; he chose not to examine hers in marrying him. She could trace her clerical ancestry for generations and liked to do so, while Mr. Doubleday's forebears had no history traditionally inspiring or useful in social intercourse and his consciousness of his inferiority in this respect may have had charm for both of them. But a love begun in the sharing of high aims and hard work was as reasonable an explanation of this marriage as most unions can offer, and whatever Mr. Doubleday's lacks and disappointments may have been, he had his compensations, and one of them was his son of whom, when Mrs. Doubleday was not there, he would speak, often and volubly, to his parishioners and friends. In her absence, the vicar's cheerfulness was presented without an effort; in her presence, it was sustained by a gentle humming of which he was not aware. It was a habit begun in the days of his courtship, when it could be interpreted as an overflowing of content, and thirty years of married life had not made him less dependent on its fictitious effect of ease. While he was dressing, when he met a servant in the passage and between the courses at meals, he broke into a series of muffled double notes, the melodic counterparts of his repetitive mode of speech, but when he entered the seclusion of his study, the humming automatically stopped. This was his own ground and Mrs. Doubleday's loyalty to his office had provided him with the very room he would have chosen. If he had not been the vicar, she would have settled him in the small apartment half way up the stairs where there was no view of the garden to encourage his curiosity about callers and distract him from his work; it was a question whether the immediate welfare of the parish

18

was of more importance than the dignity of the Church; Mrs. Doubleday decided in the Church's favour and Mr. Doubleday had his room on one side of the front door. The long straight path from the gate diverged, a few feet from the study window, for the tradesmen's entrance just round the corner, and it was quite easy to see whether the butcher had brought beef or mutton; when his window was wide open he could hear snatches of conversation which were of great interest to him; he enjoyed the cook's flirtation with the grocer's young man, who called for orders oftener than Mrs. Doubleday knew, and the vicar was distressed when the young man came less often. He was troubled, too, by a succession of new errand boys, for these changes argued bad employers or a rising generation without a sense of duty, and then he would tell himself he must talk to Sproat about it, get him to round up the youth of the parish, see that its leisure was healthily occupied and keep an eye on the conditions of its service. Callers privileged to use the front door bell actually passed Mr. Doubleday's window and while some of them caught a glimpse of the vicar's head bent over his desk, others were greeted with nods and smiles. He was warned of an approach by the clicking of the gate and, watching from behind the shelter provided by Mrs. Doubleday's thick lace curtains, he had plenty of time to decide between the bent head and the smile, plenty of time to notice a new dress on an old friend, an interesting looking parcel, the expression on a face, or a pair of shoes needing repair, for he was very observant. He gathered a store of somewhat disconnected facts from the vantage point of his window and to him who was a sociable being and never had his fill of easy, gossiping talk, these facts had a value which had nothing to do with any use he might make of them and, because he knew this, he was careful not to betray himself by passing on the information. He liked his study

19

and the long path had its merits, but he would have been better pleased if the house had been a little closer to the road and if the privet hedge bounding the garden had been less thick. He could see the tops of passing motor cars and carts above this hedge, figures flashed across the open ironwork of the gate with regrettable swiftness and, thwarted thus, he was often constrained to make work for himself outside the house, but on this September morning, he was in his study when Cecil Sproat strode up the path and with a suppressed sigh, he went to his desk. Sproat represented action, conscience and zeal. He was a hard worker and relieved his vicar of many a labour but, on the other hand, he had a genius for suggesting new undertakings in which Mr. Doubleday would have to bear his part, and Mr. Doubleday was inclined to agree with his wife, though for different reasons, that Sproat had been in the parish long enough. Only three weeks of his month's holiday had gone by, yet here he was on the doorstep.

'Well, Sproat, well Sproat,' he said and he noticed that his curate's smile had a new quality, a suggestion of amusement. That girl has done him good already, he thought, as he said heartily, 'You're not due for another week, you know. I shall consider this as a ghostly visita· tion.' He enjoyed his joke. 'A ghostly visitation. You're not really here, you know. You're still down in Devon-shire, isn't it? Fine weather? That's good, that's good. Well now, be off with you. I don't want to see you till next week. If I know anything of ladies, Mrs. Sproat will find plenty for you to do. Hanging pictures, laying car-pets, no nails in the house, that sort of thing. She'll keep you busy. And, by the way, when you do return officially there are some presents for you. There's one from the Men's Club and I believe the Ladies' Working Party has another, Ah, my dear,' he said, as Mrs. Doubleday appeared, 'here's Sproat back before his time and I'm just telling him about the presents. There'll have to be some sort of a little ceremony, I suppose?'

'I'm afraid so,' said Mrs. Doubleday, giving Cecil a limp hand. 'The men must do as they please and I've done my best to avoid embarrassment for Mrs. Sproat, but of course all the women, and even some of the ladies,' she added in genuine astonishment, 'are anxious to meet her. They were disappointed that the wedding was not in Upper Radstowe. I've explained that as best I could, but they are determined to give the present personally. So, if you'd rather she didn't make a speech, you'd better be there to do it for her.'

'I'd very much rather she did it herself,' Cecil said, keeping his voice under control and doing his best to pretend he missed her meaning and, under cover of Mr. Doubleday's tactful assurances that ladies were generally good speakers, generally good speakers, he carried his anger out of the house.

'First blood, I suppose,' he muttered, and he went for a short walk and strenuously smoothed out his frown, before he returned to Dahlia.

CHAPTER III

HE reflected, as he walked, on the waste of energy resulting from so essentially insignificant an activity as Mrs.
Doubleday's mind. Here he was, marching round the
hill, ignoring the changing colours of the trees on the
other side of the river, using himself up in anger against
that woman and the petty conventions of his world. He
was foreseeing further slights to Dahlia, little annoyances
that might be great in consequences, patronage from Mrs.
Doubleday evoking defiance from Dahlia, or disparagement that might give her pain, and these uneasy thoughts
were quite unsuited to a day when she was making their
narrow house into a home and the early mist had discreetly
retired before the mellow sunshine. And such absurdities,
such frets, to say nothing of real sin and sorrow, were
being created or endured by nearly every human soul; he
was as much subject to them as other people, though he
tried to despise them, and life was as bewildering to Cecil
Sproat as it was to Mr. Doubleday, but the younger man
was not satisfied with the mere statement of a mystery; he
wanted to solve it, to understand why life could not be
begun, continued and ended as a great adventure in
which the whole race was involved, in which each actor's
honour impelled him to generosity and courage and unselfishness. And there, he thought, was a good notion for
a sermon, the first he would deliver after his marriage
and one, he hoped, that would please Dahlia. He paused,
framing his sentences, drawing analogies to explorers in
a new world, bound together by such common dangers
and difficulties that the indulgence of personal desires
and irritations was impossible; dramatically he described

22

hardships, self-sacrifices and final victory, but when he imagined himself standing in the pulpit and uttering these words, he feared he would appear rather comic and sound sentimental to Dahlia. There were ideas that could be thought and lived by, but could hardly be spoken in public by anyone, and surely not by him. A poet could present nobility and keep it noble in the light of a fierce beauty; an ordinary curate was doomed to make it trite. What, after all, could he say securely and who was he to say it? He could not answer his own question and he went to the railings and looked down the steep slope of the cliff to the road and river below. Down there midget beings with worse troubles than Mrs. Doubleday and no such happiness as Dahlia, were going about their business or their pleasure. The tide was out and there was no traffic on the thin stream banked by mud glistening in the sunshine and promenaded by gulls, and the emptiness of the river, the thickly wooded opposite cliff with its massed green brightened, here and there, by a splash of yellow, or the pale trunk of a silver birch, the blue sky and the warm sunshine, produced a feeling of peace in the spirit of Cecil Sproat. The distant sounds from the docks only added to it and now and then, close at hand, he heard the sighing of a leaf as it fell slowly through the still air. This, he thought, was the peace of God; it was what all men needed, it was to be had for the taking, yet he knew it would not have been his, even amid this beauty, if he had been wanting Dahlia. The beauty was increased by the fact that she was near and the very sunshine owed something of its brilliance to her. He could give himself no credit for his receptive state, but he thought he had a hint of the solution to life's problem, though he did not know how to work it out. He could take the peace of God and resign himself to His will when he was alone here on the hill and the chief wish of his life had been

23

granted, but could he keep it if he lost his happiness or if it was blurred by the small vexations of his daily life? Again he could not find an answer to his question and he turned homewards, heartily hoping he would not be tested and more mercifully inclined towards his fellows than was his custom, for in his character was the severity of a man who had settled his beliefs early in life and whose experiences had not yet shaken him out of his rigidity. Lately, however, he had been conscious of a tremor. Marital infidelity, of which he believed Dahlia's mother to have been guilty, was more shocking to him than other forms of faithlessness. His horror of it was linked up with a personal fastidiousness, the thought of illicit love offended him like the thought of a debauch; he could not believe it might have dignity and beauty and he did not know that the outfacing of convention, even in a moment of passion, could have an astringent, purifying bitterness. It was outside the law and outside the Church and he could think much more calmly of loveless marriage sheltered by both, yet, through loyalty to Dahlia, he was involved in loyalty to her mother, whose sin he detested, for whose character he had respect. It was an old sin and ought long ago to have been forgotten, but it had lately been discovered in Upper Radstowe. Louisa's marriage to her fellow sinner would not silence a bitter tongue, and while the religious side of him applauded Louisa's action which was like a declaration of penitence and a prayer for forgiveness, from a practical point of view he had to admit its inconvenience. He had scoffed at Dahlia's statement that she would hamper him in a worldly sense, he knew that even Mrs. Doubleday could not refuse the evidence of breeding in Dahlia's pretty ways and speech, but Louisa Grimshaw was across the bridge, his own sense of filial duty could not entirely neglect her, while his marriage to Dahlia, at his home and not hers, had, as it were, already disclaimed her mother's rights, and been, he thought now, an error in tactics, made in a moment of confusion. Louisa was secretly married to a man who was demanding her company and to whose house neither girl would go; Jenny, on the rebound from her sad love affair, had half promised herself to another man and that man her mother's late lodger, and accepted the occupation offered to her in his home; Dahlia had neither home nor occupation. It had been a difficult situation, but Cecil Sproat was his mother's only son and his wishes were hers, and to her Dahlia had gone and by her been welcomed and there they had been married. Louisa had refused Mrs. Sproat's hospitality for the ceremony. 'I reckon I've done harm enough,' she said, and Dahlia's family was represented only by Jenny, a grave-eyed guest and one to reinforce Mrs. Sproat's content with Dahlia, but one who seemed as if she had forgotten to bring her spirit with her. It was a solemn little wedding, as in Cecil's view was seemly; he disliked the pagan suggestion in finery and feasting, but he resented the lack of sisterly joy on Jenny's face, he knew that Dahlia's silence, as they drove away, was not caused by maidenly reserve or awe; it was caused by concern for Jenny, by grief at leaving her and the longing to protect her. She held his hand firmly, but he thought her real grip was on Jenny and all her subsequent sweetness had not completely overlaid his jealous pangs.

Some of the peace of God, too easily gained, departed from him as he walked home, thinking of these matters. He had been under its wing but he had not touched it and he forgot about it altogether, forgot his need of it, when he saw Dahlia ankle deep in the paper she had been tearing from his study wall.

'It had to be done at once, while I'm feeling enthusiastic,' she said in excuse. 'I thought I could bear the dirt,

25

but I can't. We'll get some distemper this afternoon and by to-morrow you'll have a room fit for supplicants and sermons.'

'I'm not having any supplicants for another week and I wish I need never have a sermon.'

'Are you tired of your job?' she inquired.

'No, I'm frightened of you,' he said.

'Oh, I shan't take them seriously,' she promised him. 'I'd never be so mean as to let them count against you. After all, I've heard some of them already and I can truthfully say that I've forgotten every word.' He saw, with some dismay, that she gave him these assurances in all earnest. 'So let's decide that they're like cleaning teeth. We don't look nice when we're doing it and I should hate you to watch me, but I know it wouldn't make you like me less. So let's decide that,' she said, gathering up an armful of waste paper. 'Otherwise, Sundays will be misery for us both, you feeling uncomfortable and me pretending not to notice. Let's have a bonfire with this paper to-night, when it gets dark,' she suggested happily. 'A kind of beacon.'

'Throwing rubbish, like my sermons, to the flames.'

'Yes,' she said, and then, 'No, I'm sure yours are not worse than anybody else's, but then I've so little to go by. I hardly ever went to church, except at school, and then, naturally, I didn't listen. Sometimes I went with father to Combe Friars, but that was just a kind of droning and underneath it you could make up things about yourself, things that didn't happen. Of course I knew they wouldn't, but they passed the time.'

'What sort of things?' He was sure she had planned no such future as the one before her and, bitter about his sermons, he wondered whether, in happier circumstances, she would have married him. 'And I wish you wouldn't hug that dirty paper.'

She dropped her burden and he noted her willingness to oblige him in small matters while, in those near his heart, she did not trouble to choose her words or spare his feelings.

'What things?' he repeated.

'Silly ones. Dreadfully handsome young men with heaps of money.'

'Not a comic curate with very little.'

'I did think you were rather comic, at first,' she owned. 'Do you remember the dolls I made, like you and Mr. Doubleday? I've got them, somewhere. We'll put the one of you on the bonfire to-night, but we'll keep Mr. Doubleday and I'll make one of her when I have time. There's a silly sort of idea that curates must be funny. I believe it's the clothes. It makes them self-conscious, like people in fancy dress. By the time they're middle-aged they've got used to them, but the young ones can't forget them. You weren't like that. I only laughed at you because you never laughed at anything yourself. But, thank goodness, you are not one of the jolly ones. I think they are the worst.'

'And where did you get all this knowledge? On your own showing, you've had very little experience.'

'Has something upset you?' she asked quickly. The coldness in his voice had never been addressed to her before.

He shrugged his shoulders in irritation. He was amazed by her lack of perception, but he tried to keep his temper and said, mildly enough, 'I'm doing difficult work. It may not be important to you, but it is to me. I don't like you to laugh at the men who are trying to do it. And I've no doubt I'm a bad preacher, but if I were a bad greengrocer I'm sure you'd try to help me. You wouldn't say it didn't matter if my goods were of inferior quality.'

'Of course I shouldn't,' she agreed amicably. 'People would stop coming to the shop.'

'And it doesn't matter if they stop coming to church?'

'No, I don't think it does,' she said. She could be wise, she could even be wily in little ways, but he and she had started their acquaintance on a foundation of honesty and, for her, it would have been a betrayal of their compact to give him anything but a frank answer; she had yet to learn that, even with him, truth need not be presented nakedly.

His voice annoyed her with its melancholy. 'You think that. I see. But I wonder how you can say such a cruel thing to me.'

'You wanted an answer, didn't you?' Why should she be blamed for an opinion? It would be as reasonable to scold her for her red hair and he would have been horrified if she had dyed it.

'Well, I must just bear it as best I can, I must manage alone,' he said, and she thought he was foolish in his resignation and self-pity. 'And, in the circumstances, I think I'd rather you didn't go to any trouble about this room.'

'Oh, that's childish,' said Dahlia. She picked up the paper she had dropped and carried it to the bottom of the garden. There she stood, with her back towards the house, until the tears had cleared from her eyes, then, adding fallen sticks and leaves to her pile, she fumbled for the matchbox in the pocket of her overall and stooped to start the fire. They could not have their happy beacon in the dusk and though she felt no desperation about the quarrel and foresaw a reconciliation before many hours had passed, she knew that something invisible was going up in flames and it was her perfect faith in the security of Cecil's friendship. Her training had taught her to distrust passionate love; she accepted his and gave him all she had, but what had been really precious to her was the inevita-

28

bility of frankness in their union and the knowledge that there was nothing in her short past and was likely to be nothing in the future that she would be afraid to show him, not because she was and would continue good, but because their liking for each other had seemed to be independent of their actions and to thrive on differences.

CHAPTER IV

THEIR midday meal had none of the gaiety of their breakfast. It had the same outward attributes of a picnic, for Dahlia's zeal in the study had taken time she should have spent in making the house generally habitable, but light hearts are necessary for the enjoyment of half-cooked potatoes and a scarcity of plates, and the pressed beef had a sordid appearance on the bare deal table. They had carried their breakfast things into what they called the garden room; dispirited now, they lunched in the dark basement room across the passage.

'For how long do you think we shall have to live in this discomfort?' he asked politely. He had been delicately though simply bred. He was not familiar with kitchens unless they were the living rooms of the poor and these, except in cases of dire poverty, had seemed to him pleasant places, with their bright open fires and simmering kettles. Here there was a gaunt gas stove, there were iron bars outside the window and though Dahlia had insisted that this room, at least, must be newly papered and painted for hygienic reasons, it was doomed, by its natural gloom, to arouse suspicions of dirt. This further discouraged an appetite that was never hearty, while Dahlia, a being, he was pleased to think, of coarser physical fibre, was making a great show of satisfying a healthy hunger.

'How long? I haven't the least idea,' she said.

'Then I think I had better go and find a woman who can help you.'

'She won't be able to come till next week. They never can.'

'I think I know of several who would come to-day if I asked them.'

'One will be enough,' Dahlia said. She was vexed by his bland certainty of getting what he wanted; it was another symptom of the conscious difference between him and other men and she said, to humble him, 'They'll want to come because they're curious.'

'Yes, I've thought of that, so I do ask you to remember that you are my wife.'

'Why should I forget it?' she asked. She smiled a little teasingly. 'How could I forget it? What you really mean is that I'm the curate's wife.'

'Yes, that is exactly what I mean. There is a general belief in the existence of sympathy between a clergyman and his wife, in their ideas, in their ideals. It would be a pity if you led a simple woman to think otherwise and made a mockery of what she has been taught to respect.' Perhaps it was fortunate that words failed Dahlia while he paused. 'I'm not asking you to be hypocritical,' he said, 'but I have a right to ask you to be discreet.'

'It would be much easier to be hypocritical,' she said untruly.

'I don't think it would,' he said in gentler tones, but she did not see or she chose to disregard the compliment.

'No, you don't know,' she replied. 'We don't know anything about each other, but we're learning, and I expect I shall learn to be discreet, too, though, as a matter of fact, I always have been. I didn't know it was necessary with you. But I was brought up in a very reserved family, a very awkward family, and I think you can trust me.'

'Oh, I know I can,' he exclaimed penitently and he kissed her. 'We're friends now, aren't we?'

'We're married,' she replied.

He kissed her again. He liked her answer; it implied the possession of all the proper feelings and when he went out to seek the willing charwoman, he was remorseful about his anger. She was very young, she had an abundance of high spirits and in spite of a disjointed sort of upbringing, with a sceptical, cultured father and an ignorant, easy-going mother, she had made for herself a standard of conduct which, he still believed, was better than his own. That moment of spiritual exaltation on the hill had come to him too easily; he ought to have seen its danger; it had given him a false sense of safety and enlarged his confidence in himself, while through it Mrs. Doubleday's poison had been subtly working and increasing his readiness to see faults in Dahlia. The faults were there, he would not deceive himself about that. Without a sense of reverence, she had an awkward tendency to tell the truth, and there was a world of difference between refusing to tell lies and insisting on the free expression of opinion, but she was intelligent and she was loyal, and he, on his part, must be patient, showing her that a religion which at present meant nothing to her, was a controlling and inspiring force to him. He tried to crush his desire that she would find her faith in his because it was his and approve of all he did because he did it. She had given him no cause to expect this acquiescence. Indeed, at his suggestion that she should be confirmed before their marriage, her astonishment was a definite refusal and almost a reproach, as though he had made an attack on her integrity, but it was undoubtedly awkward to have a wife who absented herself from Holy Communion. The vicar would not be disturbed and perhaps Mrs. Doubleday would approve of a wife who stayed at home to get the breakfast instead of going to early celebration and, with luck, would not notice her failure to appear at the altar rails when Holy Communion was included in the morning service, but it vexed him to have to make these calculations: it was a real sorrow that he could not share

32

the sacred experience with her, nevertheless, he believed there was no comparable woman in the world, even to-day when she had angered him. He could therefore hope she was concealing like feelings with his own success, but what he forgot or did not know was the immense advantage her beauty gave her over him, or rather, the disadvantage his lack of beauty was to her. It is easy to forgive offences when every movement of the offender is pleasing to the eye, when the senses are comforted by the curve of a lip or roused by it into forgetfulness of mental separation.

When Dahlia watched Cecil leave the house, she had no pleasure in his physical appearance, no certainty that his touch and the sight of him would always soften her. She liked the look of him but it did not prevent her from thinking him stupid in misinterpreting her statement that they were married. She had been pointing the difference between that condition and what she considered the nobler one of a friendship in which marriage could be included, the greater embracing the less, and his complacency annoyed while it amused her. He should have the discretion he wanted; she would have a secret satisfaction in using it, but she knew it would be a barren satisfaction, for she was a sharer by nature. She knew, too, that she could not long sustain her anger; it was not rooted deeply enough for permanence, yet something else had taken seed in her mind, a little distrust of herself and of him. Until now she had been cautious, she had reserved any expression of her deeper feelings, she had followed his lead in this new relationship and the first weeks of marriage had been an instinctively artistic performance on her part, with every outward circumstance to aid it, but its success and his delight in her had caused a slight slackening of her watchfulness, as Cecil's elation on the hill had done for him, and she was so free of personal vanity and belief in her own importance and therefore so little sensitive to slights, that she had not expected him to be otherwise. It did not occur to her that his own doubts about the value of his work might make him sturdier in its defence and more hurt by her attacks. She had not meant to attack it, she had, indeed, honestly meant to help him where she could, she would still help him in the ways expected of her, but an organized religion and the homage paid to its ministers roused her humorous defiance. These men were set apart and they were dressed as beings who were different; they were like policemen, she thought crudely, with more privileges and less muscle, and she wished Cecil were really the green-grocer of whom he had spoken. Why was there not a uniform for greengrocers? Why was there not a special sanctity about selling the good fruits of the earth? She wished she had explained to Cecil that a tradesman thrives according to the wares he offers, while a clergyman is credited with good ones before they have been tested; his wares are standardized, they are a monopoly to be left or taken, and if anyone tests them, finds them wanting and goes without them, the fault is supposed to be with him. These thoughts, never clearly formed before, somewhat surprised her, but she was chiefly conscious of a sense of desolation and again she wanted to see her mother, but this time it was for her own sake. She would find a welcome on the other side of the bridge and a physical presence like a warm fireside and a dumb love that asked for nothing in return, a love that was like a shelter. It might be a barely furnished shelter with no ornaments in it and no books, nothing to satisfy the eye or stimulate the mind, but it was just the place to creep into if one were cold or unhappy.

'But I'm not unhappy, I'm only cross, and I've got to wait for the sanctimonious charwoman,' Dahlia said aloud, and she left the study with its carpet rolled back and the furniture in the middle of the room. She would attend to it to-morrow but, instead of distempering it in a warm yellow colour as she had planned, she would get a cold grey for the walls, paint the picture rail black, wash the frieze with a dead white and see whether Cecil recognized his less formal suit of clothes, his waistcoat and his collar. 'If he won't laugh with me, I shall have to laugh by myself,' she said, going into the room behind the study which was her little parlour. Here, as elsewhere, the furniture had been pushed into its appropriate room, under Cecil's directions, before the marriage, and now Dahlia recovered her good temper in arranging it to please herself. Here was the demure little Victorian settee with its accompanying pair of chairs, given to her by Edwin Cummings, the upholstery framed in an edging of wood, the legs somewhat tortuously turned. This type of furniture, he explained in his letter, was not fashionable at the moment, but he foresaw a future for it and, what was much more important, it fitted the period of the house and the workmanship was good. 'Properly speaking,' he wrote, 'the house has no period, and all you can aim at is a harmonious effect, so when I found we'd got these in the shop I saw at once they were what you wanted.' He was right. They looked as though they had been made for the little room with its gold encrusted paper which was not fashionable either but, like the furniture was good, and Dahlia decided not to strip it. Time had toned down its grandeur and left it modestly festive; it belonged to no period worthy of the name, it matched the house and the ornamental marble of the mantelpiece, she was sure Edwin Cummings would approve of it and, if he approved, it could not be wrong. He had unerring taste. That was why his admiration had passed her by and fixed on Jenny. Jenny had the shapely austerity he adored in works of art and, as Dahlia paused in her labours with a

35

hand on the back of the settee, she felt a sudden wave of pity for him. Jenny was like a fine museum piece he could never possess; only by accident would it come into his keeping, and though his care of it would be scrupulous and loving, he would not have the joy of really owning it. Dahlia had not much faith in Jenny's power of adapting herself to her conditions. From a distance, the shop with the old furniture, the parlour leading out of it and then into the garden, the workshop at the back of that, had the charm of a quieter world; flowers and cobbled paths and the sound of leisurely, careful labour appealed like a beautiful retreat to a wounded spirit, and Jenny, who had found her lover weak and faithless had turned to the man who could neither deceive nor be deceived, although, or because, he loved her. He saw her faults as clearly as he saw flaws in furniture, in his company she could relax and that, at the moment, was what she wanted, so, when the illness of the elder Cummings made it necessary for Edwin to take charge of the second-hand shop, she had gone with him to the little Somersetshire town to help his sisters with the house and business, while he wandered about the countryside and haunted sales for the discovery of antiques. What moral obligations Jenny took with her, Dahlia did not know. There had been an unusual glow about her when she left Beulah Mount, the look of a person who had chosen the better way, but the glow had gone when she appeared for Dahlia's wedding and Dahlia had felt ashamed of her own happiness. At the back of her mind was the thought that, for one day, Jenny might have pretended all was well with her: there was no denying her selfishness, the tragic atmosphere in which she could wrap herself and Dahlia wondered how those practical Cummings sisters were dealing with her.

'I must go and see her,' she was thinking when the

ringing of the front door bell announced the charwoman, a brisk, comely woman who removed her fur tippet while greetings passed and immediately set to work, thereby rousing in Dahlia some respect for the practical uses of religion, and not long afterwards, Cecil appeared, hiding behind a bunch of golden chrysanthemums the serious expression he wore when he was pleased. The success of his mission and the inspirations about the flowers had cheered him.

'She's a nice charwoman,' Dahlia said, 'the flowers are lovely, I like you and I hate myself. I didn't mean you when I made fun of clergymen. I don't think churches and sermons make much difference, but I think you do. I apologize. I'm going to be perfection. Kiss me, please, but not in a forgiving, holy way.'

It was the first request of the kind he had had from her and he was able to respond so satisfactorily that she repented of her plans about his study. The walls should be a warm yellow after all.

CHAPTER V

FOR the rest of the afternoon, Dahlia and Cecil and the charwoman were hard at work, moving furniture, emptying packing cases and arranging books and china, and by the time dusk had fallen there was a semblance of order in the house and a bright little fire in the sitting-room and Mrs. Bailey carried away the remains of the pressed beef and Dahlia's good opinion. Not once had she protested against the reverend gentleman's menial labours or paused to expostulate with Dahlia for standing on the top of the steps to hang the curtains.

'I like that woman,' Dahlia said. 'Does she go regularly to church?'

'No, but she sends her children to Sunday School.'

'Good idea!' Dahlia said heartily, then, lifting her eyebrows ruefully, she glanced at Cecil. It was the wrong comment, but he was careful not to notice it.

'She has to cook the Sunday dinner,' he explained.

'And so shall I have to. But,' she added quickly, 'it will be the kind of cooking that doesn't need much attention. A stew's the thing. It's quite happy if it's left alone. Isn't it a mercy we shan't have to be careful not to give the servant trouble?'

'I wish we could afford to have one. I don't see how you'll manage to keep the house clean.'

'I shan't. Not very. But it's going to look pretty when I've finished with it and, once a week, Mrs. Bailey can come and scrub.'

'But there'll be callers soon,' he said, 'lots of callers. What are you going to do about them?'

'What would you like me to do?' Dahlia asked. It was

38

a good question and a wifely one and she was proud of it. She had bathed and changed her dress and now she sat neatly on one of Edwin's chairs and it may have been through the influence of the furniture that she put this question instead of answering his. What she wanted to do about the callers was to pretend to be out and hide in the kitchen whence she could watch the skirts and feet coming, with anticipation, up the garden path and going down in disappointment. It was what she might do in the end, but she had offered the decision to him and when he said, with helpless generosity, that what she did was certain to be right, she had learnt another lesson in the amenities of married life. Yet she felt as though she cheated him with her gravity and she feared she might have to discipline it into a habit until she became one of those good earnest girls who were indifferent to the shape of their hats and the hang of their skirts, and her love of fun and her sustaining tendency towards nonsense were overlaid by the anxiety, or the necessity, to please him. She had a vision of herself dancing off in one direction while he walked steadily in his own, and it seemed to her that either they must turn and meet half way, or she must run after him, a little breathlessly and resentfully, and then walk soberly beside him, refusing the temptation to dally by the way. She turned a sigh into a yawn.

'Tired?' he asked slowly, looking up from his book, and he managed to put all his loving kindness into the word and to assure her that, whatever the outward details of her life might be, she had here something worth keeping, something she would not find elsewhere, to which she would be wise to adapt herself if she could, and there flashed through her mind the startling knowledge that she could never put love for him into a single common word like that. Strangely enough, it was the most passionately revealing thing he had ever said to her, she realized that his love for her unconsciously affected his very accents and she was humbled and remorseful. If she could speak to him in such a tone, she would not be doubtful of the future; every moment would be a delight because it was shared with him. She felt, too, a pang of envy. It was good to be adored, it might be better to adore, and that was what she could not do, and, slipping from her chair, she put her head on his knees, pressing it against them, hiding there her fear that she had not dealt fairly by him, and emphasizing the strength of her affection and her need of him.

'It was a silly quarrel. You'll have to be patient with me,' he said unexpectedly.

'No, it's the other way round,' she murmured. 'But,' she looked up, 'I'm only twenty-one and I was happy, and when I'm happy that's how I go on.'

'Then go on doing it — with me.'

'Can I? I'd made up my mind not to and I expect you'll get tired of it, or perhaps,' she threatened him lightly, 'I shall stop being happy. But I wasn't thinking about the quarrel. I was just — thinking.'

'I know, but I believe it's going to be all right,' he said, reassuring her with his lack of alarming certainty and with the suggestion that, at present, they were travelling side by side. Thus, in one day, she experienced the sensation of slipping from a hold, then of recovering it from another angle and finding that though she was not in exactly the place from which she started, she had not lost much by the fall and was actually in a better position for the next step, and she thought she could go on firmly now, not knowing that in this most difficult of relationships, there must be, if it survived with any beauty, this periodical slipping and recovery and advance in a slightly different direction.

She took a step forward. 'You'll have to tell me what

you want me to do to help you. Apart, I mean, from being nice.'

'First, you'll have to receive a wedding present, from the Ladies' Working Party, and you'll have to make a speech.'

'Do you know what the present is?' she asked, and he noted that the prospect of the speech did not alarm her. 'Because,' she said, 'it may be one of those things that you can't hide, that they see when they come to call and you see all the time and hate.'

'I don't know what it is. Mrs. Doubleday told me it was to be given to you.'

'And what else did she tell you?'

This, he thought, was a moment for justifiable evasion. 'There is a present for me from the Men's Club.'

'That will be all right,' Dahlia said. 'They won't give you a standard lamp with a pink shade. A pink shade, in this room! But perhaps it would cost too much. Let's hope for something smaller. And after that kindness, I suppose I shall have to go regularly to the working party, and I don't sew well and I can't cut out, but I expect it's Mrs. Doubleday who slashes up the flannel.'

'They are working, now, for the bazaar,' Cecil said unwillingly. His involvement in such affairs was one of the trials of his calling.

'Oh! The bazaar,' Dahlia said. She had forgotten all about it, though it had its place in her history. She had been helping Miss Morrison, another of her mother's lodgers, in work for that bazaar on the night when she made the little caricatures of Cecil and Mr. Doubleday and learnt that Cecil could be generous when he was hurt, but they were both silent about Miss Morrison, each aware of her admiration for him, neither sure that the other knew and both incapable of reference to it.

'The stallholders', Dahlia said solemnly, 'were to be

41

dressed as shepherdesses.' She looked at him sideways and decided not to ask him whether he and Mr. Doubleday were to be shepherds; she forbore from remarking that perhaps they considered themselves so costumed already. He was frowning; his lips were pursed up in a way she did not know but liked for its sudden boyishness.

'I hate these bazaars,' he said. 'Spending a shilling to make one and twopence and fools of themselves into the bargain! Those good women wouldn't give the cost of their fancy dresses to the mission fund; it's not the fund they care about.'

'But so long as you get the money . . .' Dahlia suggested.

'I know, but I don't feel like that. Think of the difference it would make to the givers themselves if they gave freely, instead of insisting on some rubbish in return.'

'You wouldn't get so much.'

'I'd rather have less.'

'I don't understand that,' Dahlia admitted, 'but then I don't mind about the state of other people's insides, not unless I like the people, and from what I've seen of the ones who go to your church, I don't think their insides matter. I think they're all clogged up, and the people at the mission will get the benefit. That's the queer part of things,' she said sagely. 'Good for one person nearly always means bad for someone else.'

'Then it must be because we don't know what good really is. And we don't know,' he said, still frowning.

'It's good to be here, isn't it? We're not hurting anyone else by being here, are we?' Dahlia asked, but she thought of Miss Morrison who might be pained if she could picture them beside their fire, talking of matters she would consider far beyond Dahlia's scope. 'And,' she went on practically, 'if you feel like that about the shepherdesses, I needn't waste money on a dress, but I don't think I can promise to give what I save to the fund. I'd rather get another kind of dress, one that you'd like me in. I think you'd better know that I'm very fond of clothes.'

To that avowal he made no response. 'It depends on how you feel about it yourself,' he said. He was vexed with the paltriness of the problem. It was not a man's business to deal with it but, unfortunately, it was the business of a curate in Upper Radstowe where Mrs. Doubleday was the vicar's wife and where Dahlia would be particularly subject to criticism.

'I think it's idiotic,' she said.

'Well, you'd better feel your way about it.'

'Why should I, when I know how we both feel already?'

'Because,' he said, 'I'm the curate and I have to present an appearance of loyalty.'

'Then I wish you'd be quick and be a vicar. And I suppose I'm a sort of curatess and Mrs. Doubleday is my superior?'

'No doubt she thinks so,' he said dryly and she cried joyfully, 'Thank goodness you don't like her, but I wish you'd say so.'

'I do not like her,' he said obligingly, 'but I don't want you to quarrel with her.'

'I won't, but if I have to dress up, I'll do it better than anybody else and she can quarrel if she wants to. But how stupid it all is!' she exclaimed. Her eyes shining, her lips a little parted, she gazed at him in a sort of wonder. With him she had more to do than present an appearance of loyalty; she had to feel loyal, too, and as she had been forbidden to separate the man from his work, that work must be included in her adhesion, and her youthful craving for perfection demanded that it should be entirely noble, so that she could see him as a hero. 'Half of what you have to do seems to be a kind of game,' she complained. 'I don't like you to be mixed up with working parties and bazaars. It isn't — it isn't suitable.'

43

'Oh, I know that as well as you do,' he said wearily. 'There are times when I wish I were anything but what I am.'

'Well,' she was eager to discuss this, 'what could you be?'

She saw no answering interest on his face. Once more she had failed to give him what he wanted and for a minute she sat quite still, looking at the fire, clenching her fists and trying to force herself into an enthusiasm she did not feel. She was prejudiced but she wished to be fair. She knew very little about his work and she had not encouraged him to tell her of it, and now, rather clumsily and obviously, she persuaded him to talk, and it was late before they put out the lights and went quietly up to bed.

It had been an eventful day; they had quarrelled and made friends again, he had talked to her freely and she had listened, making no comments but giving, now and then, a little nod of understanding, and, sensitive to his effect on an audience, he knew he had impressed her. This was true; she appreciated his labours for his fellow-men; she warmed towards him when he spoke of material conditions which must be changed; the thought of slums and ill-fed children roused all the mother in her, but what made her feel unusually heavy on the stairs was not the weight of unnecessary woe endured by human beings, it was not her share of responsibility towards these sufferers; it was the knowledge that while her practical sympathy was with Cecil's efforts, the fount of his inspiration was quite dry for her and when he spoke of it she felt uncomfortable and did not want to look at him.

CHAPTER VI

CECIL's breakfast was rather overdone next morning. The fried egg was encircled by a crisp brown fringe, the rasher of bacon had to be arranged on the plate with the pinker side uppermost, and Dahlia thrust Jenny's letter into the pocket of her overall. Then she took it out again and laid it carelessly on the table. There had not been time to read it, for it was long; a hasty glance across its sheets had been enough to spoil Cecil's breakfast and she did not want to have Jenny even indirectly blamed. Still less did she want him to read the letter, for Jenny's self-betrayals were not of a kind to enlist masculine sympathy, and certainly not Cecil's, but there was an element of deceit in hiding it and, as he had withheld advice when he was asked for it, so he might refuse to read those open pages.

She was not disappointed. He ate his breakfast uncomplainingly, she lightly kissed the top of his head in reward and if he connected the scorched food, the letter and the caress, he gave no sign. He said simply, 'When I woke this morning I felt sorry for everybody else in the world.'

Dahlia could not make quite such a comprehensive declaration, it was not she who had found the perfect listener, but when she considered the small circle of her acquaintance, she found no one to envy. She was more fortunate than her mother and than Jenny, and much more fortunate than Mrs. Doubleday, yet, on this morning, though no one knew it, Mrs. Doubleday was in a state of secret bliss and because it was secret it was the more blissful. She, too, had had a letter. Always, on this morning of the week, she rose earlier than usual so that she might first touch the envelope addressed in the beloved

45

handwriting, and always she had the same scorn for her husband who made no effort to secure this privilege and often actually forgot the importance of the day.

She was able to read her letter without interruption, for she had a cook in the kitchen, and Reginald's letter was much shorter than Jenny's. Slowly she read it twice and then, as she heard Mr. Doubleday's humming approach, she put it in her own desk which he had never been known to open.

She seldom noticed that humming. It was as familiar and as much disregarded as his round, rosy face and the busy chafing of his hands advertising his pleasure in a new day.

'Sunshine, sunshine,' he said, going to the window.

On the other side of the road there was a short row of fine, flat-fronted old houses, plainly seen now, when the flowering trees in the gardens had lost their thickness, and Mr. Doubleday could appreciate the solid dignity of the buildings, the intricate structure of the branches and the leaves still hanging like the work of a craftsman in bronze and copper, beaten into transparency and shaped with inspiration. A little farther to the right and opposite the church, The Green began and stretched gently upwards to the hill overlooking the river, and though Mr. Doubleday only had a partial, sideways view of it, he could see the massed colour of the trees, amber and gold and brown, more metal wrought by the same artist into a great chased bowl to catch the autumn sunshine. Mr. Doubleday liked the appearance and the feeling of a mellow autumn. Outside the sun was bright, behind his back a small fire crackled in the grate, the fragrance of coffee was in the room and his general pleasure was increased by the thought of Sproat with that pretty girl in the house behind the trees.

'Yes, yes,' he said approvingly, and turned hastily to

the letters beside his plate, to give the impression that his double affirmative was an address of welcome to the labours of the day.

Mrs. Doubleday had letters too and she was unusually communicative about their contents. It was her laudable practice to spare her husband the small details of her own part in parish affairs. She could deal with them competently and the vicar, as she often said to other people, must not be distracted from his more important work; thus, he was deprived of many a little enjoyment. Words of disapproval would drop naturally from her lips, but the full, gossipy story of her difficulties and her problems was seldom given to him. She may have believed in the worthiness of her motives, but the eagerness of his response to her remarks this morning, his little exclamations of sympathy or surprise, should have taught her that while her reservations might be wise, they were not kindly. He was pleased with her fragments of information, still more pleased because she gave them, and, in the enduring hopefulness of his spirit, he foresaw a continuance of this interchange. Why should it not continue? was the half-formed question in his mind, taking the place of the other, subdued but ever present, that asked why it had not begun before. The vast space separating them at table seemed to have contracted, it shrank to nothing when she appealed to him for advice and this he gave, after a moment's due consideration, for he wanted to be prompt but not hasty, and then, for the first time in many years, he looked her fairly in the face. He noticed its length, the heavy nose, the dark eyes set a little too near it, the strong hair streaked with grey and brushed back from a high forehead, and he decided that it was a good face, not handsome, but sensible, and the lips, normally pushed forward as though ready to let out a puff of reproof, were drawn back in the beginning of a smile.

47

'But you know best, you know best, my dear,' he said, anxious to preserve the smile and, walking with his light, bouncing movement, he went contentedly into his study.

Mrs. Doubleday was not a self-indulgent woman and she had few temptations, but when she gave way to them, hardly knowing that she did it, they had a rare delight. Her son's letter was in her desk, he would be at home for Christmas and she was keeping the knowledge to herself, cherishing it, knowing it would lose some of its wonder when she shared it and taking a delicate pleasure in expressing her happiness in a form entirely deceptive to her husband. Partly to prevent him from remembering that this was the day when Reginald's letter came, she had shown him an amiability which was all for her son, and he had taken it for himself. The pathos of his eager response was lost on her, the complacent folly of it amused her. She did not analyse her emotions and she could not have brought herself to believe that they were her subtle revenge on him for having married her, for being able to call himself her husband and Reginald his son. Yet she was well enough pleased with her position and she would not have changed it; she would not even have changed Mr. Doubleday; he suited her, at this stage, very well as he was; she was sure of her superiority and enjoyed it, but because she was convinced of that, she would never forgive him the physical intimacy of their youth, though Reginald was the result. She had an unacknowledged, unreasonable feeling that she had been insulted.

Soon, however, he would have to know of Reginald's unexpected return. To-morrow, at breakfast, she would tell him in a calm voice, but she would have had her secret for twenty-four hours. It was like being alone with Reginald and, as she looked back over the thirty years of his life, she realized how seldom that had been possible.

During the short time before he went to school there had been little leisure to give him. She had worked hard, then, in the house, because she could afford less help, and she had been busy in her husband's first parish, urging him on and trying to fire him with her own ambition, but the few sparks she raised only spluttered feebly and went out. He was content to be a vicar for the rest of his life, and she had wasted time on him that might have been Reginald's, the only time, from birth to preparatory school, when her jealousy of possession would have been satisfied. Preparatory and public schools, the university, an appointment abroad, had left her with short periods of his company when all his interests and his friends were like shadows menacing her supremacy. Reginald as a separate individual hardly existed for her and if she had been asked for an outline of his character, some indication of his tastes, she would have been at a loss; all she knew of him was summed up in the fact that he was hers and it was enough, but she wished she could recover those early days, the loss of them was another count against her husband and looking back, now, she saw the folly of looking forward and planning for the future, even when it was for her son. She ought to have lived in the moment and taken what it gave her: she took this one and refused to have it spoilt by the knowledge that a bad attack of malaria was sending him home before his time.

With a tread as heavy as Mr. Doubleday's was light, she went upstairs to inspect Reginald's bedroom. It was always in perfect order, but she thought she might get a more comfortable armchair for him, she was pleased to imagine signs of wear in the carpet. Then she pulled the lace curtains into better folds and marched out again, without lingering to look at the school and university groups on the walls; she had seen them before, once, when he brought them home, and they did not interest

49

her, while the carpet and the armchair were important because she was to buy them for him.

From the shelter of his study, Mr. Doubleday watched her go down the garden path, basket on arm and wearing one of the tall hats she affected, and in spite of his happy breakfast, the click of the gate released his spirit. He sighed, felt guilty, murmured 'A good wife, a good wife,' and turned to his own affairs.

Mrs. Doubleday's shopping expeditions had the nature of an inspection and not only of the things she wished to buy. She looked in the windows of shops owned by nonconformists, but she did not pass those thresholds. She ignored definite outsiders, like the lady of the manor neglecting villagers of the wrong political party, and though, occasionally, for her own convenience, she invaded neutral territory, she was loyal to those who were loyal to the church. She took an interest in their personal affairs and they found it hard when they had to own to a child with measles or chicken pox, for she gave the impression that the parents were to blame, but she could be relied on for help when it was deserved, she was practical and not unkindly in the proper circumstances and her sense of her own duty was as severe as the one she expected in other people. To-day, her elation did not make her forgetful; she asked questions which were not always welcome and gave suitable advice, she bought her meat and vegetables with her usual care, but when her business was done she did not go home at once to answer letters and compare estimates for turning the parish hall into a pastoral scene of the bazaar; she walked on rather slowly, enjoying the sunshine and making instinctively for open spaces. She paused, however, in front of the big fruit and flower shop in The Barton. She was sensitive, this morning, to its festive air. There were grapes and choice apples in one of the windows, the grapes

50

misty with bloom, the apples gleaming with polish; tall jars of chrysanthemums stood in the other, fluffy white ones looking as though they were made of tissue paper, stiff ones with every curled petal in its place and others dark and dishevelled, as raggedly handsome as gipsies. A few long-stalked roses, a few carnations, very shapely and aware of their beauty, were in slim glass vases and, within the darkness of the shop, in basins on the floor, there were bunches of late roses fresh from country gardens, Michaelmas daisies and marigolds.

It was a constant surprise to Mrs. Doubleday that a shop dealing almost entirely in flowers and fruit should prosper in Upper Radstowe with the steadiness of more important institutions. Through good and bad times, the homely flowers were in their basins on the floor, the choice ones preened themselves in the window. The shop was as firmly established as the Church and though Mrs. Doubleday failed to see what was common to them both, for beauty had no connection with religion in her mind, she remembered that funerals and weddings, ceremonies conducted by the Church, accounted, to a great extent, for the survival of the shop, and this gave her a sense of patronage and the right to linger on the doorstep, though she bought nothing. Behind the counter at the back, the owner, eyeglasses balanced on her nose and secured by a cord to her bosom, was busy wiring flowers for a wreath or a bouquet. She worked quickly, hardly looking at what she did, and peered over her glasses to watch the activities of the son and daughter who dealt with customers. She wired, peered, gave orders, answered questions, missing nothing, remembering everything, calm and confident, mistress of her world, and yet, as those waxy white flowers gratifyingly demonstrated, dependent on the one represented by Mrs. Doubleday. Another woman who had a passion for an absent son

51

might have envied this one a business shared with her children, but Mrs. Doubleday's imagination was not accessible to absurdities and she did not grow wistful over a picture of herself wiring flowers behind the counter while Reginald weighed grapes for customers.

She had to move aside for a young man in a grey suit who carried a large paint brush insufficiently wrapped in brown paper, and strode towards the counter saying, in a voice she recognized, 'Here's the money for the flowers I bought yesterday, Mrs. Stone.'

Mrs. Stone spared time to smile at him and nod in acknowledgment of the money and, still wiring and looking over her eyeglasses, she watched his hurried departure from the shop. Mrs. Doubleday watched it too. He had gone by without seeing her, he was wearing a soft collar, he had bought flowers yesterday, he was too much absorbed in something else to notice his acquaintance in the street and Mrs. Doubleday, liking none of these signs, thought this was the proper moment for an informal call.

CHAPTER VII

CECIL's long legs and his love took him very rapidly up the street and across The Green. He had already done several errands and he was willing to do more. He liked leaving the house for the sake of coming back to it and finding Dahlia there, always busy but also always ready to stop work and talk and tell him how the house would look when she had finished with it. She had none of that concentration on the task in hand which proves the ruin of so many homes and, with her bright hair hidden under a coloured handkerchief, her features seemed to gain in value. The faint powdering of freckles on her nose was more apparent and more charming and the generous curves of a mouth inherited from her mother claimed more attention, and he was in the mood to find her faultless. The talk of the night before had broken down the last barriers and, feeling now that he was truly married, he could allow himself to be riotously happy, though he had the wisdom to appear calm. He knew enough about himself to believe he would be ridiculous in an ecstasy and Dahlia's sense of humour would not be likely to miss absurdity simply because it came from him.

Dahlia's control was the antithesis of his. She was not happy; she was worried about Jenny and while she was honest in her desire to keep the day unspoilt for him, a stronger motive was her family loyalty, the habit of years which could not be forgotten in three weeks of marriage. With any criticism of Jenny he might offer, her common sense would probably have agreed, but her affection, her protectiveness would have resented it. She would not be moved, except to anger, by irrefutable arguments. It was strange to her that Cecil had never been touched by Jenny's elusive, wholly feminine charm; his fancy had ignored her air of fastidiousness and reserve and lighted on the gayer sister, but for those, like Edwin Cummings and Dahlia, who had once been stirred by her, she remained appealing and lovely and forgivable. Dahlia was glad Cecil had not taken his chance to read the letter. She was justified, now, in concealing her uneasiness, and each time he returned to the house with a packet of nails, a supply of distemper or a paint brush, she thrust back the visions Jenny's letter created in her mind. She would not think of the small figure standing forlorn in the midst of furniture which was second-hand much more often than it was antique: she would not hear the dragging footsteps of old Mr. Cummings, who was partially recovered from a stroke, and the difficult, broken speech which passed his twisted lips. 'Sometimes he wanders about in the night', Jenny wrote, 'and there isn't a lock on my bedroom door. I don't know what he says and I know he means to smile at me but he's really making faces. I can't bear it. Kitty and Fanny don't seem to mind, they don't mind touching him, they kiss him every morning. And meals are horrid. But it's a beautiful kitchen, so clean, with shining pots and pans, and flowers on the window sill and a canary, and I could be happy with Kitty and Fanny. I like it when Mr. Cummings has gone to bed and we sit beside the fire and plan about next summer when we're going to have teas in one side of the shop and just good furniture in the other. That was my idea and they like it and all the horrid old fenders and things like that are going to be kept next door, in a little shop they're renting for it. I can't get interested in iron fenders and ugly ornaments and bedroom china.' This was underlined. 'I think it's disgusting to have it in the window but Fanny says you must let people know

54

you've got the complete set. Fanny is very practical. She's letting me pay something every week because I'm not much use at present, so I'm very glad Mother made us have Father's money. Kitty is like you, a little. She laughs a lot and doesn't care what anybody thinks. I wish I could be like that. There are hardly any flowers left in the garden. I always felt as though the lavender would be blooming all the year. I suppose it will come again in the summer but the winter will be very long, and we only have lamps and candles. I wish I had a light I could put on quickly when I'm in bed. I often think of our room in Beulah Mount and how lovely it was to have you in the other bed.'

It was like Jenny to regret circumstances which had been bitterly resented at the time, to forget her past unhappiness in exaggerated present woes, and though Dahlia understood her shrinking from anything physically unpleasant, she felt a strong desire to shake her, she had half a mind to send a telegram bidding her buy nightlights and be sensible, but what most troubled her was the absence of any reference to Edwin Cummings. 'Nothing about young Cummings,' their mother had written of Jenny's letters and there was no mention of him in this one. What part did he take in those evening talks round the fire? And how much had the bedroom china, the iron fenders and the shuffling feet of his father affected Jenny's gratitude for his devotion? 'It isn't fair,' Dahlia murmured, but at the sound of the opening door she went to take the paint brush and at once she dipped it in the distemper.

'I think it's going to be very difficult not to get this smeary,' she said. 'I'll begin in a dark corner. I expect this economy will cost us dear in the end, but never mind, it's fun, I'm always willing to pay for my fun.'

'I'll pay for it gladly,' he said, thinking it would be

hard to refuse her anything she wanted and believing in the modesty of her demands.

'We'll both pay. We'll share,' she said.

'Everything,' he agreed.

'Then why didn't you buy two brushes? What are you going to do while I'm doing this?'

His immediate duty was to answer the front door bell: his misfortune was to find Mrs. Doubleday on the step, and the courtesy of long experience in unwelcome interruptions almost failed him in this case. He tried to pilot her past the study's open door in the tidiness of the little sitting-room, but Dahlia herself frustrated his attempt to spare her this visitation and with the particularly wide smile which neither Cecil nor Mrs. Doubleday yet recognized as a danger signal, she stepped into the passage and invited the caller to come and view her handiwork.

Mrs. Doubleday raised one foot and then another over the obstructions on the floor and Dahlia, holding her head high and looking like a proud child, glanced from the patch of distemper to Mrs. Doubleday's high hat and back again. There was little enough on which anyone could comment and Mrs. Doubleday made a more general remark.

'I understood that poor Mr. Sproat got the house all ready for you before you were married. That is what he said he was doing,' she added with emphasis.

'He's a truthful person,' Dahlia said gently and the subject under discussion felt uneasy. Dahlia still smiled but the brush in her hand had somehow assumed the appearance of a weapon.

'I've known him a good deal longer than you have,' said Mrs. Doubleday, and Dahlia said solemnly, 'Yes, but I'd like to go on believing in him if I can.'

'Of course, of course.' Inadvertently Mrs. Doubleday fell into her husband's trick of repetition. She felt unaccountably confused. 'I was just thinking it was a pity to undo all his work. A man finds it difficult, but I suppose it couldn't be helped in the circumstances.'

'No, it couldn't be helped,' Dahlia said cheerfully, and he admired her clever obtuseness. 'But he wasn't responsible for the grimy wall-paper. The man who put that up must have been dead for a very long time.'

'Well, Dahlia, I always advised you against the house.'

'You did,' Cecil said with a certain grimness, 'so I'm sure you'd like to see the rest of it.'

'No, do your business first, in the sitting-room,' Dahlia said, 'and then we'll all go over the house together. I can't have people looking at the house without me.'

'But I didn't come on business. I just came to ask how you were getting on.'

'Oh, I see. How nice!' said Dahlia, putting down her brush. 'Then I'll go and make some tea and we'll have a party.'

'Not for me,' Mrs. Doubleday said firmly. 'I don't take tea in the middle of the morning. It's what I'm always telling the women in the parish they shouldn't do, but they were bred to it and I can't break them of the habit. You must see to that, Cecil, or Dahlia will lose her com plexion and have her digestion spoilt.'

This was another of those implications best met with obtuseness and Dahlia did it so successfully that he almost thought Mrs. Doubleday's shot had gone too wide in that direction. It had hit him fairly enough, but he could not let Dahlia know it so he held his angry peace and she said innocently, 'Oh, I never have it in the mornings. I thought you might like it.' Then with a slight change in manner, a touch of dignity, she asked Mrs. Doubleday to follow her up the stairs.

She was admirable, Cecil thought; she was capable of dealing with all the gossips of Upper Radstowe, but when

57

the visitor took her leave, having remarked on the deficiencies of the cistern, warned Dahlia that, no doubt, people would soon be calling, and given her some information about the way she should behave, there was a different brightness about Dahlia's eyes.

'Does she try to be horrid?' she asked slowly. 'Or can't she help it? I don't mind, it makes me laugh, and I do wish Jenny could have seen her turning out her toes when she came down the kitchen stairs, flat-footed, like this. Jenny would have looked disgusted, as though it was indecent. A person who walks like that ought to be very careful to be pleasant. But I'm sorry for the poor old thing. I don't suppose she has anything to make her happy. And we have.'

The statement was almost a question and his answer was quick and unmistakable.

'So long as you don't mind,' she murmured. Then, freeing herself, she exclaimed. 'It's so old-fashioned! I didn't know people bothered much about one's parents, nowadays. Except people like the Merrimans,' she added.

'You don't yet know your Upper Radstowe,' he said. 'We're a long way behind the times and physical violence in return for insult would hardly be an anachronism here. I shall hit her one of these days.'

'It would be a great pleasure,' Dahlia said gravely. 'And I'm glad you want to do it. It makes me like you very much. But the best revenge is not understanding what she means. Let's get on with the distempering and pretend we're daubing Mrs. Doubleday. I wonder if she's nice at home.'

She thought of her own mother, uneducated, inarticulate, outside the social and moral world of Mrs. Doubleday, but incapable of meanness, tolerant, possessed unknowingly of a wisdom derived from the country in which all her days had been spent, where she had seen the seasons come

58

and go, the crops spring up and fall under the reaper, bareness where once there had been woodland and fertility overcoming waste, while the rocks and the shape of the land, the wind and the rain remained the same. It was a training to reduce the senses of personal importance, to show that death for one might be life for another, and she had been willing to sacrifice herself for Jenny. She had not given her action so grand a name, she had not seen, perhaps hardly felt it as a sacrifice; it was the natural thing to do and she had done it in that spirit.

'I shall go over the bridge very soon,' Dahlia said.

'Yes, I should,' Cecil said heartily.

'All the same,' she said, giving him the brush and watching him critically for a minute, 'all the same, I do wish Mrs. Doubleday could have seen my father. He would have paralysed her. And I wish you'd seen him, too. It would have been nice for you to know that part of me came from him.'

'I don't need any such assurance. It's quite apparent. I think what annoys Mrs. Doubleday is that she can't patronize you.'

'Poor thing,' Dahlia said again. 'Some day I shall begin boasting to her about my grand aunt in Herefordshire. I've got one, you know.'

'You never told me.'

'Because it doesn't matter. Or does it matter? Perhaps it does. Perhaps I'm more of a snob than I think. What rubbish it all is! But tell me Mrs. Doubleday's Christian name. We seem to be on Christian name terms, so I'd better know it.'

'Yes, I noticed that. Well,' he was almost apologetic, 'she's called Flora.'

'Perfect,' Dahlia said contentedly. 'I shall enjoy calling her that.' She noticed, with amusement, a gleam of anxiety in his eye. 'And she called you Cecil. First Mr.

59

Sproat — it really is a dreadful name — and then she decided on Cecil, so now we know we're all good friends. And Mr. Doubleday's name is Norman. That's good, too. I wonder what they called their son.'

'No idea,' Cecil said indifferently.

CHAPTER VIII

IT was not long before Dahlia heard that name, though Mr. Doubleday was conscientious about this last week of Cecil's holiday and refrained from interrupting it even to give his happy news. It was a week of perfect weather, with slight frosts in the morning, sunshine and blue sky afterwards and enough chill at night to make sitting by the fire a comfortable, drowsy ending to their day. Early each afternoon they went across the bridge and walked in the country so familiar to Dahlia and almost unknown to Cecil. They went over fields belonging to the Merrimans and over the stiles set in their neat fences and so came to the Monks' Pool and saw that quiet water so strewn with fallen leaves that there was hardly room for any reflection of sky or tree. When they stood still, they heard the plop of a water rat, the quacking of the ducks at the far end of the pond and the crashing of wood pigeons among the branches and, with a shifted foot, the dry leaves crackled under it. It was a secret place; all the neat fences and signs of improvement were out of sight: under these trees the monks must have sat when they came to take their carp, the descendants of those fish were in the water, the wood pigeons had a long lineage, yet the past seemed to have no influence there. It was a breathless present that overhung anyone who stood there, it was a lovely thing created for the moment, with the appearance of having been like that for ever and the certainty that it would last only as long as it was seen and must do its best to hold the observer for the sake of its own life.

Dahlia and Cecil turned and went very quietly along

the rutted road and round the corner. Already that bubble of gold and brown and blue must have broken, and they had not heard a sound. A little farther on there was a farm, a busy woman in a white apron, geese stretching their necks at the intruders, and Dahlia said in relief, 'I like this better. I like ordinary things. That place — it was enchanted. Beautiful, but enchanted. I've seen it often before, but not quite like this. Perhaps I'm different. It seemed as if it didn't want to let me go. I was a little frightened.'

'I'm much more frightened of these geese,' Cecil said. 'D'you think they mean anything? But yes, the pool was beautiful.'

'Don't make a sermon out of it,' Dahlia begged quickly, and then, 'Oh dear, oh dear! I've done it again, but you've forgiven me. Make a sermon out of these geese and us.' Throwing her hands in front of her, she ran at them. 'Dangers boldly faced will disappear and that sort of thing. You see, they've gone.'

'But,' he said, 'you mustn't think I'm turning everything I see into a sermon . . .'

'I won't,' she said with prompt docility.

'Most of the time I'm thinking how pretty you are and how you match the woods with your hair and those brown clothes.'

'That's very satisfactory,' she said. 'I expect I match because I was born near here. I'll show you the house soon, but I don't think we'll go close to it. I believe it's empty still, except for ghosts. I shouldn't like to look in at the windows.'

'We needn't look at it at all.'

'But I want you to see it.' She was glad he was not laughingly comforting about the ghosts. She knew they were there; her father as he was in his last years, and Jenny and herself as small children, lying in bed and hearing

62

the lorries laden with war material go thundering down the dark road, knowing that their absent father was somehow concerned with the thundering, so that, for them, his part in the war was that of a man constantly riding on a lorry through the night, while inside the house, doors opened and shut and there were murmuring voices and laughter they did not want to hear. She could not bear to see and hear those ghosts, she could not speak plainly to them of Cecil; it was a shame even to remember them, for, not far off, the mother who had stolen out into the little orchard to meet her lover was living with him on his farm and though she had failed to help one daughter, she was determined not to hurt the other. Dahlia hated the ghosts, but she could understand that episode in her mother's life. In her own character there was the same recklessness, the same impulse to take happiness as it came, but she was her father's daughter, too, and here was Cecil, walking by her side like a companionable guardian angel who had no work to do. She felt contented and secure, secure enough to say, as she pointed, 'And Thomas Grimshaw's farm is in those trees. It wouldn't take us long to get there.'

'No,' he said, 'these are our days. Don't let us have other people in them.'

She nodded her acquiescence. She did not say that she found it impossible to exclude the two others for whom she cared, she did not ask whether he would have been more willing to call on a different kind of mother, and, as she looked at his severe profile which could soften so charmingly for her, she knew she could get no further into his mind than he could go in hers and, lighthearted and happy though she was, she had a moment's panic, realizing that each was bound to an essential stranger and that she was almost completely dependent on his care.

She slipped her hand under his arm, he squeezed it against his side and the friendly contact gave her comfort. It was good to be here with him, mounting a lane that followed the edge of a bare field, with the sun shining and a little wind teasing the sere stalks in the hedge and chasing the crisp leaves. The field ran up to the skyline without a break and it seemed that it must be hiding something wonderful, and as they rose to a level with its top and found only a gentler slope of the field, the tree-studded pasture land dropped away on the other side to give them a view of the Channel and the hills beyond. The beauty expected on one side had not been there, but it was given on the other, and they leaned over a gate and saw the sky pale over those faint hills but deepening in colour as it approached, until it overhung them in a blue made more brilliant by the whiteness of clouds derisively sailing by. The grass had a peculiar vividness of green, there was a shining blackness or a gleaming pallor on the trunks of trees; the leaves, hanging or fallen, made tall flames or fires creeping along the ground, and a fir copse in the distance was like a cold, dark lake.

'Is it as beautiful as we think it is?' Dahlia asked.

'That's a very difficult question. It's what the philosophers quarrel about. Would it be there at all if we were not here?'

'The Monks' Pool isn't there any longer,' she said, 'but it will come back the next time I want it. I don't think this goes away. This isn't magic. But would it look so lovely to us if we didn't know there were slums in Radstowe, if we weren't thinking that, in a day or two, our holiday will be over?'

'I don't know. I know this time with you has been perfect, but I'm quite ready to begin work again.'

'So am I,' said Dahlia.

'Well, then——' he said and she did not continue the

argument. She was not afraid of work; for her the end of the holiday was not so much a cessation of leisure as the beginning of a new life and, perhaps, a new Cecil. She had known two of him already. There was the earnest young man at whom she had laughed and whom she gradually came to see as the one she needed; there was the married lover who, except for that short quarrel and his succeeding confidences, had set aside all his preoccupations and given everything to her; and the day after to-morrow, there would be the clergyman in a stiff collar, saying things in public which made her feel uneasy, being a special kind of person in the eyes of others, often doing and always meaning to do good, but making it necessary for her to adjust herself and her conduct, and her opinions if she could. She would do her best, but again she wished he were that greengrocer, going early to market, coming back with things which were definite in their value and giving people what they wanted instead of what he thought they ought to have. She had not considered all this before she married him and she saw the unfairness of allowing it to influence her now. The man's profession was an accident as far as she was concerned but it was none the less her duty to accept the consequences. Moreover, she knew she was setting her prejudice and ignorance against definite convictions and she wondered how far her father's tacit cynicism had affected her in religion and other matters. She had never set store on him, like Jenny, as a symbol of their birthright from one side of the family: she had had less communication with him than Jenny had enjoyed, and that was little enough, but there he had been, a distinguished figure in a wholly unsuitable setting, with a quiet manner of speech from which all the life had departed, a walking mistake who could not see himself as anything else, an exile with all his hidden thoughts on home and a bitter anger for the conventions from which he had broken but of which, fundamentally, he could not rid himself.

'Would it be bringing other people in', Dahlia asked, 'if we went to the village and the churchyard? I should like you to see the stone that Edwin Cummings designed for father.'

'Let's go by all means,' Cecil said.

She wanted to go, but she was disappointed by his willingness. It would have been more consistent if he had refused, it would have been less like a criticism of her mother. Perhaps he agreed only because he did not like to deny her twice. She hoped it was that, while she knew he secretly shrank from meeting her mother. She guessed that, in spite of himself and for all his courtesy, he could not forget she was a woman who had been a sinner, of the kind for which he felt most repugnance; that the memory made a dark background against the thought or sight of her. Dahlia was young to be so quick but, since she was a little girl, she had been watching for, and pretending she did not see, that disapproval, and she had been able, at the same time, to say and to believe she did not care. It was easy to defy criticism in the next door neighbour or the woman who lived three broad fields away; it was harder to suspect it in Cecil and chiefly hard because she would see it as a failing in him, and she was very anxious not to find failings in him. 'He's too good to understand a thing like that,' she told herself, but his criticism seemed to her like labelling a grown-up person as a glutton because he had made himself sick with overeating when he was five years old.

'I don't think we'll go to the churchyard,' she said.

'Tired?' he asked, and she said 'No', and walked on faster. She wanted to tell him everything that was in her mind, to make sure of what was in his, to have everything clear between them, and she stood still and opened her lips to speak and let out nothing but a breath.

66

'I'm sure you're tired,' he said. 'If we go to the village we might find a car to take us home.'

She was not tired; she had simply decided against taking a risk and that went against her nature; she was engaged in the arduous task of refusing to draw inferences from that decision and she could not keep a note of anger out of her voice, though she laughed as she spoke.

'I'm not tired and if I were on the point of collapse I shouldn't dare to go home in a car. All the old ladies in Upper Radstowe would talk about it. They'd think I was delicate — and what a hindrance to poor Mr. Sproat — or lazy, or extravagant. And Mrs. Doubleday would come round in the morning to inquire and I don't think I could bear that. No, we'll tramp home at a great pace, full of energy and talking in ringing voices. Don't you hate people who so obviously don't mind letting other people hear what they have to say? Perhaps you don't, but you do hate Mrs. Doubleday and that's a great bond between us.'

'I should be sorry if that was all we had to trust to.' He was a little puzzled by the mixture of amusement and bitterness she presented.

'It's a very good thing to be going on with,' she said.

CHAPTER IX

THE Ladies' Working Party was held in the house of Mrs. Bagshot in The Avenue and thither Cecil was to escort Dahlia on the afternoon of the presentation. This was on the Monday after their holiday ended. Her first public appearance had been in church the day before, when Mr. Doubleday was the preacher, but she had accompanied Cecil to the Mission hall in the evening and found the less conventional service much more to her taste. Mothers could take their babies there and she thought she might become interested in the Mission, though she disapproved of Cecil's ambition to build a church for it. It would be better, she thought, to put the proceeds of the bazaar towards improved heating arrangements in the hall and more comfort in the smaller rooms attached to it.

'So Mrs. Doubleday says,' Cecil said slyly.

'Well, that's a pity, but she's quite right,' Dahlia said fairly. She felt rather more enthusiastic about the working party, and she was setting her hat at its most becoming angle when she heard footsteps on the garden path and, looking from her bedroom window, she was in time to see the top of Mrs. Doubleday's tall hat and of Mr. Doubleday's soft, low one. The bell was rung. Cecil opened the door and Dahlia pulled a little more of her bright hair into view, examined her appearance in the long glass and ran downstairs.

In the study, Mr. Doubleday, holding his hat behind his back, was making a show of interest in Cecil's books, Mrs. Doubleday sat in a grudging manner on the edge of the armchair, there was an odd expression on Cecil's face, but Dahlia, all smiles, waved a clean pair of gloves and said, 'We're just starting for the ceremony.'

Mr. Doubleday turned willingly from the books to look at this gay young figure and he put out his hand for hers, while Mrs. Doubleday said firmly, 'Yes, we've come to fetch you.'

'It's a great occasion', said Mr. Doubleday. His hand was soft and warm, but friendly. 'We must all be there, all be there. Mrs. Bagshot's making quite a party of it.'

'It's the sort of thing Mrs. Bagshot enjoys and she doesn't get many opportunities,' Mrs. Doubleday said caustically. 'But we work afterwards. Until half-past six. You must bring your thimble.'

'Thimble, thimble,' Dahlia said, looking round busily. 'In my workbasket, Cecil, in the sitting-room. Would you like to see my sitting-room?' she asked the vicar. 'I'm very proud of it.'

'Some other time,' Mrs. Doubleday decided. 'We must not be late.'

'Punctuality — yes,' Mr. Doubleday murmured vaguely.

'It's a big house, Dahlia that's — why we have the working party there — but you'll find nothing imposing about Mrs. Bagshot.'

'A kind little body,' Mr. Doubleday said. 'Butcher's shops all over Radstowe at one time. Business sold when Bagshot died. Plenty of money.'

'But unfortunately the name was part of the goodwill and, in any case, it couldn't have been forgotten. So you see . . .'

'You mean that I mustn't mention meat,' Dahlia said, and Mr. Doubleday chuckled. 'How difficult these things are.'

'Yes, but you'll soon get used to them. I just wanted you to know that Mrs. Bagshot, in spite of the house, is not one of the important people in Upper Radstowe, so you can be perfectly natural and you'll find it will all go quite easily.'

'Quite easily,' Mr. Doubleday echoed, nodding kindly.

'And now, if Cecil's found the thimble, we'd better start.'

'And it's a very nice present,' Mr. Doubleday said in Dahlia's ear, as they passed into the narrow hall. 'Yes.' He spoke in a whisper from behind his hat. 'Soup tureen — silver-plated.'

'Lovely!' Dahlia whispered back. Her sitting-room was safe.

'You've got to be surprised though.'

'Of course!' she said.

It was not much more than a long stone's throw to Mrs. Bagshot's house and the little procession walked slowly, Mrs. Doubleday and Cecil in front, Dahlia with Mr. Doubleday who talked happily about his son.

'We shall have to have some parties,' he said. 'Christmas time, you know.'

'Does he like parties?'

'Well, he's young, he's young. Can't help liking them, can he? But . . .' he realized that perhaps it was not wise to promise parties; they were not for him to give or to withhold — 'he's been ill, pretty bad, so we shall have to see. Malaria. Nasty thing. Now, here's a pretty scene.'

They had turned into The Avenue and the wide road lying on a slope between the houses and the trees that gave the place its name, was edged with coloured drift from the elms, and the path under these and the grass beyond were encrusted with gold and bronze.

'It's like a jewel,' Dahlia said.

'Yes, but mind these damp leaves underfoot. Flora!' he called, 'mind you don't have a slip. Give Mrs. Doubleday your arm, Sproat. Ah, my wife's very independent — and sure-footed, fortunately. But you take mine, my dear. That's right.' She did not know how much she

70

pleased him with her quick response. 'Nearly there, nearly there,' he said.

At the big gate, hospitably thrown open, Cecil waited, while Mrs. Doubleday stalked towards the door. With a half-smile he raised his eyebrows to ask if all was well and she gave him a little nod. She knew he was proud of her and she passed through Mrs. Bagshot's grand portals without trepidation.

It was certainly the largest house she had ever entered and plainly the parlourmaid would have not served Mrs. Bagshot if the family had still been in the butcher's trade; as they followed her towards the drawing-room they had a glimpse of a laden table in the dining-room and Mrs. Doubleday said, 'Too much food, as usual,' in a loud aside. The hall reminded Dahlia of a shop in which the goods had been indiscreetly massed. She had an impression of rugs, brass gongs, palms in pots and carved furniture of a kind to make Edwin Cummings shudder and, on the outside and inside of the doors, heavy velvet curtains swung on gleaming rods.

'Cosy, cosy,' Mr. Doubleday said, doing his best for Mrs. Bagshot.

Mrs. Bagshot looked like an unwelcome stranger in her big room where already a number of women had gathered. Very small and neatly dressed, with childish blue eyes and a little, nervous face, she stood beyond the threshold, raised a hand towards Dahlia and wisely dropped it in favour of Mrs. Doubleday.

'I'll take her round and introduce her to everybody else,' Mrs. Doubleday said in a loud voice, but Dahlia stood beside her hostess for a minute, listening to her nervous congratulations and smiling thanks for them.

'Come along, come along,' Mrs. Doubleday said with an attempt at coaxing and Mrs. Bagshot, looking guilty, patted Dahlia's arm and let her go.

71

'We'll have a talk afterwards,' she whispered.

Dahlia shook twenty hands, smiled twenty smiles and looked frankly into twenty pairs of eyes during the next few minutes. She was not shy because she was much more interested in this assortment of women than in herself; for the same reason she was neither glib nor clumsy; she faithfully obeyed Mrs. Doubleday's order to be natural and Mrs. Bagshot, gazing up at Cecil almost tearfully, informed him that he was going to be very happy.

'So pretty and so sweet,' she said.

He knew there was an active brain at work behind Dahlia's gentle manners and afterwards he was astonished to find that she hardly misplaced a name and could add a suitable epithet to each one, but she was in that company a good deal longer than he was, for after the presentation of the soup tureen and a rich tea in an over-heated room, the two clergymen took their leave and left the women to their labours. Hats and coats were removed and put on the lace coverlet and pale blue eiderdown of Mrs. Bagshot's bed before the party settled down at a long table in a room upstairs. Mrs. Doubleday went to the cupboards in the walls as though she owned them and drew out bundles of calico and flannel, and Dahlia sat with her thimble in front of her until she was supplied with some puzzling parts of a shirt.

'Tack up the seams,' said Mrs. Doubleday, 'and then take them to Miss Fairweather to be stitched.'

Miss Fairweather, with an ostracized expression, sat behind a sewing machine at a small table apart. When she was idle, she looked straight in front of her; when she was supplied with work she bent her sharp nose over it, guided it under the needle with a firm, bony hand, turned the handle rapidly with the other, snapped the cotton, dropped her hands to her lap and waited for the next garment. She seemed to have a personal animosity for each thing she touched and an unemotional satisfaction in driving the needle through it. Not once did she join in the general chatter and now and then, as Dahlia struggled with her seam, she found herself compelled to watch Miss Fairweather.

'Funny, isn't she?' said a large woman in the next chair, with a half wink towards Miss Fairweather. 'But I expect you think we're a queer lot anyway. So we are. Hard on you, I call it. There's not one of us isn't old enough to be your mother and if it was me, I'd have an engagement every Monday, I would really. I come myself because I'm a friend of Mrs. Bagshot's and I'm always ready for a good tea and a nice fire, not being well off myself, and she likes to have me, but at your age you wouldn't have seen me inside a sewing meeting. It's not natural. Let me have that shirt, dear, you're putting the side to the tail.'

'I don't know how to manage shirts,' Dahlia said in a sort of despair.

Suddenly she felt tired and lonely. The kindness of this fat Mrs. Matthews made her want to cry. She was surrounded by strangers who had done their duty towards her and were now talking busily about people and affairs of which she had no knowledge and they were all middle-aged or old, set in their opinions and habits. She thought they looked like houses without windows, and as she watched all those fingers, fat and thin, and heard all those voices and the waspish whirr of the sewing machine, she wanted to be back in Beulah Mount with Jenny and her mother, she longed for the relaxation of being with people she had known all her life. These women looked dryly competent and useful; only Mrs. Matthews and Mrs. Bagshot seemed to have eyes for more than the work in hand, or interest for more than their own small importances; Mrs. Doubleday was no doubt secretly rejoicing over the failure with the shirt and, raising her voice a little, Dahlia said, 'But I can dress dolls. I could make all sorts of things for the bazaar.'

'Then I should do,' said Mrs. Matthews. 'And I suppose you'll get yourself up as one of these shepherdesses. And I must say, you'll be the only one of this lot to look it. But they're going to get some young girls, outsiders, you know, to help.'

Suddenly an authoritative voice boomed over a large bosom at the end of the table. 'We must have sideshows. The success of the whole thing will depend on the sideshows. Fortune tellers, little plays, competitions — we can get the young men to manage them and they'll bring in all their friends. What we want to avoid, Mrs. Doubleday, is making this a parochial affair. We want to attract the whole of Upper Radstowe. Even some of the other suburbs,' she conceded. 'People from across the Downs, people from Combe Friars. We must concentrate more on the sideshows. That's where we shall make the money. If we're not careful, this will be nothing but a Sale of Work. A Sale of Work!' She gazed round the table and only Miss Fairweather kept her bleak and detached stare. 'What's the good of that?' she demanded.

Mrs. Matthews curled her fingers round her mouth and leaned towards Dahlia. 'Mrs. Tothill,' she said. 'Ought to have been an M.P.'

'If I hadn't been away from home, I should have seen to this before, but if you give my sons a free hand, I guarantee they make a success of it.'

'Big contractors,' Mrs. Matthews said, knowingly squeezing up her eyes. 'And she's quite right.'

The assembly on the whole agreed with Mrs. Matthews that Mrs. Tothill was quite right, and it interested Dahlia to see how, under the assault of this managing character the personality of Mrs. Doubleday seemed to dwindle.

Within the limits of her authority and experience, she had a sort of power; outside these, she looked slightly bewildered in her stubbornness.

'I must hear what the vicar thinks about it,' she said.

'There'll be no difficulty with the vicar,' said Mrs. Tothill, truly enough. 'The only pity is that your son won't be back in time to help us.'

If possible, Mrs. Doubleday's face hardened a little; to that remark she made no reply and Mrs. Tothill turned her attention to Dahlia.

'Mrs. Sproat, you can help us in this and get all your friends together.'

'I haven't any,' Dahlia said quietly, aware of a quickening of interest round the table, 'but I could paint scenery and make dresses.'

'Good. I'll send my boys round to see you later on.'

'That'll keep you out of the sewing meeting,' said Mrs. Matthews. 'Good thing, too,' and under cover of an eager discussion about sideshows, reminiscences of other bazaars and stories of Tothill successes in amateur theatricals, Mrs. Matthews kept Dahlia so well amused that she forgot to feel forlorn. It seemed that both Mrs. Bagshot and Mrs. Matthews had been against the soup tureen as a present.

'Just another thing to clean, we thought. Mrs. Bagshot was all for a good eiderdown — she has a beauty herself — but then we didn't know whether it would be one large or two small. There's always that nowadays. And Mrs. Bagshot never speaks up in company. Nervous, you know. I must say, you said your piece very nicely, not too much of it, either, and no gush. And Mr. Sproat looking so pleased. You're going to be a good help to him.'

'I hope so,' Dahlia said sincerely, and her wish was more strongly influenced by the remembrance of him in the drawing-room, than by any sense of duty or feeling of affection. Mr. Doubleday had been the vicar with a jovial or sympathetic word for everybody; Cecil had been an ordinary gentleman among acquaintances. So far, at least, he was not tainted with a sense of his special position and, when she stood up to offer her simple thanks, she had seen him leaning against the wall, wearing a half amused and wholly confident expression which had warmed her. It would be good to escape from these chattering women and tell him, with a reasonable amount of caution, what she thought of them, and she was thankful when Miss Fairweather viciously put the cover on the sewing machine.

She had to thank her hostess for sparing her the walk back with Mrs. Doubleday. Mrs. Bagshot drew her into the drawing-room, patted her hand, told her to run in any time she liked and timidly suggested that she should take home some of the superfluous cakes.

'Mrs. Matthews always has some of them on our Mondays. But perhaps you'll be offended — perhaps Mr. Sproat wouldn't like it — and oh dear, you've got the tureen to carry back already.'

'But we can put some of the cakes inside it,' Dahlia said.

She had taken his arm and made a friend of Mr. Doubleday; she had accepted Mrs. Bagshot's cakes and made another friend of her.

CHAPTER X

CECIL's lack of real interest in details was a surprise and a disappointment to Dahlia. Her few close relationships had been with women who have a natural appetite and need for minute descriptions and exact reports of conversations and she found that he neither wanted them nor knew how to give them to her. He would tell her briefly what some one had said to him and what he had said in reply and expect her to understand whatever significance there might be in the remarks or the situation. An inquiry as to the actual words used was unproductive; yet to her these were all important, these were revealing. No doubt Cecil himself had received impressions subtler than the ones he conveyed, he might even tell her what these were and ask for her agreement, but she wanted the tones of the voices, the gestures and the words before she could give an opinion. He could not, or would not, remember them and he seemed to think that her desire for them, like Mr. Doubleday's, was allied in some way to the traditionally feminine love of gossip. He would listen with amusement to her own stories but sometimes she thought he was like a mother who enjoys the prattling of her child while she has her mind on something else. For Dahlia, the remark of the grocer who handed her a packet of tea, people's faces, house and clothes, were part of the stuff of life; they were also interesting in themselves, as the experiment of a scientist may be to him, and, like him, though with a much less conscious purpose, she was co-ordinating her knowledge and anxious to share it. Thus, when she returned from her first visit to Grimshaw's

Farm, there was a double reason for disciplining herself; Cecil would want to hear as little as possible about her mother and, even if the visit had been to someone else, he would not have wished to know how the furniture was disposed or the shape of the garden.

Tired after her long walk, she sat at the bottom of the stairs and took off her muddy shoes before venturing further into the house kept clean by herself, with the weekly help of Mrs. Bailey, and when Cecil found her there, put the proper question and received a cheerful answer, he assumed that she was as well satisfied as he was. He saw the big bunch of flowers at her feet and gave it a little nod of appreciation, but he asked no questions, and again Dahlia longed for Jenny. Hearing about Grimshaw's Farm, she would wear her little look of distaste, because it was his; nevertheless, she would listen and Dahlia would be able to present her picture to another mind and get an inexplicable content. She wanted to tell someone how snugly the farm was backed by sycamores and flanked by outhouses and how the garden, whence came these flowers, had that air, most pleasing in gardens, of having grown up with the house and received no more attention than was strictly necessary. The long front of the house had weathered to a beautiful dull red, its roof tiles and those of the barns were cushioned, here and there, with green and yellow moss, and while everything looked comfortable and water-tight, some liberty had been allowed to time. The rose bushes were overgrown and the blossoms suffered in quality, there was no scheme of colour or kind in the plants under the low windows, but there was something better than a planned beauty in the place; generations of men had made a hard-won living from it and their women, working as hard or harder, had found time to sow a few seeds, to put a flower root in the ground and keep the beds clear of weeds. The beauty had

78

come, as it were, from rare moments of leisure, it had survived and increased and was all the greater for its subor-
dination to homelier necessities. Inside the house there
was the smell of stored sunshine, of a kitchen fire, chiefly
fed by wood, that had been burning, summer and winter,
for a century, of apples and baking bread and damp cloth
under a hot iron. The threshold was worn by the passage
of heavy boots, the kitchen flags were worn, too, and in
places they had sunk a little so that only familiar feet
could cross the room without uncertainty. It was the
typical living room of a farmhouse built when there was
no grudging of space or labour and the women were as
little likely to complain of many yards to scrub as the
men of broad acres to plough, and though there was no
need for Louisa to be on her knees about that business,
this, as Dahlia saw at once, was the house of a woman
who made sure that it was done. In the little white house
where they had lived until their removal to Beulah Mount,
she was not notable for domestic activity; in Upper
Radstowe, too, the house had been just clean enough; in
both of them she had been misplaced, but here, in the
atmosphere of her own girlhood, she seemed to have
recovered the best traditions of her forebears and to have
taken on those of the Grimshaw women.

'My father only rented his farm,' she said to Dahlia,
'but I don't know when this didn't belong to Grimshaws.
And the Merrimans still wanting to buy it! Well, let them
want! I suppose they'd give it to that lad if he got married.'

'And how charming they would make it,' Dahlia said,
with an irony lost on Louisa.

'It's all right as it is,' she said. 'And I've been thinking,'
she went on slowly, a little shyly, 'I was a bit soft to fancy
they'd ever have looked at Jenny.'

This was the only reference she made to the circumstances of her marriage. There had been time and

opportunity, during these months, for learning that, apart from an old village scandal, a man who habitually soiled his hands in his own land was no fit relative for the Merrimans, who could not understand, or resented in a working farmer, the passion with which he held it. They had a land hunger of their own, but it was of a different kind. They were enlarging for the future, he was preserving the past as well as enjoying the present, and he must have revealed some of his sentiments to Louisa, for she said proudly, 'There were Grimshaws here before ever the Merrimans got out of their little back shop in Radstowe.'

This was quite unlike any other remark Dahlia had heard from her and there was comfort in remembering it. She would not have quoted Thomas Grimshaw if she had disliked him; there was no doubt she liked her dairy and her home and, for one of her nature, perhaps the conditions of her life were more important than the actual personality of her husband, so long as that was not definitely antagonistic.

'I took to butter-making as natural as though I'd never stopped,' she said, but she did not offer any of her produce to Dahlia. With her lazy, powerful movements, she stooped and picked the flowers from the beds. The colour she had lost in the basement kitchen of Beulah Mount had come back into her cheeks, the sloping sunlight burnished her hair; what had been a little flamboyant in her appearance there, was perfect in this setting, and it seemed as though some ruthless heavenly artist must have arranged matters with the sole purpose of bringing her here, where she looked like the human expression of the house and the farm and all their scents and sounds. And, with an aesthetic success, he had inevitably made a spiritual one, for there was apparent in Louisa a satisfaction that went below the face of things, except when she spoke of Jenny.

'I've seen your house. When are you coming to see mine?' Dahlia asked, and she heard a forced note in the question, though the wish behind it was genuine.

'I wish I could see Jenny in one of hers,' was Louisa's reply. 'I don't like for her to be down there. And he's a nice lad enough, but it's not natural. And her never so much as naming him in a letter.'

She threw a look over her broad shoulder at the house drowsing in the mellow afternoon and the look was like a comment on all the empty rooms behind the blinking windows and on the impossibility of persuading Jenny, who lived with strangers, to enter one of them. Then she met Dahlia's eyes and, for a minute, they looked at each other across the shadowy figures of the people who had been concerned in their lives, the shifting scenes which came from the memory or the imagination of both and, during that minute, they were completely united in the conviction that, for good or evil, those people and those scenes had brought them where they stood and sent Jenny into the little Somersetshire town.

'Oh well . . .' Louisa said.

As Dahlia walked home, she realized that Thomas Grimshaw and Cecil had only been mentioned in passing, she guessed that her mother spoke of Jenny to her husband as little as Dahlia did to hers, and life seemed to her like a great stretch of open country, beautiful and exciting, but blocked, here and there, by stone walls which might, indeed, come to pieces, but would hurt her in their fall if she tried to climb them, and though their height would be lessened, the stones would still lie in an unsightly heap. It was better to pretend they were not there and shift her course a little, but while she saw the wisdom of avoiding difficulties, her youth demanded the right to march on unhindered. There was no sense in building walls of prejudice and reserve and secret con-

81

demnations and old resentments, in saying one might pass this way but not that, yet when she pictured all humanity in a state of brotherly love, going across that open country with no obstacles before them, like a vast and conscientiously happy picnic in which there was no diversity of opinion about the place and hour for the opening of the luncheon baskets, no quarrelling about necessities that had been forgotten and no petty animosities to spice the meal, she decided that a life of such cheerful progression would be a dull affair. Sin and disease and aching hearts were deplorable in themselves and she was sorry for the sufferers but, among all the other ingredients of life, they had their place, and she remembered how she and Cecil had looked over the brilliant fields to the Channel and the hills and wondered how much of that beauty depended on their realization of contrast. Even the sewing meeting which, in return for the tureen, she felt obliged to attend, was bearable because most of its members, as individuals, were not: Mrs. Doubleday, treating the cupboards as her own, Mrs. Tothill, throwing up a window without so much as asking Mrs. Bagshot's leave, indications that some of the ladies who had welcomed Dahlia so kindly had now learnt that her mother had kept lodgings in Beulah Mount and were prepared to be patronizing or painfully delicate about certain subjects, these little happenings and states of mind were what kept Dahlia's humour satisfied and her brain alert. A company of entirely lovable needlewomen would have been much more formidable than the one she had to face; a husband without danger zones would have been too tame a companion, and when she sat on the stairs and saw him giving his little nod, acknowledging the flowers with their scent half-bitter, half-sweet, earthy and damp, but, as it were, closuring any information in connection with them, she stifled her injured feelings. Things had to be judged in the whole, not in part, and the whole was mainly good. She was not yet accustomed to seeing his face change when he looked at her, she had the recurrent pleasure of remembering that he loved her, of surprising him with a look or an attitude he had not seen before. That was a game in which she was the only conscious player and, in a sense, though she was naturally forthright, the whole of her existence in its new conditions, was a kind of game. Still essentially Dahlia Rendall, she had to present Dahlia Sproat to her new acquaintance; when she received visitors or carried messages for Cecil or went with him to the Mission, half of her self was watching the other and seeing that it played its part in a seemly fashion, and sometimes, because she was very young, in a way that might be interesting to others. She did not look towards the time when she would not be so pretty or so young and when her new experiences would have become deadened into a routine, and there was no reason why she should, for she was definitely interested in human beings and they would last as long as she did. They were like the printing on the leaves of a book with a leaf for every day; she could read it with expectation, disappointment or indifference and she could turn back to study it again; she could guess how the story might develop, but she was not allowed to see clearly beyond her daily page. It was a story crowded with characters, and a long way further on she might find her own children.

At present she was awaiting the arrival of the Tothill brothers, eminent for amateur theatricals and the impossibility of failure: later, Reginald Doubleday would appear and go again, not without leaving some impression. There must be hundreds, perhaps thousands, of men and women, as yet unknown, who would have an influence on her history, and always there would be Jenny and her mother or the thought of them, hovering on each page and she could not tell whether they would grow or lessen in importance. There would be passages of comparative dullness and there would be sad ones, and she was prepared for those, some day. Now, she was eager to hurry on to the place where she was painting scenery and designing dresses, getting a good deal of amusement for herself and perhaps creating some surprise, even in the famous Tothills. Each evening she dressed with more than her usual care in expectation of these brothers. She had told Cecil they were to come and he had grunted. He did not know them, it was astonishing how many people he managed not to know; he disliked the fuss and waste of time involved in the bazaar, and she hoped he would be out when the young men arrived, for she knew what they would think of him — they would be wrong, but it might be difficult to set them right.

CHAPTER XI

'I THINK,' said Dahlia, 'he'll be a cross between a camel and a baby elephant.'

She was sitting on the floor by the study fire while Cecil worked at his desk. He had a shaded light burning there and the fire gave enough light for Dahlia whose hands were idle unless she picked up the poker and arranged the coal to keep the fire shapely. He was sorting and writing matter for the parish magazine, a task he had willingly taken over from Mr. Doubleday whose jauntiness became exaggerated and did not appear well in print. Now he made a vague sound and looked towards Dahlia, hardly seeing her at first, his mind still on his work, and then becoming truly aware of her fire-gilded person on the hearthrug, and the turn of her head, showing him her profile and the knob of hair on her neck. The luxury of having her there, in the home she had made, gave him a guilty feeling. The days of furnished rooms and landladies were gone; it was no longer necessary to make a passion of his work because he had no other and, in this constant companionship, he had almost forgotten the loneliness of a man who did not easily make friends. He was ashamed of the little he had done to earn these riches and he remained where he was, as a form of penance.

'Yes, I think that's the mixture,' Dahlia said, tapping the coal. 'Camel and elephant. Old camel and young elephant. If that's possible,' she added. Then she looked up. 'I'm sorry. I didn't mean to interrupt, but I've been perfectly quiet for three-quarters of an hour.'

'I know. You're an angel. Somehow you make quietness quieter.' He left his desk and sat in the armchair on the other side of the hearth. 'What are these animals you are talking about? Is it some idiocy of the Tothills?'

'No!' She chuckled. Then she became earnest. 'But it wouldn't be a bad idea to have a comic zoo or a circus, at the bazaar. It isn't too late. But no. I agree. It would be too uproarious. Tony Tothill . . .'

'Tony?'

'He's the fat one,' Dahlia said.

'But — Tony?'

'The other one is called Simon. Tony might be a little too funny with a comic zoo.'

'Do you call him Tony?'

'With a mister in front. To distinguish them. I can't be totting hills all the time. That,' she explained gravely, 'is the kind of joke he makes.'

Cecil moved impatiently. 'I don't know how you bear it.'

'I like it,' Dahlia said. 'He makes me laugh. Much oftener because he's silly than because he's funny, but he doesn't know that.'

'It might be a good thing to tell him.'

'Why?' Dahlia asked, and she seemed to want an answer.

'Conceited young ass!' was all Cecil could find to say.

'But so babyishly conceited. I like him.'

'And the other one?'

'He is different.'

'And how,' Cecil asked, 'do they address you?'

'Tony calls me Mrs. Spro-at or Mrs. Sper-ote. That's funny too!'

'I call it impudence, but I suppose we must be grateful that he gives you a title.'

'Oh,' she said, 'don't spoil it. I'm enjoying it and I'm really managing him very well considering I've never known any young men. None!' she said in a sort of surprise. 'Except Edwin Cummings and he hardly counts.'

It was Cecil's turn to say 'Why?' and Dahlia's to find a difficulty in answering. She saw at once that to give as a reason his attachment to Jenny, to say he was too sober or she felt sisterly towards him, would suggest an unsuitable pleasure in the company of young men who were unattached, gay and far from brotherly.

'I don't think Edwin was ever really young,' she said.

'Like me, I suppose,' he said sourly, and she exclaimed, 'Ah, don't!' She leaned towards him, and put her hands on the arms of his chair, enfolding without touching him. 'You are you,' she said.

'And I wonder what that means,' he murmured, but by this time she was on his knee and he was already solaced.

'Well, it means this, doesn't it?' she said.

She was happy in his arms. She had the sense of security his love always gave her, but its quality had changed a little. He seemed to be holding her against the approach of other people and this increased her value for herself and he knew that the character of her response was different and they both held to their moment, savouring it and, perhaps, mistaking it.

It was when he went to his desk next morning that he remembered the camel and the elephant. They had intruded on his work, they still seemed to be on his desk and as they had led indirectly to some supremely happy hours, it seemed ungrateful to pay them no attention, so he took the trouble to go downstairs where Dahlia was washing the breakfast dishes in the dark kitchen.

'You never explained about those animals,' he said.

'Animals?' said Dahlia, intent on the prongs of a fork. 'Animals? Oh yes, that was my boy Reginald — the camelphant. Ha! Tony would think that very good, but I suppose I mustn't tell him.'

'I don't understand.'

87

'Haven't you heard about my boy Reginald? When I took that note to Mr. Doubleday yesterday, he talked to me for hours about him. Mrs. Doubleday was out — I waited till I knew she would be — but he saw me coming up the path and opened the door himself. He knocked at the window and made me understand, with nods and becks and all the things that come in that bit of poetry, that I wasn't to ring the bell.'

'H'm. Afraid of losing the chance of a chat.'

'Yes. I think he's pathetic,' Dahlia said.

'Pathetic?'

'And frightened, rather.'

'Frightened? He's lazy.'

'Pathetic,' Dahlia insisted. 'Don't you think it's sad to have to call me in to talk about his son? He was bubbling over with him. And I know why. It's because Mrs. Doubleday is a very tight cork.'

Cecil thought there might be another reason. Though he did not listen with much interest to the details of her stories, he knew, from his own experience, that Dahlia herself could listen very well.

'Of course I'd heard about him before,' she went on, 'but only in snatches. Double snatches. Haven't you?'

'I think he has mentioned him once,' Cecil said rather reluctantly. 'The fact is,' he seemed to excuse himself, 'I always escape as quickly as I can. He wastes so much time.'

'Oh! Don't you think time likes to be wasted now and then?' Unintentionally showing him how pleasingly this could be done, she leaned against the kitchen table, the drying cloth hanging from her hand. 'I hate to think of it blown up like a bladder and nearly bursting. Mr. Doubleday was nearly bursting with Reginald. I think his passage is booked, so it's getting rather exciting

88

and if it's possible for a fly to feel fairly comfortable in a spider's web, that's how I felt in Mr. Doubleday's parlour. I couldn't get out and I was afraid the female would come back and eat us both. The females do, you know.'

'But — ' Cecil leaned in the doorway and wasted time with a good grace. 'I still don't understand about the larger animals.'

His adjective pleased her and she laughed but she said, shaking her head, 'It wouldn't interest you a bit. It was just nonsense. Oh well, if you must know,' she said quickly, 'I was trying to imagine what Reginald would look like and I decided that it would be camel from mother and elephant from father. Camel face and feet, elephant body.' She returned to her dishes. She felt a little embarrassment at revealing her absurd imaginings and Cecil's silence added to it. She took a look at him and seeing him in a state of solemn surprise, she exclaimed, 'I wasn't trying to be funny! I just saw him like that. I couldn't help it. And I told you it was nonsense.'

'Yes. But what puzzles me is how you could deliberately sit down and make up that sort of thing about a person you'd never seen.'

'It was because I hadn't seen him that I could. And it wasn't deliberate. It just happened. And it isn't worth discussing.'

'I don't know. I think it's rather serious in a grown woman.'

'I hate to be called a grown woman,' Dahlia said. 'It sounds so well developed. And I always think about people like that. I suppose it's silly to wonder what Miss Fairweather does when she isn't prodding flannel shirts and what Mrs. Matthews has for supper. But I do.' She offered him her widest smile. 'You must think of something better to occupy my mind.'

He was beginning to suspect that smile. 'I'm afraid you think I'm very stupid.'

'No, you're more clever than I am, but I can always amuse myself and that's a very good thing and it's a good thing for us to be different, I think.'

He was not so sure about that. He wanted their minds to run on parallel lines; these odd and rather senseless collisions worried him. He found her adorable in all her moods, but he was troubled by her constant desire to be entertained. She was intelligent and he thought her pleasure in the society of Tony Tothill was an abuse of her wits: she was good, he had no doubt of that, and for him, her bright hair was the halo of a merry and unaffected saint, yet she was entirely without his urgency of service. Her hard work for the bazaar had no thought for the cause behind it; when she went to the Mission, she made a difference to the atmosphere of the dingy hall, she made a difference to what he said, for he was always aware of her alertness and more critical of himself, but she seemed to forget the place when she left it. In his dreams about his marriage he had seen the slums of Upper Radstowe as the domain in which he and Dahlia would find their common interest and strongest bond and he would not give up his dreams, for these, as he recognized, were early days, but he decided that he must find some definite work for her to do when the excitement of the bazaar was over. That bazaar was a bad introduction to her future life which would necessarily be of a sober kind and though it was ridiculous to feel jealousy at her association with those young men, he could not rid himself of his annoyance. He had an old-fashioned prejudice in favour of homekeeping wives, unless they were engaged in helping their husbands. Dahlia ministering to the poor and unhappy and the wicked in a dirty tenement was a vision from which he did not shrink, but he saw her

90

dignity, and his, assailed by the inventive foolery of the Tothills.

It was Mrs. Doubleday who proved of assistance to him here. When he went, that morning, to take his parish magazine matter to the vicar, there were no nods and becks from the study window, there was no friendly rushing to the front door which, however, opened before he could ring the bell and Mrs. Doubleday was behind it. Her remarks assured him that she had been watching for his arrival and he had time, even in his rage, to realize with what economy she could convey a great deal of meaning, to wonder why youth and beauty should inspire her to spitefulness; he remembered Miss Jewel, his old landlady in Beulah Mount, who had hated the Rendalls with a bitterness too strong to have come from the mere fear of losing a good lodger, and he thought that even Mrs. Doubleday, for all her self-assurance, might be conscious of having missed the most satisfying kind of homage. He could have no idea that as her son approached the joy no one suspected in her was half a torment. While he was far away she could at least imagine that she possessed him: in Upper Radstowe, everyone who spoke to him would rob her, and Dahlia consorting and making herself popular with the gayer elements in the place, from which in any case, her antecedents should have banished her, had risen in Mrs. Doubleday's mind as a glittering danger.

'People,' she told Cecil, truthfully, but with a false implication, 'are talking about her already.'

'Then they must be getting a great deal of pleasure and still more good,' he said, glaring at her. 'And I shall be grateful if you'll mind your own business.'

Mr. Doubleday, hovering near his door, heard the sound and some of the words of this altercation. He sighed deeply and tiptoed back to his desk. 'Pity, pity,' he muttered. There was a disagreeable day in front of him.

CHAPTER XII

IT was strange that a heavy-handed woman like Mrs. Doubleday should have a comparatively light touch when she chose — or had she been inspired by a subject completely to her taste? — and Cecil could not but admire the skill with which she had indicated her acquaintance with Louisa's old story and warned him of Dahlia's possibly inherited tendency to lightness of behaviour. This was abominable but, unfortunately for his comfort, he could not be single-minded in his anger. Mrs. Doubleday's spitefulness was only one of the tributaries to the stream of his indignation at the conditions which were bound to interfere with the work he had to do. And they were all caused by women. At this thought he had a temporary return to his belief that the clergy should be celibate and, without humour, with a new realization that he and Doubleday might have points of contact after all, he wondered whether the vicar ever considered celibacy with envy. And he refused to give Mrs. Doubleday the credit for his own righteous feelings of disgust with Louisa Grimshaw. No, for some reason most mysterious to a man and like Miss Jewel, she seemed to take pleasure in being disagreeable to youth and beauty, and he suspected that a plain and humble Dahlia would not have been dowered with her mother's faults. He owned that with him the fault itself would more easily have been forgiven if it had not been accompanied by a country accent. It savoured too much of the casual village encounter for his pride, the dignity of his profession and his campaign against sexual transgressions in the parish. And Dahlia herself had been guilty of mild indiscretion in her glad association with the young Tothills and their friends who had nothing to do with the church and never entered it. Mrs. Tothill was fairly regular in her attendance and generous with money and advice, but Mr. Tothill played golf on Sundays and his sons rushed about the country in motor cars; their activities for the bazaar were only occasions for amusement and the curate's young wife would have behaved in a more seemly fashion if she had stayed at home and plied her needle for the good cause. He could not tell her, but he felt strongly, that her unfortunate position in Upper Radstowe before he married her, and her still more unfortunate mother, should have instructed her to be very cautious and self-effacing in everything except the occupations proper to his wife, for though Upper Radstowe was the chief suburb of a large city it had the character of a little country town, where the business of one person was the gossip of everybody else. Carts came trundling across the bridge with produce from Combe Friars and beyond; Thomas Grimshaw's poultry, eggs and butter, doubtless found a market within a short distance of the Reverend Cecil Sproat's house; for all he knew, half the people in the place looked at him with changed eyes since he had married Dahlia and though it was difficult to believe they could criticize her character, they must inevitably remember that she had not always been the curate's wife.

He felt easier in the mean streets towards which he had been making his way. This slum was like a foreign growth on the respectability of Upper Radstowe. Here, people living from hand to mouth were not concerned with much beyond their struggles and the scandals of their own streets, there were no signs of the feudalism still apparent in the manners of the shopkeepers, and their interest in the curate's marriage was a purely sentimental one. He would have been surprised to know that many of these slatternly women with far too many children and insufficient food and house room, had felt more pity for him and his evident loneliness than for themselves, and that now he seemed less inhumanly determined to help them. In his choice of a wife as young and pretty as Dahlia he had raised himself in their opinion by showing he was capable of the emotions which had caused some of their distresses. Dahlia was no disadvantage to him here where there was a far more generous welcome for contrast than for the similarity which would have been offered in the person of the dowdy drab-coloured sort of woman whom the reverend gentleman might have been expected to favour.

There were kind inquiries after Mrs. Sproat in some of the houses he visited this morning and he was more than ever convinced that this was where she would find her truest self when she had had her unimpeded fling with the Tothills and their like: she should have that without a staying word from him and in deliberate defiance of Mrs. Doubleday, but much of the work he did was rightly a woman's and she would do it well. He knew he was a dark presence in a sick room; Dahlia would be a bright one, not given to prayerful consolation, but the personification of encouragement, and seeing her so, his spirits lifted a little. He thought he could return for the midday meal without betraying his recent agitation and, in the rash kindness of a person happier than he expected to be, he went a little out of his way to have a friendly word with Mrs. Bailey, chiefly, perhaps, because Dahlia liked her. He shared her approval of Mrs. Bailey. She had had the good sense to marry a steady man, her house was spotless, her children were clean when they left it in the morning and the dirt they gathered during the day was merely superficial; her eldest girl had lately been persuaded into

94

domestic service and Cecil also approved of that, but he found a constricted look on Mrs. Bailey's sensible little rosy face this morning. It was a look he had often seen on other faces, sometimes increased in the hope of searching questions, and in this case the sign of a determined reserve, but he would have considered himself lacking in duty if he had respected it in silence and she was at last constrained to admit that Ivy had been getting herself into trouble. The influences of the good home she had left and the other she had entered had not prevailed against the temptations of the flesh.

'Shameful!' Cecil exclaimed.

He might have been more tactful if the shadow of sexual complications had not been pursuing him for hours, and he saw a further tightening of Mrs. Bailey's expression; he was shocked to hear her say that it was a common occurrence and a natural one, though very awkward.

'But Mrs. Bailey . . .' He checked his expostulations and, becoming practical, asked for the name of the other sinner.

'That's Ivy's business. You'll have to go to her for that. Anyway, she's not marrying him, so she says.'

'But he must be made to marry her!'

'He's ready enough and I don't wonder, for she's a good girl.' Mrs. Bailey was not daunted by Cecil's frown. 'She says he was all very well for a bit of fun . . . .'

'Fun!' Cecil ejaculated.

'But,' Mrs. Bailey went on perseveringly for, having been forced to start, she intended to go on, 'she's not tying herself up to him for life. She'd rather have a real bad time for a month or two than drag along with a chap like that for ever. And there,' Mrs. Bailey said firmly, 'she shows sense, though what her father'll say I don't know. He's always set a lot of store on Ivy and, man-like, he'll think you can cure one wrong with another. It'll be "What'll the neighbours say?" with him, but it's Ivy I'm thinking about.'

'And the child?' Cecil inquired.

'The child's not here yet and I never could see that a bad father's better than none. Nor a bad husband.'

Cecil's arms were folded across his chest and his face was grim. Mrs. Bailey was not the woman he had thought her, he was not used to hearing the opinions, when they opposed his, of people in this rank of life and Mrs. Bailey's independent views caused a great part of his displeasure.

'Mrs. Bailey,' he said, 'a bad husband and a bad father, and let us hope he will be neither, must be regarded as part of Ivy's punishment. I'm astonished that you take the matter so lightly.'

There was a slight trembling of her lips but she controlled it. 'Sir,' she said with dignity, 'I'm in trouble and I'm bound to do my best for the girl. These things don't come the way of folks like you, but I've seen them happen time and again and time and again I've seen misery let loose when a girl's married against her will — and often enough when she hasn't. And I'll force no girl of mine to save her respectability for a year and lose it for ever afterwards. She won't need any more punishment than she'll get, you may be sure, if it's any comfort to you, without fastening her up to a lad who's never done a day's work and never wanted to. You're a young gentleman,' she said forgivingly, 'but I've lived in this street for nearly twenty years and I know what I'm talking about.'

There was a polite but decided dismissal in her manner and Cecil unwillingly accepted it. He was not wanted in a house where, hitherto, he had been welcomed; he had failed, somehow, and he could not believe it was his fault; he had said what he believed to be right and what the

Church would approve of and he was grievously upset by Mrs. Bailey's indifference to authority. The best woman in the parish had flouted it and he had a horrible sense of impotence and of effort wasted.

It was unfortunate that Dahlia had chosen this moment for fitting herself with what was supposed to be an Arcadian head-dress, while she kept a less interested eye on the pots and pans, for the sight of her standing under the electric light and in front of the mirror, with a smaller mirror in one hand and some pins in her mouth, was hardly soothing to Cecil at the moment.

She removed the pins on his arrival and asked at once: 'Has Mrs. Doubleday been annoying you? You've got rather a Doubleday look.'

He had temporarily forgotten Mrs. Doubleday but the remembrance of her had some effect on his reply. 'I've just come from your friend Mrs. Bailey,' he said sharply, 'and you look ridiculous with that thing on your head.'

Dahlia was hurt. No attack on her character would have been so painful, but she did not remove the cap and she looked at him calmly. 'Mrs. Bailey was your friend first,' she said. 'Now that you call her mine, I suppose she has done something you don't like.'

'That,' he said, 'is a very mild way of putting it.'

'Well, when you've told me all about it, perhaps I shall feel fiercer.'

She could not, however, share his disgust with Ivy or anger with Mrs. Bailey. She was sorry for them both and she made a sympathetic murmur which, even if it was meant for him, was not what he wanted.

'This is the sort of thing', he said, 'which makes me despair of my work.'

Without looking at him, Dahlia gave a little nod. She was picturing Mrs. Bailey's face with trouble on it, she was imagining the mingled fear and defiance of the girl.

97

'They pick and choose,' Cecil went on. 'They take what you have to give when they like it, they pay lip-service to religion, but they simply reject its teaching when it doesn't suit them. I'm almost more outraged by the mother than by the girl. She hardly listened with decent respect to what I had to say. And I'm not thinking of myself,' he added, protesting against a comment Dahlia had been wise enough not to make, 'I'm thinking of what I stand for. What's the good of all this preaching and teaching? What's the good of it?' he demanded.

'I don't know,' Dahlia said and, quickly, she went on consolingly. 'But you must remember all the girls who don't have babies when they shouldn't. There must be a lot of them.'

She did not refer to the satisfactory mothers who persuaded their bad daughters to marry men they did not like. She felt sorry for Cecil, too. There was something childish in his distress and she was acute enough to guess that, protest as he might, he was personally piqued by Mrs. Bailey's rejection of his counsel.

'You must think of all the dreadful things that might happen, if it wasn't for you,' she said.

He responded at once to this suggestion which she had feared would irritate him with its simplicity and, seeing him brighten with such pathetic readiness, she was honestly grieved to have to refuse a request.

'But how can I?' she asked. 'How can I interfere? I've never seen the girl and, just because I'm married to you, how can I dare to give advice to Mrs. Bailey? She's nearly old enough to be my mother. She knows far more than I do.'

'It's not a question of knowledge or experience. It's a question of right and wrong.'

'That's what I mean,' Dahlia said. 'I don't know which is which.'

98

'But I've told you!' Cecil cried.

Dahlia was good-natured, but all the implications of this remark were too much for her independent spirit. Her reply was sharp and his was sharper and, before they had time to steady themselves, they were deeply in a quarrel and, in retrospect, the quietness with which it proceeded after the first outburst was one of its worst features. They might have been able to laugh at each other's violence and make friends again, but neither could doubt the sincerity of the coldly uttered statements passing between them. There was his disappointment and her lack of sympathy, there was her amused impatience for the seriousness with which he took himself: there was her frivolity and his lack of humour. She approved of Mrs. Bailey's attitude and he was enraged by her disloyalty to him and to the religion which, as she pointed out, she had never professed and never would profess, if its view of marriage was the same as his. She could not feel his horror for Ivy's sin and, in an evil moment, he attributed her laxity to the early influences of her life and all his bitterness against Louisa Grimshaw was in his words and tone.

A pained amazement at this reference kept Dahlia silent until she could say stammeringly, 'But you promised! You promised — before I married you!'

'Then I've broken my promise,' he said.

She looked at him, honestly, and gladly hating him. 'Ah yes — and more than that,' she replied.

CHAPTER XIII

LIKE many people highly sensitive about themselves, Cecil under-estimated the sensitiveness of other people, and Dahlia's gay independence had misled him. He forgot that indifference to the opinion of a Mrs. Doubleday did not imply callousness to his and, during the ensuing miserable hours spent chiefly in avoiding each other, he thought much more about the home truths he had heard than about the ones he had delivered. He felt that his were justified and pardonable because they were true, while Dahlia's unfair criticism rankled badly, but he was troubled by his breach of faith and ready to ask forgiveness when she gave him an opportunity and he could bring himself to take it. He knew she would accept an apology, but he did not suspect her shattering sense of loss, her loneliness and family loyalty, nor could he measure the strength of an allegiance first begun in defence of herself and Jenny, developed into a habit of protection towards their mother and lately grown into the tribute which must be paid to goodness. There was nothing in Cecil's decent family history to superimpose such a feeling on ordinary affection and though he had known loneliness and rejoiced in this new companionship, he did not properly understand her isolation and how happily she had swung to the safety of the anchorage he gave her, or realize that one of the links in the connecting cable was her certainty that he would keep his promise to remember no count of inferior birth or conduct against her mother. And when they met, perforce, for the next meal, he had to acknowledge that she had inherited no fault in manners. She was cheerfully conversational and he found himself craving for some of the nonsense he had occasionally deplored, and at night, when he saw her, straight and slim, in her nightgown, it seemed to him that the time had come for reconciliation. He could forget the hard things she had said, though he might remember them to-morrow, and all their differences must be melted in the warmth of an embrace.

Unfortunately, his appearance had not the same softening effect on her. If he had looked like a god, her mind would still have resisted him and unless her mind was satisfied she had nothing physical to give him. Her response came of his gratifying adoration of her beauty, but chiefly from a sense of their firm friendship and that had gone, so they lay stiffly apart and after he had let out a few heavy sighs, meant to provoke pity, he fell asleep.

Dahlia stared into a darkness that gradually became grey and showed her the shapes of the furniture she had chosen when she was happy. There was a certain consolation in telling herself she would never be happy again. She hated the bed she lay on; it was outrageous that she must share it with Cecil, but there had been something a little too dramatic for her sense of humour in betaking herself to the spare bedroom, some satisfaction in mortifying herself with his neighbourhood and in being able to detest him at close quarters. And, in her anger, she could persuade herself that this quarrel had its advantages; she was under no obligation beyond keeping house for him; she would be less restraining with Tony Tothill and more interested in his much more attractive brother and, as once before, in her early acquaintance with Cecil, his coldness had hardened her, she now decided that there was no adequate reward for being good. For the first time, she had a complete understanding of her mother's lapse from virtue; it was an act of defiance created by lack of appreciation and encouraged by the need for excitement and a natural ardour. Dahlia was suffering now from the consequences, but she felt no resentment: she had always suffered from them and determined that their cause could never be worth the price others had to pay, and though she was under no immediate temptation to excess, or desire for it, the idea of tempting other people, and annoying Cecil in the process, was attractive. And then she thought of Ivy who had done what she wished to do, but more nobly, without any self-preserving caution, and sordid as that affair might appear to people who were personally more dainty and nicer in their speech, Dahlia could understand that there had been romance in it for Ivy and she felt a renewed anger against Cecil who could feel passion, even in this hour of estrangement, and find nothing repulsive in that because the Church had blessed it, and yet had so little mercy for unlicensed lovers. He was right from a practical point of view. Trouble for Mrs. Bailey, for Ivy and the child, for Cecil and herself, had or would come of it, but Dahlia felt sure it was not God who willed the trouble. No doubt he approved of self-control; it was an aristocratic attribute and must be his. It must, she decided unwillingly, also be her own. She would not be a vulgar flirt, even to vex Cecil, she would give him no excuse to blame her mother, but she would take any harmless pleasure that came her way and give up struggling to make her conscience agree with his. She had very little respect left for his conscience. He had broken faith with her and broken it because he was narrow-minded, because he had not troubled to look beyond her reserve and see how much feeling it concealed, how much dread of his lack of sympathy and consideration for himself.

She lay at the extreme edge of the bed, very sore at heart and lonely. She had too much sense really to believe that the edge would always be her portion; at the moment she could not imagine herself elsewhere, and knowing that the extremity of this bitterness would also pass, she allowed herself to indulge it. In the morning, when the small concerns of life had to be met, she would realize that the world held more than Cecil and herself, that there were people who had more cause for sorrow, and she would gradually grow used to disappointment, to being alone, like Jenny and her mother, and she thought of her mother who, however much — and it would not be much — she might be annoyed with Thomas Grimshaw, would never allow her feelings to interfere with the comfort of her bed; she thought of Jenny, lying in hers, listening for the shuffling feet of old Mr. Cummings, and it seemed to her that they were a sad trio, each with a man to love her and each dissatisfied with him, the three of them united yet separated by more than distance and incapable of doing each other much service, but Louisa Grimshaw was probably the happiest of them all. There had been no self-seeking in her marriage and though the one great expectation from it had failed, she was in the right place, she accepted what she did not like as part of the common lot, she was spared the capacity for analysis of herself and others and, in her partnership with Thomas Grimshaw, there were few but practical problems to settle. Right and wrong, in their occupation, was a matter of wise or foolish sowing, reaping, breeding and marketing. There were no tiresome moral questions to settle and no differences of opinion to cause a heartache. It was absurd that such differences should cause one. Why must her views coincide with Cecil's? Why should she be punished when they did not and why had he more right than she had to exact coincidence? She smiled against her pillow when she remembered the reversal of this situation in the Doubleday household and she decided that her own was better, though for what reason she could not tell.

Centuries of men's real and conventional predominance made a too masterful woman seem like a grotesque, an object for cruel laughter, probably because there was often in such a woman an actual physical reflection of the mental state. Beauty was of great importance to Dahlia. She saw it when she looked in the glass, she was used to it in each member of her family and she would have resigned much to keep it. If looking like Mrs. Doubleday had been the price of her independence, she would have accepted slavery, but she knew that in no circumstances could she blindly adopt the opinion of another until she had proved its wisdom for herself. She regretted this inability, though she had her pride in it. Life would be a much simpler matter with her will, her thoughts and her footsteps following Cecil's, but how very dull this docility would be, how bad for both of them! She was as little willing to face a future of constant sparring and, to her common sense, it seemed ridiculous that they could not agree to differ and find, perhaps, that they could love with a lasting excitement because parts of each other were just out of reach. That was what she had expected of her marriage, it was what happened during her short engagement, what ought to continue, in spite of a wedding ring, and in a little burst of temper, she removed that ring, with a vicious pull, and sent it spinning across the floor.

Cecil stirred at the sound and she laughed silently. It was a fine gesture but, in the morning, she would have the undignified task of peering under the furniture to find the thing. She would not advertise her defiance, but it was pleasant to think that when Cecil put the ring on her finger, he imagined, in his old-fashioned way, that it would remain there until, after becoming grievously embedded in the increase of years, it dropped from her dead bones with just such a tinkle as it gave when it found rest on the floor. And then, there would be no one to hear the sound, and at this sudden realization of her mortality and his, she put out a hand, the one without the ring, to touch him and assure herself that her ultimate utter loneliness was still far off.

He waked at once and she was moved by his perpetual consciousness of her nearness and when he had caught her hand and held it against his lips, murmuring, 'I'm sorry!' she released it to give his shoulder a friendly little pat. It was a great deal, after all, to have this human warmth beside her, it was still more to know how soon she could restore his happiness. It was a power that made her humble and kept her forbearing in the morning when his manner assumed that yesterday's misery was all forgotten, when he announced his discovery of compensations in quarrels.

'It's like beginning all over again,' he said.

'But if we do that too often, we shall never start.'

'Oh, I think we shall start, I think we have started,' he said with gentle gravity and she knew, as plainly as though he had told her, that he had decided on taking a new direction and leading her by an easier slope to the heights they must occupy together. He was tactfully unexpectant of her company to the Mission hall that evening, she purposely said nothing of the rehearsal to which she had been bidden at the Tothills' house and her overnight resolutions did not prevent her from feeling some compunction, for she was not needed at the rehearsals. There had been a decision against painted scenery, the girls involved in the performances did not want her advice about their clothes: she went because she enjoyed the gaiety and liked to laugh, because she was the curate's wife only when Tony Tothill chose to remember it and tried to shock her. She was a girl among other girls and, still greater novelty, among young men, and in the big room, once the nursery, at the top of the Tothills' house, she seemed to be capturing those rights of girlhood which had been denied to her.

As though anxious not to waken vigilance in the quiet little house, she moved rather stealthily as she brushed her hair into a burnish and changed her dress, but she broke into a happy run when she had banged the door behind her. Skirting The Green for a little way, she took a turning to the left and passed the stables where the clock never changed its time, and she was still running easily down the hill when a car stopped by her side.

'I nearly missed you,' said a voice she knew. 'I came round, by The Avenue to fetch you, just too late. But get in now, won't you?'

'I like running,' Dahlia said.

'But I can't let you run while I drive and I can't run with you because the car doesn't know its way home, and,' he seemed to divine some criticism of his manners, 'I can't get out and be polite because I'm not sure of my brakes.'

'Then what happened when you rang my bell?'

'I didn't ring it — and anyhow that's level ground — I saw you turning the corner, so I followed.'

'It was very kind of you,' Dahlia said and she crept under the low hood of the car, 'but I don't want to be fetched, you know.'

'It was my mother's idea,' he said disappointingly. 'My mother has a mania for action, delegated action. She's sent Tony off to fetch some of the others, just because we were both comfortable in armchairs and drinking coffee. But, of course, I was very pleased to come. And the moon's up so we'll go round the Downs first if you would like it.'

'We shall be late for the rehearsal.'

'That doesn't matter. We've nothing to do with it, really.'

'No,' Dahlia reluctantly agreed. 'But I hope you're not trying to give me a treat.'

'Giving myself a treat,' Simon said. 'And, my word, I need one! Besides, there are times when I get tired of Tony's high spirits. Perhaps,' he said, 'I'm jealous because I'm not so funny. And there's nothing more beautiful than the gorge in moonlight.'

'Nothing more beautiful in any light,' Dahlia said.

'I'm not so sure of that,' he said, disregarding his steering for a moment, and then, just avoiding the pavement and looking straight in front of him, he told her that the Monks' Pool pleased him better.

'But that's my place!' Dahlia cried.

'Sorry, but I'm older than you and it must have been mine first.'

CHAPTER XIV

THE Downs were as pale as a silver lake and on it, here and there, a figure was miraculously walking; the hawthorn bushes were dark islands, the elm trees seemed to be rising above a flood, a heap of fallen leaves had the look of ruffled water and the white roads might have been causeways built across it. The moon observed her effects with the indifference of a complacent beauty. These things came by no will of hers; she was not responsible for her loveliness, for increasing happiness or making the sad more desolate. Slowly she swept across her shining floor and, far below her, the light cast by Simon's lamps had a vulgar feverishness. It streamed from two greedy, searching eyes that watched the edges of the road with the eagerness of a hungry, predatory beast, ready to lick up the smallest morsel and the noise of the engine was its purring voice.

They went fast, over the causeways, round the encircling roads and back again, and Simon seemed to have forgotten any anxiety about his brakes. Hunting something that might at any moment emerge from the lake with a swiftness as great as their own, they could not slacken pace, but nothing rose from the quiet water: it ridiculed their hurry as the moon ridiculed their lamps and Dahlia, excited by the speed, yet soothed by Simon's almost sensuous handling of the wheel, had a feeling that he and she were defying all that was ordered and secure, but when she glanced at him and saw him carelessly leaning back, she realized that their worlds were different. Many a time he must have driven a girl in the moonlight; never could he have known this glad, guilty feeling of truancy. This was no adventure for him, and she settled down to pretend it was none for her but, in the hottest burst of their speed on the shore of that still lake, she was compelled to cry, 'Oh don't! This is like singing comic songs in church.'

'Just what I feel like doing,' he said, but he took his foot off the accelerator and the car slid to a standstill at the railed edge of the cliff. 'But I suppose I oughtn't to say that to you?'

'Why?' Dahlia asked.

'Because you've got a sort of proprietary interest in the church, haven't you?'

'I suppose so. But not so much that I mind what anybody says about it.'

'Well, I feel rather better tempered. I don't want to say anything — about anything. Let's have a look at the river.'

The tide was out and the water was like a sluggish snake making its slow way at the bottom of the gorge. The lights marking its windings for the guidance of ships looked impotent under the moon, but when she slipped behind a cloud, they changed, as though at a signal, to a bright gold and, in the same moment, the wooded opposite cliff became deeply black. Then the cloud passed, the lights went pale again and the trees resumed their different intensities of colour.

With startling suddenness, Simon clapped his hands in applause and the sound came back in a faint, derisive echo.

'Very well done,' he said. 'Tony ought to have seen that. His stage effects are not nearly so well timed.'

'You're spoiling this, too,' Dahlia murmured.

'Yes. On purpose. I'm afraid of getting sentimental.'

'It's the right feeling for moonlight,' Dahlia said.

'Yes, if you can keep it concentrated on the moon, but you can't.'

'Oh yes, I can. I'm the most unsentimental person in the world,' she said with an untruthful caution which was not necessary for when she turned and sat on the stone coping of the railings, she saw that though he looked at her he was thinking of something, or someone else. 'And anyhow, why concentrate on the moon?' she said, feeling quite safe and wishing she did not, for he was attractive with the collar of his great-coat turned up, his hands in his pockets, his bare head shapely and his features saved from ordinariness by the whimsical set of his nose and mouth. 'The moon is so far off,' she said.

'That's the reason,' Simon said. 'Hopelessly and comfortably out of reach.' He came a few steps nearer and looked down on Dahlia and she looked up at him, trusting that the absurd, nervous twitching between her eyebrows was not apparent. 'You are very kind to let me talk,' he said.

'But you've hardly talked at all!'

'Haven't I? I'm really not quite sure what I'm saying and what I'm thinking. I'm hellishly miserable, so you must forgive bad manners. I want to tear round the roads and smash things up. I want to profane the sanctuaries. But it's what they call execrable taste to refer to one's feelings. Let's get back into the car and I'll drive more discreetly.'

'No,' Dahlia said. 'Tell me why you're miserable. You'll feel better afterwards.'

'Shall I? Well I don't think it will make me more ashamed of myself than I am already and I know you won't look sympathetic the next time we meet. And you're married, and that makes a difference. But don't tell the parson.'

A little flare of loyalty to Cecil gave place to resignation for herself. She was married and that state, which seemed to have changed her real self so little, had set her in a charmed circle for this young man. He was outside it but she was fit to receive his confidences and adapting herself to this privilege, she said gravely, 'Have you done something wicked?'

His denial was half laugh, half shout. 'I'm seeking a lady in honourable marriage and she won't have me.'

'Oh!' This was a trouble with which someone who was not married would have been more competent to deal. 'I'm sorry.'

'But I'm not.'

'Then I don't understand.'

'It's rather complicated,' Simon allowed. 'I'm in love with her but I don't like her. I'd hate her a week after I'd married her — Oh, before that. I'd loathe her, but still I want to marry her because I can't get her any other way. And I loathe myself already because I know she's a selfish, kind-hearted little beast, but she happens to have the kind of beauty that makes me mad, not beauty, exactly, either. She's saving me from a lifetime of hell and I can't forgive her.'

This was more interesting. Here was an extreme example of passion existing in spite of an alienated mind. Were all men like that? Dahlia wondered and, aloud she said, 'What kind of beauty?'

'Rather demure, rather sad, dark, pale, very red lips, but that's artificial, small — I don't want to talk about her.'

'It will do you good,' Dahlia persisted. Her curiosity and her ignorance of a young man's mind were more important than his pangs. It was this girl, then, that they had been hunting round the roads. 'Does she live in Radstowe?'

'She'd die in Radstowe. That would solve the problem, if I could get her here, but no, I'm much too small beer. Her father's in our line of business but he has a handle to his name and she wants a bigger handle for herself.'

'It's not her fault if she can't like you enough.' Dahlia had to be just to this girl who, rather disturbingly, sounded like a more exotic Jenny.

III

'But she does — very nearly.'

'And it's no worse to want a title than a woman you don't like. It's only a different kind of greed and I don't think you'll be unhappy for very long.' This was the voice of a young matron who sat and looked judiciously at her folded hands, but when she glanced at him and saw him trying to cover his distress with a humorous petulance, she could not remain judicious and she said, a little brokenly, 'It must be terrible while it lasts.'

This he could interpret as the voice of a happy lover who contrasted her state with his, but she heard it herself with the dismayed knowledge that she had missed something and that she envied him. Jenny had not missed it. It was odd that this boy should be the one to teach her what her sister had suffered, and now Dahlia knew for a certainty that Jenny would not marry Edwin Cummings. She was still too young to be content with safety. 'And I am too young,' Dahlia said woefully to herself. Wide-eyed, she stared at Simon and he laughed to reassure her.

'It's not so bad as all that! What made me tell you? Part of my madness, I suppose. I'd better take you home. It's too late for the rehearsal.'

'Yes, too late,' Dahlia said. 'But go slowly.'

He went slowly and she watched his hands and, after a time he said, 'D'you know, I think I must have meant to tell you when I followed you. I must have known you'd be a — a febrifuge. You're a very kind lady,' he said, leaning round to look at her. 'You see, I've just come back from London this afternoon and — oh, well, never mind! One gets used to things and then forgets them. Life's a mess but it does clear itself up if you give it a chance. Here we are and thank you. Some day will you come with me to the Monks' Pool? Some Sunday? No, I suppose you can't come on Sunday. Some Saturday?'

'Shall I?' She seemed to consult him, then she shook

her head. 'You mustn't go there until you've quite recovered. It's a queer place. That will be the sign. When you've recovered, you can come and fetch me.'

She had hardly shut the front door behind her when she heard Cecil's key in the lock. He kissed her cheek. 'How cold!' he said. 'Have you been to the post? It's a lovely night.'

'There was a rehearsal,' she said.

'Oh!' The quick shadow of his disapproval crossed his face. She had been watching and half hoping for it. It absolved her from saying more. If he had been kind, she would have been constrained to tell him about her drive and the Downs like a lake in the moonlight, and she did not want to tell him. He would be still more vexed. There was some excuse for going to a rehearsal while he went to the Mission, there was none for driving with Simon Tothill, none that he would understand, but fear of his displeasure did not influence her. Some of Simon's trouble had left him when he spoke of it and she did not want the same release. For a little while she would be glad to keep this unhappy stirring in her heart. She was too young to be content with safety, after all. It had been the chief thing she wanted and it was not enough. She was too young to be afraid of giving pain a welcome and, as yet, the pain was only a promise of romantic sadness, of being a novitiate in the fellowship Simon and Jenny unknowingly shared. She wished they did not share it, she wished Simon's hard-hearted lady was not pale and dark, yet this fact was quickly turned to advantage. There could be no harm in going to the Monks' Pool with a man who had that taste in beauty. She would be quite safe, she seemed doomed to be safe, it was Jenny who would be in danger, but Jenny was a long way off.

Cecil saw a proper contrition in Dahlia's attentions, her busy stirring of the neglected fire, the hot soup she brought him and her intelligent questions, but how much of this was a way of making secret amends, how much it was designed to keep him from questions of his own, Dahlia herself did not know. She studied all his gestures, she tried to imagine that she was stealing a precious hour with him; she looked critically at his hands and noticed how vague they were in their movements and she did not want to watch them; she saw his hair touching the back of his collar and disliked it; her voice was pleasant but there was no surprise in anything he said and, before she knew they were in her eyes, there were tears trickling down her cheeks.

He paused, astonished and a little irritated. There had been emotion enough yesterday to last for a long time; he had apologized and now, though the grievance was all his, he had ignored it, yet she was crying, but when she said piteously, 'I'm so terribly sorry for you,' he told her ardently that there was no cause. Holding her in his arms, trying to still her convulsive sobbing, which surely should have stopped at his first kiss, he felt very tender and determinedly patient, and she was glad to be held there. He did not understand this passionate weeping and she was amazed that she could cling to him after yesterday when, for her, their friendship had been broken, after to-night when she had learnt that neither mind nor body belonged to him as it should, yet there was nothing essentially inconsistent in the pressure of her wet cheek and her nervous twisting of the fingers that had no charm for her. She felt the meanness of going to him for comfort and taking him when she needed him, but she was also giving him what she could, she was acknowledging his love for her and her certainty that it was enduring. It was enduring but it was not comprehending; she knew he was not puzzling out reasons for her abandonment; he was simply accepting it because it was hers and loving her for the best of all reasons, because he could not help it.

CHAPTER XV

MRS. DOUBLEDAY had chosen the carpet and armchair for her son's bedroom and arranged that they should be delivered at a time when Mr. Doubleday would be from home. His chirruping excitement at these preparations would have been more than she could bear and she was less than ever inclined to give him pleasure, in this or any other direction, since her quarrel with Cecil Sproat. She spared him small distractions when she could, but she had a natural inclination to consider important what was disagreeable and of such matters it was her duty to keep him well informed. Moreover, she knew that he must have heard the sounds of altercation, so, giving him time to make inquiries about them, to act chivalrously towards a woman and a wife, she waited in the pleasant certainty of his weakness, she enjoyed his adroit but, to her, quite obvious avoidance of dangerous subjects, his hope that this trouble would blow by, his experienced fear that, sooner or later, it would break over his head.

There was a permanent spring of hope in Mr. Doubleday's breast. Though it sank low at times, it had never dried, and this had prevented him from learning that often the best defence is in attack. There was always the chance that defence would not be needed, always the chance, hummed his secret mind, and, as the hours passed, the odds appeared to be in his favour. He did not reckon with Mrs. Doubleday's artistry, he was not aware of its existence, and if he had wished to find an explanation for the postponement of her story, he would have decided that she was trying to get the better of her anger. She was waiting, however, for the hour when he would be hoping to enjoy his evening meal.

'Very unfortunate, very unfortunate,' he said, tapping the table, when she had said her say.

'What?' Mrs. Doubleday demanded.

His answer needed care. Truth and tact are an uneasy pair to drive: he could persuade them to jog along if they were not startled, but Mrs. Doubleday always had a disconcerting effect on them. He made a great effort to keep them together. 'What you have just told me, my dear.'

This was too flagrant a ruse to deceive anyone and she was determined to hear something more precise. 'Then I shall expect you to take action.'

'Action?' He seemed to look for it. He heard his own questioning tone and knew it would not do, and he repeated the word on a thoughtful note. 'Action — yes, well — But not without your advice, Flora.'

'You won't like the advice I shall give you.'

'I have always found it valuable.'

'Yes, to keep, but not to use, unless — ' There was a queer strain in her voice which was pitched higher than usual; it had a goaded sound and Mr. Doubleday, troubled but innocent, was obliged to look at her. 'Unless you can get someone else to handle it for you. What I suggest,' she said slowly and bitingly, 'is that you insist on an apology and try to behave, for once, like a man.'

A miserable change came over Mr. Doubleday's round, rosy face. In the thirty years of their married life no remark so crude had been made by either and it arrived now with the impetus of release after long repression. He could not deceive himself. She was angry but she was sincere and when she threw her missile, she broke down the careful structure of illusion to which he had added, day by day. She saw it fall herself and she was frightened into an attempt at laughing her words into a joke; she realized, too late, that a flimsy shelter was better for them than none, but they were facing each other across the ruins and they could not be raised by the mirthless sound she made. Laughter, from her, only served to emphasize the strangeness of this occasion and it was followed by a few seconds of taut stillness. Then Mr. Doubleday picked up his knife and fork and finished the food on his plate.

She had less command of her appetite. It had gone with the certainty of her dominance and she was bewildered by that certainty; there was insufficient cause for it, but she knew it had gone in those few seconds of stillness. Nevertheless, she felt herself to be cruelly wronged by the absence of those placatory remarks which she despised but to which she was accustomed, by her husband's ability to eat and to be silent. He did not hum between the courses or hover near the fire for a few hopeful moments before he sought his study. He took with him a painful sense of liberty and left her extraordinarily desolate, for she knew she had lost one of her favourite occupations and, with a very little more caution, she might have kept it for ever.

Mr. Doubleday was aware of all this, yet he had no sense of triumph and no comfort in facing the truth at last, but he did look at it with the manfulness she had refused him. He had always been afraid of her, she had not willingly given him a single happy moment, he had always taken the easy way, to her injury and his own, he definitely disliked her and she despised him, but she had been the only strength he had and he preferred his old state to this. He thought enviously of Sproat and his pretty wife, who at this moment were deep in their own quarrel, and Mrs. Doubleday thought of them, too, trying to find in them the cause for letting loose the accumulated resentment of years and knowing they were only the occasion.

She felt like a stranger in her own house. These rooms were not acquainted with a woman who owned to an error in judgment. She had to subdue the heavy possessiveness of her tread and she could not settle down to her usual evening reading of the newspaper. She was chiefly preoccupied with the awkward, almost indecent necessity of eating and sleeping in the presence of a different Norman Doubleday, and as other thoughts flitted through her mind, such as discontent with this person or that in matters connected with the rapidly approaching bazaar, she realized that there was no one now to whom she could voice her complaints unless habit proved stronger in her husband than remembrance of the blow that had made his face crumple like paper in a rough hand. For an instant and for her own sake, she played with the thought of apology and retraction; she decided that she could more easily bend the poker; moreover it would make no difference. She had sense enough to gauge the stubbornness of a hurt, weak man; she would be restored to her old position only when some folly forced him to seek her aid or when in this matter of the Sproats, or in some other, she was found to be abundantly right, but, before anything of the kind might happen, Reginald would arrive and she saw with dismay, that a Norman no longer in subjection might enlarge his claims on his son. Her mistake was growing in importance and, at about the time when Dahlia threw her wedding ring across the floor and Mr. Doubleday, like Cecil Sproat, was sleeping, Mrs. Doubleday was very wide awake.

By nature unimaginative, she found it hard work to picture herself to-morrow, deprived of Norman's eager conciliations; she remembered, with congratulatory relief, that in the presence of other people she had always sustained him in his part, and on the next public occasion their rift would not be evident.

This occasion was the bazaar and among her consoling thoughts about it, was her conviction that Dahlia had little tactical sense. The parish had shown a lamentable disregard for the fitness of things; Louisa Grimshaw's daughter had been accepted for her own youth and charm, Mrs. Tothill's house was open to her, she had been made welcome at the somewhat dull entertainments offered by sober members of the church, yet foolishly, from her own point of view, she was helping Mrs. Bagshot and Mrs. Matthews, socially the least desirable of all the stall-holders, at the bazaar, and Mrs. Doubleday could only explain this strange choice by the sympathy of like for like. Mrs. Bagshot was generous and, materially, the stall would be a good one, but the important buyers would not frequent it. Dahlia was unlikely to have the privilege of wrapping up parcels for Mrs. Merriman, who was to open the bazaar. The ultimate distinction would not be hers. To Mrs. Doubleday, who had a bishop among her forebears, Mrs. Merriman was chiefly important because other people thought her so, because she was rich and therefore useful at such a time. She would be more valuable still if she taught Dahlia the difference between the Tothills, without landed property, and the Merrimans whose bailiff probably had to badger Dahlia's stepfather for the rent. It was a pity Mrs. Merriman was not in the parish; then Mrs. Doubleday might have explained the situation and seen that Dahlia was properly neglected, but it would not do to discredit the curate's wife to an outsider, and Mrs. Doubleday had to rely on the obvious vulgarity of Mrs. Matthews and the gentility of Mrs. Bagshot for ensuring that Dahlia was not noticed as she must wish to be. Mrs. Merriman would pass that stall as quickly as she could.

It was difficult, however, for anyone to avoid seeing this radiant young woman in her bunched petticoats. There was nothing half-hearted, though she knew there was a good deal that was absurd in her appearance. The

Dresden china shepherdesses were all showing their own hair and wearing muslin caps instead of powder, for on this compromise Mrs. Doubleday had insisted, arguing that powder might damage the goods offered for sale in a most unpleasant manner, while wigs were expensive and theatrical. Dahlia's hair was more brilliant than that of anybody else, but in spite of this distinction, her pleasure in a very well defined waist and extravagant skirts was spoilt by the incongruity of the cap and she wished she were merely a spectator who could enjoy the scene without any sense of responsibility for what was ludicrous. Mrs. Doubleday had always been opposed to the shepherdesses and the only pastoral symbol to which she would condescend was a crook adorned with a knot of ribbon, and Mrs. Matthews, in black silk, said, in her vulgar way, that Mrs. Doubleday with a bell round her neck might easily have been taken for the wether.

'I always said we'd look a funny lot, but when the crowds gather we'll show less. Some of the girls look pretty in their fancy silks, and you're prettier in your cotton, but it's a fact that in this world people like to laugh. They'll get more fun out of Miss Fairweather than they'll get pleasure out of you.'

'I can't get fun out of Miss Fairweather,' Dahlia said.

'No more can I, but there's some will.'

Separated from the sewing machine, standing at apparent loss under the green paper festoons designed to give the parish hall a vernal look, and dressed in a rather soiled but authentic peasant costume which, perhaps, was the spoil of foreign travel long ago and had some connection with Arcadia in her mind, Miss Fairweather was so sad a figure that Dahlia nervously approached her in the desire to remove her forlornness and gradually persuade her into a less conspicuous position in the almost empty hall.

'That's right, dear,' Mrs. Matthews said encouragingly. 'Better for her and for the bazaar if we can get her behind some of the hangings, anyhow till the place fills up a bit. Ask her to come and help us here. I'm big enough to hide anybody.'

But Miss Fairweather was neither in need of help nor anxious to give it and if she was aware of her incongruity in the Arcadian scene, she was indifferent to it. She seemed to have her own secret resources, though she looked like a pale, crumpled leaf adrift in the parish hall, and Dahlia returned, a little abashed by her presumption in imagining she could set Miss Fairweather at her ease.

'She's perfectly happy,' she reported. 'We needn't feel sorry for her. How muddling people are! It would be much more convenient if they'd match their looks.'

'Well, here's the vicar,' Mrs. Matthews said. 'You can't make any mistake about him. Though,' she added, with her confidential wink, 'it's always beaten me how he manages it, because, dear, between you and I, she'd turn the cream sour. But there's no accounting for tastes and p'raps he wouldn't be happy if he didn't have his cross. If Mr. Sproat wants one he'll have to look for it outside his house, won't he, Carrie?'

Mrs. Bagshot agreed with her friend and the modesty of Dahlia's smile changed to uneasiness when Mrs. Matthews playfully accused her of watching for Mr. Sproat's arrival. She had not been conscious of her frequent glances towards the door in her watch for someone else of whom she was likely to see no more now that the rehearsals were over, unless he came and told her he was ready to visit the Monks' Pool. And watching for him at this early hour was foolishness; she well knew that it was foolishness at any hour, but it was exciting; it raised the standard of everything she did, in case he should chance to be looking at her. However, he would not come yet and, in the meantime, she could give her attention to the advent of Mrs. Merriman. She was curious to see the woman who had played her part in Jenny's love affair.

She was already overdue and the youngest shepherdess was half-concealed in a corner of the platform, and anxiously supporting a large bouquet, against a painted background of a youth in doublet and hose, and a good deal out of drawing, who piped to a group of inattentive maidens. Dahlia's two partisans were of opinion that it was she who should have given the bouquet. It would have been a pretty compliment to the curate's bride and one that ought to have been paid.

'I should have enjoyed that very much,' Dahlia said. Nothing could have better pleased her sense of irony than forcing flowers into Mrs. Merriman's hands, but she would have to find some other use for it, and a general flutter among the stall-holders, Mrs. Doubleday's heavy march and the vicar's light tip-toeing towards the door, were signs that the great lady had arrived.

CHAPTER XVI

To the disappointment of the vicar who marshalled Mrs. Merriman, with fine impartiality, from stall to stall, and to the surprise of Mrs. Doubleday, there was no sign of Dahlia when Mrs. Bagshot and Mrs. Matthews were presented. Offering the bouquet would have been a pleasure, taking Mrs. Merriman's hand was more than Dahlia could manage when she remembered Jenny's stricken little face.

From the other side of the hall, Mrs. Doubleday observed her husband. She could guess what he was saying in praise of the newcomer to the parish, she could see him glancing here and there in search of her, and with rough, hurried movements, his wife rearranged the goods on her stall as though she hated them. Angrily she shook up the embroidered cushions and pulled the table centres into more conspicuous positions. Her whole world seemed to have shifted a little under a tremor of her own making. She could not despise her husband with her former whole-heartedness; she had few obviously feminine qualities, but she had the traditional reaction to neglect and though he was incapable of rudeness, he was neglecting her in the way she found most painful. He had lost his conciliatory nervousness, she deeply resented his performance of what, for her, was no less than a miracle, and if she had foolishly given him the impulse, it was Dahlia who had first inspired her.

What lay behind her dislike for Dahlia, Mrs. Doubleday hardly knew and did not try to discover. The lodgings in Beulah Mount, the undesirable mother, might have been forgiven and made into opportunities for kind patronage

123

with a young woman of meeker disposition, as Cecil Sproat had been acute enough to guess, but Dahlia was so flauntingly an independent person and so little oppressed by her disadvantages, and other people were so unobservant of them, that Mrs. Doubleday was not only denied a pleasure but presented with a grievance. There was no one definite reason for her antagonism. It was an instinct encouraged, perhaps, by the fact that Dahlia, like her mother, had the kind of beauty to arouse suspicion in respectable bosoms. Aware, but seldom conscious of it, yet influenced by it as she was bound to be, she had a charm and a frankness of approach very irritating to her superior in the parish, and to the mother of a son. Though he was too much her son, as she believed, to be more than mildly interested in a woman married to another, Dahlia would certainly supply a contrast and might cause comparisons and, later in the day, when the hall was invaded by the Tothills and their friends, who lingered beside Dahlia's stall, or took her into the refreshment room, after buying anything she offered, Mrs. Doubleday remembered and hoped her husband would not misinterpret her desire that he should try to behave more like a man. She had a sudden conviction that there was danger in the simplest speech, but here her little-exercised imagination was overdoing itself; in its stiff jerks it went too far. Mr. Doubleday's envy of Sproat was a retrospective one and though he might wish there had been a Dahlia, instead of a Flora, in his own youth, his present view of her was a paternal one. He had not forgotten the daughterly way in which she had taken his arm, her friendly touch had warmed his heart and, if he could have wanted Reginald to be different, it would only have been to change him into a girl like this one, and as he tripped about the hall, showering smiles, jokes, sympathy and praise, he refreshed himself with an occasional glance at her. She was a good

saleswoman, giving serious attention to her customers'
needs and, because the young men had none, she made
them buy what she thought would suit their mothers.
Mrs. Bagshot's takings promised to be heavy and Mrs.
Matthews, sighing but cheerful as she stooped, was
obliged to bring out reserves from the boxes concealed
beneath the stall.

'Her heart's in the work, because it's for him,' Mrs.
Bagshot said with sentiment.

Mrs. Matthews thought Dahlia was enjoying the bazaar
on its own merits, and the only care she had herself was
the fear of being beaten by Mrs. Doubleday. 'And I'm
not so much afraid, either,' she said, standing with her
hands on her hips and moving her head this way and that,
to get a glimpse of their rival. 'I mean, well, you've only
got to look at her. And she's keeping her eye on us,
too.'

Mrs. Doubleday was certainly missing nothing and
Dahlia was undoubtedly enjoying the bazaar. She liked
the bustle and her own success, she was happy in the
company of these two good-natured women and the
shrewd vulgarity of Mrs. Matthews amused her. She was
essentially akin to Mrs. Matthews in whose speech she
could hear, without embarrassment, an echo of her
mother's homely accents. She was experiencing again the
popularity she had known at school, for the girls, as well
as the young men, concerned in the Tothill sideshows,
were ready to be friendly, yet, when she saw Cecil gravely
making his way towards her and remembered that he was
the one person in the world who really needed her, the
only one on whom she could make claims, she was glad to
see him. Mrs. Doubleday, noticing their friendly greeting,
pushed her lips further forward in their pout, Mrs. Bagshot smiled almost coyly and nodded her pleasure, Mrs.
Matthews assured him, somewhat inaccurately, that

Dahlia had never paused in her work except to look for his arrival.

'And now,' she said, 'you'd better take her for a nice cup of tea.'

'I've had several nice cups and two ices,' Dahlia said, 'and I didn't pay for any of them. If you and Mrs. Bagshot will go and have a rest, Cecil and I can look after the stall.'

'Very well, dear. I'll be glad of a sit-down. I'm beginning to feel it in my feet. And don't forget there's still that good Indian tablecloth to sell. Perhaps Mr. Sproat would like to raffle it.'

Mr. Sproat would object very strongly, though he did not say so until Mrs. Matthews' broad back was turned.

'I know,' said Dahlia, a little surprised that he had missed a more public opportunity to protest. 'I'll pin it on the front of the stall and if the first performance of the play is a success I'll make Tony Tothill buy it. I'm sure he has an aunt who would like it. The Tothills have thousands of relations. Of course, they would have. Indian tablecloth kinds and others, and that's very useful at a bazaar. We've made heaps of money for the Mission. We shall be able to warm the hall properly.'

'Or start building a church.'

'Warmth and fun — that's what the Ivys want,' Dahlia said.

They had not mentioned the girl since the night of their quarrel and he recognized her wisdom in doing it now. 'Perhaps,' he agreed.

'It's what we all want,' she said, 'and I'm getting it today, and much more warmth than I care for.' She found her handbag and looked at the little wrist-watch he had given her. 'Nearly time for the first performance.'

'Why aren't you wearing the watch?' he asked.

'Because I'm a shepherdess, and I tell the time by the sun or I blow dandelions. I couldn't possibly wear a watch.'

'Or your wedding ring?' he asked quickly.

'Or my wedding ring,' she said. 'Oh, Cecil, don't look cross! Mrs. Doubleday will be so pleased. Say Ha, ha, loudly.'

'Ha, ha!' He could not keep back a smile, but it was a swiftly passing one. 'I'm hurt,' he said.

'Then you're very silly. Silly to be hurt and silly to say so.'

'Surely I can say what I like to you.'

'But not in the middle of a bazaar! And it may be a mistake anywhere.'

'We ought to say everything we think . . .'

'Oh no!' Dahlia interjected, 'I've tried that already.'

He exercised his masculine privilege of a slight deafness when it was convenient.

'I thought the ring was there for ever,' he said sadly, and she thought she could hear it tinkling across her bedroom floor.

'I can't help it,' she said stubbornly. 'I'm sure no one was married in Arcadia.'

'That's unkind, too.'

'You're very difficult,' she said patiently. 'You know I didn't mean to be unkind, but I can't wear a wedding ring when I'm pretending to be a virgin shepherdess.'

He did not like this language and, careless of Mrs. Doubleday, he frowned heavily. 'You don't look like a shepherdess and you're quite inconsistent. What shepherdess ever went to a bazaar?' he asked without humour.

Mrs. Doubleday heard Dahlia's laughter, she also saw Cecil's frown and she was sorry when it was smoothed away with Dahlia's next remark.

'Yes, it's all inconsistent and though I think you're

127

fussy about the ring, I'd put it on now if I hadn't left it at home. Oh, I know, I know! I ought not to have been parted from it, but when I dress up I can't help wanting to do it properly. Now I think you ought to smile at me very nicely and go and talk to Mrs. Doubleday.'

'I'm not on speaking terms with Mrs. Doubleday,' he said, regretting his words at once, but before he could reply to Dahlia's highly interested, 'Aren't you? Why not?' Simon Tothill had arrived.

'The room's filling up,' he said, 'but I've kept a seat for you.'

Dahlia could not understand why Cecil should seem so much pleased to meet a Tothill. The quicker beating of her heart made his cordiality pathetic and, in pity for him, she chose to be self-denying. She shook her head and spread her hands; she could not leave the stall.

'Nonsense!' Cecil said. 'The others will soon be back and I can take care of it until they come.' Gaily he waved them away.

'You are an angel,' Dahlia said sincerely. She had not the clue to this apparent recovery from ill-temper. She would have liked him all the better if she had known that he challenged Mrs. Doubleday when he gave his blessing to this companioned departure but, as she went, she was a little worried by his faculty for making trouble out of unimportant matters, a little guilty in her happiness as she walked through the hall with Simon, conscious that, in his presence, all her senses were curiously and delight-fully sharpened. Her footsteps and his were easily dis-tinguishable among the varied noises; she walked lightly, threaded her way easily and avoided collisions with satis-faction in the answering of her body to her will. Dexter-ously and on purpose, she passed between two large women holding laden baskets and, pressing down her petticoats, touched neither of them. She enjoyed, without trying to explain, the perfect physical response which comes at certain moments, and though she did not look at Simon, she knew that her muslin cap made her a little taller than he was, that, without it, the top of her head would be on a level with his ear. The improbable Arcadian decorations seemed just as absurd as before, but now they were more excusable, the funny shepherdesses were funnier and the pretty ones more charming, the thickening atmosphere was faintly blue and kind even to Miss Fairweather, but when they were in the passage leading to the smaller rooms and Simon indicated a doorway through which there came shouting and cracking noises, and said, 'Young Merriman's in there, running the Aunt Sally, with a heap of coco-nuts he can't get rid of,' some of Dahlia's elation left her. Here, close to her, was the man who had caused Jenny so much suffering, and Dahlia's anger against him made a wide sweep to include the unknown, foolish, wasteful girl who could not appreciate Simon Tothill, and as she looked at him who, unlike Jenny, was cheerful and charming in spite of his grief, she gave a silent testimony to the superior courage of men under affliction.

'Would you like to have a shot?' he said.

Hardly hearing the question she looked at him for signs of that affliction and she noticed, at the outer corners of his eyes, small lines that creased attractively when he smiled.

'How old are you?' she asked.

'Twenty-nine,' he said.

She gave a little nod. She was glad he was as old as that. She felt more honoured in his confidence, she liked to believe his knowledge and experience were greater than her own.

'Why did you ask?' he said.

'Because I wanted to know.'

'Well, that's an excellent reason, but I was asking you if you'd like to have a shot.'

'I don't think I want one,' she said. 'If the Aunt Sally was my Aunt Sarah – I've got one and she's horrid – I'd try to hit her with pleasure. I'd try lots of times, but, as it isn't, I'll just have a peep.'

The fair young man who was exhorting the ladies and gentlemen to walk up and try their luck, three shots a penny and a coco-nut for a hit, stopped his encouragements and grinned rather sheepishly when he saw Simon and Dahlia in the doorway. He could make a fool of himself with strangers for audience but, in the presence of an acquaintance, he lacked confidence in his powers, he was not a determined amateur jester like Tony Tothill who, earlier in the evening, had dragged a toy lamb about the hall, to the disgust of Mrs. Doubleday and the very mild amusement of the few spectators who were aware of the performance. He left his customers for a moment and came towards the door, forestalling possible criticism by turning it on himself. His bashfulness was combined with a slight stubbornness of aspect, explaining much to Dahlia, and when he bowed at the sound of her name, she could not help looking at him gravely and saying clearly, 'Yes, but I used to be Dahlia Rendall,' and then she turned away in sympathetic embarrassment for his confusion.

Simon was puzzled, but he asked no question. The play was about to begin and he was not concerned in the affairs of Merriman or Dahlia. It would have troubled Dahlia to know how very little he was concerned.

CHAPTER XVII

THERE were whoops of delight from the children in the front rows each time Tony Tothill tripped over his own feet. Girls from the Mission shrieked with loud, half derisive laughter at his clowning and if Tony suspected the derision, it only cried him on to greater efforts. He would certainly buy the Indian tablecloth, Dahlia thought. He was absurd but he was happy and giving happiness to other people. They were not being elevated by art or noble sentiments but, in the release they enjoyed, one of the purposes of art was being fulfilled and she was glad Cecil was not with her. She would have felt ashamed of her own laughter and, to make another of the contrasts she half-enjoyed, half-repudiated, she took a glance at Simon who sat close to her on the crowded bench. He had reduced his width by folding his arms across his chest but, through her thin sleeve, she could feel the texture of his coat and it was easy to make the friendly contact firmer as she shifted her position for a better view of the stage. Simon's brows were raised as though he were bewildered by his brother's capacity for buffoonery, his mouth was twisted in good-natured amusement: his expression, Dahlia thought, was exactly right. There was tolerance in it and generosity, and there was also adaptability which seemed to her a most desirable quality. She drew a deep sigh and perhaps exaggerated it purposely, making it more of a tremor than a sound.

Simon responded to it at once. 'Bored?' he asked.

'No. Thinking.'

'It must be the first time Tony has made anyone do that.'

131

'It's the noise that helps. It makes a kind of shelter. Don't you ever want one?'

He shook his head slowly, looking straight in front of him and she felt she was rebuked for lack of tact. Of course he did not want a shelter for his thoughts, he wanted to forget them, and why, she asked herself sadly should he be interested in hers? Youthfully, she wished she could have presented herself as a person whose inner life was more profound, more complicated, than anyone would suppose, but, in any case, she could not have confided in him. She could not tell him of her satisfaction in his nearness, the movements of his hands, the way he smiled, her certainty of his sympathy in any problem. Moreover, her pride, at war with her senses, insisted that she must make a success of her undertakings. Had not he said himself that life, though a mess, would clear itself up in time if it were given a chance? No one, looking at him, would know he had his secret trouble and no one should ever know of hers. She was dramatizing herself a little, a course foreign to her spontaneous nature, but the spontaneity had latterly been checked by the reserve Cecil's disapprovals had forced on her. He disapproved of a good deal, she decided, and especially of her mother and of Jenny. She could not speak freely of them to him and yet they were constantly in her mind. How could she suddenly forget those two who were the background of her life and, remembering them intensely, remember also not to mention them and yet feel no resentment for the restriction? He had effectually silenced her about her mother, but the sight of Cyril Merriman had made her very conscious of Jenny, exiled with the Cummings, her future uncertain and unsatisfactory. Was she to be left there indefinitely? Was nothing to be done for her? Was a friendly consultation impossible with Cecil? She smiled a little sourly as she remembered his protest about frankness but, with her habitual fairness, she owned that she had made it difficult for him to talk about his work. She sighed again, but this time she took care to control the tremor. Something had gone wrong, and perhaps Cecil was luckier than she was because he had so much pleasure in her physical appearance, but perhaps not: it might, she saw, be worse for him, yet, if it could be perfect for neither, why should it not be better than it was at present, with their silly little misunderstandings and reserves? She would do what she could. Cyril Merriman had wasted Jenny, that girl with the red lips was wasting Simon, another woman, such as Miss Morrison, might well think Dahlia was wasting Cecil. It must not be, she thought, with her courageous optimism. She would go to him at once and start again. She would hold his hand as they walked home and crossed The Green under the bare trees, and talk to him about Jenny and ask for his advice. Asking advice was always mollifying. She would not look up to see whether he frowned and she would not frown if his words displeased her. They must accept each other's differences and be patient or ignore them and love each other none the less, yes, and at once, she added in a panic, as Simon turned and smiled and whispered, 'You are not laughing. Are you thinking still?'

'No,' she said with decision. 'No, I've finished.'

'So has the play, or very nearly.'

She allowed herself a long look at the face that pleased her. The play was nearly over, there would be no more rehearsals, he was not likely to come her way again, and Cecil was sitting faithfully by the stall and watching for her. She was grateful for the love no one else wished to give her and as the audience pressed into the corridor she managed to slip away from Simon. She wanted to find Cecil immediately. All her goodwill and her desire to love him with a full return were in her quick step and her

133

bright eyes. She was looking for the man, who, when a few hours had passed, might truly be her lover, but when she entered the hall she could not see him. There was a clear space between her and the stall where Mrs. Bagshot and Mrs. Matthews were chatting comfortably; the Indian tablecloth still hung in disregarded invitation; more than half the customers seemed to have disappeared, for it was the dinner hour for those who dined, and presently the hall would be thronged by those who were waiting for the lower entrance fee. Mrs. Doubleday was not in sight; a few people strolled from stall to stall in an indifferent, critical manner, proclaiming their unwillingness to be coaxed; they would only buy when and what they liked and the stall-holders had correspondingly relaxed their efforts. Dahlia felt a sinking of her spirits and a little anger against Cecil for not being where she had put him in her picture, but her two friends nodded and smiled at her like happy mandarins.

'In the refreshment room, dear. There's a nice surprise for you. Mr. Sproat's taken her to have something to eat and drink. She was looking very wan.'

'Jenny?' Dahlia said. To no one else of her acquaintance could that adjective be applied and Dahlia saw her as she must have been when she came into the hall, white and wide-eyed, half resentful of the conditions in which she found herself and creating that atmosphere of distance and reserve which was peculiarly her own.

'Been travelling all day, it seems,' Mrs. Matthews continued. 'Found the house empty, but saw the flags across the street and came on here.'

Dahlia did not try to collect or to control her thoughts. She knew there would be no perfect concord with Cecil for her that night. Choosing her own time, Jenny had come at the wrong moment, but Cecil's probable vexation, the near neighbourhood of Cyril Merriman, her

134

own disappointment and the new problem this arrival indicated were worries which were forgiven in the protective love that sent her swiftly to the refreshment room.

'Now, I wonder,' said Mrs. Matthews, 'What d'you think all that means, Carrie? Mr. Sproat didn't look too pleased, either. Trouble for somebody, I fancy.'

'It won't be of Mrs. Sproat's making,' Mrs. Bagshot said. She had infinite faith in the sweet sanity of the girl who had not been too proud to accept her cakes.

'No, and the little one's not a patch on her for looks.' Other people might not have agreed with Mrs. Matthews, though Jenny was not seen to advantage at this moment. Her hat concealed the smooth, shapely head and her creased coat the slim fineness of her shape. Cecil had plied her with food and drink, but he had no brotherly companionship to offer, no solicitous questions to ask. He knew the answers would be unsatisfactory to a person with a sense of duty, and her little face, so attractive to some people, had no charm for him. Already in a state of irritation with Dahlia and Simon and Mrs. Doubleday, he was in no mood for Jenny who had probably run away from something she considered disagreeable; she was not even eating with the grateful appetite she ought to have shown and it was a relief to both of them when Dahlia, vivid and quick, broke into the sombre company.

'Oh, Jen!' she said. The words began as half a question and ended in a joyful catch of the breath, and forgetting Cecil, she exclaimed, 'I didn't know how much I'd missed you!' She slipped into his empty chair without noticing that he had gone.

'The house was empty and all dark,' Jenny said, 'but I saw those awful banners and I remembered the bazaar.'

'I like the banners,' Dahlia said stoutly, 'and they brought you here, so you should like them too. You

135

might still have been sitting on the doorstep. Why didn't you tell me you were coming?'

'Because I didn't know,' Jenny said. 'Can we go back to the house now?'

'You could go with Cecil,' she looked about for him, 'but I think I ought to stay.'

'Then I'll stay too.'

'I don't think you'd better,' Dahlia said quickly. 'You'll be so tired and there'll be a fire in the study. Have you brought any luggage?'

'A little case. The large woman said she would take care of it.'

'Mrs. Matthews. She's a darling and so is Mrs. Bagshot. That's why I can't desert them. Let's go and find Cecil at once.'

Dahlia stood up, trying not to betray her anxious haste to get Jenny out of danger, but, as she spoke, she saw Jenny's eyes fixed on the other end of the room. A little flush waved over her cheeks and left them very white and, as fresh ripples in the sand appear as the tide recedes, her faced quivered into a smile, friendly but distant, and it seemed to ask a question.

Too late, Dahlia stepped in front of the table. 'I'll come home with you,' she said, but Jenny said calmly, 'There's no need for either of us to go. I'll stay and help you when I've taken off my hat and coat.'

CHAPTER XVIII

THE air was cool on their flushed faces as they walked across The Green. The bazaar was over and the goods left over had been carried away or covered with dust sheets for the night. The floor of the parish hall was strewn with paper, string and dust and the ends of forbidden cigarettes. Mrs. Bagshot, almost tearful at the girls' refusal to be driven home, had rather timidly directed the proud chauffeur to Mrs. Matthews's lodgings and that stout lady, undaunted by any minion in livery, had been jocularly regretful about her size and the little room it left for other people.

'Ah, it's only because they want to be together,' Mrs. Bagshot said with tender sympathy.

It was after eleven o'clock and the streets were almost empty. The Green, with its steadily burning lamps under leafless trees, was like a garden decorated for a fête and robbed of all its foliage by some stroke of witchcraft which could not subdue the fairy lights. The shadows of great branches made black barriers across the paths but they flattened themselves and offered no resistance when they were approached. Light shone through the fanlight of the Sproats' front door and, more dimly, behind the curtains of the study, and Jenny said, as they reached the gate, 'When we used to look at this house, we never thought you were going to live in it. There are all sorts of things like that in front of us and we can't tell what they are.'

'That's what makes life so exciting.'

'Frightening – for me. But it will be comfortable and happy for you, I expect,' Jenny said and Dahlia smiled at her sister's usual assumption that the worst must always be for herself. 'Could we go up to the hill for a few minutes?'

'I must air your sheets, Jen.'

'Oh, don't be so practical,' Jenny said and Dahlia smiled again. She was more concerned about Cecil than about the sheets. Jenny had postponed, or stolen, the critical moment – a day later and all would have been well – but to-night, Dahlia feared she would pile sweetness upon Cecil, merely to placate him. It was hypocritical, it was base, it suggested a discourtesy, a boorishness of which he could not be guilty, yet her trust in his power to hide annoyance and disapproval was weaker than the necessity to make Jenny welcome, and since there was not time to explain that this was as important to her as the saving of a soul to him, she must resort to such little wiles as her honest life had never known, and she felt the familiar, loving exasperation with her sister.

'For a very few minutes, then,' she said.

They left Jenny's suit-case within the gate and walked up the winding bush-bordered path and, when they reached the top, they leaned against the railings and looked across the river. Was this, Dahlia wondered, an indulgence of sentiment on Jenny's part, or a declaration of indifference to the man she had met in those steep woods and the fields beyond? Had she decided to stay at the bazaar to show Cyril she felt no discomfort in his presence? Had she taken off her hat and coat, emerging from those coverings like a pale flower from its rough sheath, to remind him of the Jenny he had loved? Dahlia could not ask; they had never forced each other's confidence and in the stillness, broken towards the city by the perpetual noise of the docks, Jenny was held by her own thoughts and Dahlia, trying to avoid hers, was reaching out to Jenny's. There was no moon, now, to make theatrical effects; the trees hung darkly on the opposite cliff, the lights by the river had no rival to drench their glow, and though the bodily Simon was absent, Dahlia could not rid herself of a sense that he was near, and as, on that other night, he had instructed her in what she had missed, so, now, he seemed to hover, telling her she would never have it. Jenny had come back to Upper Radstowe in an ill-chosen moment and, for all Dahlia's hopefulness, she had little faith in the recapturing of an inspiration: Jenny, behind the stall, in an unusual brilliance of animation, had brought a reminiscent expression to Simon's face and it had stayed there until it changed to one of pleasure.

Dahlia tightened her hands on the topmost bar, but she let them go limp when Jenny began to speak.

'I knew he would run away,' she said, 'I hoped he wouldn't, but I'm glad he did. I was perfectly certain I didn't like him when I said good-bye, all those ages ago, but afterwards, I wasn't, quite. And now,' she drew a breath, 'I know I don't care any longer.'

'But if he'd stayed?'

'Ah, if he'd stayed, he would have been a different person, the one I thought he was at first. I'm glad he ran away.'

'But Jen,' Dahlia said quietly, 'haven't you run too? Or,' she said when there was no answer, except a stiffening of Jenny's figure, 'are you going back?'

'I can't go back!' Her cry sped across the river and the tree-tops as though it would reach Merriman House in the village and Grimshaw's Farm beyond, the places where she should have found shelter, but one of them had been refused to her and the other she would not take. She turned, and there was light enough to see her outraged face. 'He kissed me,' she whispered and she seemed to be blaming Dahlia.

'Edwin?'

'No. Edwin wouldn't have mattered – much. It was

old Mr. Cummings.' She brushed her hand across her face. 'And he has a beard, straggly. And his lips show, all crooked. I think he forgot I wasn't Fanny or Kitty. It wasn't meant to be a nasty kiss. He's not like that.'

'Perhaps he counted you as a daughter, poor old man. You can't have run away because of a kiss.'

'No, but Fanny wouldn't let me stay. She said I was unkind to him. I never said a thing, but perhaps I showed I hated it.'

'Perhaps!' Dahlia exclaimed.

'Well, I can't help having that kind of face, can I?'

'Neither can he.'

'I wasn't unkind, I was sorry for him. I just used to go away when he came near me. And they are a very loyal family.'

'So are we,' Dahlia said, 'and we know what it's like to have unkindness.'

'Yes, but we're all nice-looking,' Jenny said in a final tone. She could forgive almost anything except a physical fault.

'What else did Fanny say?'

'Oh, heaps of things, and I suppose they were mostly true.'

'And Edwin?'

'They meant to be gentle with me and they were, Kitty and Fanny, but they showed quite plainly they didn't want me. Nobody wants me.'

'And Edwin?' Dahlia persisted.

'So you see, I haven't really run away. I've been sent.' The bitterness of failure was in her tone. 'And there was nowhere else for me to come to.'

'Oh Jen, couldn't you have stayed and tried to be different? Didn't Edwin ask you to stay?'

'No. He just looked at me. That,' the words came with difficulty, 'is why I went so suddenly. I couldn't bear it.

Because he's good. Because, I suppose, I've cheated him. And I did mean to like him, but how could I tell, then, when I was so unhappy? It seemed to be the only thing to do. I thought I should be safe with him, like you with Cecil.'

'Yes,' Dahlia said, 'we both wanted to be safe.'

'But it isn't enough,' said Jenny, and the words sounded like an echo of Dahlia's thoughts. 'And I'm not quite twenty,' Jenny told the silent and indifferent night. 'Can't I be forgiven for a mistake?'

The vague powers she addressed gave her no answer. The woods were black and non-committal, the lights below were intent on their task of marking the river windings; impersonal clangings and shoutings from the docks increased the isolation of the girls at the cliff's edge and a leaf, turning on the ground under a faint stirring of wind, seemed to sigh its ignorance and resignation.

'Edwin will forgive you,' Dahlia said at last.

'I'm sure he's done that already. Oh, he's good, he's good. Too good for me. Fanny,' she spoke in a low voice, 'Fanny told me I think of nothing but myself.'

'Well, that's nearly true, isn't it?' Dahlia changed her weight from one foot to another. It had been a tiring day and there was still Jenny's bed to prepare.

'Yes, but it wouldn't be if I really loved somebody,' she said and with great simplicity she asked, 'What is it like to do that?'

'I thought you knew.'

'That was a dream,' Jenny said. 'That doesn't count. I mean the kind that lasts.'

'It's the same kind,' Dahlia said and though she spoke with authority there was no life in her voice, 'but it goes on. It's being able to disagree without quarrelling and not being embarrassed about anything, anything at all,' she said with emphasis and she saw Jenny nod. 'I mean when you are together, because there are no secrets. And it's feeling happy when he's near, even if he isn't thinking of you, and taking each other on trust and not saying do and don't. It's liking the way he holds things and the lines round his eyes, and loving him without his loving you.'

'But,' Jenny forgot herself in this moment, 'Cecil hasn't stopped, has he? He couldn't!' And because Dahlia did not reply at once, she said again, 'He couldn't!'

Stiffly, Dahlia turned her head. 'Cecil? No!' She laughed a little. It was as though she had been listening to a disembodied voice, and not her own, making a secret avowal to the darkness. 'He likes me so much that he'll be very angry with me for staying out so late!'

'And he'll blame me,' Jenny said.

'And he'll be quite right,' Dahlia said gaily. She slipped her arm through Jenny's. 'And I'm so tired that if I don't run down the hill, I shan't be able to get home at all.' But, before they started, she added gravely, 'Don't think about love, Jen. You are too young and what you want is some hard work to do.'

'I know. But not too hard,' she said and, suddenly, she was able to see her own absurdity. Her rare laughter startled a bird from the rocks below and the intense blackness of wings, as it swooped, made the night look grey. 'If I'd had work to do I shouldn't have been so silly about Cyril, I shouldn't have needed to go with Edwin. We hadn't half enough to do in Beulah Mount and so, of course, we had to fall in love.'

'Of course,' Dahlia agreed.

'And then . . .'

'I know.'

'I just took the only place there seemed to be for me.'

'I know,' Dahlia repeated impatiently. 'We both know. Don't talk about it.'

'But I had to tell you.'

'There was no need. Let's run. And stop me at the gate, because I shan't be able to stop myself.'

They went quickly, with long easy strides, and Cecil, going once more to the door to look for them, heard the steps keeping time before he heard their light voices and saw them, linked but running freely, Dahlia's stiffened petticoats under her coat making her figure belie her youthful speed.

He was before them at the gate and in his jealousy of Jenny and the anger of his anxiety, he said, 'Where on earth have you been? I was sure you would come back with Mrs. Bagshot or I should have fetched you.'

He knew he ought to have been softened by their quick change from gaiety to the aspect of timid children chidden by a stern parent, he wished he could take an arm of each and, in this friendly fashion, lead them to the house, but he had an unconquerable fear of being lenient when severity was due; he wanted to know whether Jenny was blameable for this sudden arrival before he could conscientiously try to feel friendly towards her. He must hear what excuse Dahlia could offer for staying out so late, and the realization that he was alone in his anger and they were two in their enjoyment was a hardening factor in his feelings.

'We wanted to go up to the hill,' Dahlia said cheerfully. 'It was very stuffy in the hall.'

'It was my idea,' Jenny said loyally.

'And who took care of you, up there, at this time of night?'

'Took care of us? On the hill? There's nothing to harm us there. We took care of each other – don't forget your little case, Jen – as we always do.'

'I don't like you to wander about at night.'

'The next time I want to do it I'll get an escort.' She

143

hesitated, then found his hand and gave it a little squeeze. 'I'll get you! Come along! I must air the sheets.'

'It's too late.' Jenny felt she must do her soothing share. 'Blankets will do.'

'Yes, it's much too late,' Cecil said, bolting the front door. 'And Dahlia is very tired.'

'In a good cause,' she said. She stood at the foot of the stairs and ticked off the hours on her fingers. 'Ten,' she said, 'without counting the preparations this morning.'

'Ten,' she said to herself, 'for the old Mission and only half of one for Jen. I shan't be able to be nice to him.' But her voice was happy enough as she called Jenny to follow her upstairs and asked whether she was sure she could sleep in blankets.

'I could sleep on the floor,' Jenny said. 'Oh, you don't know how lovely it is not to be afraid of waking in the night.'

CHAPTER XIX

DAHLIA changed her crushed frock for a dressing-gown; she found her wedding ring and put it in her pocket and she went downstairs rather slowly, vexed that policy should have mastered her sense of hospitality. A chat by a warm fire, something hot to drink and a lingering good night were what she should have given Jenny, but an eye beyond the immediate present had seen the wisdom of an unceremonious bundling into bed and the same eye directed her to stand beside Cecil on the study hearthrug, to look up at him prettily and say, 'Aren't you going to thank me for all the hard work I've done for you?'

'Was it for me?' he asked.

'Who else?'

He did not answer for a moment. 'Need it be for a person?'

'Everything – I mean, the very little – I do, is always for persons.'

'So it seems.'

'And the Mission is persons, isn't it?'

'But were you thinking of the Mission?'

Smiling still, in case he should look at her instead of at the fire, she decided that he was very stupid not to realize how his scant welcome of Jenny had turned this hearthrug into a possible volcano and, seeing him in this mood, she felt most disinclined to use the intended wiles which would take them both out of danger.

'Were you thinking of the Mission?' he repeated and, as she grew still more resentful of this catechism when a kiss would have been so easy, she became gladly careless of eruptions.

'Are you asking because you really want to know, or are you beginning a little sermon?' she inquired. 'Well then, I didn't feel any noble fervour for the Mission. I didn't think of it except in wanting to please you. And I enjoyed the bazaar because it was fun. And I sold that ghastly tablecloth. No one else in the hall could have done it!'

'No one else was so pretty.' His tone turned this praise into a condemnation.

'We must use the gifts God gives us,' Dahlia said brightly. 'Would you like me better . . .'

'I couldn't like you better.'

'Like me better,' Dahlia continued, 'if I were a good earnest girl, forgetting all about you in the Cause?'

'I've said I couldn't like you better.'

'Scold me less, then,' she said wearily.

'I haven't scolded you!'

'You are trying to lift me to a higher plane and that's much worse. I want to stay on earth. It's a good place. Oh Cecil, why are you so cross?'

He did not know what to say. The small grievances were too trivial to be mentioned, the big ones were too important. His little quarrel with Dahlia, the heat and noise of the bazaar, his absurd dealings with tray cloths and knitted baby clothes, had all contributed to his ill-temper, but his real trouble was a sense of isolation. Dahlia's joy at seeing Jenny, the quick intake of breath she had never given him in welcome, and later, the ease with which she responded to the chatter and nonsense of the Tothills and their friends, had thrust him into another world. But he believed his own world was better and while he wished to be where she was, he was naturally prejudiced in favour of her following him to the higher plane at which she mocked.

'This,' said Dahlia, sinking to the hearthrug as he remained gloomily silent, 'is much more tiring than airing sheets.'

'Because you would have been doing that for your sister,' he said sharply.

'I've been slaving for you all day!'

'Because it amused you.'

'Jenny amuses me too,' she said, 'so there's nothing in that.'

She must put a stop to this nonsense. What were they quarrelling about? She was horrified at the rapidity with which they had slipped into this little dark pit where reproaches crawled like poisonous snakes; it seemed that the marriage state had a tendency to lead one to its edge and much care was needed not to fall, but that state has an advantage over other threatened friendships in a readier power of recovery. It can renounce reason, and so find it, in unabashed demonstrations of affection, and though Dahlia, too, had been adversely affected by the happenings of the day, she knew that here there was something worth nurturing carefully until its roots went deeper. The result might not be exactly what she wanted but it would have a value of its own, Cecil and she had not so wide a choice that they could disdain the one at hand, and she was beginning to lift her arms towards him when he spoke.

'I don't find Jenny at all amusing.'

'Well no, perhaps it was the wrong word,' Dahlia said pacifically.

'I find her very disquieting.'

'Then don't talk about her. I'm going to bed.'

'But we must talk about her.'

'No,' Dahlia said with smiling decision. 'I won't listen. I'm too tired. But I wish you could be glad, just because I am, that she's here. When you have a spare bedroom—

what a queer expression that is; it sounds so grudging –
it's fun to have some one in it.'

'Fun! How often you use that word!'

'Gratifying,' she said, and solemnly she turned her
eyes to the ceiling, 'to all one's instincts of service and
hospitality.'

'I hope I'm not inhospitable,' he said quickly
'but I don't know whether we ought to welcome her.
There must have been some trouble with the Cummings or she wouldn't have arrived unexpectedly like
this.'

'And why should you suppose Jenny made it? But
people are always ready to believe in strangers, rather
than in their friends.'

'It depends on their experience with their friends.'

His dry tone was too much for Dahlia's carefully
guarded control. 'And what experience have you had
with Jenny? You don't know anything about her. You've
never wanted to. All these weeks, these months, you've
made me feel that I mustn't mention her or mother.'
She paused, trying to get rid of a tightness in her throat.
'The only time you've spoken about my mother it was to
be unkind and now, when you think you can find fault
with Jenny, you're taking an interest in her. I'm not
like that with your family.' Her lips quivered and she
said childishly, 'I write a long letter to your mother every
week. I know she wants to hear the little things about
you that you wouldn't tell yourself. It has never occurred
to you to write to mine.'

The idea certainly astonished him and he was just in
time to stop himself from saying that he would find a
difficulty in choosing language simple enough for Louisa's
comprehension. He contented himself with murmuring
that the cases were not parallel.

'I won't ask why because I think it will be better for

148

you if you don't tell me,' Dahlia said, 'but what really surprises me is that you've been able to leave her in peace. You're such a sin hunter – and you're after Jenny now – that I don't know why you haven't tried to make my mother a better woman.'

'Oh, this isn't fair!' he cried, but to that she made no response and left him.

She cried without tears while she undressed. She found the loneliness of trouble in marriage greater than its joy when all went well, for happiness need not be concealed. The success of marriage calls for proclamation, its failure must not be acknowledged and now she could not creep into Jenny's bed, as she wished to do, and warm herself and find comfort in a love that needed no explanation. Their silence about the things they did not like was founded on understanding of them and of each other; their differing attitudes and intensities of feeling were accepted without argument, and Dahlia's criticisms of Jenny – which were much the same as Cecil's – could not diminish her affection. It seemed to her that the things Jenny did or left undone were like rain or sunshine on a familiar landscape. They were accidents which dulled or beautified, they were sad or pleasing, but the scene kept its beloved essence. Yet, in spite of this union, she could not get into Jenny's bed and dishonour Cecil in her eyes; she did not know how she was to endure his neighbourhood and, like a lost soul, she stood uncertainly on the landing. Then, very quietly, she opened the spare bedroom door and went, bare-footed to the bedside. Jenny was like a cocoon in the blankets. The curtains were withdrawn – a country habit – and there was light enough to see the dark head on the pillow and the paired semi-circles of dark brows and lashes, before she waked with a whimpering cry.

'It's only me,' Dahlia murmured and her tender heart

149

ached at that sound of fear. 'It's only me. You're quite
safe here.'

'Yes. Lovely!' Jenny sighed in immense relief and
drew the blankets closer.

'Jen,' Dahlia whispered hopefully, 'would you like me
to get in beside you, because you're frightened?'

'No room,' Jenny said. 'Too comfortable. And I shan't
be frightened any more.'

Baulked in this design, Dahlia went to her own bed
and, too tired for thought, continued anger or contrition, she fell asleep. She never heard Cecil's stealthy
movements or knew that it was hours before he came
upstairs.

He needed hours for all he had to do. He had to
examine the wounds she had inflicted and recover from
the first sharp pain before he could consider his other
griefs and find that though Dahlia outweighed them all,
the greatest was the quality of her affection for him. He
tested it in a vain attempt to imagine her quarrelling
violently with Jenny for his sake. He knew she would
never do it and he forgot that the very closeness of his
tie with her implied the existence of a sympathy which
she could forego in other relationships without injury
to them, that hard words from Jenny might be laughed
aside while those from a man who, until a little while
ago, was a stranger and one on whom she was now dependent for much more than her bread, must first strike
her cruelly and then rebound on him. He had not yet
established his right to a perfect, inoffensive frankness
which, if it does not spring, full grown, from a mental
union, must be brought to birth with infinite care. The
marriage service and a ring cannot immediately create it
and some suspicion of this truth tapped at his mind until,
at last, he allowed entry to another thought which he had
been repulsing, the certainty that Dahlia, in her ignorance

and need, had married the wrong man. Whether she was aware of this he could not tell. He hated the remembrance of the Tothills, younger men than himself, hiding any seriousness of purpose they might possess behind light ways and language which seemed to be native to her. He saw every street corner in Upper Radstowe as the spot where she might come face to face with the man she wanted, but, as he sat beside the dying fire, he did not waver in his belief that he had married the right woman and, renouncing his hope of shaping her, here and there, to match himself, he saw the necessity of wooing her anew and in another guise. That necessity was perhaps the only power capable of making him face her accusations and see some truth in them, yet, in effect, it was none the less a conquest over spiritual pride. He owned to a sort of pleasure in discovering and condemning sin; he went further and confessed that, in Louisa Grimshaw's case, his sense of her fault was emphasized by the awkwardness of her humble origin, and, first hoping that this weakness, at least, might be kept from Dahlia's knowledge, he ended by praying that it might pass from him and with it that care for Jenny's duty to which he would hardly have given a thought if Dahlia had loved her less.

Having started on this examination, he did not spare himself. He saw how his youthful anxiety to be worthy of his calling had fixed him in a rigidity which accorded little with his Master's mind, and how, in his faithfulness to the Church, he was in danger of being unfaithful to the One in whose name it was founded. By the time the fire was cold he was sufficiently humble. He had to be that or desperate with the fear of losing her and he remembered how, before they married, she had seemed like the embodiment of honesty and laughter, the woman with the qualities he needed. In some secret way, physical possession had made him less conscious of her virtues and more satisfied with his own. Now he had the not unhopeful consolation of realizing that he had never truly possessed her, and he felt all the excitement of adventure in the prospect of a new pursuit. Beyond that, encompassing it and inherent in it, he knew there was another, a search for values and standards which would not necessarily be those of his Church and while he shrank from it with all the strength of a nature that found comfort in codes and creeds, he accepted it as one of the bitter gifts of love.

CHAPTER XX

Mr. Doubleday, at the other end of The Green, had come to certain conclusions about his own marriage and certain determinations in connection with it, but they were different from those of Cecil Sproat and he was not the man to sit in a cold room or lose his sleep in the consideration of any problem. In that critical moment when his wife revealed her feelings and stripped the veneer from his, he looked manfully at the remains, saw them for what they were and after the first shock he settled down to live with them as comfortably as he could. Nothing but the stubbornness often found in apparently weak characters could have combated the habits of many years. He astonished himself and her with his success and he began to enjoy a mental freedom which demanded no long flights and was content to hop and flutter near at home with a new sense of safety. Fortunately for his ease, the nature of Mrs. Doubleday's attack had no disturbing connection with his religious beliefs, indeed, these were impregnable because they were practically non-existent. He was a clergyman, he had once subscribed to certain settled formulas and he gave them no more thought. He took for guide the natural kindliness of his heart and, instead of hating sin with Cecil's fervour, because it was, first of all, an offence against his religion, he merely regretted the inconvenience which was usually the result, to others and himself, and his tolerance was not accompanied by any desire to look for causes or adjust his views to his experience. The humming which had almost stopped in Mrs. Doubleday's presence would certainly have come between him and any spiritual doubts, for it was the screen which he could put to many uses. But he had no doubts. Mrs. Doubleday had raised none that concerned more than their own small affairs and, as he had never had and no longer wanted her approval, there was a simpler, though less inspiring task for him than for Cecil Sproat. Mrs. Doubleday, too, had married the wrong man, but Mr. Doubleday had married the wrong woman. That had been tacitly agreed between them, or so he thought, and to the mind of neither was any outward disturbance imaginable. The street corners of Upper Radstowe had no alarms for him and Mrs. Doubleday would never stand, like Dahlia, on the hill and address the night with a description of perfect love. They would continue to share a home until death took one of them and each would have felt still more uncomfortable with some one else at the other end of the table.

It was she who suffered more, for she had erred signally in judgment and she had to watch his confidence increasing to the point where he could talk of Sproat without embarrassment and of Reginald as though he were as much the father's as the mother's son. Always, hitherto, Norman had been the third and unconsidered person in the trio, quietly taking the inconspicuous place he was given, but could he be put there now, or would he stay there? Behind the long face with its protesting mouth, her thoughts were troubled. She saw herself sitting alone by the drawing-room fire while Norman and Reginald sat in the study; she imagined them going down the long garden path together, pleased with each other's company; she put her husband's new view of her into the eyes of Reginald, little guessing that he had always thought them an awkward pair and hoped he need not feel sorry for his father, and she almost had it in her heart to wish he were not coming home.

True repentance springs from detestation of an offence

and implies the determination to sin no more, and though Mrs. Doubleday considered herself to have been temporarily incautious rather than offensive, and feared she would have no more opportunities to commit the same kind of mistake, she did repent, in a fashion, but she also felt that she had been unfairly treated. Norman had given no sign of latent rebellion, she had grown to think of him as a target and not a human being, she had been misled by his elasticity to rebuffs and, suddenly and subtly, her hand was paralysed and, while her eye was as true as ever, she could not draw her bow. She did not understand the change for she had always been occupied with her opinion of him and her own dissatisfaction, and concerned herself not at all with what he might think of her. She was ignorant of the fact that he had refused to think until she forced him to it by such a slip of the tongue as might have happened any day in any of the years they had spent together, and thus gave him the independence of a dislike he could acknowledge.

At this period, as she would have been humiliated to learn, there was a faint likeness between her situation and Cecil Sproat's. His love for Dahlia necessitated an altered mental attitude; her need to recover power over Mr. Doubleday was almost persuading her to some form of conciliation. But she was much older than Cecil and she had no capacity for humility; her mind and her spirit were set and stiff and there was torture in trying to bend them. She was very unhappy and when she presided at committee meetings, or made her curt inquiries for the sick, or marched about the streets with her shopping basket on her arm, she knew she had left a more cheerful person in the study. She had deprived him of so little and herself of so much. Looking back, she realized how seldom he had talked to her, while he had supplied her with an outlet for those small irritations which, in their expression, were an important pleasure in her life. She was fortunate, however, in being able to trace her present trouble to the Sproats. Doubts of her wisdom in reproaching Cecil for his wife's frivolity and so putting him on the alert for something worse, were balanced by the hope that Dahlia's hereditary laxness would be stronger than his care and teach him to see marriage as something more than a personal satisfaction. The choice of a girl notably pretty was unsuitable in a clergyman. It suggested the frailty of other men, especially when her origin was remembered and he had set a bad example to the parish, which, indeed, had shown itself somewhat insensitive to social differences. Mrs. Tothill had said, 'Tut!' when Mrs. Doubleday sought her sympathy soon after the marriage. 'We may be keeping lodgings ourselves before we know where we are. Who cares about such things nowadays? The girl knows how to speak and how to behave and I like to look at her and I think all the more of Mr. Sproat for having married her. There must be something in the man to want her and still more to get her. I always thought he'd marry one of those women with limp skirts, running about like worried dogs with their tails between their legs. The church can't afford that sort of thing, it's in a bad enough way already. If Mrs. Sproat still takes an interest in her clothes five years hence, she'll do the church more good than dozens of revival meetings.' Mrs. Doubleday's reminder that the church was not the Salvation Army was cheerfully ignored. 'In the manner of an advertisement,' Mrs. Tothill went on. 'If you look happy and prosperous, you prosper. Anybody in business will tell you that. My husband doesn't get his contracts by looking as though he needed them.'

'I don't see the connection,' Mrs. Doubleday said. She was always mild in the presence of this hearty woman.

'Ah well, just think it over. You've got to make people
156

want what you have to give them, so you've got to give them the sort of thing they want. And you can tell Mr. Doubleday I said so.'

'I don't think it would disturb him,' Mrs. Doubleday said with dignity and truth and, in this belief, she kept the conversation to herself.

Mrs. Tothill represented the important members of the church and those whose Easter offerings were largest; the others were only fit for Mrs. Doubleday's patronage and, looking round now for a friend who would be sympathetic in such of her troubles as she wished to disclose, she could not find one, and the conviction of her loneliness struck her like a chill wind. When this knowledge comes to youth it seldom fails to bring a warming hope with it, but it was unrelievedly cold for her. As though it had really been a physical assault, she stood still in the street to meet it and found herself facing an unattractive middle-aged woman in a high-crowned hat, whose expression was not ingratiating, and she recognized the figure as her own, reflected by a mirror in the doorway of a shop.

She turned aside and marched on sturdily, carrying that vision of Reginald's mother with her. When she went to the looking-glass to do her hair, she was prepared for what she saw and she was used to it; but this unexpected, full-length representation of herself was a cruel addition to her distress, she saw in it an excuse for Norman's obduracy, and the niggardliness of nature promised to succeed where other influences had failed.

Men and women are more affected by actions than by motives which must be left to the judgment of a higher wisdom, and it is doubtful whether Mrs. Doubleday, meeting Dahlia a few minutes later, received credit in Heaven for an heroic effort to be pleasant, though a generous young mind was willing to believe the best of her.

'She's out of practice,' Dahlia said afterwards to Jenny, 'but it was meant to be a smile.'

'Then,' said Jenny, more sceptical, 'I expect there was a smut on your nose or a hole in your stocking.'

'But there wasn't. Perhaps she's not as bad as we think. I've always been afraid I might get fond of her. Or perhaps she's just excited about her son. He's coming home soon from some place where they get malaria.'

Jenny frowned. 'Has she a son? What a horrid idea!'

'I know. I felt like that, too, but, after all, it's a long time ago. He must be about thirty.'

'I shan't like him,' Jenny said.

'Poor Reginald!' Dahlia said with gentle malice. 'I told Cecil he'd be a cross between a baby elephant and a camel and he just looked puzzled, but you see what I mean, don't you?'

'Of course. I don't think Cecil has much sense of humour.'

'He sometimes laughs when he knows it's a real joke.'

'I haven't heard him laugh once since I came, but that may be because he doesn't like me.'

'Oh Jen, he was cross the first night, but he's been sweet to you.'

'That just shows,' Jenny said with some acuteness, 'how much worse you expected him to be. I don't want to stay and be a nuisance, but what else can I do?'

'The first thing you must do is to go across the bridge. Mother will be wondering why she hasn't had your letter.'

'I know, but couldn't she come here instead? I don't like going across the bridge.'

'It isn't much to do for her.'

'No, but I won't see that man!'

'Then go this afternoon because it's Saturday.'

Together, but in silence, they remembered the Saturdays in Beulah Mount, when Thomas Grimshaw, wearing a flower in his coat, would drive into Upper Radstowe to see their mother.

'It's different now, perhaps,' Jenny said.

'No. He still comes. I've seen him. It's his weekly treat.'

'Then I'm sure to meet him.' Jenny looked reproachful and aghast and Dahlia said patiently, 'And it won't matter if you do. I should think he'll pretend not to see you'.

'He gives me such queer feelings,' Jenny muttered.

'Oh, forget them!' Dahlia cried.

But, in spite of her words, Jenny did not want to forget them. For once, her thoughts and Dahlia's had separated and Jenny's were on that day when Thomas Grimshaw had made her cry and she had found shelter in a green and golden field and there Cyril had found her and she had seen him as a god. The bitterness of the ensuing experiences had gone and, slowly, their glamour had returned, making her memories like a little gilded shrine and, though she could no longer pray there, she saw it as a symbol of the ideal which might yet be discovered somewhere and could never be supplied by Edwin Cummings.

Dahlia watched with anxiety the softening of Jenny's face. Was her declaration of indifference to Cyril only the reaction to disappointment? Was she hoping to find in the old scenes a renewal of the old love? 'I wish you were young enough to be put in a perambulator and left safely in the garden,' she said.

'Why?' When Jenny flushed, the colour came slowly and faintly from below her skin, as though a rosy flame had been lighted there.

'Because I don't think you're fit to go about the world alone.'

'Come with me, then. I wasn't planning anything. I

159

was just thinking. Did mother ever tell you about when she was young, younger than I am? Well, she loved someone, too, and he was a good young man and wanted to marry her, but he was the young squire and she ran away from him because she knew it wouldn't do.' Jenny laughed a little. 'It was the other way round with me! She likes to remember that she loved him enough to think first of him, and I like remembering Cyril, though neither of us really loved each other at all. That's what I was thinking about. I wasn't planning silly things.' She looked for approval at Dahlia and saw a face full of sorrow.

'Because,' Dahlia explained, 'I don't believe she's ever had a single thing she wanted.'

'There are lots of people like that, I suppose.'

'Yes, people who couldn't help themselves, but she refused when she might have taken and afterwards, for you, Jen, she took when she might have refused. And she doesn't think it's strange at all. She thinks it's the natural thing to do. And yet——' She did not finish her sentence. She was stifled with indignation against Cecil for daring to sit in judgment on such a woman.

CHAPTER XXI

IF Mrs. Doubleday's mental and spiritual throes could have been translated into sound, they would have resembled the creakings and groanings of a strong tree forced by the pressure of a gale to bend its branches, or to resist and lose them, and though there was no doubt about the choice, it could not be accepted without writhings and pain.

She had managed to smile at Dahlia and she had been inspired with the idea of buying a new hat of a more sheltering design. She could subdue her pride into discarding the helmet-like structures she had worn for years and asking the advice of an expert in millinery: it was harder to devise and carry out some little act of graciousness towards her husband. It would have been a great convenience to find him suffering physically, for unusual attentions could then have been given without self-consciousness. A serious illness with ultimate recovery and the traditional reconciliation was beyond her dreams; that was one of the easy things that do not happen. She would have been grateful for a mild complaint, but Mr. Doubleday had the defiantly good health of a man who takes no exercise and eats what pleases him. She realized, with a sense of injustice, that Providence was not likely to intervene, but something had to be done to regain her headship of the family and prepare a home where Reginald could not discover a lack of harmony for which, most unfairly, she might be blamed.

'I suppose,' she said, her voice and face accusing poor Norman of indifference to his son, 'I suppose you wouldn't care to come and see what I have done to Reginald's bedroom?'

'But I should, I should,' he said, a trifle anxiously, and he followed her upstairs, distrusting any decorative expression of her welcome.

'The old carpet was shabby,' she said, as though she grudged the cost of a new one, 'and the old chair was not comfortable enough for an invalid.'

Mr. Doubleday had the audacity to test the new one. 'Yes, pretty good,' he said, adding slyly, 'for a lady's choice. Not quite enough leg length, and he's taller than I am.'

'A good deal!' she said indignantly.

'A good deal,' he agreed.

'Then I suppose I shall have to change it.'

He would not give a decided opinion about that, but said mildly, 'If you do, you might as well get one to match the carpet.'

'They are both green,' she protested.

An odd smile flickered across his lips. 'And we are both human beings, my dear.' The sound of his daring startled him into a few bars of humming. 'They are both green, but they clash badly, clash badly. Reginald wouldn't like that. He has an eye for colour. Always had, you know.'

She did not know, and she said crossly, giving the chair a push, 'You must choose it yourself. I've done my best.'

'No, no, it was your thought, your thought, but I'll help you with pleasure,' he said, and lightly, almost noiselessly, but for the jingling of his watch-chain, he tripped downstairs and left her to the puzzled contemplation of the warring greens.

With a roguish smile at the corners of his mouth, he settled himself by the study fire. He had made his preparations for Sunday, no duty called him forth on this gusty afternoon, and, when he had taken the precaution of arranging by his side a small table laden with papers, a pen and some serious-looking books, he drew a volume of detective stories from behind the cushions of his arm-chair. He might read or he might doze, but, at a knock on his door or footsteps on the garden path, that volume would automatically drop between him and the cushions, his hand would reach out for pen and paper and the vicar would be discovered in the midst of his unceasing work. Though he had dared to criticize his wife's taste, he was not altogether a free man for he was still lightly encased in his conception of what he ought to be and other people thought he was.

His curate, meanwhile, was bicycling into the country on the other side of the river in a small company of what are always called lads in his profession. It was a mode of progression he disliked, even when there was no wind, and now there was enough of it to make his eyes water and force his body into those earnest curves which always appear a little ludicrous to observers.

Jenny, on foot, did not smile as he overtook, without seeing, her. His nose was red, there was a grim set to his mouth and there were metal clips on the ends of his trousers. No doubt it was good of him to remove these youths from the dangers of an idle Saturday afternoon, but Jenny, for whom love was an emotion without humour, hoped Dahlia had not risked losing her romance by watching Cecil on his bicycle, and inevitably her thoughts went to the bright figure on a horse which had ridden into her own life and illumined this familiar scene of woods and river with more than its own brilliance.

To-day the sky was dull, the river looked grey and sluggish, the wind was doing its best to rob the cliffs oi any colour except the persistent green of firs, but when she stood still to look citywards, she found colour there in the big red factories, the funnels of ships lying at the wharves and the tramcars rattling along the rails by the waterside. From this point, from all the high points in the neighbourhood, and even when there were no flowers above ground, the city was like a garden with its massed roofs in every shade of red and of grey slipping into blue, with trees pricking up in unexpected places, church spires that might have been deliberate decorations and the ugliness of an industrial age changed by distance into beauty. And there were always the ships and the cranes serving them, the bare masts and spars and the funnels, crisscrossing in what seemed an inextricable tangle, to change the docks from a place of noisy labour and dull routine into one which, for centuries, had held memories and expectations of adventure.

This, thought Jenny, was better than the little cobbled street in front of the Cummings's shop; it was better than the garden behind the house where the lavender had stopped blooming; there was room, here, for hope, and if she remembered that this was the sustainment of which she had deprived Edwin Cummings, it was chiefly with impatience for human entanglements much like those apparent in the docks but, unfortunately, incapable of such skilful clearance. Somebody had to suffer and she knew herself well enough to be sure that were she the chosen one, others would soon be involved in her distress. Self-sacrifice for the sake of Edwin Cummings would have been his immolation. She had not the qualities necessary for cheerful martyrdom and now, as she approached her mother's home, without having met Thomas Grimshaw on the way and with some fear of finding him at the farm, she longed for an act of God, not injurious to herself or anyone she loved, to prevent the pursuance of her journey.

Dahlia had taken her to the gate and watched her out of sight; she had found Cecil's trouser clips and from the study window she had seen the handful of boys gather outside the house while he wheeled his bicycle up the side path from the basement. He looked back and waved, and they all made off across The Green, wheeling their bicycles until they met the road.

It would have been possible to see ironic amusement in the bowing of the elm branches as they passed and in the patter of the dry leaves following hard at their heels, like street urchins mocking what they did not understand; easy to feel a superior pity for this man's small attempt at doing good in a world of major difficulties, but Dahlia believed he was threatened with a cold and knew he hated bicycling, and though he had not much money to spare, he would pay for the passage of the bridge and a big tea somewhere in the country and come back tired, through the gusty darkness, in time to be at the Mission for the Saturday evening gathering. She softened towards him a little, for if he was hard on others, he never indulged himself. Her mind acknowledged many of his virtues, her heart demanded something to which she could give no name, and, as she looked to the left and saw the austere church, built in the Early English style and the modern manner, without traces of personal, devoted labour, she saw in the narrow windows and the steeple, much that was repulsive to her in Cecil's religion. It was aspiring but it had no breadth; it forbade the mind to wander beyond the limits it had once set, and ignorant as she knew she was, she could not make that a reason for acquiescence. 'Grow upward, but not outward, the church seemed to tell her and the anachronistic clock ticked away the minutes as though it were giving her a certain time in which to make her choice. But downstairs she could hear the activities of Mrs. Bailey who was still in a reserved state of resentment against Cecil, and Dahlia was reminded of her own grievances and strengthened in her revolt against the cramped windows and thin loftiness of the spire. She remembered trees in the meadows near her

165

early home, with their generous lateral branches growing at the same pace as the upper ones and those under the earth, she thought men foolish and presumptuous in refusing the example God had made for them. And she, no doubt, was presumptuous too, in rejecting a collective wisdom which was almost as much greater than her own as God's was greater than the priest's, yet she knew she must travel by her own light. Ardently she wished that Cecil had the power to make her follow his, for it would have implied a love for him transcending reason and that was what she craved, if only for a brief hour. She would be ready to laugh at herself afterwards, like Jenny, like Simon, by this time, perhaps, but she would have known a great feeling instead of these teasing dissatisfactions, these endeavours to believe there was high good fortune in still having Cecil's love. Everything he had was hers for the taking and she could not yet school herself into accepting what she liked and pretending not to see the rest

The grey, gusty day was not enlivening to her spirits. She felt like an elderly woman left at home, while Jenny walked her three miles and back and Cecil pedalled his twenty or twenty-five, and, like an elder, she had to deal with the problem of Jenny's future. Between them they had enough capital and more to pay for any training she might choose, and the rigorous life of a hospital was the one Dahlia felt inclined to recommend, for Jenny, under her slimness and her pallor, was as strong as a young tree, and discipline and an enforced recognition of her negligibility were what she needed, but she would blench at the thought of blood and bandages and nothing would induce her to face them. She was much more likely to favour going abroad and learning languages so that she might teach them, perhaps under the headmistress she had so much loved. The prospect of seeing something of the world would surely be attractive and Jenny could hardly turn up her nose at Miss Headley's profession. At one time, that lady was her standard of feminine perfection, a sort of counterpart of her father, but Dahlia doubted whether Jenny could now find happiness in the somewhat conventual atmosphere of the school. Somewhere, somehow, she must find it for herself. She was too young, and so was Dahlia, to know that happiness must always elude the searcher because it is not born with a separate substance and comes slowly and unawares upon those who have cheerfully resigned it. To their imagination it was a gorgeous flower waiting to be plucked and worn if they could light on it, instead of a humble, creeping plant dependent for its existence on other, most unlikely growths and found among them by chance.

Dahlia looked at the fallen leaves, changed, now, from their rich, damp colours to a uniform dull brown and crisped by the morning frosts, and unguardedly she was wishing she had Jenny's opportunities to see a greater world, when a car slid between her and her immediate view and, in some mysterious way, enlarged it. She knew the car and the hand which was the first part of Simon to appear and she thought it would be a windy walk to the Monks' Pool, and the water, thickly burdened with droppings from the trees, would not reflect the red trunks of the firs and the grey ones of the beeches.

'I thought you and your sister might like to have a drive,' Simon said.

He looked broad and strong in his heavy coat, he carried big leather gauntlets and she thought there was something vaguely heroic in his appearance and definitely secular. He was not labelled with his profession, but there was no doubt that it was an entirely masculine one and she looked at him with eyes as uncritical as Jenny's had been when she first saw Cyril Merriman. But she could criticize herself for a recklessness of emotion which was not beyond her control and in which she deliberately indulged because it was what she wanted, and if she had needed an excuse, she would have found it, paradoxically, in what she considered made her most blameworthy, and that was her safety from any encouragement on his part.

This knowledge made her smile a little stiff as she led him into the study and hospitably broke the coal into a brighter flame, but, consolingly, she saw herself as the woman he had chosen for his confidences and, though he had included Jenny in his invitation, out of courtesy, she could still hope he had really come to tell her he was cured of his infatuation, and it was the telling that was important, not whether he were healed or no.

'Where did you think of going?' she asked.

'Oh, I don't know. To the sea – or what they call the sea. There might be a few waves, with a wind like this.'

'To the sea?' Dahlia said thoughtfully.

'Or anywhere else you like,' he said quickly.

'But Jenny's out.'

He looked at once towards the window as though he watched for her return and Dahlia, with a widening smile he did not see, spared him a waste of time and hope by saying that Jenny would not be back till after tea.

'Next Saturday, perhaps,' he said. 'Or,' and this was obviously a politeness, 'would you like to come without her?'

She had been resisting the memory of his interested gaze on Jenny at the bazaar, but she submitted to it now. 'No thank you. I think it's too cold for a drive.'

'Yes. Thoroughly beastly, really,' he agreed.

He had no reason to stay longer, but he had a young man's usual difficulty in getting to the door and she followed him persuasively, like someone coaxing an animal through a gate, and with an exaggerated shrinking she

168

hunched her shoulders against the wind when she opened the front door.

'Poor Cecil!' she said. 'He's bicycling with some boys, over the river.' She allowed Simon to descend two of the five steps before she added, raising her voice, 'And Jenny's there, too. She has gone to see our mother – at Grimshaw's Farm.'

He nodded with animation and she had a wry pleasure in thinking how cold a time he would have if he decided to patrol the roads. She wondered if she had been malicious in circumventing possible diplomacy on Jenny's part about her maternal parentage. Had she done it for his sake, for Jenny's sake or her own? Her thoughts following Simon and Jenny on the familiar roads, paused when they reached the White Farm where she was born. There and in the little orchard behind the house, her mother and Thomas Grimshaw had met and laughed and whispered and the children sometimes woke to a stealthy opening and shutting of doors and cautious voices. And in the conviction that there was no danger, only something they must pretend not to hear, they never exchanged a comment on the knowledge and the feelings they shared. That early experience and all that came of it had taught Dahlia that no one can live to himself alone. She had always wanted to be good because she would not willingly bring suffering to another through her pleasure. Now she was being compelled to virtue only because Simon was not her Thomas Grimshaw, now, when she no longer cared about being good.

She sat on the hearthrug and stared into the fire until Mrs. Bailey came and claimed her wages.

CHAPTER XXII

'THAT Tothill man brought me part of the way home,' Jenny said. 'It was clever of him to recognize me in the dark. At first I didn't take any notice and tried not to run, and then he told me who he was and I remembered his voice so I got in, but I should have been much warmer if I'd walked and nearly as quick. It's a very slow car.'

'Is it?' Dahlia said and, for a giddy moment, she was whirled round the Downs in the moonlight. 'Are you coming with Cecil and me to the Mission or staying here alone?'

'Staying here with you. Oh well, I suppose I must come.'

'You'll have to play games with the girls. I won't take you if you're going to sit in a corner and look grand.'

'I don't look grand!'

'You can't help it when you're uncomfortable.'

'I didn't know,' Jenny said remorsefully. 'Do you think that Tothill man could see my face in the dark?'

'There are heaps of lamps on the bridge.'

'Yes, and we stopped to look at all the other lights. If you kept shutting and opening your eyes, Beulah Mount looked like a shooting star. You know,' she said, wrinkling her brows a little, 'the farm suits mother better. She seems right there, so perhaps I needn't feel so bad about it, after all. And he came in and we shook hands. His hand is horrid and I put mine under the tap as soon as I could, but he looked nicely at her and spoke nicely, and he didn't look at me as if I were a heifer, and I think she's happy. And,' Jenny said on a lifted breath, 'she didn't ask any questions.'

For Dahlia there was infinite pathos in those words. Their mother had a timidity with her children which had increased with her conscious love for them. She could never forget that they were already half their father's before he sent them to a school fit for his daughters, but not for hers. She could see him in all their movements and hear him in every word they said and it may have been that she refrained from asking questions because she feared the answers would puzzle her into a greater distance from her children. It was not because she had no curiosity and this restraint was part of the dumb patience which could easily be mistaken for stupidity.

'Well,' said Dahlia. 'I hope you told her things without being asked.'

'What things?' Jenny asked with a hint of defiance. 'And I don't like people who hope you've done what they know you haven't. You wouldn't have said that before you married Cecil. You would have asked me straight out, or else said nothing. I hate that gentle way of teaching and reproaching.'

Dahlia considered the accusation fairly. 'Yes,' she said, 'so do I, but you needn't think I got the trick from Cecil, because I didn't. Sorry, Jen. It's what Miss Headley used to do and it always made me squirm.'

'Miss Headley never did it with me.'

'Oh, you were the good girl. I was the bad one. "I hope, Dahlia dear, you were not rude to Miss Whoever it was," she used to say, smiling trustfully, and, all the time, she knew I had been. Silly! And calling me dear! It would have been much better to have caned me.'

Jenny's eyes widened. 'Better? If she'd tried that with me, I should have killed her.'

'Would you? I shouldn't have minded a bit unless it hurt,' Dahlia said and revealed a fundamental difference between her and Jenny. With far more real independence of character, she was free from consciousness of anything special in her personality, and her dignity was so little on the surface that it was not easily offended. She looked with amusement at Jenny's disgusted expression and said lightly, 'But she hadn't a cane and she wouldn't have known how to use it. She would have held it neatly between a finger and thumb, like somebody conducting an orchestra. Would you like to go back to school? I'm sure Miss Headley would have you – as a mistress.'

'How could I? I don't know anything.'

'No, but you could learn. You could go abroad and learn languages and see places. You always wished you could do that.'

'Yes, I'd like to see places,' Jenny said and, as Cecil opened the door, he heard Dahlia's merry laughter. It was a long time since he had heard it and not since they were married had there been in it quite that care-free note. He wondered what Jenny had said to produce it, not realizing that the proper reception of a remark creates half its humour. In Jenny's words, he would have found cause for gravity and not for mirth. Entirely occupied by that sad admission of indolence, he would have missed its engaging frankness. Dahlia knew this and, still laughing, simply shook her head when he wanted to share the joke.

'It was just Jenny's nonsense,' she said. 'It's not worth repeating. It was the way she said it.' Then, offering him, a little anxiously, the compensation she thought he would best appreciate, she said, 'We're both coming with you to the Mission.'

Though such companionship was what he had believed he most desired, he would have exchanged it for the power to make her laugh and, later, when Jenny had gone upstairs to the room now properly equipped as the guest chamber, with the best sheets on the bed, and he saw a

172

sort of film come over the brightness of Dahlia's face, he made an heroically foolish suggestion.

'Would you like Jenny to stay on with us here?' he asked.

'For always?'

'For as long as you please.'

'But you don't like her.'

'I don't see what that has to do with it.'

'A great deal,' she said, and her emphasis was somewhat daunting to his good intentions.

'She makes you laugh.'

'And cry,' said Dahlia.

'Cry?' he repeated.

The sharpness in his voice quickened her into instinctive protection of Jenny. 'Because she's such a baby,' she murmured.

'But would you be happier if she stayed here?'

'No, I should be happier if she went away,' Dahlia said. The answer came quite truthfully, and unexpectedly to herself, from feelings of which he had no suspicion and, as she gazed at him in dismayed recognition of what those feelings were, he naturally attributed her woeful look to complete distrust of him, and she, absorbed, for once, beyond the reach of his reactions, never noticed how his face seemed to close up with a snap. He was doing his best, but love does not eliminate pride or irritation, yet, because he was always earnest in his undertakings and suspected that more misunderstandings are prolonged by silence than by words, he made another effort to associate himself with Dahlia's concerns and do his duty as a brother-in-law.

'But where can she go?' he asked.

Slowly Dahlia returned to the necessities of the moment. 'I'm making plans,' she said. 'But they won't succeed. They don't deserve to.' Here she was not fair to herself, for she had made those plans before they became important.

'I don't understand,' he said plaintively.

'Of course you don't.'

'And I want to.'

'Oh, no,' she said, shaking her head and smiling wisely. 'Oh no, you don't.'

'I'm telling you the truth!' he exclaimed indignantly.

'Yes, but I know what it is,' she said and with a movement strange to one who was not inclined to be dramatic, she spread her hands under her throat as though the truth were concealed, and must be kept there. Then she dropped them and went slowly to the door.

'Are you never going to talk to me again?' he asked.

She came back. 'Why yes, of course. About the parish and the Mission – the things that interest you. And so I'd better tell you now that I went to see Ivy this afternoon. Mrs. Bailey said she badly needed a few kind words, so I went with Mrs. Bailey when she'd finished her work. It was rather difficult to be kind, and loyal to you at the same time, but I think I managed it.'

'I wonder how,' Cecil said and his bitter tone was not for Dahlia.

'I suppose it was rather a negative way,' she admitted. 'We didn't go into the morals of the question. I didn't say she was wicked and I tried not to give her the impression that I didn't think it was as bad as you do. We chiefly talked about the things she should make for the baby, and we went and bought some wool and a pattern book and we had tea in a tea-shop.'

Cecil could not change his character and his convictions in a day, and he felt bound to remark that such a treat rather savoured of encouragement.

'Yes, I knew you'd think so and that's where I wasn't quite loyal, but I was hungry. Yes,' she continued more to herself than to him, 'absurd as it seems, I was hungry, and there was nobody at home, so we had toasted buns. And after all,' she said, 'you took those boys out to tea and I expect they had boiled eggs! And, for all you know, they've been just as naughty as Ivy. And, for all you would have known, Ivy would still be a good young woman if she hadn't been too ignorant to stop having the baby. And in your heart,' she said, ignoring Cecil's frown, 'I believe you think she's much worse than what you'd call her fellow-sinner.'

'No, but it seems worse in a woman.'

'Why?' Dahlia demanded.

'Because we expect women to be better.'

'But you've no right to!' Dahlia cried. 'You've simply invented that for your own convenience.'

'No, from our experience,' he said. 'How can I help comparing a girl like Ivy with – with you, for instance.'

'It isn't a fair comparison. There are conventions in these things. And it isn't in yours to be improper before you're married.'

Cecil's frown deepened. 'It's more than a convention. It's a question of morals.'

'And morals are conventions – most of them. The only ones that aren't are the ones that have to do with unselfishness and kindness. There's nothing much more that matters.'

'Well then, have it like that; has Ivy been kind and unselfish to her mother?'

Dahlia sighed and, like Jenny earlier in the day, she decided that there was always someone who must be hurt. 'No,' she said, 'she's giving her mother all the opportunities! But,' she went on, almost in a whisper, 'perhaps she was kind and unselfish to the young man.'

'I don't believe that,' Cecil said, determined to show his sinner no mercy.

'Neither do I,' Dahlia said and she chuckled. 'But with some women it would have been unselfishness.'

'With no true woman,' he said, and Dahlia asked with interest, 'Is there such a thing as a true man?' Scornfully she answered the question herself. 'Of course there isn't! There are all sorts of good men and only one kind of good woman for old-fashioned people like you. I believe, if Mr. Doubleday wore petticoats and was a good deal younger, he would be just what you want, ready to accept your opinion and much too unadventurous to do wrong.' Suddenly her face twisted, but quickly she smoothed it out. 'You see,' she said with quiet despair, 'we begin about the parish and even that isn't safe.'

'I'm listening as patiently as I can,' he said. 'As far as I am concerned, this isn't a quarrel. Shall we call it an exchange of ideas? I think yours have the crudeness of youth, but if they are those of your generation, it's as well for me to know them.' The coldness dropped out of his voice. 'I respect your judgment more than you can guess,' he said with difficulty, 'but, on this subject, aren't you making too great a point of being broad-minded? I think you've rather forced yourself into this position.'

She held up a hand. 'Be careful!'

'No,' he said, 'you needn't be afraid.' He was not going to refer to Dahlia's mother. What I mean is that young people nowadays won't even admit the existence of sin.'

'Oh yes, I do,' Dahlia said, 'though I dislike the word. The people who use it always sound so holy. And I expect the sins at the top of my list would be at the very bottom of yours.'

'No, the fact is,' he said and to her his smile seemed rather fatuous, 'you are so incapable of doing wrong yourself, that you have to find excuses for people who are wicked.'

The shocked look she gave him before she ran out of

the room might have come from a sense of her unworthiness; it was actually one of exasperation and scorn for his stupidity. He knew too little about her to believe that, without reason, in the full knowledge of her own folly and the certainty of disaster, in spite of the lessons of her youth and her passionate desire to hurt no one by her actions, she was ready to follow a beckoning finger and if this were indeed wickedness, she thought she was already punished because, for her, that finger would not be lifted.

CHAPTER XXIII

DAHLIA's father had exiled himself in the country, lost his friends and resigned his hopes of a career for the sake of a magnificent young woman with brilliant hair. He saw her first, at a restless moment in his life, and she appeared to him as the representation of ideal natural beauty and what he imagined to be the serene simplicity of pastoral life. Here, for a man ascetic in habit from a fastidious fear of his appetites, was a symbolic figure which seemed to change his ordinary human desires into something finer. His passion needed explanation before he could accept it without a sense of guilt and it told him that she was life, reproduction, death, the rise and fall of the sap, the tender shoots of the young corn and the wheat when it was threshed; she was the complement to his intellectual, over-civilized nature and even the burr of her native accent was charmingly sylvan in his ears.

Dahlia was the first product of this marriage, but Jenny was the child of disillusionment and physical ardours of which he was ashamed, yet he need not have been ashamed if he had taken Louisa for what she was and resisted the common temptation of trying to mould her into an alien form, a process embittering in its failure to him, and in its implications, to her. His irritation at her ways and speech and the extraordinary limitations of her knowledge, prevented him from recognizing her fine qualities or giving them a chance to develop, and Cecil, taking the other view that Dahlia was a superior being, with faults only incident to youth, was in danger of producing the same result. No woman wishes to be loved for any special reason and, in particular, not for any virtue. Some unexplainable attraction of the whole personality, surviving, and thriving on, differences, quarrels, moments of physical and spiritual ugliness; some deeply rooted satisfaction in the other's essence is the only enduring security for love, and this was, in fact, Cecil's way of loving her, but he was hampered by a conscientious necessity for finding what he thought a better cause and, having found it and told her what it was, it was bewildering to find himself in worse case than before. She could not sulk, her tempers were quickly over and her method of being unfriendly was one of polite gaiety in which he fancied there was mockery, and of sudden enthusiasm for the Mission in which he imagined a reproach.

When he came home and found Jenny in the house to stir up the fire for him and make his tea, and heard that Dahlia was out on some parochial errand, he felt none of the expected content in having an under-curate for a wife.

'Was she sent for?' he asked.

'No. She's gone,' Jenny said with marked disapproval, 'because one of the Club girls had a cough on Saturday and she seemed to think she ought to go and ask about her. A horrid, spluttering kind of cough, too, and it doesn't deserve any kindness. It was like a rocket. You could almost see the germs falling.'

'Do you really think it was infectious?'

'I don't know, but I gargled when I came back.'

'Will you see that Dahlia does?'

'I'll try to make her.' Jenny looked at him gravely. 'Our father died of pneumonia,' she said. 'I don't think clergymen ought to marry people they love. It must make them so anxious when they go into dirty places. Mr.

Doubleday is lucky, in one way. It can't matter a bit to him if people cough and sneeze at Mrs. Doubleday all the time.'

'How do you know he doesn't care for her?'

'Because she's ugly,' Jenny said simply.

'What a heathenish idea!' Cecil exclaimed and he looked in the mirror over the mantelpiece and quickly looked away again, to hear Jenny saying gently, 'But Dahlia doesn't mind about looks so much as I do.'

'I hope not,' he said.

'I can't help it . . .' Jenny began.

'I wasn't thinking about you. Why should you suppose so?'

'I expect it's because I think so much about myself,' she said without regret.

'It wasn't because I'm a fault-finding kind of person?'

'No. Are you?'

'Ask Dahlia,' he said.

'That's no good. She always talks as if you were perfection.'

'Always? How often?'

'Oh, just when anything crops up.'

Jenny was sewing. Her smooth head was bent over the fragments of muslin and lace which she was fashioning into the demure cuffs and collars she affected. She sat neatly in a low chair with her feet crossed and he was soothed, almost against his will, by the precision of her movements. She took a tiny stitch and drew the thread out to its length, slowly, as though she performed a rite, and when the thread was finished, she snipped it with her shining scissors.

'Dahlia bites,' Cecil said.

'Bites?'

'I mean,' he explained hurriedly, 'the cotton or whatever it is.'

'I know. It would set my teeth on edge.'

'And generally,' he went on, 'she sits on the floor.'

'I know that, too.'

'And sews much more quickly.'

'And much worse,' Jenny said.

'Well, she can make dresses. She made the one for the bazaar and it was the best dress there.'

'And whose was the second best?'

He ran his fingers through his hair. 'How on earth should I know that?'

Jenny laughed. He saw no cause for her amusement, but these girls always laughed unexpectedly. He liked the sound, however, even from Jenny, for though her laughter had not Dahlia's rich note, it was pretty, too, and now, with her cheeks a little flushed and her mouth relaxed to show her even teeth, he could see that she had charm, he had to admit that, given the right mood, and he was in it, there was something femininely beguiling in all she did and Jenny, immediately conscious of this concession, found herself feeling very friendly towards him and pressed her advantage in the right place.

'You never saw her frock at all,' she said. 'You only saw her face. And it's a nice face to look at. When you see it, it's like coming home. How lucky you were to marry her. If you hadn't been so quick, someone else would have done it.'

This was not exactly what he wished to hear. Some remark suggesting the inevitability of the union would have been more pleasing and he said, 'You are making Dahlia very passive in the matter.'

'Well, it's tempting to have someone in love with you.'

'And she gave way to the temptation. I shouldn't have thought that was a very good description of me.'

'She saw beyond,' Jenny said with gentle candour. 'She can do that.'

'And what,' he asked, trying to keep a light note in his voice, 'do you think it was she saw?'

'Ah, you must ask her yourself,' Jenny told him and, seeing him relaxed in his armchair, his eyes on the fire, a more human brother-in-law than she had yet encountered, and one who might be sympathetic, she said, 'I thought I could see beyond, too, but I looked too long, and I knew I couldn't live in that country. If I'd married Edwin when Dahlia married you, I might not have had time to know that I should hate it.'

'So that's how it happened,' Cecil said. 'And suppose you had married him and found out afterwards?'

'I should have made him very unhappy,' Jenny said with great simplicity and certainty. 'Because I can't help showing when I'm miserable. And I don't try. I'm not like Dahlia.'

'Dahlia?'

'Yes, but she's never miserable. She has a sort of store of happiness inside herself and, if she lost it, you'd never know. Well, I suppose you might, but no one else would. That's what she's like. And here she is, coming up the path.'

'I know that! I heard her before you spoke.'

He would yield to no one in acuteness concerning Dahlia, yet, when she appeared, wrapped in the frosty brightness a person brings in from a winter's night, controlling a smile just enough to make Jenny ask her what had happened and smiling more broadly at the question, he had to admit Jenny's greater quickness at interpretation and he felt all his old jealousy of the instructive experiences these two had shared. For him, Dahlia's smile was one of genial greeting; Jenny knew better; she could distinguish one kind of curve from another and, when this one was explained, she seemed to find nothing odd in Dahlia's amused interest in Mrs. Doubleday's new hat. Impatiently he marvelled at his wife's preoccupation with anything so trivial; wisely, however, he refrained from uttering a reminder that life was real and earnest, and he settled himself more deeply and unobtrusively in his chair. But Dahlia had felt his silent criticism and, grave for a moment, she turned to him.

'It's very important,' she said. 'The hat is a different shape.'

'Well,' he said, 'tell us about it.'

He could not, it appeared, from her changed expression, have said anything to please her better. There was a flash of surprise in her eyes, a happy lift of her brows and, still puzzled, but anxious to understand, he gave a little nod of encouragement.

'A different shape,' he said.

'Yes, with a brim that hides quite a lot of her face.'

'Oh! Poor thing!' Jenny said.

Over the joined tips of his fingers, Cecil watched and listened, as though this were a little scene of a play in which the ideas were alien to his normal state of mind but, perhaps, as Dahlia said, important in ways he had not dreamed of, and through his abiding consciousness of sin and trouble beyond these walls, his own cares within them and his insistent desire to set things right, he felt a new and, he feared, a regrettable pleasure in a mood which had closer union with Dahlia for its only earnest-ness.

'Poor thing!' Jenny said again.

'But why?' The question was Cecil's and she turned to him, courteously ready with an explanation.

'Because she must have seen, or someone's told her that she's ugly. Just imagine what she's feeling! And there's not a hat brim in the world wide enough to hide her feet as well. I think it's terrible, even though she's horrid. But perhaps she doesn't know, yet, about her feet.' There

183

was a depth of sorrow in Jenny's voice. No news of bereavement or disaster could have increased it. 'This,' she announced, 'will make her nastier than she was before.'

'No. Nicer,' Dahlia said. 'That's why it's important. It shows she isn't made of cast iron after all, and, some day, she may even get to like me, and that will make things easier for Cecil.'

'But it will be much less complimentary to you,' Jenny said.

'I wonder whether it was the vicar who broke the news?' Cecil said.

'He wouldn't dare,' Jenny said.

'He wouldn't be so unkind,' said Dahlia, and she sent a look of gratitude towards Cecil for his suggestion. 'But I expect he thinks it's a pity, a pity. And anyhow, this story about the hat was only a sort of introduction to something else, someone else, the person who was expected to like the hat. I've seen a cab full of Doubledays and, fortunately, just as it stopped at the Vicarage gate, I had trouble with my shoe lace.'

'You might have thought of something more original.'

'Easily, but it wasn't necessary. Mr. Doubleday was chirruping to Reginald and Mrs. Doubleday was counting the boxes as though she thought the driver was hiding one of them.'

'And it wasn't very nice of you either.'

'If I hadn't attended to my shoe I should have walked straight into the family party. Mr. Doubleday would have been pleased, but she would have hated me more than ever. And I slipped behind the cab when I'd seen all I could. It wasn't much. Just a heap of overcoats, because of the malaria. I expect he's shivering now. It's a very cold night. So whether he's more camel than elephant, I still don't know.'

'And it doesn't matter,' Jenny said. 'I wish you'd go and gargle.'

'Why? Malaria isn't infectious. And it does matter. Everything matters. How do you know that the camelphant won't come prancing or tramping into our lives?' And she added slowly, 'As if we were in a jungle and only had a little flimsy hut to shelter us.'

'Camels don't live in jungles. It's deserts. And when they meet elephants, it's in a circus.'

'Circuses are dangerous, too,' Dahlia said thoughtfully. 'People sometimes fall off the trapezes and miss the nets they thought would catch them, or the nets break, or they lose their nerve.'

'Go and gargle,' Jenny said again. 'That's the way I used to talk and you used to scold me.'

'Oh, but I'm not frightened.' She picked up her gloves and went towards the door. 'I'm interested.'

'And take your temperature, too,' Jenny called after her. She looked at Cecil when the door was shut. 'She did sound a little frightened, didn't she? Why should she be? You are a nice, strong net for her to fall into.'

'Why should you think she is?' he asked. He got out of his chair and impatiently moved the ornaments on the mantelshelf. 'It seems to me that you and Dahlia are far too much inclined to tear everything to shreds. You find significance in any nonsense.' He tried to laugh as he made a sweeping gesture with a little china figure in his hand. 'Gossip about hats and elephants and camels! Don't you think it's rather absurd? Rather a waste of time?'

'We didn't talk about them for more than five minutes,' Jenny said with dignity. 'And do be careful with that little ornament because Dahlia likes it. Talking about the people you know is always despised as gossip, but if you talk about the masses of them you've never seen, and hope you never will, you're supposed to be doing some good. I don't know why. And as for wasting time, I know I do and I like it, but Dahlia is always working. She used not to be like that. She used to be so comfortably lazy. No, not lazy, but leisurely. Just strolling about and taking a good look at things and enjoying them. Now she rushes about as though she were afraid to stop.'

He retorted with Jenny's own question. 'Why should she be?'

'Perhaps', Jenny said after a pause, 'it's because she wants to please you, but what a pity it will be if she turns into one of those busy women. It's so much more important to be nice.'

CHAPTER XXIV

DAHLIA was right about Mr. Doubleday. He would have seen no intrusion in her presence on the pavement and she would have made amends for some of his disappointment at the station. There his happiness would have been as near completeness as his modesty and experience had taught him to think possible, if he could have encountered numerous acquaintances while he waited for the train, and introduced his son to them on his arrival, but, look hopefully as he did, with his bright professional glance, into many faces, and ready as he was to accept greetings from perfect strangers, there was no one to give him the pleasure of explaining why he was on the platform, no one to cheer him with the remembrance of his public character. Mrs. Doubleday had betaken herself to the ladies' waiting room, out of the reach of draughts. That, at least, was her stated reason for retirement, and though Mr. Doubleday might, if he had chosen, have seen in this seclusion a protest against his presence, his happiness and excitement made him quite indifferent to the possible workings of her mind. Never before had he been allowed to meet Reginald on any of his returns and he stood on the platform by right of his own valour.

'He won't expect you,' Mrs. Doubleday had said. He remembered her quick frown of annoyance when he proposed to accompany her to the station at the end of Reginald's first term at his preparatory school. Quickly, then, he had looked in his engagement book and found another, more pressing duty, and he had been finding such duties, or having them found for him, ever since. Now, while he watched the signals and pretended they referred to Reginald's train, though it was not due for a quarter of an hour, he calculated the number of times he had denied himself this joyful anticipation, this foolish belief that the lights glowed with vivider reds and greens in his and Reginald's honour, and that the engine, thundering somewhere out in the darkness, was making special efforts for his sake. He was strengthened in this belief when he looked at the other people on the platform and saw them standing listlessly beside their bags and bundles or trying to read their newspapers under the poor light of the lamps. The gloom of the dirty station seemed to oppress their spirits and Flora, poor thing, was missing all the fun. Well, he had missed his own on something like forty occasions, and he was making the most of this one. He spoke to a porter. Three minutes late! He almost wished it had been more. These minutes were precious, but he spared one of them to trot to the waiting-room door.

'Signalled, my dear,' he said. 'Now, shall we keep together or take different ends?'

'Keep together,' said Mrs. Doubleday.

No one would have suspected the rapid beating of her heart and the pulses it had set going in her limbs, and she had quite enough command over herself to consider tactics. Separation was all in Norman's favour. Heedless of his dignity, he would rush up and down the platform and the chances were that he would discover Reginald first. 'He will be looking for me, so you'd better be where I am,' she said. 'He knows where I always stand.'

Mr. Doubleday had no time to resent this implication of his parental neglect. He was thinking that of all the forms of transport contrived by man, nothing seemed less dependent on him than a great railway engine. To see a ship under sail or steam is to think of the men who guide and humour her and though an aeroplane may look like a bird or butterfly, it insists on remembrance of the controlling hands. It, too, is a reminder of human danger, but the engine, much less at the mercy of storm and mischance, seems to move by its own determination, to slacken its pace and glide into a station in the consciousness of a fine achievement, doubly fine, this evening, because it had brought Reginald home, and with modest pride in its great bulk and strength, it stopped with no more fuss than a few panting breaths.

Mr. Doubleday was smiling broadly in anticipation of his son's face at a window and the smile had to be sustained for some time, while Reginald, who did as he would be done by and seldom realized the aridity of that precept for other natures, slowly gathered his traps together, shuffled into another overcoat, signalled to a porter and made his way to the customary meeting place. Chivalrously, Mr. Doubleday stepped back and surrendered the first greeting to his wife, but even before the awkward kisses were exchanged, Reginald had a cheerful word for his father, and, in the confusion of hearty handshaking and instructions to a patient porter, Mrs. Doubleday resigned her intention of remarking acidly on the strangeness of her husband's presence. To be heard, it would have been necessary to shout, for now the engine, as though exasperated, was letting off steam with an angry shriek and she followed the men and the laden barrow with a sense of grievance.

Reginald was not talkative in the cab. He answered questions about his health and responded adequately when his father pointed out a new building here, or the place where an old one had stood, and his comfortable conviction that he need not bestir himself while the old man prattled, was interpreted by Mrs. Doubleday into her own disgust at Norman's intrusion. On other occasions Reginald had told her about his journey and made inquiries about herself and her activities and together they had maintained a more or less steady flow of talk. Now she was ignored in her corner until, as they passed under a bright arc light, she heard Reginald uttering approval of her hat.

'Very nice, very nice,' said Mr. Doubleday, taking a hasty look, and Reginald, with a reminiscent chuckle, told her how he had always wished she would wear hats more like other peoples'.

'When you used to come and see me at school, you know. I was always afraid the other chaps would jeer at them.'

Mrs. Doubleday laughed heroically, but she could well have cried. What other criticisms had there been in his young mind? What might be lurking in his maturer one?

'No, no,' said the vicar. 'Your mother always had great dignity, great dignity.' And, searching his vocabulary, he added, 'Distinguished.'

'Queer things, boys,' Reginald said and then, uneasily aware that his remark had not been altogether fortunate, he owned to a like feeling of shame when his father played cricket in the parents' match, and then hoped he had done his duty by both of them.

Mr. Doubleday could laugh without an effort. Missing catches long ago was a less painful reproach than the one his wife had received: few things are harder for a woman than the discovery that her personal appearance has seemed ludicrous, and she remembered her lately acquired knowledge of Reginald's eye for colour and wondered in what other ways she had offended. Rapidly she reviewed her past and present wardrobes and she considered the furnishings of the drawing-room with misgiving.

Nevertheless, as Dahlia had witnessed, she was able to count the packages. Nothing was missing and she was denied the pleasure of blaming Norman for an appropriate disaster. Norman, altogether, seemed to be in luck's way. Upstairs, in Reginald's bedroom, where a bright fire was burning, the shape and colour of the new chair represented her husband's taste and there was another unintentional little stab in Reginald's appreciation.

'You must thank your father,' she said, poking the fire roughly. 'He wouldn't let me keep the one I bought for you.'

'Wouldn't let you!'

She could not tell whether this comment were in her favour or not. 'He said it wasn't big enough.'

'Well, it takes a man to choose a man's chair. And it's all very nice and I'm glad to be back again. And you look years younger in that hat.'

'But I'm three years older. And so are you.'

'It makes no difference at your age,' he said.

It had made a difference at his. With the realization of a new assurance in him, she went into her room and removed the becoming hat. Three years ago he had seemed little more than the reserved youth she had known since he went to his public school, the fancied replica of herself with the attributes of her own choosing, and suddenly, she could not tell why, he seemed to be a man, not resembling his father in character or appearance, but indubitably an example of the same species. She had a fear that the enemy was reinforced and, for the first time in her life, she wished she had a daughter, but she was not the woman to be daunted by numerical superiority or to see no alternative to a pitched battle and, as these thoughts passed formlessly through her mind, she paused, with her hand on the wardrobe door. What had caused this atmosphere of antagonism, this necessity for warfare? The question was most unwelcome. It came upon her stealthily, cunningly choosing the moment when her fancied hold on Reginald was loosened and her nerves were shaken; it threatened all the convictions by which she lived, and she did not know whence it had come. Just for a moment she stood rigidly in her stout petticoat and neat cambric bodice, before she jerked a dress off its hook and hurried into it. Only the necessity for Reginald's approval, only the hope that, in his maturity, he would understand her natural irritation with his foolish father, forced her face into some semblance of amiability as she went downstairs. For months she had been living for this day and all the anticipated savour had gone out of it. And it was Norman's fault. He sat at the end of the table, rubbing his hands, smiling, fussing about the fire at Reginald's back, apparently unaware that he had robbed her of the first precious hours and, by his manner claiming an equal share – more than his share – in the boy. And she who, until lately, had never criticized any of her works, was painfully anxious about the table decorations. With unusual lavishness, she had bought pink carnations, to make the proper contrast with the green silk shade of the central light, and put them in slim silver vases, and though her eyes could find no fault with the scheme, she did not know how it affected Reginald's. Pink and green was a common enough union in nature and could hardly be wrong on the Vicarage table, yet, perhaps, a bowl of bronze chrysanthemums would have looked richer and, at the same time, more homely.

Reginald turned to her with a smile. 'Good, wholesome, English food,' he said.

She was pleased, but she had never had doubts about the quality of the food she offered. She would rather have received praise where she was less certain of deserving it, in those strange, newly-discoverd aesthetic regions where she was bewildered.

'And how's the pretty lady with the red hair?' Reginald said next.

In the act of carving another dainty piece of chicken for him, Mrs. Doubleday stopped with uplifted knife and fork. She saw, she could not be mistaken, a shade of embarrassment on her husband's plump face.

'Very well, very well,' he said hastily. 'A little more chicken, my boy.'

'What pretty lady?' said Mrs. Doubleday.

'Mrs. Sproat, my dear.' The vicar had recovered himself. 'And now there's a pretty sister staying with her.'

'Two of them? What luck for the parish! More red hair?'

'No. Dark,' said Mr. Doubleday. There was a stubbornness about his lips when he shut them on the words.

'I shall see them in church, I suppose.'

'H'm,' said Mrs. Doubleday. 'I don't call Mrs. Sproat a very good churchwoman. I've never yet seen her at Holy Communion and I should make some inquiries about that if I were on better terms with Mr. Sproat.'

'Not on good terms with Sproat?'

A shade of embarrassment now crossed her own face, she saw a flicker of amusement on her husband's. She had made another mistake in reminding him of that quarrel. The Sproats were fated to involve her in discomfort yet, in self-respect, she could hardly abandon the subject immediately.

'I suppose,' she addressed the vicar, 'you haven't noticed that she's never there.'

'My dear!' Mr. Doubleday assumed a somewhat shocked expression. 'It's not the moment for noticing who and what and when. But I know Mrs. Sproat is generally at morning service and she goes to the Mission in the evenings.'

'She'll feel more at home there, of course,' Mrs. Doubleday said.

Reginald was interested. 'Did the curate find her at the Mission?'

'Certainly not!' said Mr. Doubleday indignantly.

'Certainly not,' said his wife with a different intonation. 'It was not the sort of place where you would find any of Mrs. Sproat's family. Far from it!'

'What's the matter with them?'

'Mrs. Sproat's mother kept lodgings,' Mrs. Doubleday said with restraint.

'Had to, I suppose.'

'I doubt it, but what I do know is that Miss Morrison, a very worthy woman and a church worker, tried living there and had to give it up. In fact . . .'

'Now, Flora . . .' said the vicar.

'Reginald asked a question and I answered it, but I can assure you that I'm very careful outside this house, for the sake of the parish. They are the last people I want to discuss. I don't know why they were mentioned. I've never told Reginald a word about them.'

'No, but the Dad has. Can I have some more of that good, fresh cabbage? Very interesting letters, too. Presentation of the soup tureen and all that. Quite funny!'

'I see,' said Mrs. Doubleday slowly. She found it hard to eat and she looked over the carnations at Norman whose appetite was not affected by the discovery of his deception. Week by week, he had slipped a short and very dull note into the envelope addressed to Reginald, week by week, she had read and scorned it, and he had been writing long, funny letters secretly and posting them on the sly! She was ready to suspect him of almost any wickedness. Had he been writing such letters for nearly twenty years, while Reginald was at school and university? If so, the really dangerous change was in Reginald who no longer cared to spare her feelings.

CHAPTER XXV

In truth, he had never spared her feelings because he had not thought about them, he had no idea what they were. When he was young, he accepted her as many children do accept their parents, as the people who arrange certain details of life and have very little connection with its reality, and his shame at her unfashionable tall hats was one of the few acute emotions she had caused him. Perhaps he had always been aware of her grim devotion and more thankful for its lack of demonstration than for the thing itself, but he was not the boy or the youth to indulge in analysis. He enjoyed life in his rather stolid way, did more than averagely well scholastically and took up his appointment in West Africa with becoming serious-ness and a secret fear of a responsibility which somewhat overpowered him, but gradually, not suddenly as it appeared to his mother, the oppression had slipped away, he knew he was equal to the responsibility and he liked it, and the consciousness of his ability to deal with pro-fessional problems, his belief that he was in the right place was like the opening of a door. He had hardly known it was shut, its opening occasioned him no joyful sense of release, but he was benefiting by his new freedom and his relations with other people were easier because he was at ease with himself. Three years ago he would not have referred to anything in his father's letters which, he had been elaborately warned, were to be a secret, for then he was still in the state when discretion was his first thought: now, though he knew he had carelessly involved the old man in unnecessary trouble, the whole thing had a triviality which seemed to him characteristic of the narrow life his parents led. He was fond of his father, and suspected him of capabilities his laziness concealed; he tried to be fond of his mother and he was young enough, in comparison with them, to believe they had passed the time when such little bickerings could hurt them: it was probably their way of being companionable. To-night, however, there was a new strain in the atmosphere. His mother had shown more enmity for these Sproats than was apparently reasonable and while he apologized for his clumsiness about the letters, he wondered unwillingly whether the vicar were taking an undue interest in young women.

'I'm afraid I stepped in rather heavily at dinner,' he said.

'That's all right, my boy.'

Mr. Doubleday had produced cigars. He seldom smoked them, but, on such an occasion as this, Flora could hardly make a protest. Indeed, as he remembered with gratification, she had made none, since that other miserable evening, when, inadvertently, she had set him free.

'Just as well, just as well. Silly to make a mystery about it, but your mother liked to think she was giving you all the news, you know. Seemed a pity to spoil her pleasure.' This was not the whole truth but retrospectively and in his new independence, he could believe it was the chief part of it.

'And what's the matter with these Sproats?'

'I don't quite know,' Mr. Doubleday replied honestly. 'Your mother picked up some old story about Mrs. Sproat's mother. I didn't listen to it. Better not. Better not. I thought she was a good-natured sort of body. Not educated. No, not educated. Kept lodgings, too. Your mother considered the marriage most unsuitable.'

'I should have thought that was Sproat's business.'

'So did he, apparently,' said Mr. Doubleday.

'And I suppose he had to tell her so.'

'I don't know. I didn't listen. Ask your mother. And if you've finished your cigar, you'd better go into the drawing-room. She'll be expecting you. Mustn't disappoint her.'

Mrs. Doubleday sat in a straight-backed chair. Her feet in low-heeled slippers trimmed with bows of ribbon, were planted stubbornly on the floor, and she was knitting with every appearance of loathing for the wool, the needles and the future recipient of the garment. She sat there and she knitted as though she had been forbidden, as though some evil power, which she was determined to resist, were trying to loosen her feet from the floor and her hands from their charitable occupation.

'Always busy,' Reginald said genially.

'Yes, I never waste time,' she said, giving the wool a sharp tug.

'No,' said Reginald.

It was not a laudatory monosyllable; it sounded like a criticism and she stiffened herself against a half-formed vision of a Flora Doubleday relaxed in an easy chair, with idle hands and plenty of time to spare for the confidences of a son. She knew he had no confidences to give her. Probably Norman had been as sly in receiving letters as in posting them and there was no knowing, only a cruel guessing, how much Reginald had told him and kept from her. They had both robbed her and she was incapable of realizing that the thing stolen had existed only in her imagination, yet, perhaps, her loss was all the greater, for she could exaggerate it to any size, and the love which had never been for Reginald, as a person, but, obliquely, for herself through a son, was very near to hatred at that moment. If she were not supreme in his regard, how could he be paramount in hers? Yet she could not resign the chief sustenance of her life without a struggle and her next words indicated the line of her attack.

'And how do you think your father's looking?'

'Blooming,' said Reginald. It was an apt word. Mr. Doubleday's face was like a cheerful, homely flower, shining under the sun and not depressed by rain. 'Better than ever. Younger, somehow. And yet,' Reginald said slowly, finding, as he spoke, an explanation of one of the subtle differences he felt in the house, 'and yet he's quieter.'

'Quieter?'

'Not so fidgety. Tapping the table. Humming. He was always humming.'

'I haven't noticed any change,' she said, but she was lying. Bitterly she had missed the tapping and humming, propitiatory and evasive, and marvelled that a few careless words could sweep away the habits of a lifetime.

'Sign of nerves, I used to think. Leave overdue.'

'And what do you mean by that?' she asked. The ball of wool had fallen to the floor and, giving it another pull to draw it nearer, she sent it rolling lightly across the room, under the rosewood cabinet which held treasured pieces of family china.

Dahlia and Jenny who, according to Cecil, found meaning in the slightest incident, would certainly have seen something symbolic in this frustrated purpose. Mrs. Doubleday merely felt vexed at the stupidity of the ball and Reginald obligingly went on his knees to recover it. Then he stood up and slowly wound the long loosened thread.

'I mean that when I see a man fidgety I think his leave's overdue. Too much whisky, too much malaria, that sort of thing. Or too much work.'

'Your father doesn't suffer from any of those complaints.'

'No,' Reginald said again.

'The difficulty is to get him to do anything.'

'Why bother?' Reginald asked easily.

'Except,' Mrs. Doubleday went on, foolish but irrepressible, 'to deceive me.'

So, thought Reginald with irritation, for his work gave him quite enough weighing of evidence and settling of domestic problems, the old man had been up to some mischief, after all. He was at the age, he was of the nature, to slip into some sort of silly trouble, and this gaunt and angry lady would not be placated with kind words and a present.

'If you know he's deceiving you, you are not deceived,' he said sensibly. 'What's he been up to?'

Mrs. Doubleday's lips shook. 'I'd no idea he was writing to you every week, more than the notes he put inside my letters.'

Reginald looked round the neat room, his mother's conception of what a drawing-room should be. He looked at the grey carpet with its pink floral design and up at the cornice where the ornamental plastering had its pattern defined with corresponding pink: he looked at the gilt frames round the pictures of herbaceous borders, waterfalls and sunsets behind trees, at the chairs covered in rosy damask. The room had the obviousness of unimaginative sanity; as a surrounding for his mother at this moment, it had that effect of nightmare which is produced by ordinary things in conjunction with the extraordinary. But the moment passed, he conquered his strong impression of being in touch with abnormality and he said: 'Good God! I thought you were going to tell me he was unfaithful.'

He expected a reprimand for such language; he had chosen it with some skill, almost instinctive skill in offering another target for her fire. He meant to give, but he received a shock. His mother's expression would have been humorous if it had not been marred by a sneer.

'Can you imagine him being unfaithful?' she asked in derision.

Reginald did not like this. He was disturbed by a remark so foreign to her prudery, and pretending not to notice the sneer, he said comfortingly, 'Of course I can't. He's the loyalest man in the world. Don't you remember what he said about you in the cab?' The words were impressed on Reginald's memory because he had been astonished by them. 'He said you were distinguished.'

Mrs. Doubleday's habitual pout increased. 'Oh, that!' she said. She did not want such tributes from Norman; she wanted cause for grievance.

'And he didn't write every week.' It seemed necessary to deal with the subject of these innocent letters, but it was certainly absurd. 'He wrote once a month and not regularly at that, just when he had something amusing to tell me, I suppose.'

This reassurance had not the intended solace. What was there amusing in the life they led? What was she missing which Norman saw and handed on to Reginald, knowing it would be welcome? 'Amusing?'

Reginald made a soothing noise and said, 'It's queer about these pictures. When I saw them again, I remembered them, of course, but until this evening, I couldn't have described them for the life of me.'

Mrs. Doubleday looked at them all and then at him, a little suspiciously, for here was this question of taste again.

'Perhaps the new wall-paper shows them up better.'

'Yes, I think it must. I shall never be able to forget them again I'm – I'm sure. When did you have the new paper?'

'Do you like it?'

'Yes, it's a good clear grey, no mauve or blue in it.'

'So I thought.' This was an escape and she adopted his

200

opinion that grey should be clear and free of blue or mauve.

Conversation was easier after this. Mrs. Doubleday continued to be vicious towards the wool, but there was nothing unusual in that, for she could not manage a rhythmic or a gentle movement, and when Reginald went to bed he almost persuaded himself that his own fatigue had distorted his mother's words and manner. Perhaps, he thought, she had always been like this and he had not noticed it. He knew his powers of observation had increased with necessary exercise and he foresaw disadvantages in this development. And, how on earth, he asked himself, was he to spend three months in Upper Radstowe? He had hardly an acquaintance in the place except the contemporaries of his parents, and he felt worn out after a single evening. It was true that he might go away and pay visits to friends, but that would hurt his mother's feelings. The absurd incident of the letters had been enlightening, it was annoying, too, and hampering, even when it was stripped of the exaggeration for which he was willing and anxious to blame himself. It was also pathetic. This only child business was a mistake, it was a two-fold burden and, to carry his share of it, he saw that he must be careful, pay his mother a good deal of atten-tion, buy flowers for her, take her for walks, submit to paying calls with her, even to appearing at social Christmas gatherings connected with the church. He would go to church, too, and try not to sleep through the old man's sermons, yet, having made this last resolve, he had an uncomfortable conviction that an interested attention would not please her, but that a gentle sleep, unnoticed by the rest of the congregation, would be gratifying to the woman who had asked with so much scorn whether he could imagine the marital unfaithful-ness of his father.

CHAPTER XXVI

ON Saturday morning there was a letter for Jenny addressed in a handwriting unknown to Dahlia though the postmark was familiar.

'It's from Kitty,' Jenny said, 'and if it's to tell me that old Mr. Cummings is dead, I'm not going to the funeral.'

'They wouldn't want you. They wouldn't tell you. But perhaps it's about Edwin, dead of a broken heart,' Dahlia said with unusual malice.

'He wouldn't be so inconsiderate. He would never do anything to make me miserable,' Jenny said earnestly. 'And you shouldn't make fun of him.'

'Shouldn't? I couldn't.'

'Or of me, then. It's not a very nice letter,' Jenny said, folding it up. 'They are going to send back father's bureau. I wanted Edwin to have it. I begged him to keep it. It would have looked lovely in the shop window. But he said, ages ago, he wouldn't have it without me, so you see, this is a way of saying he doesn't want me any more.'

'You ought to be glad for him.'

'I might be if I believed it, though I don't think I ever liked him enough to wish he'd stop liking me. And, anyhow, it's hard to lose things, even when you don't want them.'

'It's worse to want things you can't have.'

Jenny's little face seemed to grow paler and thinner, her grey eyes were wide with reproach. 'You needn't remind me of that dreadful time!'

'I wasn't thinking of it,' Dahlia said. 'The bureau will look very nice in the drawing-room.'

'Oh, the drawing-room's full of Edwin already! It's

rather awkward to think that he sent you the sofa and chairs because of me.'

'It wasn't because of you. It was because he likes me and because he knew what the house needed. Edwin's an artist.'

'I wish he really were,' Jenny said with some fervour.

'Jen,' Dahlia spoke seriously, 'would you marry him if it wasn't for the shop?'

'It's not only the shop; it's all sorts of little things. He doesn't walk about as though he owns the world,' Jenny said.

'Why should he? He doesn't own it.'

'Neither did father. You know quite well what I mean, but, perhaps, if I'd never seen his father, or the photograph of his mother – coloured, too, with a locket and a large bust . . .'

'Well, considering that Edwin has seen our own dear Aunt Sarah and that we've got an Uncle Albert, somewhere in the country who's probably much worse, I don't see why you should be so pernickety. I don't suppose,' Dahlia went on slowly and with enjoyment, 'our Uncle Albert has had a bath in his life, not since he was a baby, even after hay-making or carting manure.'

Jenny shut her eyes and put her fingers to her ears. Then, dropping her hands and opening her eyes, she exclaimed, 'I don't know how you can bear to think of it! And you know it's quite different. We're not like that on both sides of the family. Think of Aunt Isabel! She was lovely.'

'Yes, lovely to look at, but I think I like what you would call common people. They are so much warmer-hearted. I know they don't behave as though the world belongs to them but, secretly, the ones who do are terribly afraid of losing it. That's why they are so particular about their acquaintances. They don't feel as safe as they look. I'm not pretending I wouldn't rather introduce Aunt Isabel to my mamma-in-law than Aunt Sarah – though I'm glad Cecil saw Aunt Sarah – but, in character, I shouldn't think there's much to choose between them. Sarah's a grasping old cat who had to fight for all she has and Aunt Isabel's a sleek, petted one who's never had to catch a mouse for herself. She's been fed with cream by the fireside and poor old Sarah has had to prowl about on the tiles! All that fuss because father was dead and not even a letter afterwards for his children!'

'She gave me her address,' said Jenny.

'And hoped you wouldn't use it.'

'I don't know about that, but, of course, I couldn't use it.'

There was a faint flush on Jenny's cheeks. She had not used Aunt Isabel's address or asked any help of her, but she had talked of her to Cyril Merriman, trying, by doing so, to establish herself in his mind in a worldly situation like his own. She was ashamed of that now. He had not been worth the effort and the cunning, yet, as she looked at the rough grass in Dahlia's back garden and the bare trees waving against a grey sky, they were transformed into the summer woods where, though time seemed to stop, it promised to endure endlessly and in perfection with Cyril. Such happiness, streaked by misery and exalted by it, she could not expect again. The buttercups of no other year would have a lustre of the same brilliance, and how, mistaken once, could she again trust her judgment?

'No, it wasn't only the shop,' she said again. 'I should rather like a nice shop, but not one with bedroom china in the window, put there by Edwin, too, quite carefully, almost lovingly, as though it wasn't something to be ashamed of! It made me feel different about him.'

'You've no sense, Jen. He loves beauty far more than

204

you do, but he knows he can't have nothing else. Nobody can.'

Jenny did not need Dahlia to tell her that; she had proved it for herself but, with extreme and teasing gentleness she smiled and said, 'You're beginning to be a tiny bit inclined to preach.'

'No, I'm trying to think.'

'Then don't. It seems to come to the same thing in the end. I told Cecil I was afraid you would soon be too busy to be nice.'

'And what did he say to that?'

'Just glared and pushed things about and then went to his desk and pretended to be busy himself. I think you'd better write to Miss Headley about me and going abroad. He very nearly likes me for half an hour every few days, but that's all he can manage.'

'You won't go because Cecil doesn't want you,' Dahlia said firmly, 'but because you have to earn your living. You must write to Miss Headley yourself. You're not a baby.'

'But I can't write the kind of letter she'd expect. I don't feel affectionate to her any longer. I couldn't say the right things, but she won't expect anything much from you.'

'She'll be hurt.'

'Then she won't ask me to go and stay with her and that will be a good thing.'

'Oh Jen,' Dahlia said once more. There was no doubt of Jenny's selfishness and her extreme sensitiveness about herself and to all forms of beauty was accompanied by a strange callousness. 'I don't know why I like you so much. It must be a habit and I can't get out of it.'

'Do you want to?'

'What's the good?' said Dahlia. 'I shall always like you'.

'I know,' Jenny said with satisfaction.

205

'And when we've done the housework we'll write the letter.'

The sounds of their domestic activities reached Cecil in the study. Voices, the rattling of crockery, the turning on and off of water, were plainly audible from the kitchen below. Then there were quick footsteps, tapping busily on the linoleum of the basement stairs, muffled on those leading to the upper stories. Over his head, short steps, here and there, forward and back, were Dahlia's as she made the bed. The carpet sweeper purred and squealed across the floor and banged against some piece of furniture, drawers were pushed in and out with a rattling of handles, a window was opened or shut, and all the sounds were repeated, more faintly, in the bedroom behind. In that flimsy old house it was impossible not to trace the movements of its occupants, but Cecil was sitting very still at his desk and possibly he was forgotten by the girls upstairs. He could hear, not the words but the tones, of their voices as they exchanged comments and reported progress and he was not disturbed by them except to feel his recurrent envy for their friendship. They could scold each other without giving offence and take orders, when they worked together, as requests. He and Dahlia could not do that. Perhaps it was impossible between any pair of people who had not passed their early years together and in amity, or perhaps the power came from the quality of their voices which seldom failed in graciousness. In character these two were poles apart, neither was influenced by the criticism or disapproval of the other, and it occurred to him that it might be this combination of love and recognized independence which produced their mutual trust, while marriage, imagined by him to be a mental and spiritual as well as physical union, was singularly lacking in this desirable fusion and not noticeable for trust.

He looked down at the notes for his sermon at the

206

Mission and drew a heavy pencil mark across them. Until lately, his little discourses had not been difficult to plan or to deliver. There were the virtues to extol and the vices to denounce, there was the assurance of the fatherly love of God to offer and the example of His Son to recommend, there were parables to be explained and Bible stories to be applied to conditions of modern life, but the much desired presence of Dahlia, which should have been a strength to him, was strangely disconcerting and he was as much afraid of her humorous view of things as of her doubts about his doctrines. He could see her, while he preached, properly grave but, for a clergyman's wife, a little too attentive and alert. She was thinking of what he said when she should have been placidly certain that what he said was right. She ought to have worn an expression indicating her proprietary rights in his remarks and a gentle willingness to hear obvious truths made plainer for simple minds, instead of showing that she was exercising her own bright, untrained intelligence. He was losing confidence in what he said and his way of saying it. Inevitably, she tested his precepts by his practice and, fearing further estrangement in the exchange of opinions, he dared not invite the comments she would not make. And how was it that he feared estrangement through their differences? Why had it been created already? It was rather unpleasant to consider that, in some matters, he was more akin to Jenny than to Dahlia. Jenny might not be shocked, but she would be suitably disgusted by the transgression of Ivy Bailey, she had a snobbishness which theoretically he deplored and actually shared, but she and Dahlia were secure in their relationship and unaffected by a divergent sense of values. He was puzzled. He knew he had deeply offended her about their mother and for that he did daily mental penance, but Jenny, offending in the same way, would have been forgiven long ago. There would, in fact, have been no question of forgiveness and suddenly he saw the parties to a marriage like two neighbouring armed states, protesting the desire and the necessity for peace and friendship but brought, by their very proximity, to a sensitiveness which, at the slightest grievance, might see cause for a shot.

The click of the garden gate drew his attention to the window. Like Mr. Doubleday, he had a point of vantage in his study and, while he gained in a shorter garden and no obscuring hedge, he had fewer temptations, even if he had wished, to look out. This was not the way to the shops for the ladies of Upper Radstowe and errand boys, tradesmen's carts, nurses and their charges were the chief passers-by. Normally he ignored the clicking of the gate and the ringing of the bell, for he had not Mr. Doubleday's curiosity, but to-day, dissatisfied with his sermon, puzzled and uneasy, half vexed with himself for allowing Dahlia to influence his convictions and faced with the fact that he had adopted them with more faith than thought, he was ready for a distraction, though the arrival of Mrs. Bailey for her weekly work was not the one he would have chosen. He had been hard about Ivy. Hers, he had slowly come to believe, was not the unforgivable sin. Unwillingly he suspected that his own capacity for passion and his unconquerable sense that, somehow or other, even in marriage, it was not holy, made him particularly bitter against a fault of the flesh, and striving to be honest and to subdue his pride, hoping he was not merely and weakly trying to please Dahlia, he began to consider ways in which he might help the girl. Mrs. Bailey, he knew, would not be receptive to his suggestions. He would have to talk to Dahlia and that would not be easy and, at this moment, she opened the door and looked in.

'Only for a second,' she said. 'I want some paper for a letter.'

'And I want to talk to you,' he said. He took the bull by the horns. 'What are we going to do about Ivy?'

'We? Nothing. It's all done. I told Mrs. Bagshot about her and she'll look after her. No, not in her own house. She can't do that because she's afraid of her parlourmaid and I don't wonder. In the country somewhere where she has friends. I think they must be related to the late butcher. Anyhow, they're kind — I believe butchers always are — and they'll see her through her trouble, as they call it, and find work for her where she can keep the baby.'

'Oh,' was all Cecil found to say.

She went towards the desk. 'Paper, for scribbling, I'm going to write to Miss Headley about Jenny and I must make a rough copy.'

He held the paper out to her but he did not let it go and, thus joined, they looked each other steadily in the eyes and it was Dahlia who first turned her head.

'Where are you going to write the letter? Is there a fire in the drawing-room?'

'No, but we shan't be cold.'

'You must come and write it here,' he said with authority.

'We shall disturb you.'

'I'm doing nothing important.'

'We shall giggle.'

'I've never heard you do that.'

'Laugh, then.'

'I hope you will.'

'If you're sure we shan't bother you . . .' she murmured.

She went away without looking at him again and left him with a feeling of elation. In all their acquaintance she had never before refused to meet his glance and he knew that, with those curt phrases and his curbed desire to hold her hand instead of the sheet of paper, he had revealed himself, perhaps for the first time, as an attractive lover.

CHAPTER XXVII

But could he sustain that character in the pulpit? He returned to his desk and held his head in his hands, apparently absorbed in parochial matters.

'Dear Miss Headley,' Dahlia said. 'Or should I say "my dear"?'

'Or "our dear",' Jenny suggested.

' "Dear", I think,' Dahlia said, rapidly making a sketch of her late headmistress in a corner of the paper. ' "Dear Miss Headley, I don't think I ever told you I am married . . ." '

'She'll send you a piece of Italian pottery.'

'I must risk that.' "Married, and now I'm living here with Cecil Sproat".'

' "Because",' Jenny commented, ' "I found I could not bear my husband".'

'Yes, it does sound like that,' Dahlia said slowly.

' "Very happily married to Cecil Sproat" is what you ought to say. Then, when she's quite comfortable about that, she can attend to the rest of the letter which, after all, is the important part.'

There was a pause before Dahlia spoke. 'It's a very middle-aged kind of remark.'

' "Married and very happy," then. That's girlish.'

'Horribly,' said Dahlia. 'Cecil, are you trying to write your sermon?'

'No, I'm listening with great attention. And timing you, too. Five minutes already and nothing done.'

'Well, these simple things are terribly difficult. Come on, Jen. Let's start again. "Dear Miss Headley" . . .'

' "Dear Miss Headley",' said Jenny, ' "I know I was not a very satisfactory pupil. . . ." '

' "Because I found your gentle way of dealing with me most exasperating. . . ." '

' "And our interviews in your chaste study. . . ." '

'I call that mean. You used to love her study.'

'I know, but I don't like it any longer. Must I be exactly the same for ever? I think it was affected.'

'Ah, Edwin's taught you that.'

'Who's mean now?' Jenny demanded.

' "Our interviews in your study",' Dahlia went on, ' "amused me very much though I am afraid they were a grief to you. . . ." '

Carefully Cecil turned his head to look at the girls. They were certainly not giggling, but their earnest amusement in their far from witty efforts seemed to put generations between them and him. He told himself he had married a child, and then, remembering her prompt management of Ivy's affairs and her pointed exclusion of him in the matter, and the mixture of spontaneity and dignity she showed in dealing with other people, he had to modify his judgment. It might be that her lack of self-consciousness or any sense of her own importance, any view of herself as this kind of person or that, resulted, at times, in a childishness so different from any stage in his own growth that, with less belief in her honesty, he would have thought it was a pose.

'It's your turn, Jen,' Dahlia said. ' "A grief to you . . ." '

' "But since I left school for a world of larger responsibilities. . . ." '

' "I often think of those care-free days. . . ." '

' "And realize how much I owe you".'

'And that,' said Dahlia, 'is quite true. I don't know what it is, exactly, but I know it's something. You breathe it in, even when you're trying not to, and I'd like to tell her so if it wouldn't sound sickly and if I wasn't going to ask a favour. It's difficult to be fair,' she said thoughtfully, 'to people in her kind of position. It makes you want to mock them,' a remark which was not lost on her attentive husband. 'Now, let's be sensible. I think I'll begin about you, and just put in a bit at the end about me, to explain the signature. Be quiet for a few minutes.'

'I'll go and do some washing,' Jenny said.

With her departure the atmosphere in the room was changed. It must always change with any coming or going, and now there seemed to be a little less air in the study, the sounds made by Cecil's pen and Dahlia's pencil were intensified. His consciousness of her drove his pen the faster and Dahlia's private thoughts delayed her pencil, but it was not long before she said, 'I think that will do. Would you mind reading it?'

'If you will read mine,' he said and he left his desk and offered her a sheet of paper.

'Have you written one for me?'

'Yes, for you, not for Miss Headley.'

'For me?' He looked tall and thin and black, standing over her and, with his back to the light, she could not be sure of his expression.

'Well, it's addressed to Miss Headley. I went on with your letter at a point where you left off,' and then, as she continued to look at him and did not take the paper, he crumpled it roughly and threw it into the fire.

'But I wanted it!' she complained.

'You should have been quicker in taking it.'

'Should I have liked it?'

'I don't know,' he said.

'Were you telling her how silly I can be?'

'You should have been quicker,' he said again.

His impulse in destroying the letter had come of a temporarily overlaid but profound distrust in such self-revelations and a fear of ridicule, for he had described himself as he thought Dahlia saw him, in appearance and in character, he had expressed what he imagined to be her regrets and dissatisfactions. It was a form of communication which, at the moment, had seemed rather poignant and dramatic: her lucky pause had saved him from an absurdity and, without calculation on his part, it had done more than that. It had made her curious, less certain of his attitude towards her and much more interested in a man who could write a letter to her while she sat in the room with him, and then threw it in the fire. Again he felt elation. This second wooing was a more exciting and delicate one than the first. The remembrance of physical experiences shared and now tacitly renounced though, for him, promised in the future if he had wisdom enough in the present, was a richer possession than their ignorant virginity and, half ashamed of the control which was a higher sensuousness, he bent down, not to kiss or hold her, it was days since he had touched her, but to push a hairpin into its place.

He did not know how to interpret her little shrinking movement, steadied at once when she realized the limits of his approach, but he knew it had no welcome meaning. Was it physical distaste, or a mental antagonism which had the same effect? His elation dwindled and, looking down at this piece of humanity on the floor, he wondered, in a kind of anger, why that particular moulding of features and the chance pigments in her skin and hair should be of so much importance. He believed in the nobility of her character – that was essential to his own comfort – but he might not have discovered it through the medium of a meagre body and a dull complexion, and this was a sad admission for a young clergyman who, until lately, had tried to satisfy himself solely through the spirit, and because her beauty had already taught him to see her warmth and generosity and gaiety, he could take no credit for his certainty that Dahlia, smitten suddenly by disfiguring disease, would remain desirable.

She was looking at the fire where there was now no vestige of his letter. 'I wonder what was in it,' she said, and she was startled by the apparent irrelevance and the irritation in his loud reply.

'I haven't done a stroke of work this morning!' he cried.

This was his protest against his weak preoccupation with a girl while the world had need of him: it came, more directly, from the collapse, when she shrank from him, of his faith in himself as a skilful lover.

'You said you were doing nothing important,' she reminded him.

'Nothing you would consider important.'

'I took you at your word,' she said. 'It's mean of you to blame me now,' and in her voice there was bitter resentment at being made to act the wifely part of scapegoat. Sympathy and soothing were no doubt what he wanted, but these she did not feel inclined to give and she despised his need of them, for she was still young enough to believe that no man worth loving ever failed in any kind of courage.

'Now! I've never ceased to blame you since you said my work was not important!'

'I said I didn't see much use in sermons. And I don't.'

'Neither Miss Headley's nor mine,' he said. 'They make you want to mock.'

'Yes,' she said and, greatly to the increase of his anger, she smiled. 'But I've forgotten all Miss Headley's sermons. I just remember how much, poor thing, she tried to help us. And that's something, isn't it?'

'Oh, a great deal,' he said, 'for the work of a man's life!'

'If you choose that kind of work, or any kind, you must just put up with its disadvantages,' she said sensibly.

'And you,' he used what she called his pulpit voice, 'could eliminate them all.'

'I? How?'

'By believing in what I do,' he said.

'Well,' said Dahlia and she took her time over her reply, 'I call that dastardly. I didn't know people could say things like that. You believed in it before you saw me, didn't you? But now, when you are beginning to have doubts about it yourself, you say it's all my fault.'

'So it is.'

He said what he believed to be the truth, but this, essentially a tribute, sounded like an insult and, indeed, at the moment, that was how he meant it. He could not always preserve a humble mind; his respect for her character as a far better one than his own was hopelessly entangled with the kind of hatred engendered by frustration, and failure with her was failure with everything.

'Then,' said Dahlia, 'you'd better change your profession. I said, ages ago, I wished you were a greengrocer and I still do. Either the vegetables would be good or they would be bad and we'd only sell the good ones. I could help you with that. There wouldn't be any doubts, there wouldn't be any cheating. We should have the scales — and scales in shops have to be tested regularly — to tell us whether five pounds of potatoes were really five pounds, and you and I couldn't quarrel about that. It would be simple. You wouldn't be hurt, not personally hurt, if we disagreed about the stock. And, every week,' she went on thoughtfully, 'there would be different things to sell. People would ask for them and be disappointed if they couldn't have them.'

The implication in these words was not lost on Cecil and the youthful, quiet, perhaps unconscious, callousness with which she struck him in his tenderest place kept him silent for a moment before he said, and it was the wrong thing to say, 'Can't you see how cruel you are?'

'I didn't mean to be cruel.' Lightly she stressed the

215

word which sounded weak and foolish in her ears. 'I'm just trying to explain.' With the fatal feminine trick of elaborating a painful theme she went on explaining. 'I sometimes think yours is rather a womanish occupation. But,' she said, defending herself against the wrath he held back with difficulty, 'I have tried to help you at the Mission. And,' she added honestly, 'I rather like it. But I didn't know I had to believe in your beliefs and I didn't expect to be blamed for anything that went wrong.'

'To my mind that is inherent in the idea of marriage.'

'What? The blaming? Well, that's very nice for you but not so good for me.'

'Now you are wilfully misunderstanding me.'

'Yes,' Dahlia said, with her broad beneficent smile, 'Of course I am. You can't quarrel properly if you're just! But I don't want to quarrel.' Her smile faded and she looked about her in bewilderment. 'Why are we quarrelling? I can't remember how this started.'

'You don't remember, I suppose, that you called me dastardly?'

'Did I?' she said and with polite weariness she shut her eyes for a moment and asked, 'Now, why was that? Oh, I know. Yes, well I think you were, but I ought not to have said so. Will that do?'

'No, it will not do!' he said thunderously, squaring his shoulders and swinging away from her with every intention of turning back in renewed power, but suddenly, he sank to half his height and, wobbling a little, he remained with knees ludicrously bent and then dropped them to the floor and bowed his head.

Dahlia rose to her own feet in alarm and she had time to feel anxiety and remorse for having brought him to this pass of physical distress — the possibility that he might be imperatively urged to pray did not occur to her — before she heard him rap out the words 'Get down!'

Instinctively she obeyed the sharpness of the command. She, too, knelt and dropped her head and, for some moments, silently awaited the arrival of a stone through the window or something else, wholly mysterious, in the form of an attack. But there was no shattering of glass, no sound from outside except the homely one of a tradesman's cart trundling by, and she dared to whisper, 'What's the matter?'

'Doubledays, father and son,' he hissed, 'coming across The Green. If they catch a glimpse of us, there's no escaping them!'

Dahlia's laughter released the tears she could not otherwise have shed and Cecil, laughing too and gratified by her mirth, since he had caused it, could still consider it somewhat excessive, but he had not seen himself standing black and gaunt and full of ire and dropping limply like a Jack-in-the-box with a broken spring, before no fiercer threat than the vicar and his son. His sense of humour was not readily evoked, he was not quick to appreciate the incongruous and, under his pleasure that this quarrel, though unresolved, had been suspended in friendly laughter, he was puzzled, and later he would be hurt, that an absurd episode had made him more companionable to Dahlia than any of his inmost thoughts.

Jenny returned to find both of them on the floor and Dahlia wiping away her tears.

'We're hiding from the vicar and Reginald,' Dahlia said. 'Cecil was afraid they would come in.'

'But what a pity,' said Jenny and, in defiance of Cecil's warning she went to the window, but she was too late for a glimpse of Mr. Doubleday tripping lightly and more than ever watchful for acquaintances now that he was accompanied by his son.

CHAPTER XXVIII

THE defective cistern, neglected in spite of Mrs. Doubleday's censure, had changed its gentle song into loud,
spasmodic gurglings. Its hiccoughing, which once had a
certain gentility, as though it put its hand to its mouth
and attempted a disguising cough, had suddenly become
blatant and unashamed, disturbing respectable slumbers
with sounds of carousal, and Cecil announced vaguely
that something must be done about it. He wanted a
peaceful night before Sunday's hard labour.

'And of course it's Saturday afternoon,' said Dahlia.
'But I expect I can manage it myself.'

'How?' Cecil asked.

'I don't know but I believe, if you take the lid off,
there's something you can push. If that's no good I'll
spend the rest of the day in looking for a plumber.' Whatever her faults, she never grudged any trouble. 'I wish
I'd asked Mrs. Bailey about one before she went.'

She tied her head in a coloured handkerchief and, taking
a candle, went up to the top story. Here there were
two unfurnished rooms and the cistern was inconveni-
ently placed under the sloping roof. She heard the banging of the front door and felt the responsive shaking of the
old house. This meant that Cecil had set out to do his
duty in which the curing of the cistern was not included,
and there was no sound of Jenny. Jenny, naturally, would
not volunteer for dirty work, but she might, at least, have
come to hold the candle. Perhaps she, too, had gone out
and, up there under the rafters, Dahlia felt as though she
were alone in an inverted pit with darkness where there
should have been light and the wintry sunshine far below

her. She had no company except that of the cistern squatting under the roof in the imperturbability of the happily drunken, chuckling amiably now in enjoyment of its reprobacy and, before she tried to deal with it, she went into the front attic to see the daylight and look down on tree-tops and people walking across The Green. It was a good attic, it had a fireplace, and, with protecting bars across the window which was commendably low, there could hardly be a better place from which to see the world go by and in her own mind, never to Cecil, she had always called this room the nursery. Cecil was not the kind of man with whom to discuss possible children in the matter-of-fact way which was the only one for Dahlia, and she had a secret fear that with a child definitely in prospect he would show the solicitude and see her in the sacred light under which, although Dahlia did not know it, her own mother, accustomed to such processes of nature, had suffered a sense of being made ridiculous. He would probably expand at the promised justification of his love, as though relieved of a guilty conscience, but he need feel guilty no longer and she need not fear embarrassment. She would have neither love nor children and suddenly, her wise defences unguarded for a moment, she asked herself plainly why she had married him, why any two people should be allowed to marry before they had tested their capacity for the strain.

'There ought to be a law about it!' she cried aloud and, after a minute, a rich chuckle from the cistern made suitable comment on her realization that she would run the risk again, she would even be foolish enough to face the certainty of regret, for the sake of a few days in which she could be blissfully unreasoning, uncritical, satisfied in eye and heart and lost to any consciousness of herself except as the complement to the beloved. Months ago, on a summer night, she sat on the doorstep of the house in

Beulah Mount and dreamed of such love under the heavy trees, and then she had allowed a lodger to kiss her, hated his kiss and seen in Cecil Sproat the friend who would give her shelter against impulses inherited from a father who had made a passionately hasty marriage and a mother who had compensated herself for her mistake. But, she had discovered, safety was not assured and it was difficult to find a friend in a man who so constantly saw himself as a husband. The mediaevalism of the church seemed to linger stubbornly in his view of marriage and Dahlia's independent spirit would not submit to merging her individuality in his, to thinking his thoughts and walking in his steps, not in Cecil's for a moment and perhaps in nobody's for long, yet if she had not married him, she would have been poorer, she would never have met Simon Tothill, she would not have had this precious soreness in her heart or the material with which to make dreams which could not come true.

'Oh well!' she said aloud.

Those were her mother's words in times of bewilderment or helplessness or resignation, but Dahlia did not hear them as an echo and the state of her feelings was no reason why Cecil should be disturbed at night, so struggling with the cistern's heavy wooden lid, pushing and pulling, she dislodged it and let it slip to the floor with a shattering noise. Again the house trembled and she thought desperately, 'I don't care if the whole place falls to pieces!' but it was a satisfaction to hear hasty footsteps on the stairs, she hoped the haste was caused by alarm for her, it would do the neglectful Jenny no harm to have a fright, yet, being essentially good-natured, she called out reassuringly, 'It was only the lid. Were you frightened?'

'Frightened?' said Jenny. She halted under the skylight. 'No. I'm vexed.'

'Well, after all,' Dahlia said reasonably, 'it's my own house and my own cistern and I can make a noise with it if I like.'

'I didn't hear a noise. I'm vexed because there's a Tothill man downstairs.'

'Oh! Is he trying to be funny?'

'Not in the least.'

Then it was not Tony, yet how could anyone be vexed with Simon? 'What does he want?' Dahlia said. She stood on tiptoe and peered into the tank. 'You could almost swim in here.'

'He wants me to go for a walk with him. A walk! Why should I? And what an entertainment with a man I don't know!'

'Perhaps,' Dahlia began, and her voice was a little indistinct, for her hands were on the edge of the cistern and her mouth against them, 'perhaps he wants me to come too.' And then, changing her posture and speaking more sharply, she said, 'Where does he want to go?'

'To the Monks' Pool,' Jenny said. 'It's miles away and I've seen it dozens of times. He seems to think it would be a treat!'

'I think he must mean me to go too,' Dahlia said, but there was no conviction in her tones, and from the safety of the darkness, she examined Jenny's face. The flush of her haste and annoyance had faded. She was pale and her hair was dark and though her lips were no redder than was natural, there might be, in her faintly haughty air, some likeness to the assisted arrogance of the other girl. But Dahlia had seen all this before. She thought Simon's cure was begun on the day of the bazaar and now it was accomplished and she was not surprised to hear Jenny saying, 'No, I don't think he meant you to come too – I don't see why you shouldn't invite yourself – because he asked me to come if you could spare me.

And that, I thought, was a silly thing to say, as though I were the housemaid!'

'I'm afraid he misunderstands your character or he was taking care to make the invitation definite,' Dahlia said, and she laughed in company with the cistern.

'And you can't spare me, can you?'

'It will be difficult,' Dahlia said gravely, 'but I must try to manage this disgusting old drunkard by myself.'

'Oh, no!' Jenny failed in appreciation of irony when it was directed against herself. 'I'll tell him you can't,' she said happily.

Dahlia stooped for the candle and held it aloft. Its light was given back by the dark water and as she peered busily for the mysterious thing which could be pushed, she was startled to see her own face, its colour gone and the bright hair hidden under the handkerchief, and it looked like a drowned face stealthily raised from the bottom of the tank to stare at her. She stared back as though she could wrest from it some solacing wisdom, or as though she must take the message it had come to give her, but she learnt no more than the accidental nature of this thing called love, for her hair might well have been black under the handkerchief and the original of this face have been as pale as Jenny's. She thrust her empty hand into the water, trying to shatter the vision, and all she could do was to distort it, but when she lowered the candle, the dim face slipped away and she thought it was she who was under the water and the girl who now heard steps and voices approaching was the semblance.

Jenny appeared first and, flashing a look of annoyance in Dahlia's direction, she said pleasantly, 'Mr. Tothill thinks he can help.'

The cistern chose this moment for making a more than usually derisive noise; it was happy in its sin and had no

222

wish for improvement, and Simon Tothill did not trouble himself to hurry. Like a doctor, he listened to the tale of symptoms and considered them at length before he suggested an examination of the patient and then, as though to set the anxious relatives at ease, he talked of irrelevant matters. He had to address his remarks to Dahlia for Jenny was behind him, leaning in affected patience against the wall, and Dahlia, careless of her expression while she remained in shadow and her voice came cheerfully, watched him with a bitter humour and a new clear-sightedness which had no comfort in it. His nose a fraction of an inch longer or shorter, a line eliminated there or etched somewhere else, a different or a more frequent smile and hands of another shape would not have solved all her problems, but she would probably never have given two thoughts to Simon Tothill. There was no more reason in her view of him than there was in his of Jenny. What did she know about him? What did he know of Jenny? She saw all three of them as the sport of some gamester who played only for amusement and tossed up these three poor human balls in carelessness of which struck which, with what results, and how, eventually, their positions were resolved.

'Oh, there's no sense in it!' she cried, irritably rapping the side of the cistern, forgetting that the real Dahlia was at the bottom of it.

'Perhaps we can put some into it,' Simon said. He took off his overcoat and hung it on the banisters and he did not look at Jenny as he passed her. For all the attention he paid her she might not have been there, but as surely as Dahlia knew he was aware of the figure against the wall, she also knew that he merely dallied with the cistern, though his sleeves were rolled up and his hands in the water. And now, as she held the candle, the drowned face came back, cheek by jowl with his.

223

'Come and hold the candle,' she said to Jenny. 'My arm is getting tired.'

It did not cost her a pang to change places, for they were all helpless and no act of hers was of importance, but Simon retreated by a few inches and Dahlia understood the movement, she thought she could understand everything except the first impulse creating this situation and Jenny's indifference to Simon. That indifference angered her, for there was arrogance in it and insensibility to Simon's due and she felt a fierce, almost maternal desire that he should have what he wanted.

Then, from far below, there came the tinkling of a bell and though Jenny, anxious to relinquish the candle, offered to go downstairs, Dahlia had vanished before the words were finished.

She opened the front door to Mr. Doubleday and Reginald, two solid men representing the sane, ordinary world she had forgotten up there under the rafters, Mr. Doubleday beaming in the certainty of a welcome as hearty as his own pleasure, Reginald more doubtful and slightly rueful in his character of a trophy.

'I can't shake hands,' Dahlia said, displaying them and leading the way into the study. 'But if you'll wait a minute I'll go and wash them. We are having trouble with the cistern.'

'Pity, pity,' said Mr. Doubleday. 'Sproat up there, dealing with it?'

'No, Cecil's out.'

'Ah, always busy!' His smile broadened. He had reckoned on Sproat's absence. A good fellow, a hard worker, but not unfailingly sympathetic. Mr. Doubleday was more comfortable without him and, nodding to Reginald, he seemed to promise him enjoyment in this visit and to assure him of Mrs. Sproat's charm, in spite of overall and hidden hair, but really Dahlia was the privileged person to his mind. Here was Reginald, unfortunately too old to be discussed frankly in his presence or made to show off his little tricks, but here he was, an object of obvious interest, yet, surprisingly, she did not make the most of her advantage and Reginald doggedly refused to be drawn into personal narrative.

'Sister in?' said Mr. Doubleday, hoping for better things from Jenny.

'Upstairs, with the cistern.'

'Ah, now I wonder if we could do anything to help you. What do you say, my boy? Shall we go up and see what we can do?'

'Oh, why should you trouble?' Dahlia said, but the vicar was already making for the stairs; he enjoyed seeing the more intimate parts of people's houses, and Reginald, who had no taste for conversation, was glad to follow him.

Dahlia lingered beside Cecil's desk, her eye caught by the fair copy of her letter to Miss Headley, sealed and stamped. She looked at it for a minute, then picked it up and threw it with a deft flick across the room, into the glowing coals. She could not make the posting of that letter agree with her sense of honour, she would have nothing to do with sending Jenny out of Upper Radstowe, and she had an absurd pleasure in not having paused to save the stamp.

CHAPTER XXIX

IT was Cecil who went to the Monks' Pool that afternoon. When he had crossed The Green and turned towards the bridge he cast a leftward glance at Beulah Mount, where he and Dahlia had once been neighbours, and he was tempted to follow its slightly curving slope, not for the sake of its romantic associations, but in pursuit of his accustomed and quickest way to the mean streets lying beyond. Those streets were his province and he could not be quite easy if he let a day pass without appearing there. Sometimes he had no definite work to do – though it was seldom that there was no one sick or sorry – but he walked through the streets as much because they drew him as in indication of his readiness to help. Where Mr. Doubleday, bouncing lightly, on his rare visits to this locality, dispensed smiles and an air of general benevolence and slightly propitiatory confidence that all was well with the world, Cecil stalked slowly, his hands in his pockets, his eyes often downcast, oppressed by his knowledge that these people were worse fed and worse housed than he was, ashamed of his better clothing, though it was shabby enough, fearful of presumption while he was eager to serve. He did not know that there were mothers who threatened screaming children with the black parson, or that he gave the same mothers a vague sense of security by the very severity of his aspect. He was not moved by piteous, unproven tales, but he had no false, optimistic consolation to offer and he did not pretend to see some higher purpose, which they were serving, in disease and drunkenness, insufficient work for the men and ceaseless labour for the women. He was better appreciated than he guessed and looked for oftener, but to-day, though habit and conscience urged him to those streets, his own needs were for once predominant and they took him across the bridge into the county where even at its very edge, within sight and sound of Radstowe, the air is different. The wind there seems to be an old wind, as old as the land itself, and it has its secret place among the hills and the grey rocks whence it comes with wisdom; a tolerant, kind wind, or a teasing one, as the mood takes it, earthy from all the wide fields it has passed, damp from the moss in the woods and lanes or soaked with the rain it carries, smelling of wood smoke caught up from farms and cottages, and of rotting or ripe apples in the orchards. As soon as it crosses the river, the air changes a little. It brings the rain into Upper Radstowe, the scent of wood smoke and apples in the autumn, a whiff of primroses in the spring, and these, though good, are the partial gifts it makes to strangers. On its own side of the water all these fragrances, whatever the season, seem to be present, and when Cecil had passed the houses overlooking, or set back from, the gorge, and found the field paths Dahlia had once shown him, he felt he was in another world, older and more peaceful, and the peace was not the child of lethargy, it did not come from the mere cessation of noises made by men's machines; it was deep in the country's acceptance of conditions and its persistence in doing what it could with them; in the way it kept its personality yet submitted, with docility, to human inter-ference. An intermittent breeze was like the pat of a gloved hand playfully chiding any preoccupation with private griefs; the pale sunshine put a polish on the jaun-diced grass, brightened the silver bark of the birches and enlivened the rich emerald of mossy boles. On the austere trunks of beeches, before they put out a branch, there were great black streaks, as though someone had

227

made them with a gigantic brush in petty irritation against this smooth grey strength, and the black was blacker than anything else Cecil had ever seen and the grey more absolute.

He sat on a stile at the edge of a wood and shut his eyes and immediately became aware of innumerable noises, rustlings in the undergrowth, the fretting of twigs under the breeze, a sudden protest, a cry or a groan, from a branch painfully twisted, the wintry chirpings of birds, the exclamation of a pheasant, and then, sitting very still, he heard far off and quite unimportant, outside this charmed circle, the thudding of motor engines on the main road. Within the circle there was sometimes a voice or a dog's bark, and a clinking as though someone in the farm beyond the Monks' Pool, were carrying pails. It was past milking time and he was roused by a little shiver from his state of apathy, a sleep without dreams or a waking without thought. The sunshine had gone and he knew he must hurry to see the pool by daylight, if he saw it at all, for Dahlia had said it existed only in her presence, it went when she went, and he would hardly have been surprised to find a dry hollow in its place, but in spite of an increased thickness of fallen leaves on its surface, there were patches of water like dull eyes, and at the farther end, the ducks paddled conversationally in their own quarters.

It was here and therefore, he thought, she must be here, too, either by projecting her spirit to this place, and he had no reason to suppose she was doing that, or simply through his foolish inability not to take her with him. The pool was here but it was different; the red of the fir trunks was subdued, there was no reflection of blue sky, the enchantment had changed in quality, and he thought there must be enough of Dahlia's presence to produce illusion and too little to give it beauty.

He did not linger, he passed the farm without remembering the geese and found himself in the bare field that had its upper edge against the sky and, following the lower edge where the earth was trodden into a path, he reached the gate where they had leaned and looked at the Channel and the hills. If she were here now, in the flesh, there would be no feeling of companionship. There would be a bright coolness on her part and on his a tendency to scold. They would look at the scenery without comment and she would not suggest a visit to Grimshaw's Farm. What had happened between them? She ought, by this time, to have forgiven his allusion to her mother but, since its utterance, it seemed as though she could not trust his heart and perhaps, in relation to everyone except herself, he had none to trust. He had tenderness for people in the mass and little for the individual; he had the fault of the reformer in a condemnatory impatience with those who hindered him; he missed the near thing in looking at the far one and did the kind thing from a sense of duty and the people helped rarely emerged as separate human beings; he looked at them from outside and saw them making or marring the world he wanted. It was the wrong way, no doubt, but how was he to change it? Officially he subscribed to the truth of miracles, but practically he had little faith in such a one as the sudden transformation of character, and this admission showed him a path he knew he had to follow.

He had to make his mental attitude as scrupulously honest as the greengrocer's scales, a harder matter than the weighing of potatoes. Often he had glimpses of this hard path and Dahlia was always in the way, stubbornly blocking it with her power of distracting him, but he had to get her out of it and he could not do that until he had actually forced the passage, a dilemma to which the only solution was that they should go together. She would not consent to do that. She had the young unconscious cruelty which believes that if all cannot be given all must be withheld and he had a suspicion that any physical attraction he had had for her, and he did not deceive himself into thinking it had been much, had changed to revulsion with mental dissatisfaction. He forced himself to consider these matters, distasteful to him in general and painful in particular, and he thought he saw an important difference between the normal man, as he believed himself to be, who could forget offences in an embrace, and the normal woman, if Dahlia were one, to whom, in that moment, the offences appeared larger and less forgivable. There was something in this to appeal to his inbred conviction that women should be nicer and more virtuous than their brothers, but it was one of those beliefs which, exaggerated by men for their own convenience, can be adjusted when the kind of convenience changes. It was easy to decide that the moment for niceness should not be chosen by the woman, and that there could be no justification for such selection in marriage, but, having gone so far, Cecil made a violent gesture of dissent and walked on, hoping to leave these unworthy sentiments at the gate. In any case, they had to be ignored. He was old-fashioned but she was not, and though she was unfair to him, he was still chivalrous; he had to win her again or lose her altogether. For a few minutes that morning he had interested her with a new manner, but it had been for a very few minutes; he had made her laugh, but that had been an accident; she despised his sermons and he could not blame her; he wished he need never make another, and he saw that it must be a very simple mind which could accept his deliverances without criticism, or a mature one which could leave the criticism inside the church and make allowances for the difficult position of mentor. She made such allowances for Miss

Headley now, when she was free of her authority, but with marriage, she had in effect been put to school again, under a different kind of authority and a more trying one. At her old school she had been expected to conform to rules as the minimum of allegiance and here he was demanding a mental coincidence which was not reasonable.

He felt happier when he had settled that and taken most of the blame himself but secretly he knew that differences of opinion would have been negligible if she had really loved him and he stood still for a minute, as once he had stood still in Beulah Mount when he discovered his need of her. Now he was contemplating the blankness of life if he could have no more of her than he had already and it was too complete to be believed in; somehow or other it had to be filled up and with a somewhat shamefaced feeling of trying to be good, of rather obviously turning over a new leaf, he made as straight for Grimshaw's Farm as his ignorance of the way allowed him.

He returned with a box of eggs under his arm and a great deal of mud on his boots, and, entering by the back way, he could see into the lighted garden room where the curtains had not been drawn. Dahlia and Jenny were setting the table for Saturday's early supper. He thought the golden rectangle in which the girls were held was like one of the lantern slides of his youth, and anyone watching from the garden would have seen his dark, passing figure as some accidental defect, spoiling the picture. He saw Dahlia's head go up, with the action of an alert young animal, at the sound of his footsteps and, as he opened the door, he heard Jenny saying, in final tones, 'Well, anyhow, he mended the cistern and that Tothill man, who's in the building business, hadn't the faintest idea what to do with it.'

'Very odd,' said Dahlia. She turned to Cecil, noticing

in her quick glance the muddy boots and the egg-box.
'We've had a party here this afternoon. Mr. Tothill and
the Doubledays — gentlemen only! All on the top landing,
very friendly, and Master Doubleday was excellent with
the cistern.'

'Camel or elephant?' Cecil asked lightly. He was proud
of this remark, it was an inspiration, and he had his
reward in the twist of Dahlia's mouth.

'Neither. Just an ordinary young man. A sterling
young man. He reminded me of Edwin Cummings.
Edwin was good with pipes and things too. Well Jen,
you know he was. I used up all to-day's crumpets and
to-morrow's muffins and about a pound of butter. It
would have been cheaper to have had a plumber. We
must have bread and scrape all next week.'

'No we mustn't. There's a pound of butter in that
box, but only half a dozen eggs. Most of them had gone
into market and the hens are not very obliging just now.
I had to tell you that.'

At this point, Jenny retreated to the kitchen and Dahlia,
with a protective gesture, put her hand on the egg-box.
There was alarm and questioning and distrust in her look
and though he supposed he deserved it, he was hurt by it.

'Have you been to the farm?' she said in a low voice.

'Yes. I went for a walk. To the Monks' Pool.'

'The Monks' Pool?' Her voice sharpened. 'Why did
you go there?'

'I wanted to see it again. I wanted to see if you were
right about it. And you were. It was only partly there.
I suppose the rest of it was in your mind.'

'Yes, perhaps, it was,' Dahlia said slowly. 'And then
you went to the farm?'

'You asked me to go there once, when we did the same
walk together, and I wouldn't go. I don't suppose you
have forgotten that. So I went to-day, instead. And I've

232

brought back all this mud and the eggs and the butter and your mother's love.'

'Yes, you've brought all that, but did you think it necessary to give her anything in exchange?'

'Not what you seem to suspect,' he said. 'I talked about you, and even about Jenny, but mostly about you. It seemed to be what she wanted.'

'Thank you very much,' Dahlia said gravely, she was ashamed of a slight feeling of disappointment.

'But', Jenny said, returning with her father's petulant little frown, 'we can't possibly eat that man's eggs and butter!'

'Don't be ridiculous! You needn't, if you don't want to. There'll be all the more for Cecil and me. We', she said, with a definite accent on the word, 'are very glad to have them.'

'And your mother took pains to tell me that the fowls were her own and she made the butter herself.'

'Oh!' Dahlia cried, 'she shouldn't have to say that!'

'No, she should not,' Cecil said emphatically.

CHAPTER XXX

'IT's quite time we had an answer from Miss Headley',
Jenny said a few days later. 'She ought to have had ours
on Monday.'

'She ought, certainly', Dahlia agreed. 'Can't you
imagine her picking up her little ivory paper knife and
slitting the envelope? I'm sure she has never opened one
with her thumb. And it's also time for the bureau to
arrive. Perhaps Edwin will bring it himself.'

'You never miss a chance of mentioning Edwin', Jenny
complained. 'You used not to be like this. You used to
be so kind.'

'Yes, I spoilt you.'

'Does Cecil say so?'

'Cecil doesn't talk about you at all.'

'It comes to the same thing. He doesn't approve of me.'

'No, it's not that. He has other things to think about.
Very surprising!' she added.

'There, that's what I mean! Why do you say sarcastic
things like that?'

'I'm not sure,' Dahlia said slowly. 'It may be that you
don't seem to have to pay for your mistakes and I'm,
well, mean about it. It may be that. I haven't thought
about it properly and I don't want to.'

'But you should,' said Jenny, 'before you get into a
nasty habit. And mistakes! Haven't I paid?' Her face
answered her emotions with astonishing rapidity. It
seemed to grow thinner and her eyes wider, reminding
Dahlia of the days when she had waited in vain for Cyril
Merriman. 'Isn't it punishment enough just to have made
them? It makes me feel smudged!'

'Then, Jen, at this rate, you'll be black all over long

234

before you die, but perhaps you will be very wise as well.
Life's very puzzling. What is it meant for? I feel as if
we ought to be doing marvellous, heroic, splendid things
and all we really do is to wash up the dishes. And then
we mind so much about our own concerns and feelings.
That can't be right, but how dull it would be if we didn't.
And no one else's knowledge is the slightest bit of use.
You can't believe in it. You have to learn everything
for yourself. It seems a great waste of all the good people
who have lived. And I think dumping us down here is
like setting a problem and keeping back some of the things
you have to know before you can possibly solve it. Cheating on the part of the examiners! So', she added, in
conclusion to this unusually long speech, 'if the examiners
cheat, I'm not going to feel guilty about my failures, and
you mustn't, either!'

'I don't feel guilty', Jenny said in her grandest voice.
'I just wish I hadn't made them for my own sake, though
I still like remembering parts of them, but what I can't
bear is for you to remind me of them – on purpose. The
worst thing that could possibly happen', she said and grew
wan again at the prospect, 'would be for us to change
about each other. It wouldn't be so bad for you,' she
said and Dahlia smiled at this characteristic remark,
'because you've got Cecil, but I have nobody else in the
world.'

'But you might have had. Sorry. I won't do it again.
And I hope I shall never change.'

'I was afraid you were beginning,' Jenny said.

'I suppose,' Dahlia began, enjoying the luxury of this
half confession, 'I get little spasms of envy.'

'Envy? Why?'

'Oh, because your hair's dark and your eyes are grey
and you look like a lily.'

'But most people would think you far prettier than me.'

235

'So did I, once, but I've decided that I'm too gaudy and I'm jealous. Come on, let's go through that play and change the damns for words like bother. We can't allow the Mission girls to use these coarse expressions. Heavens! I wonder what they say among themselves! And what they know! You and I are just unborn babes. I always think they must be laughing at me. Still, I do know a little more about acting than they do. How would it be', she said slowly, 'to ask Mr. Tothill to help us?'

'Why Mr. Tothill?'

'Because he knows a lot about it.'

'I think it would be very stupid and the girls would giggle.'

'They giggle already. He could produce the play and prompt on the night while you and I dress the girls and push them on to the stage and shout at them to come off.'

'I'm not going to help to dress them,' Jenny said, lifting her nose. 'That's where I draw the line. And you couldn't ask Mr. Tothill, or anyone else, to help with a dreadful little performance like that.'

'Couldn't I? People mixed up with good works don't mind what they ask of anybody. They learn not to be sensitive.'

'But they needn't be idiotic. And if Mr. Tothill is as good at theatricals as he is with cisterns – D'you know, there hasn't been a single gurgle since Saturday?'

'Yes, there can't have been much the matter with it.'

'Then why . . .' She broke off. 'Mrs. Doubleday', she said in dismay, 'is at the gate.'

'Alone?'

'Yes.'

'In the new hat?'

'No, it's like a tower.'

'That's a bad sign.'

'Let's pretend we're out.'

'Certainly not. She's my superior officer. What can I

236

have done wrong?' And she added tenderly, 'Poor thing!' as she went towards the door.

Mrs. Doubleday acknowledged Jenny's presence with a grim nod and announced that she had come on parish business, and having said that, she stood in the middle of the room as a person stands and waits for a reluctant dog to take his dismissal. Then, when Jenny had gathered up her belongings and shut the door very quietly behind her, Mrs. Doubleday sat down and Dahlia sat opposite, in polite attention.

'Is that your sister?' Mrs. Doubleday inquired.

Dahlia did not reply at once. It was an unnecessary question; it was meant, in some way, to be insulting, but Dahlia was not insulted. She was sorry for this woman. She had a dim idea that Mrs. Doubleday was angry with Jenny for being charming and well-mannered, for moving quietly and with the grace informing all her actions. 'Yes, Mrs. Doubleday. That's my sister. You've seen her before, I think.'

'Oh, have I?' Jenny was dismissed for the second time. 'Well, what I've come about is this play for the Christmas treat at the Mission. We were surprised to hear of it. And the vicar is a little, a good deal, hurt. He has not been consulted.'

'I'm sorry,' Dahlia said. 'It's a harmless little play. Cecil approves of it.'

'But I – but we are not always of one mind with Mr. Sproat.'

'No,' Dahlia said, 'that would be dull. And he is very particular.'

Mrs. Doubleday's pout was reduced in a smile which Dahlia very well understood, but she was determined not to allow this woman to offend her and she said brightly, 'If Mr. Doubleday will be at home this afternoon, I'll bring the play round for him to read.'

237

'The vicar has gone out on business for the day. Now, Mrs. Sproat, this play at the Mission is an innovation and I don't think it is a good one. An entertainment would be much more suitable.'

'I was hoping the play would be one,' Dahlia said.

'Recitations,' Mrs. Doubleday said, ignoring Dahlia's remark, 'recitations and songs would be better for them and much less exciting.'

'Oh much, but I don't think their singing would be – would be humanizing. They have such awful voices. They are not so bad in the hymns on Sunday because they don't think of what they're singing, they just enjoy the noise, but love songs . . .'

'I should bar love songs,' said Mrs. Doubleday.

'What else can girls sing about?' Dahlia inquired. 'All the sensible songs are for bass voices.'

'They could be sung an octave higher, I suppose. And I don't like to hear you criticizing their voices. It's not the right spirit. The thing for you to do is to try to improve them.'

'I do,' Dahlia said meekly. 'But they begged for a play. Mrs. Doubleday, couldn't you persuade the vicar to let them do it?'

The effort to steady herself against the picture of a stern vicar and a pleading Mrs. Doubleday gave Dahlia's eyes a fixed look which could be mistaken for anxious hope and there was a slight lessening of Mrs. Doubleday's antagonism. She was not so hard to mollify, after all, Dahlia thought. She would not yield too soon but, in the certainty that consent would be given, Dahlia lost her wariness, she hardly knew how much was needed, and tried to strengthen her position.

'And when I was talking to him about it on Saturday, he didn't seem to mind.'

'On Saturday. Oh, you saw him on Saturday.' Her

238

clasped hands, enclosed in thick, smooth kid of clerical grey, jerked upwards and fell heavily back to her knee. 'I don't think he can have been attending to what you were saying.'

'Perhaps not,' Dahlia said, but she had a very clear vision of Mr. Doubleday, smiling and nodding encouragingly over his crumpet.

'People won't leave him alone. He can't take a walk without being pestered about business. It's too bad,' Mrs. Doubleday said and she had her own wry satisfaction in this representation of the vicar's willingness to be waylaid. 'So don't do that again,' she said, half playfully and at a venture, and she would have learnt what she wished to know, for Dahlia was already opening her lips to explain that Mr. Doubleday and his son had called, if she could have resisted saying. 'When Mr. Sproat or rather, if Mr. Sproat is lucky enough to get preferment, you will understand what I mean.'

'I understand already,' Dahlia said. 'No one could work harder than Cecil. Nobody does.'

Now she looked frankly mutinous. She was fond of Mr. Doubleday, he had been kind to her from the first and she indulged a half daughterly pleasure in charming him, but he took shameful advantage of Cecil's zeal, and loyalty was very strong in Dahlia. And then, to her own intense surprise, to her later shame and amusement, she heard herself telling a lie. It simply took possession of her, she did not know where it came from and, as far as she knew, she had not so much as considered the possibility, worthy of Jenny, which she now revealed to Mrs. Doubleday.

She said, quite glibly, 'I don't know whether Cecil wants to be a vicar, but there's a living in my uncle's gift in Herefordshire', for the moment she had forgotten the surname of Aunt Isabel's husband and the first one she had never heard, 'and I suppose Cecil could have that,

239

some time, if he wanted it. But his real interest is in poor people and he isn't worldly.'

'Oh! I thought all your relatives were local people.'

'Not all of them,' Dahlia said with a kind smile, but her heart beat a little faster. She would bear with a good deal from Mrs. Doubleday but any rudeness about her mother would meet with its deserts.

Fortunately, and Mrs. Doubleday also was glad of the diversion, for she wanted to escape and consult the pages of *Crockford* and consider other matters of more immediate importance, the gate clicked and there were footsteps on the path. In a winged armchair and with her back to the window, she had not Dahlia's view of Reginald, but she rose at the sound of the bell.

'I mustn't keep you from your household tasks, or,' she added, 'from your visitors.'

'It's the plumber,' Dahlia said lightly. Jenny would bring him in and there would be explanations, there might even be laughter and Mrs. Doubleday would go away in a good humour but, after a murmuring of voices, there was a tramping on the stairs and when Mrs. Doubleday had made the usual remarks about plumbers and referred to her early warning about the cistern, it seemed to Dahlia that the little joke would fall extremely flat and, as she was in no mood to be snubbed, she allowed Mrs. Doubleday to take her departure in ignorance of her son's presence on the top landing.

'And in any case,' said Mrs. Doubleday, as she went down the steps with the peculiar action caused by the set of her feet, 'there must be no trousers.'

'Trousers?' said Dahlia.

'In the play. You must manage with top coats and leggings,' she said and she marched down the path and banged the gate.

DAHLIA was impatient to tell Jenny of this ultimatum and she decided to hasten Reginald's departure, but when she was half-way up the stairs she heard his voice in the steady flow of narrative, momentarily stemmed by an eager interjection from Jenny, and the sound of this rare eagerness sent Dahlia down again, to sit on the bottom step with her head against the banisters. She would not interrupt the story; neither the teller nor the hearer would be pleased, and she felt unreasonably vexed with both of them and very lonely until Cecil turned his key in the lock. She remained in her somewhat forlorn attitude and when he looked down at her with grave consideration, she looked up at him a little pathetically, making unfair use of him when she needed him. He had had his hair cut and she liked him the better for that; indeed, during these last few days, since his visit to her mother, and because he had ignored as much as he had noticed her, she had liked him a good deal and she was only restrained from deliberately feminine provocations by her unwillingness to accept the consequences.

'I've had a very difficult, complicated morning,' she said. 'Rather funny, though. Mrs. Doubleday . . .'

'Yes, I met her.'

'Oh! Then that's settled.'

'Quite.'

'Did she say anything about my relations?'

'No, I stopped that sort of thing a long time ago.'

'I'm sorry you had to do that. Why didn't you tell me? She really is an old – word I shouldn't think of using! Isn't she? Do say she is! It's rather important.'

'Has she been worrying you?'

'No, I think I've been worrying her. Are you frowning? I can't see you very well.'

'Then come into the study where it's lighter.'

Dahlia threw the window wide open and shook up the cushions which Mrs. Doubleday had pressed. Cecil was not frowning and she said solemnly, 'I've told a lie.'

'Wasn't that rather difficult?'

'It told itself. I didn't mean to do it. It took possession of me. Now I understand all about evil spirits. She's a dangerous woman.'

'What has she been doing?'

'Making me tell lies, of course, and it might be awkward for you, so I'd better warn you, but I don't want Jenny to know about it.'

He raised his eyebrows. 'So you can tell me something you can't tell her?'

Taking that in, Dahlia replied to it indirectly. 'I pretended that Aunt Isabel's husband . . .'

'Aunt Isabel?'

'Father's sister, you know. Pearls, and smells of violets and wears her furs as though she wouldn't mind much if she lost them. Not vulgarly. Just to the manner born. I could never do that. I should hook them on firmly, like people who have safety chains on their best brooches. They do, you know, but I don't suppose you've ever noticed. Well, I said . . . and it wasn't me, it was the evil spirit – that Aunt Isabel's husband – I can't remember his name, but Jenny knows it – ' She paused, biting her lip and exaggerating her regret, 'I said he has a living in his gift and you can have it if you want it.'

'I wonder if he has,' Cecil said thoughtfully and most unexpectedly, and again his eyebrows went up, for Dahlia was laughing and looking at him with appreciation.

'And I thought you'd scold me!' she said. 'You're very funny sometimes and perhaps, in the end, it doesn't really matter that you don't mean to be. Perhaps it's all the funnier.'

He was not slow to read past dissatisfactions into those words but, for the moment, he was glad to enjoy the radiance he had produced. When she was happy her hair looked brighter, there was a glow under her skin; he noticed the variety of shapes her big mouth could take. Those changes alone would ensure his never wearying of her and if, by accident or design, he could supply her constant and inexplicable demand for laughter, he thought she might not weary of him.

'I told Mrs. Doubleday you were not worldly,' she said.

'I don't think I am, particularly, but I wish I could have a year or two with plenty of time to read something a little more invigorating than the parish magazine. I suppose even the busiest doctor manages to keep up to date in his profession. He has to, if he doesn't want to lose his patients and his income. My income,' he said in a peculiar tone, 'is hardly noticeable, but I have no anxiety about it – none whatever. I don't need skill and I don't need knowledge for my living. I was supposed to have enough of both when I was dressed up like this and turned loose in a parish, and I'm not required to increase either of them. It's rather humiliating. I haven't reconsidered my position since I was ordained!'

'Does anyone want you to?'

'Of course not,' he said with some irony. 'Simple faith and plenty of zeal are enough. Or even simple faith alone! Look at Doubleday! Nothing will ever move him out of his comfortable little corner! He's there for life.'

'Unless,' Dahlia said, 'he murders Mrs. Doubleday.'

'And, upon my word, I believe it would do him good and nobody else any harm.' He was too much in earnest to notice Dahlia's broadening smile. 'He's as safe at present as an infant in a cradle and not, I should think, so

243

intelligently active. And I'm not much better. Oh, I run about more, I run about more, but I'm really of no more use, I'm no more expert, than any of the good ladies who help in the parish. They can do all I do.'

'No they can't,' Dahlia said stoutly.

It seemed as if she had only needed his discontent to remove her own, but the new sense of liberty he gave her with this confession was not altogether satisfactory. In loosening her bonds by admitting that he shared them, he put her on her honour not to desert him.

'You do more good than you know,' she said.

She turned away and, having shut the window, she stayed by it with her doubled hands pressing on the sill. She did not want to see him, rather boyish and endearing, sprawling in a chair much too small for his length and wearing an expression of annoyance which was all for his own shortcomings. She wanted to resist the sympathy he was rousing in her and the desire to set him right with his world. She was reluctant to resign her feeling of alienation for, if that went, she would be more bewildered than he was. She might be forced back to her earlier wisdom of accepting imperfection as the reasonable human lot, and that would be falseness to the ideal she had seen. She had never expected to see it, she had thought it existed only in her mind and could, accordingly, be ignored, and little as she was inclined to complain of circumstances, she felt that life had deceived her in producing it. The examiners had cheated twice; she had refused as insoluble one of the problems they had set her and now, cunningly, they were making it a little easier and persuading her to attempt it, and there was no guarantee that they would not cheat again and change the answer just as she seemed to find it.

'Your greengrocer could do as much good without my pretensions,' Cecil said. 'It's the pretensions I don't like.'

'Why,' she asked, turning quickly, 'are you suddenly saying all this?'

'It's not so very sudden. How long have we been married?'

'Ah, then it's my fault. I didn't think you would take any practical notice of my opinions,' she said, in a faint dismay which had its echo in his question.

'You are not sorry, are you?'

'Yes, in a way, I am,' she said.

He was slowly removing the grievances she had against him, he was increasing her obligations and she, unwittingly, had helped him, and she was glad when he said with masculine obtuseness, 'You mustn't think you have made me unhappy. It's rather – ' he looked at her a little oddly, 'rather exciting'.

Between the feet stretched in front of her and the supporting hands on the window sill behind her, Dahlia's lithe young body swung free. 'And all this time,' she said, addressing the points of her slippers, 'Master Doubleday and Jenny are sitting on the top of our cistern. There's nowhere else for them to sit and they've been there for ages. I'm glad I didn't dust it.'

'Master Doubleday? What's he doing here?'

'I've told you,' Dahlia said with patience.

'They must be very uncomfortable.'

'I hope so,' she said.

He was puzzled by the quickness of that reply and he said, as though he offered her consolation, 'I never had a chance of sitting in such a cramped position for your sake, but I must have walked miles to and from the pillar box. If there were several letters to post I made a journey for each one and if there weren't any I used to write unnecessary ones. There was always the hope of meeting you or seeing you through the window.'

'Need you have written the unnecessary ones? Couldn't you just have pretended?'

245

'Not successfully. I should have looked guilty.'

'And you felt guilty! Because you knew you only liked me for being pretty. You didn't know a single thing about me. It wasn't reasonable!'

'No, it wasn't reasonable, but it was right.'

'Just to trust a face?'

'Not only a face. It was everything about you.'

'Yes,' she said, and then she sighed. 'That's how it happens.'

'And do you think that's what's happening to Master Doubleday and Jenny?'

'It mustn't be that!' she cried. 'No, no! He's only hiding from his mother.'

'There's no reason,' Cecil said in mild reassurance, 'why he should have any of the family characteristics,' but Dahlia was facing the window again, attracted by the pleasant and increasingly rare sound of heavy hooves and rumbling wheels, then the jar of a brake and friendly admonitions to the horses.

'It's the carrier's van with Jenny's bureau come back from the Cummings. She won't like that!'

'Then let's smuggle it into the drawing-room before she sees it.'

She gave him a quick look, not the one with which she usually rewarded his concessions, but one that had seriousness in its mischief. 'There's no hurry,' she said.

She signed the receipt and talked to the carter who had leisure to spare. He was not possessed by any false idea of the necessity for haste, conspicuous in those who deal with mechanical transport, and when Dahlia went with him down the path to superintend the unloading of the bureau from the back of the van, where there perched a small boy, important but consciously lacking in muscle, he accompanied her willingly to the horses' heads and waited conversationally while she patted a rough, damp neck in its winter coat, and stroked soft, distended nostrils.

Cecil had occasion to observe once more her easy way with many kinds of people, her sincere response to the man's remarks, her vivid, immediate interest in the man himself and her appropriate manner with the anxious boy, and he resented the carter's marked respect for the gentleman in the clerical collar. The clerical gentleman was not to be troubled with the handling of the piece of furniture swathed in sacking by Edwin's careful hands and largely labelled as fragile, but the arrival of another gentleman, obviously not clerical, was a relief to the carter. He had no objection to accepting the assistance of Reginald Doubleday and, without accident, the bureau was carried up the steps, shepherded by Dahlia who carefully avoided Jenny's eyes and made no reference to the bureau when Reginald, having helped to unwrap it, insisted on dusting it and lingered to pick up stray straws and bits of paper, had taken his departure.

She went into the kitchen to prepare the overdue midday meal and was presently aware of Jenny in the doorway.

'Why don't you say something about it?' Jenny asked irritably. 'You're making it much worse by saying nothing.'

'I don't know how to please you. I wish you'd go and lay the table. What shall I say? Edwin had packed it very carefully and Master Doubleday was very tender with it. He seemed to appreciate it. He's like Edwin in that, too. It looks lovely in the drawing-room.'

'I shall never go into that room again!'

'Well, we don't often, do we? We have to be economical with coal. We shall use it more in the summer.'

'And I shan't be here. It's queer that Miss Headley hasn't written.'

247

'Not a bit. I didn't post the letter. You must write it yourself, Jen. It's too childish for me to do it. Did Reginald know his mother was in the study?'

'Yes, I told him, and he said he'd go and look at the cistern. I don't think he's a bit like Edwin.'

'What did you find to talk about all the time?

'Oh,' Jenny brushed a hand across her forehead. 'Crocodiles and things,' she said vaguely.

CHAPTER XXXII

To say that Mrs. Doubleday ought to have been a man is not necessarily to assign the more disagreeable qualities to the male sex, but, in an authoritative position of her own making, even in Norman's position, her natural sourness might have been partially sweetened by a sense of achievement. Some authority she already had and it was galling that she could not assume all she wanted without revealing Norman's sins of omission and thus, indirectly, losing more than she would gain. As the head of a large institution, she would have been a terror to underlings and a great satisfaction to herself: married to an energetic and successful man, she would have been spared the secret ignominy of her failure to push Norman's plump softness, with its surprisingly hard core, to an elevation worthy of herself. Her dislike for Cecil Sproat had been aggravated, though it had not been caused, by his marriage. She had always detected in him something of her own feeling for his vicar, and such a feeling was an intolerable liberty to take with what, unfortunately, belonged to her, but, for compensation, she knew how insupportable he found any interference on her part and it was a pleasure to see him coming, more slowly than usual, across The Green. She had stated that he and she were not on speaking terms, but quarrelling hardly came under that designation and she was ready and anxious to make him angry about the Mission play.

She did not succeed, however, in her amiable purpose. She planted herself in front of him, she felt she was formidable, but his dark frown did not appear. Usually, he glared straight into her eyes; to-day his own wandered with a sort of mild interest round and about her face. It was a little disconcerting. He was, in fact, thinking of things so much more important than Mrs. Doubleday, and some of them so much pleasanter, that he managed, unawares, to seem a little sorry for her in his assurance of having already secured the vicar's consent to the performance of the play. It occurred to her that the living in Herefordshire must be within his grasp. Nothing else could account for a manner with a baffling hint of condescension in it, and she reflected that unlikely though Dahlia's story was, its claim to truth lay in that capacity for vexing her which she had come to expect in anything connected with the Sproats.

Life was puzzling to Mrs. Doubleday as well as to Dahlia. She could not understand why what she did not like should be allowed and she thought with sympathy of Job who had suffered undeservedly though he, too, was good. It was consolatory to be in spiritual partnership with him, but she was too practical a person to linger long on the similitude. She found it difficult to imagine him otherwise than scantily clothed among the potsherds, in a scene of general disorder and the spotless white curtains at the Vicarage windows marked a difference between her material lot and his. They even told a little in her favour, for they were symbolic of her excellence and efficiency and when she had rung her bell, for she seldom used a latchkey and liked to be admitted properly by the parlour-maid, she found more evidence of her character in the neat dining-room, with its bright fire and tidy hearth, and the clean luncheon cloth and shining silver, happily laid this morning only for Reginald and herself.

Mr. Reginald, she learnt, had not yet returned from his morning walk, and realizing that *Crockford* would not be enlightening until her information was more exact, she sat down with the newspaper, paying little attention to what she read and using the sheets as though they had offended her. Now and then she looked at the clock, grudging every minute of which Reginald's unpunctuality was robbing her, but when she saw him strolling up the garden path her jealous greed for his company was changed to a momentary feeling of pure satisfaction in her son. His head, moving slightly from side to side, seemed to keep time to a tune, his lips were pursed for whistling and she was infected by his air of happiness until she wondered what had caused it. Once she would have flattered herself that it was produced by the prospect of some quiet hours with her; now she decided to be content if his cheerfulness owed more to his father's absence than to her presence. He was very good and dutiful to his father, rather more so than was necessary, but she thought it would be a much less sensitive person than Reginald who did not feel the improved atmosphere of the house when Norman was not in it. Sensitiveness was a meritorious quality and therefore it pertained to her son, but it failed him on this occasion. He did not take his seat at once and when he was bidden to it he suggested that he should first fetch his father from the study. He had not felt the changed atmosphere after all, and it was absurd of him to suppose that his father was ever too much absorbed in business to forget the time for a meal, but she controlled her annoyance and accounted for his cheerfulness by the improvement in his health.

'You are looking better already, very much better,' she said. 'This air is doing you good.'

'I don't think much of the air,' said Reginald. 'It's rather enervating.'

'Then,' said Mrs. Doubleday, disappointed, but constrained to be sharp though she might have to pay for it, 'you'd better have a few days somewhere else, by the sea.'

'Too cold,' he said.

'If you're not satisfied here,' she added.

'But I am. I like the place. I like the way it's been left high and dry and peaceful.'

'You've seen it before,' she reminded him.

'Yes, but I never looked at it. It's full of surprises, but nobody's surprised, or hurried. The motor vans dash about and try to look busy, just to be in the fashion, but it's all pretence. And there are still real country carts jogging across the bridge.'

Mrs. Doubleday was not sure that she liked to hear the scene of her activities thus described, but she asked amiably, 'And where did you go this morning?'

'Not very far,' said Reginald.

'That's right. Don't overdo it.'

'Not far, but high,' he said, taking a look at her.

'You were out for a long time,' she said. 'You mustn't get chilled.'

'Oh, I wasn't chilled. But I felt a bit cramped,' he admitted.

She did not understand his allusions; that was plain from the comparative placidity she showed and, while it was a pity to disturb it, he could not prolong his playful deception.

'I've been attending to the Sproats' cistern.'

'The Sproats' cistern?'

'They were having trouble with it on Saturday when we called . . .'

'Oh! You called on Saturday! I thought you were going for a walk.'

'So we were. We just popped in and the cistern, well it delayed us.'

'You never mentioned it. Either of you. I suppose you agreed to that.'

'Certainly not! But what was the good of telling you? We both knew you wouldn't like it.'

'Ah, you both knew.' There was pain for her in their common knowledge. 'Then why did you do it?' she asked angrily.

Reginald carefully considered his reply. 'You don't like the Sproats,' he said slowly, 'but the old man does and so do I. You surely don't want us to ignore them because you have a prejudice against them. That's carrying family loyalty a bit too far, isn't it? Besides, you mustn't have war in your own camp. Sproat's the curate and he seems to be a good one.'

Mrs. Doubleday's voice was mournful, but it was almost meek. 'Did you have tea there?'

'Yes, a very good tea. Crumpets. And I think they are delightful people and that red-headed one's a charmer and if you'd seen as many black ladies as I have, you'd understand how much I enjoy looking at pretty white ones.'

'Ones?' said Mrs. Doubleday.

'The other one's pretty, too,' Reginald said crossly.

'I can't see it myself. Too pale. I don't think she looks healthy. Mrs. Sproat, of course, is very – very flashy, but you've only to see her mother – And she said you were the plumber!' she cried. 'I was in the house when you came and she said you were the plumber!' Was that intended as an insult? No, far more likely it was a plan for securing the son and getting rid of the mother. In any case, Mrs. Sproat was not to be trusted and Mrs. Doubleday felt a great relief. She could safely disbelieve in the Herefordshire story.

'That was her little joke, I suppose. You see, I was rather successful on Saturday. I knew you were in the house. The other one told me.'

'Oh, she told you.' Mrs. Doubleday was disappointed.

'But I thought I'd have a look at the cistern while you were talking business and when I came down,' he said disingenuously, 'you'd gone.'

'The cistern must have needed a lot of attention.'

How unwise she was! Her inner monitor, persevering though always disregarded, warned her of her folly. A few careless words had made Norman independent of her and now she was showing herself tart and captious with Reginald, when she should have been interested and sympathetic, but she had no idea of holding without gripping and the effort of changing her mental processes would have been analogous to wrenching every stiffened muscle in her body.

'It didn't take long', Reginald said, 'but after that there was a bit of furniture moving to be done.'

'They've been making you very useful!'

Paying no attention to that remark, Reginald stared at the sideboard, adorned with silver goblets of his own winning, a biscuit box and a silver tray and coffee service presented by the parish on the twenty-fifth anniversary of the Doubledays' wedding. He looked at the chairs and cast a glance over his shoulder at the desk near the window. The chief merits of the furniture were its solidity and its escape, though it was made of oak and considerably carved, from any attempt at imitating the antique in colour or design.

'If you want to keep me out of mischief while I'm on leave,' he said, 'and if you have a hundred pounds to spare, you'll commission me to buy you some old furniture.'

'This is quite old enough for me. Do you dislike it?'

'I don't like it, but it's harmless.'

'I think it's decidedly handsome in a quiet way,' she said; but she looked at it in puzzled doubt.

'And I don't know that I could do much with a hundred pounds,' he said and smiled at her disarmingly. 'Two hundred would be better.'

'If I had two hundred pounds you should have them,'

she said and under her grim manner he knew there was affection too awkward for his handling.

'I really believe you would,' he said, 'but I have some savings of my own and I think I'll prowl round the shops and see what I can find. It's a harmless hobby and it isn't expensive. You look at things much oftener than you buy them. I've always been interested in old things, you know,' but she had not known, 'and that bureau I helped the Sproats to unpack has set me off again. A lovely thing, walnut, like ripe fruit, like chestnuts, I can't get one as good as that. It has been in the family ever since it was made, I suppose, and it has just been sent here from the country.'

'From Herefordshire?'

'I believe it was Somerset.'

'Ah yes, that's where they came from. I expect it has been lying about in some farmhouse or cottage. Those girls come of very humble people you know, though that's nothing to their discredit,' she said with false magnanimity.

'Nothing,' said Reginald with complete sincerity.

'But,' she said, not pleased by his ready agreement, 'unfortunately their mother is very handsome . . .'

'Unfortunately?'

'It's unfortunate in a certain class, the class she belonged to, and I've heard rumours from a most respectable person who lived next door that she really wasn't any better than she should be.'

'It depends how good she ought to have been, doesn't it? And we don't know. And it's not our business, thank goodness, though no doubt the respectable person enjoyed the idea.'

Mrs. Doubleday pouted heavily. 'I don't like to hear you talking flippantly about such things.'

'No, we should not talk about them at all. Leave the poor woman alone. And, anyhow, she ought to have a

255

medal from a grateful country for reproducing her good looks.'

'You think too much about looks. Men do,' she said, flapping her napkin before she folded it. 'It's character that's the important thing, character.' She pushed the napkin into its ring. That, at least, she seemed to say, was where it should be and where she wished to have it. 'And there's a saying about what's bred in the bone, you know.'

This was not altogether a comforting reminder for Reginald. Though he tried to observe the conventional decencies in which he had been trained, he could not produce those feelings which are a mother's due. He did not doubt her love for him, but daily he was more clearly realizing its strange nature and the jealousy which had no skill and no gentleness to aid it. He was sorry for her; she was unfortunate; she had no physical graces, he had yet to discover compensating moral attributes and, remembering another proverb, he wondered if it were true that beauty went no deeper than the skin, whether the possession of it, in a person of sensibility, might not create a correspondence in the mind, because anything else would be a kind of aesthetic outrage. A beautiful woman ought to fit her character to her face as carefully as she chose her hats for it; a plain one must start from the other end, and make her face reveal her virtues, and that he regretfully believed, would be a hard task for his mother.

CHAPTER XXXIII

OF all the church festivals, Mrs. Doubleday liked Christmas best. Whether its message and meaning had any particular appeal for her, only Mrs. Doubleday knew, but its practical obligations involved her in an orgy of organization in which she was not hampered, as in the affairs of the bazaar, by the divergent views of a committee. There were meals to be arranged for the mothers, the old people and the children from the poor parts of the parish and, when the curate had produced his list of those who should be fed, it was she who yearly planned the feasts, bargained for them, examined the viands and helped to dispense them. Untiringly she carved joints and ladled gravy and issued her sharp orders to the helpers who had less important dealings with cabbages and potatoes. She sat behind steaming tea urns in a mist like that surrounding the Delphian priestess but, unlike her, Mrs. Doubleday was not moved to speech. She was too busy turning the taps, lifting lids, signalling for more hot water and keeping an ungrudging eye on the consumption of buns, and probably she did not see the guests as individuals to whom she could give or from whom she could get anything in conversation. They were there to be fed, to have a Christmas treat, they were having it without stint and she had done her duty in providing it and seeing that it was good. The vicar chatted and made jokes, the curate knew the names and private affairs of the guests, nothing was lacking to their enjoyment, and she was singularly free from any wish for popularity or thanks. What she liked was doing things efficiently, delegating minor employments to her lieutenants, collecting money from the rich parishioners and gifts of goods from the tradespeople. She was generous herself and gave more freely than anyone suspected, but she found a peculiar pleasure in asking Mrs. Tothill, with her nearest approach to tact, for a large donation, and entering shops with the plain intention of staying in them until she had the promises she wanted, a charitable form of brigandage which may have satisfied submerged ancestral traits.

Another of her enjoyments, at this season, was viewing the accumulated labour of the Ladies' Sewing Parties, sorting the clothes into their different kinds, consulting more lists, assigning shirts and chemises to the deserving poor and adding to them the packets of tea and sugar she had wrested from the shopkeepers. For this purpose she made free of the big room in Mrs. Bagshot's house and there Miss Fairweather sat at the sewing machine, looking as though she had not moved since the last meeting, pushing seams of half-finished work under the needle, turning her wheel with the rapt eagerness of someone performing a cruel but necessary rite and then waiting, void of will or emotion, until the next victim was produced. But Mrs. Matthews, not to be hurried, keeping a shrewd, observant eye on Mrs. Doubleday, seemed to pour oil on the wounds inflicted by Miss Fairweather when she put the finishing touches by hand. She was present at this select gathering by reason of her friendship with Mrs. Bagshot who, nervous and propitiatory, was inclined to interrupt serious business with suggestions for Mrs. Doubleday's comfort, a window to be opened or shut, a few biscuits and a glass of sherry, or a nice cup of tea.

It was the custom for the curate to make out his list of aged people and large families to whom presents of clothing might be given with no danger, that terror to the charitable, of bestowing anything on the unworthy, and

Mrs. Doubleday and her helpers were doing their best to deal justly.

'And before Mr. Sproat's time,' Mrs. Matthews confided to Dahlia, 'the curate used to come himself! Did you ever? A shy young man, too, and there was no calling things by their proper names. Well, shirts would pass, of course, and nightgowns at a pinch, but when it came to anything with two legs we'd have to call it a garment. What d'you think of that? In these days, too! And I've seen some of our maiden ladies put a pin through the garments for fear the legs got loose before his eyes. If ever I got a chance, I used to hold them up and shake them out and have a good look at them. Such rubbish! Well, it was a bit of fun, anyway.'

Mrs. Matthews had Dahlia's own appetite for amusement but, in the absence of the shy curate there was not much to be had. Holding the list, Dahlia sat at Mrs. Doubleday's left hand and Mrs. Bagshot, at the other end of the long table, made neat piles of the clothes and labelled them according to directions. Patiently Dahlia enumerated the children, testified to the sobriety or excess of the father, the thrift or bad management of the mother, and she was not always strictly truthful, she made large allowances for difficult circumstances. She hated Mrs. Doubleday's assumption that poverty, a fault in itself, demanded a specially high standard of morality and that, with this, it almost became a virtue. It was certainly an excellent opportunity for her patronage, and by the time all the clothing and groceries had been allotted, she was in wonderfully good humour. But, long before that, Dahlia's normal willingness to be useful, to make the best of things and find entertainment in them, had given place to a sort of panic and rebellion. She looked at these women who were all older than her own mother, and saw herself caught in the midst of them and constrained to make their sober interest hers when she should have been playing with young men and women of her own years. The thought came to her, with a pang, that she had never been to a real evening party, never dressed for a dance more exciting than the ones at school and had now no prospect of greater gaieties than domestic and parish work, occupations not to be despised but substituted too soon for the youth she should have had. She wondered whether Mrs. Doubleday and Miss Fairweather had once been gay: she could well imagine Mrs. Bagshot fluttering to her parties and Mrs. Matthews robustly flirting at hers, and she was sure none of the three matrons had passed from school to two years of complete isolation in the country and so to a marriage of such sobriety as hers. Even Mrs. Doubleday, earnest in church matters from youth, must have had some of the experiences Dahlia missed. The rehearsals at the Tothills' house had been her liveliest moments, but the young people she met there had not troubled to pursue her further. If they belonged to any church, it was not to the one on The Green and they had no enduring interest in the curate's wife. Simon alone had persevered in the acquaintance, but it was for Jenny's sake and now, also for Jenny's sake, his mother had sent an invitation for a dance and Cecil had not considered the possibility of accepting it. He did not know how to dance and, more disastrous to Dahlia's hopes, the evening was one on which they were both expected at the Mission.

There had been a delicate pleasure in refraining from a sigh, or a suggestion which should have come from him, in being able to feel aggrieved at his calm assumption that she did not want to go, or could not go without him, and this sustained her in her disappointment. She longed to dance with Simon. It would be misery but it would be rapture, too. If she might once dance with him, she thought she could be good for the rest of her life, but it must be a long dance, and bowing her head and shutting her eyes against the room with its piles of flannel and calico and groceries, and the four middle-aged women, she saw herself moving to music in perfect accord with him, and she fancied how, as if by accident, she might put her cheek against his shoulder for an instant.

Mrs. Doubleday's voice made a loud discord in that music. 'How many girls in the family, Mrs. Sproat?'

Dahlia looked at her list; she could not find her place in it.

'We're doing the Trotters,' Mrs. Doubleday said sternly.

'And we're nearly at the end of the alphabet,' Mrs. Matthews said comfortingly. 'You're tired, my dear.' She turned to Mrs. Bagshot. 'The child's tired,' she repeated. 'She's had too much running about with all this Christmas fuss.'

Mrs. Doubleday pushed out her lips. 'It's a busy season for all of us, Mrs. Matthews. How many girl Trotters?'

'Two little ones and the Trusts have three,' Dahlia said, anxious to steal ahead and go on with her thoughts.

Why did she want to put her head on Simon's shoulder? Why had Cecil been so active in posting unnecessary letters in the hope of seeing her? He had trusted a face, a voice, the movements of a body and though it was not reasonable, it was right. So he had said, but it was only right for him and, in this case of Simon which was also unreasonable, it was only right for her, and Simon was wrong for Jenny though Jenny was right for him, and perhaps they were all mistaken. Yet it went against the grain to admit this mistake on Cecil's part. She depended more than she knew on his regard for her. It was like a home not greatly valued when things went well outside but waiting for her in case of need and, slowly, some of her objections to using it permanently were being removed, as though a devoted, old-fashioned parent had hidden

261

away the antimacassars and wool mats in deference to a modern daughter's taste, and pathetically wondered what was now amiss.

'No,' she returned to her list, 'there are no children. Mrs. Watkins is a very old woman and she hasn't any teeth either, not one.'

'We are not a dental hospital. We can't supply her with any,' said Mrs. Doubleday, condescending to be humorous.

'She doesn't want them. She hasn't had any for twenty years and she's much happier without them. She says her gums . . .'

'Next, please,' said Mrs. Doubleday.

'Oh,' said Mrs. Matthews, 'let's hear about the gums.'

'They can do anything except crack nuts,' Dahlia said, and she sent a mock reproachful glance in the direction of Mrs. Matthews' chesty chuckle. 'And she doesn't like nuts. The next is the Watsons. There's a little boy in hospital with a mastoid.'

This seemed to be a magic word, loosening tongues and uniting hearts. Mrs. Bagshot had known several sufferers from this disease, some child remotely connected with Mrs. Matthews had died of it and Mrs. Doubleday had saved the life of another through being wiser than the doctors. It was only Miss Fairweather who did not quote an instance. She had been idle for some time and no one thought of dismissing her. Her hands rested loosely on her knee and she stared in front of her. Was she using this talk, Dahlia wondered, as a cover for thoughts and memories more romantic than anyone could guess, did her stillness come of apathy or, under her starved, pointed look, was she feeding on these details of diagnosis and operations and death? She was surely past the age when she could feel Dahlia's impatience with the present and fear of the future, of a time when her jaded enthusiasms would be revived at a mastoid's clarion call. And Jenny

was going to a dance in a new frock: she would dance with
Simon and treat him to the coolness she was showing for
all his little attentions. She was too busy to go and see
the factory which the firm of Tothill was raising on the edge
of the city, never too busy to inspect a piece of furniture
which Reginald Doubleday had discovered somewhere.
It seemed strange to Dahlia that the old furniture should
not repel her with its associations, considering her sensitiveness about the bureau in the drawing-room, but Jenny
was annoyingly dignified in protesting her abiding love
for beautiful things made by men's hands and her detestation of red brick factories designed to house hatefully
efficient, soul-stultifying machines.

'Then you should have stayed in the Cummings's shop,'
Dahlia told her.

'If you'd seen the Cummings's shop, you wouldn't be so
stupid. And the whole point about these things is that
they're here, not there. Besides, how could I possibly be
interested in a factory?'

That, for Dahlia and perhaps for Jenny, was the same
as saying she could not possibly be interested in Simon
and, as Dahlia recalled all that made him charming, she
thought Jenny was both extraordinary and cruel. She
ought to be ready to sacrifice herself to make him happy.
His happiness was more important to Dahlia than her
own. She would feel no jealousy, or very little, if Jenny
loved him, but she was helplessly angry at this indifference,
and though she was aware that she demanded of Jenny
what she was refusing to Cecil, her attitude was not
changed.

'And so,' said Mrs. Doubleday, 'I never pooh-pooh an
attack of earache.' She thrust out the lips which were
already permanently set for that expression of disdain and
Mrs. Bagshot and Mrs. Matthews murmured approval.

But she would help Jenny to make her dress; indeed, she

263

knew from experience that most of the labour would be hers, and she would stay at home and no fairy godmother would come and waft her to the scene of revelry, but fairy godmothers, she supposed, would offer no aid to a faithless wife, they were all on the side of virtue. 'But I haven't done anything!' Dahlia cried within herself. 'I haven't had a chance!' But now she did not say she would follow a beckoning finger if it were raised for her. She remembered that Cecil, too, had trusted a face and as she did not want to know disillusion, so she wished to spare him from finding that face was false.

'Dreaming again!' said Mrs. Doubleday. 'We've finished the Watsons.'

'The child's tired,' Mrs. Matthews repeated and Mrs. Bagshot nodded knowingly. The meeting would soon be over and she kept a modest cellar.

MRS. DOUBLEDAY refused tea or refreshment of any kind and, accompanied by Miss Fairweather who wheeled a bicycle, she marched down Mrs. Bagshot's drive. A strong light from the porch shone on the gravel and was met midway by the light from the lamps on the gate posts. Mrs. Doubleday considered these lamps somewhat ostentatious of Mrs. Bagshot's indifference to electric light bills; however, they had their convenience, like many of the uses to which Mrs. Bagshot put the wealth derived from the shops which still bore her husband's name.

'A kind-hearted little woman,' said Mrs. Doubleday.

Miss Fairweather was silent. Faint whirring and clicking sounds came from her bicycle, but none from her until, pausing outside the gate before she mounted to ride down the hill, she said questioningly, 'Mrs. Sproat?'

'No, Mrs. Bagshot,' was the sharp reply.

'Oh,' said Miss Fairweather, with one foot on the higher pedal and her thin shoulders raised to help her to the saddle, 'that's easy. The difficulty is to be young and kind too. When you get to our sort of age if you're not kind-hearted you might as well be dead. I'm going to start myself, in a few years time. Yes, I shall fall back on being very kind-hearted before long,' she said, and with a farewell that sounded weirdly jaunty to Mrs. Doubleday's already astonished ears, she sailed down the hill, between the rows of bare trees casting their gigantic shadows on road and pavement.

Mrs. Doubleday watched her out of sight and was glad to see her go. She did not like surprises and an expression of opinion, a theory of conduct from Miss Fairweather not only upset her ideas about the woman but forced her to the discomfort of reviewing all past transactions with her and seeing them as they might appear to the person who went off on her bicycle like a witch on a broomstick. She might even know more about mastoids than Mrs. Doubleday herself! It is always disconcerting when an apparently negligible person shows signs of individuality and though, naturally, Mrs. Doubleday did not make any personal application of Miss Fairweather's remark, her pleasure in a successful afternoon's work was slightly ruffled. The business had been done with dispatch and without opposition and Mrs. Sproat's occasional absence of mind was rather pleasing than otherwise. The veteran was standing the campaign better than the recruit who, no doubt, was now being petted and pampered by Mrs. Bagshot and Mrs. Matthews, as though the chief burden had been hers. But, of course, Mrs. Doubleday thought, as she stood where Miss Fairweather had left her and unconsciously absorbed some of the beauty of the wide road splashed with black shadows and the elm-bordered path on the other side, of course birds of a feather flock together and Mrs. Sproat must feel more at home with these women than she could with her, but she had to admit that this partiality for the vulgar was the only way in which Dahlia betrayed her origin. Her unfortunate mother was carefully kept in the background and that, though politic, was hardly dutiful, in fact it had a savour of deceit which ought not to be countenanced by Cecil Sproat. Mrs. Doubleday liked people to pay the full price for their mistakes and it seemed to her that the curate was still in debt. Yes, she decided, turning and stamping up the hill, he was evading payment; his mother-in-law had vanished as completely as though she were dead. But she was not dead and this fact gave Mrs. Doubleday an undefined feeling of satisfaction which restored her to good humour.

All arrangements for the Christmas festivities were well in train; Reginald had been charmingly helpful with her private shopping, advising her about her gifts and always deciding on the shapes and colours she would not have chosen herself and so involving her in swift changes of opinion which left her a little bewildered but entirely trustful. He had an eye for colour and he had good taste. So she often told herself, forgetting that these were Norman's statements, believing she had made the discovery long ago. She was glad, too, of his interest in antiques. It kept him occupied and though, as far as she knew, he had not made a single purchase, he always had plenty to tell her when he came home. She could not be jealous of tallboys and sofa tables and, while he helped her to do up her parcels, she listened amiably and with half her attention to the distinguishing marks of Sheraton and Hepplewhite; the other half was given to his general excellence and his dexterity with brown paper and string: the smell of hot sealing wax was always to be associated with the happiest hours she had ever had with him. His old habit of reserve, of which she had necessarily approved at the time, had changed to this superior friendliness, unflecked by any personal element except what they themselves supplied and, to preserve this sense of union and his evident content, she was prepared to sacrifice her dining-room furniture and let him do the best he could with the meagre proceeds of the sale.

The top of The Avenue met The Green and, on her left hand, she could see the Sproats' house in darkness. The Vicarage, also, was in sight, though it could not easily be distinguished across the whole length of The Green with its screen of tree trunks and bare boughs, and Mrs. Doubleday's nearest way home was to follow a little diagonal path which ended nearly opposite her own gate. Instead of taking this, she made off at right angles for

The Barton where Mrs. Stone had her fruit and flower shop. Fresh fruit was very good for Reginald and there was a special Christmas brilliance in the street this evening. The shops would be open later than usual and coloured lights shone on the decorations in the windows. There were no special lights in the flower shop. Mrs. Stone was sure of her Christmas sales, and there she was, with mittened hands, sitting behind the counter, stabbing sprigs of holly into a mossy circle, looking over her eyeglasses at the customers, correcting or confirming the statements of her sons and daughters, registering orders in her practised mind. The shop was bushy with evergreens; on the floor, strewn with berries from holly and mistletoe, jars and basins were crammed with chrysanthemums; on shelves there were bowls of growing waxy Roman hyacinths and pots of heather. Orchids, lilies, roses and carnations and massed bunches of dark violets stood in one window; in the other there were bunches of grapes, silvered with bloom, and peaches lying in nests of cotton wool.

Mrs. Doubleday bought a pound of apples, reminded Mrs. Stone that evergreens and flowers would be welcome for the church decorations and continued down the street, which was particularly characteristic of Upper Radstowe. The shops, which were chiefly on one side, had been built against the lower part of tall old houses and, from a distance, the severe pediments of these could be seen above the smaller, later growths. And the shops, too, were characteristic. Except for the flower shop and a fishmonger's, they were small and unpretentious; their owners were not agitated by requests for commodities they did not keep, or zealous in procuring them. They continued to be amiably regretful and the shops continued to survive, as though this were a village without a rival within many miles. Among them there was certainly one which had nothing to fear from any rival, here or else-where, for nowhere else were such cream cheeses to be found, more cream than cheese and wrapped in snowy muslin, or butter of such excellence, straight from the farms across the river, and Mrs. Doubleday, who liked the shop well enough to break her rule of neglecting non-conformists, had often unknowingly enjoyed butter from Grimshaw's farm and, even now, there was some of his wife's making on the counter. There were crusty loaves of home-made bread and, twice a week, there were cakes of a great size, to be bespoken in good time, knobbly where they had risen above their tins and stuffed with clean and well-stoned raisins.

Mrs. Doubleday entered for a cream cheese and left without one. A cream cheese would also be good for Reginald, but the little woman, like a robin, behind the counter, was smilingly unable to promise one on any definite day. She offered no substitute; she supposed the lady knew what she wanted and she should not be pressed to take something else. This courtesy, or indifference, was traditional in the older shops of Upper Radstowe, but the lady, known to everyone as the vicar's wife, was evidently turning things over in her mind, for though she left the shop, she remained just outside it. Then she came back, a little flustered, and sat down.

'Butter,' she said. 'I'll have some butter.' She seemed to have no clear idea of how much she wanted or whether it should be fresh or salt. 'Half a pound of country butter,' she said at last, but she did not tell herself that this, too, would be good for Reginald. Apples, cream cheese and butter were alike useless against the menace she had seen, and it was still there, on the other side of the road, in front of an antique dealer's window, when she left the little shop. It was the slim form of Jenny Rendall standing beside the bulky one of her son. The two figures had not moved

269

since she first saw them and the stillness, the similarity of the intent attitudes, gave Mrs. Doubleday an extraordinary conviction that the thoughts of these two, though they might only be concerned with the furniture, were keeping the same pace and direction and, as she watched, their bodies betrayed a corresponding sympathy, for they turned simultaneously and went slowly up the street, a foot or two between them and their heads still bowed consideringly.

Mrs. Doubleday might have followed them without fear of detection, but the sight was too abhorrent to be prolonged. She was swept and submerged by a wave of indignation and woe, but she lifted her head above it to cry within herself that her dining-room furniture – and she returned to all her old allegiance for it – should never, never be the occasion for more window gazing with Jenny Rendall. And but for this timely accident, that young woman, the daughter of the woman who had probably made the butter Mrs. Doubleday was carrying, might have had the choice of the table off which the Vicarage meals would be eaten, the very chair in which Mrs. Doubleday would sit. And this, she thought bitterly, as she went homewards by another route, was the explanation of Reginald's fortunate hobby and of his cheerful chattiness. It was a gross deception and there was not one of her Christmas parcels, waiting to be posted, that was not stamped in sealing wax with his deceit. The happiness of the busy hours she had spent with him was a mockery; his share in it was in no way due to her and, as a little drizzling rain began to fall, she thought of Norman, rosy and contented by the study fire, with a new, sad sense of comfort, and she wished with all her heart that she could tell him everything and cry unstintedly. Her recognition of this impossibility was a lesson to her in this extremity. She must command herself, she must not alienate Reginald too; and, if she could, she must secure Norman's sympathy. The simplicity, the lack of self-consciousness with which she made this decision, was the measure of her misery. He would not agree with her in condemnation of Jenny Rendall; she had no hope of that, but she had an urgent desire for kindness and consolation. She knew now, definitely, that she would never get the love she wanted from her son; it was, perhaps, not in the nature of a son to give it. Her only anchor had failed her and she went instinctively for the one harbour she could make.

Mr. Doubleday, not warned by a knock on the door, was caught with his detective novel in his hand and, out of habit, not in hope, he slipped it between the arm of his chair and his plump thigh.

'You're wet, my dear,' he said, for little beads of moisture were shining on her clothes.

'It's only a drizzle,' she said, giving her coat a clumsy shake. 'It's the usual Christmas drizzle.'

'But a happier Christmas than usual, I hope, a happier Christmas.'

She turned mournful eyes on him and, if he had seen them, he must have been startled by their strangeness and have asked a question which would have brought her to a still more startling tearfulness, but he seldom looked higher than her shoulders.

'I think Reginald ought to have a change,' was as near as she could get to her trouble.

'What's the matter with him? Not a touch of malaria?'

'He says this air is enervating.'

'So they all say! So they all say! I've never noticed it. But if he wants something stronger, he can have it, can't he? Take him away after Christmas. Take him to the sea. Take him,' there were no limits to Mr. Doubleday's generosity, 'take him abroad. We must get him well before he goes back to Africa.'

'Yes,' she said slowly, 'we must do that. Where would you like to go yourself?'

'Me?' said the vicar. For a moment his face was boyish, then it became grave. 'No, my dear, you'd be happier without me, happier without me. You go off with him and enjoy yourselves together.'

'But he'd like it better if you came,' she said.

It was a great admission, a great surrender, but he did not know what to do with it, he would rather have been without it, and he gave an awkward little cough as she turned brusquely aside.

CHAPTER XXXV

Mrs. Doubleday determined to be threatened with a chill and merely to be threatened was enough to make caution necessary in view of the work before her. She knew that bed was the safest place for her. She could not trust herself with Reginald yet, she could not produce the maternal sympathy he had been wrongfully receiving from her lately, she was afraid her tongue would betray her humour. She retired at once and created quite a commotion in the household for neither the cook nor the parlourmaid nor the vicar could remember another such occasion. It was simply as a precaution, Mrs. Doubleday kept repeating firmly; but in the kitchen there was an interesting belief that the mistress must be much worse than she allowed, and Mr. Doubleday ventured to suggest a visit from the doctor. No, she would not have the doctor and when she had been supplied with a hot water bottle and a cup of soup, she was left alone, at her own request, until Reginald quietly opened her door and asked if there was anything he could do for her. It was an ironical question to her ears and, answering in a subdued, negative murmur, she hoped his conscience hurt him.

'I shall get up as usual in the morning,' she said.

'You'd better not do that. You must be careful,' he said and she retorted in exasperated sharpness, 'That's what I'm here for.'

She found being careful very difficult. She had no bodily discomfort to distract her from the memory of those two figures companionably intent outside the shop and turning away at precisely the same moment without so much as looking at each other. It would have been a much more bearable memory if one had lingered and called the other back and if there had been talk and gestures between them. She did not know why, but she knew it was so, and hardest of all to bear was owing her happy hours with Reginald to his happy ones with that girl. His friendship with any girl would have distressed her, but to choose Jenny Rendall was base ingratitude and cruel deception. What was she to do? Opposition in such cases was notoriously foolish, but, as she lay there seeking a solution, to the accompaniment of voices rising from the dining-room below, she never considered the possibility of allowing Reginald to have his way and being glad with him. She had no tender recollections of her own youth to give her sympathy; she and Norman had never strolled about the streets in silent concord; moreover, Reginald was not a youth and, here her spirits revived a little, he ought to have known better than to form a friendship with a girl he could not marry. It was not fair to the girl and she must tell him so, yet she knew that form of persuasion would go a very little way if Reginald really meant to go further in the opposite direction.

Flinging herself from her side to her back, she blamed Cecil Sproat once more for his snobbish neglect of his mother-in-law, but, perhaps, at this season, the family would be united and Mrs. Doubleday knew she would sing very heartily of peace and goodwill if Louisa Grimshaw accompanied her daughters to church. She would gladly ask them all to her Christmas dinner, on condition that both Grimshaws were of the party. She would leave no stone unturned to save the descendant of a bishop, a dean, an archdeacon and two canons from such a misalliance, and she remembered a certain stone which, turned skilfully, might reveal just what she wanted. It was not a precious stone, in spite of its name, but it might

274

be precious to Mrs. Doubleday, for Miss Jewel had been the Rendalls' neighbour when they lived in Beulah Mount.

'Well, I'll try her,' she thought, without a moment's doubt about her conduct. The end justified the means when Reginald was in question and, as she had always lived in the happy certainty of her Christian qualities, she never indulged in criticism of herself.

She heard her husband leave the house and, remembering that he had an engagement, she forgave his desertion of her on her sick bed, but she never heard her son's departure, for Reginald had taken the precaution of turning his key in the lock and shutting the front door without a sound loud enough to reach his mother's ears. It was strange that parental authority should still have some effect. He was thirty years old, a person of some importance and responsibility in his own world, yet he felt a little uncomfortable when he shut the door and muffled his footsteps on the grass, a little uncomfortable but quite determined to do what he liked without interference and fuss and he had not much time to spare. When he remembered how many days of his leave were already spent he could hardly restrain himself from breaking into a run, but he managed to present himself calmly at the Sproats' door. He had an excuse for calling. He liked to have one, for he was old-fashioned. It might deceive no one, but it seemed to him more seemly and respectful to produce it, and he seldom parted from Jenny without some important thing left unsaid, or the hour of their next meeting undecided. Mrs. Doubleday was right in believing he had made no purchases among the many things he admired; he was too wise for that and risked being considered a vacillating character for the sake of the opportunities his indecision gave him. To-night he had a definite errand. He wanted advice about a Christmas present for his mother who, tossing and turning in her wearisome bed, would have thought this almost the final insult.

Dahlia and Jenny did not exchange a glance; it was not necessary to tell each other that this was a glorious opportunity for mirth of which they could not take advantage. They could think of so many things for which Mrs. Doubleday would be all the better, and it was difficult to treat the question with proper gravity, but they succeeded, for they never failed in courtesy, and Cecil, knowing the kind of nonsense they wanted to be talking, listened to their remarks with admiration and thought Master Doubleday must be somewhat lacking in humour.

'What sort of things does she like?' Dahlia asked, but Master Doubleday did not know.

'Then I should give her heaps of flowers,' Jenny said. 'All the flowers we ought not to be having, roses and lilies and lilac. Lilac is lovely at Christmas.'

'Yes, but it doesn't last.'

'That's the best of it.'

'I don't think my mother would think so. I think she'd like something useful and all the shops seem to be full of rubbish. What,' he asked hopefully, 'are you giving your own mother?'

'I've made her a nightgown,' Dahlia said, 'but you can't do that for yours.'

'A nightgown?' Jenny said, in shocked surprise. 'I think that's most unsuitable,' and turning to Reginald, she explained simply, 'Because we don't like her husband.'

Amazement at such frankness from Jenny held back Dahlia's laughter for an instant; then it burst out as she realized the full meaning of this disapproval. 'Oh, Jen!' she cried. Through her tears she saw an embarrassed smile on Cecil's face. His sympathy was with Jenny, but he could not help being rather prudishly amused; moreover, Dahlia's laughter was infectious. Reginald, longing to laugh, too, but watching Jenny's serious dignity, settled his mouth into a neutral curve.

'But we like our mother,' Jenny explained, 'very much.'

'Oh dear!' Dahlia wiped her eyes. 'I always laugh much longer than I should, longer than anybody else, and it makes me seem so silly. It must be Mrs. Bagshot's champagne. I'd never tasted it before and I shouldn't have known it wasn't cider.'

'Good Lord!' said Reginald. He seemed distressed. 'It must have been very bad. My mother was there, wasn't she? I wonder if that's what has upset her.'

'But she didn't have any. Is she ill? She seemed quite well.'

'I don't think there's much the matter.'

'I expect she's tired. There's so much to do. Mrs. Bagshot says I can have her car whenever I want it, so we'll take our presents to the farm to-morrow, and bring back the turkey. And there's a rehearsal in the evening, the last until after Christmas. For the girls' play at the Mission,' she told Reginald.

Here was another opportunity, 'Do you want any help with it?' he asked.

'We shall want heaps on the night,' Jenny said, 'and for several rehearsals before that. We really need someone to prompt and do the stage managing. I think the girls would take it all more seriously.'

'All right, I'll come, but I don't know anything about it.'

'Neither does anyone else,' Jenny said.

'We're forgetting about Mrs. Doubleday's Christmas present,' Dahlia said.

Cecil thought there was a new note in her warm, genial voice and he saw that she made an effort to be interested in old mahogany tea-caddies and knife boxes, but at last Jenny and Reginald decided on a tea-caddy and arranged that she should choose it with him in the morning. Then, when he had said good night and they had all seen him off, Jenny ran upstairs to bed, without returning to the study, and there was something gay in the quickness of her step and a desire to be alone in the banging of her bedroom door.

Dahlia sat on the hearthrug and picked up the poker, Cecil stood near her, his arm on the mantelshelf. 'I've been thinking,' he said, 'that we ought to have asked your mother here for Christmas Day.'

'Mrs. Bagshot has asked us to go there and I've half promised. I'd much rather not have to cook a dinner. You'd hate it if mother came and so should we and so would she. We should have to have him, too, you know, and as Jenny said, we don't like him. We should all be very uncomfortable. But she has too much sense to come. I'll tell her you wanted her, if you like, and it was nice of you to think of it, but don't,' she begged unkindly, 'get so embarrassingly good!'

'It's very difficult to please you,' he said stiffly.

'I know. Everything's difficult. I'm sorry.' She reached up a hand for his and, holding it tightly, she twisted it while she spoke. 'Do you realize that Jenny told Master Doubleday we don't like Thomas Grimshaw. And she didn't mind talking about mother! And I shouldn't be a bit surprised if she asks him to come with us to-morrow. She doesn't seem to mind what she says to him. And, a little while ago,' there was a strain in her voice, 'a little while ago when I suggested getting someone to help us with the play, she said we couldn't, she said the girls would giggle, and now she says they'd be more serious! And I don't believe she remembers what she said before, or else she doesn't care.' Dahlia ended with what sounded like an accusation. 'She's just being perfectly natural with him.'

'And do you mind?'

278

Very near the tears she had hardly known before her marriage, Dahlia nodded.

'But, my blessed child, why should you? Can't you spare her to anyone?' he asked impatiently.

Dahlia turned very red, but she still looked at him and still clung to his hand. 'Not to him,' she whispered.

'I don't understand,' he said and he loosened her hold. Suddenly he was afraid to understand, but he could not help remembering the night of Reginald Doubleday's arrival and Dahlia's insistence on its possible importance and, first like a prick, then as a sharp pain, he admitted the suspicion that she was beginning to love the fellow. He would not look at her as she sat there, the tears now rolling slowly down her cheeks, her mouth drooping, her eyes asking for kindness. It seemed to him that she was strangely callous in her behaviour and it seemed to her that this was the moment when he should put his arms round her and kiss her. She wished he would; but, instead of taking that wise and difficult course, he settled himself at his desk and made a typically masculine show of having urgent work to do.

CHAPTER XXXVI

As soon as Dahlia went upstairs, Cecil left his desk and made up the fire. He was not attracted by his narrow share of the bed he had chosen in bashful determination and against the advice of the shopman, who had murmured something about the convenience of single beds in case of illness. Remembering this, Cecil realized the wider experience of that man with the suave manner and waxed moustache; no doubt he was thinking of other occasions when separation might be welcome. And here was one of them. He had been willing to endure the discomfort of lying stiff and straight when it was a penance imposed by himself with the prospect of future reward: it became a different matter when the careful space between him and Dahlia was filled by the thought of someone else. His jealous anger, with its desire to deal cruelly by her, was kept in check by shame for so primitive a feeling which he could never have turned into action, and just as strongly by a profound doubt of his own suspicion. Though Dahlia did not love him and might well love another, he could not believe in Reginald Doubleday as a rival. He had no reason for this scepticism except his belief that he was not the man to move her. Yet what else could account for her tears, for her distress at this happy friendship between Reginald and Jenny? Did she see in it something she had missed herself and grudged to Jenny? But she grudged Jenny nothing. And why had she clung to his hand and twisted it, with the action of a child who begs something from its mother?

He started from his chair and sat down again. Her tears would be dry by this time and her heart hardened: he had missed a moment which might have been a happy one; but, on the other hand, it might have precipitated him into a misery for which there was more than enough time. And how could he be altogether selfless and forget that, whatever the cause, he was being badly treated? She was cheerful and friendly, she worked hard in the house and out of it, she did not complain of tasks which must have been very dull if she had not put her own liveliness into them, she had no fault except her failure to love him properly, and when he considered how hard he had tried to please her, how humbly he had tried to learn from her and adapt the lessons to his conduct, though they had affected the prejudices and the faith of his whole life, he did not know what more he could do to ensure their common future. Perhaps he could do nothing, perhaps it was already out of his keeping and, while he sat there, he came to the important and astonishing conclusion that, whatever she did, he could not think ill of her. She had the very essence of goodness in her and even if she should trespass in the way which had always been most abhorrent to him, he would not be able to condemn her; he would only be able to pity and despise himself for failure to hold all that vitality and humour, or wake the passion for which another had the right touch or word. He was passing altogether beyond the condemnatory attitude. He had not been able to sustain it with Louisa Grimshaw when he had once tried to see the real woman, and he acknowledged the impossibility of applying a fixed judgment to totally different human beings. He ought, with his experience, to have learnt this earlier, but the sins and sorrows of those he tried to serve had affected him as a priest, not as a man: he knew what he was supposed to think about them and he thought it; he felt the proper emotions, but they were not strong enough to alter an opinion, a personal trouble was necessary for that. And he had not wished to change, there had been safety in acceptance and, looking back at himself as a boy who avoided certain kinds of knowledge, as a young man who consorted exclusively with people of like mind, as a candidate for Holy Orders and later, when he was ordained, he saw that he had fenced himself very securely and been careful not to look over the palings. His very severity of aspect and rigidity of mind had been created in self-protection: his indignation with Dahlia's criticisms of his religion and its rites had been that of fear and uncertainty: but he had looked over the palings and seen her and tried to lift her into his refuge and keep her there. She had refused to be lifted, she had forced the palings and made not only an entrance but an exit, and her goings and comings had so widened the breach that soon there would be little else. He owed her his liberty. He had not yet decided what to do with it, but he was no longer afraid to consider his position and he was not ashamed of his debt to a young girl who had no knowledge and made no claim to it; his difficulty was in paying it to her satisfaction.

He shut his eyes and his mind stopped working, but it admitted pictures of past happenings and possible future ones and he did not know when these slipped into dreams. He woke to see Dahlia kneeling on the hearthrug and cautiously replenishing the fire.

'I didn't know where you were,' she said. 'It's half-past one.' She touched his hand lightly. 'You're very cold. I'm going to get you something hot to drink.' She went out and returned immediately with his overcoat. 'Instead of a rug,' she said, 'because we haven't one. I suppose Mrs. Bagshot has dozens. Her house is like a shop. It's so dreadful that I feel I must be polite about it, but there's no need, really, and if you praise anything she wants to give it to you. She must think this house is very empty.'

'Does it feel empty to you?'

'No, not empty. There's plenty in it. Yes, plenty,' she repeated and she added thoughtfully, 'if it's used properly.'

'Well,' he said, 'tell me how I can use it better.'

'You? I wasn't thinking of you.' He frowned and made an impatient gesture and she said sadly, 'You mean, I never do.'

'I don't mean anything of the kind. I mean I'm so much in the habit of preaching that I imagine everyone else is doing it, too. I'm going to give it up.'

'Are you? What bliss!'

'Would it be?'

'Well, comparatively,' she said honestly. 'I think the time I hate most is when you turn your back and say those words at the end of the sermon.'

'But they are good words. And I mean them.'

'Yes. Well, wait till I come back and we'll go on talking. I don't think we're going to get cross with each other to-night.'

She returned with a jug of cocoa and a plate of biscuits. 'Fattening, but soothing,' she said. 'You look just like a man sitting up all night in a railway carriage. At least I suppose that's how he would look. I've never seen one doing it, I've never seen anything, or been anywhere. I'm not complaining. I'm just, perhaps, explaining. Not even to church very much! I wasn't brought up to it and at school it was just part of school, one of the things we did. If you're not brought up to it I don't see how you can help thinking it's rather a funny old performance, in costume. Quaint!' she said with a small grimace for the word. 'At least, it's funny when Mr. Doubleday performs, but when you do it makes me feel uncomfortable. Father was brought up to it and though he didn't believe in it, he thought it was beautiful. I suppose he liked the language and then he was interested historically. You are

being very patient,' she said. 'What I want you to understand is that it just doesn't touch me anywhere. Can I
help it? I don't see what the Church teaches that you
don't know already. Am I missing something? What is
it,' she asked gravely, 'that inspires Mr. Doubleday? Poor
little man! And poor Master Doubleday! I don't think
he can have much sense, or he wouldn't take Jenny to
choose a present for his mother. He can't like her, can
he? His mother, I mean. I think perhaps it will be better
for everybody if I don't turn religious.'

'You think one in the family is enough?'

'Oh,' she said, 'you're not nearly so bad as you were.'

She sighed and at the sound he said, 'That ought to
please you.'

'Yes. No.' She looked at him as though it were he who
could explain her to herself.

'Do you want to go back to bed? Are you warm enough?
Then,' he said with an odd smile, 'will you listen to the
story of my life?'

'Is it exciting?'

'Beginning to be.'

'Yes, I'll listen,' she said and when she had settled herself closer to the fire and was staring into it, he thought
there was rather a stubborn set to her mouth, and, in
fact, she was telling herself she had been foolish to come
downstairs, she ought to have stayed up there with the
remembrance of his coldness. She was risking the faithfulness to which she held with the love of the creator for
what he has made, she was in danger of renewing the
faithfulness she had resigned, she did not know to which
she should be loyal. She had a suspicion that somewhere
there was a sort of falseness in her and she was afraid to
look for it. When she found it she would lose something
else, for it was a law of life that gain and loss went together, and the thing she would lose was precious. As a

284

spider has the matter for his web within himself and weaves it to fit his purpose, though it will break at an alien touch, so she had spun her love for Simon out of her own romantic, passionate needs and she knew her web was very fragile, but no one except herself, unless it were Simon, could destroy it, for it was safely hidden, yet she felt as though she were slowly being led to the hiding place and constrained to see the flimsiness of her structure. But she listened to Cecil fairly and soon she turned to watch him while he spoke, with all her critical faculties alert for words and mannerisms to which she could make objection.

Wisely, Cecil did not look at her. He knew he might be abashed or influenced by a twist of her mouth or amusement in her eyes, yet, as it happened, his caution was unnecessary. She could recognize sincerity and she felt the humility of a sensitive person who is trusted with the confidences of another. And part of his story seemed to her very pathetic. When she tried to picture him as a little boy, she could not help seeing him already in a black coat and clerical collar, the only son of his mother, delicate and timid, and she wished she had him with her now, to make him laugh. But, in truth, she had him here, in this room, a good deal older and still in need of laughter. It was a great responsibility for she was very young and her instinctive judgments leapt far ahead of her knowledge and experience, yet they enabled her to understand how his timidity had become courage in the beliefs he had never questioned and how that courage was changing into one of a finer quality and seeking safety in no authority under God. And she appreciated the restraint he used when he talked of her and acknowledged his past feelings about her mother. He had made no mistakes on this occasion, not one, she admitted with another, but a silent sigh.

'So that's where I am,' he ended. 'What a relief!'

'To be there?'

'Yes, and to have told you.'

'Thank you for telling me. I don't know why you wanted to.'

'I suppose,' he said briskly, 'it's because I love you very much, but not enough to keep my troubles to myself.'

'If you love people properly, you tell them everything,' she said.

'Then I love you properly.' He looked at her, hesitated and decided to go on. 'But you don't tell me your trouble.'

'It isn't a trouble! It isn't a trouble!' she cried. She would not have it called that. It was beautiful and precious and she clasped her hands against her breast, defying him to rob her.

'It made you cry,' he said. 'Now go to bed. It's nearly three o'clock. I shall finish out the night in the railway carriage.'

'But you can't do that.'

'I can't do anything else,' he said abruptly.

'Ah,' she said, with a quiver of amusement in her voice, 'that's another advantage the rich have over us. I'm sure Mrs. Bagshot has dozens of beds, too. We shall have to get rid of Jenny.' Then, in compassion and gratitude, she knelt beside him and rubbed her cheek against his hand. 'Kind friend,' she said. 'Kind friend.'

'I've been thinking', Jenny said next morning, 'that I oughtn't to have promised to go out with Master Doubleday. It leaves you with all the work to do.'

'Yes, but there's nothing new in that.'

'I know, but I'm rather thinking of turning over a new leaf.'

'Wait till the new year.'

'I wish I could, but I'm afraid I must start at once. I stayed awake for a long time last night and I've decided that I'm very selfish and always have been and what I really mind most about it is that everybody else must have known all the time.'

'Everybody?'

'Yes,' Jenny said ruefully, 'I think so.'

'And, if it hadn't been for everybody, you wouldn't have made this great discovery! You're very funny and I like you as you are.' She looked at the small, pointed face and thought its air of pride and fastidiousness was its chief attraction for those who were at all susceptible to her charm. 'I think you'd better not try to be different. It might spoil you.'

'I shan't go as far as that,' Jenny said seriously. 'But shall I tell him to choose his present alone? What's the good of giving her a tea-caddy? She needs a new face and new feet and new everything. Isn't it a heaven-sent mercy,' she said fervently, 'that Master Doubleday hasn't inherited the feet?'

'Mother's have cancelled out Father's,' Dahlia said, 'but what would you have done if they hadn't?'

'I should have missed a lot of nice walks,' Jenny said demurely.

Here, thought Dahlia, was another instance of the chanciness of love. If Reginald Doubleday had turned his toes in or out, Jenny would not have wished to be unselfish, she might have looked more kindly on Simon Tothill, she would not have said now, with the faintest stain of colour in her cheeks, 'Would you mind if he came with us in the car this afternoon?'

'To the farm? It's a very nice old house and he seems to like old things, but what shall we do with him when we get there?'

'Take him in,' Jenny said.

'It will spoil it for mother.'

'He needn't stay long. He can find evergreens for the church till we're ready to come back.'

'He mustn't pick holly. We can't have Mrs. Bagshot's car scratched. And, you know, Thomas Grimshaw may be there.'

'Yes, I hope so. You see . . .' she began frowning a little, and Dahlia said, 'Oh, yes, I see.'

There was to be no deception with Master Doubleday and Jenny was being wise in time. Now, if necessary, she could retreat in good order; if she waited a little longer the retreat might be a rout, but what was most astonishing was her comparative indifference to a situation which had once been torture to her. Jenny was trying to be unselfish, but she was not sufficiently practised to be offering a view of her relatives for Master Doubleday's sake alone, she was not doing her best to stop a love she could not return, she was guarding herself against possible pain, but, to test her, Dahlia said, 'Are you going to take all your friends to the farm? Are you going to take Simon Tothill?'

'I'm not going to take him anywhere. I don't like him.'

'Why not? He's much more attractive than Master Doubleday.'

288

'No,' said Jenny, 'he's too much like me. Always thinking about himself. And talking, too. I don't do that. Oh,
he doesn't bore you about what he's doing, but he's always
edging on to the subject of his feelings.'

'Only because he likes you.'

'No, I think he'd do it with anyone. It's his favourite
topic. He wants to be interesting and a little tragic. Oh
yes, he does. I know, because I should behave like that,
too, if father hadn't been what he was.'

'Has he told you about a girl he used to like?'

'And half hated? Of course!' Jenny said, with scorn.

This made Dahlia unwillingly thoughtful. For the first
time she saw something a little strange in his confidences
that night on the Downs, and something a little theatrical
in his behaviour. He hardly knew her but he had persuaded her into his car, driven with a fury inviting
speculation, and told her of his unsuccessful love, and she
began to suspect that she had been duped for his benefit
and had subsequently duped herself for her own. To how
many other simple young women had he told his story?
And what other stories had he told? Under her frankness
there was a reserve which, as Jenny rightly said, was
inherited from their father, and she wondered now that
she had not missed it in Simon. A flush of heat ran up
her spine. She had been guilty of bad taste in seeing none
in Simon's conduct and an error in taste was one of the
hardest things to forgive in him or herself. It was comforting to believe that his interest in his story must have prevented him from noticing her foolishly rapt attention.
Then she became angry with herself for this readiness to
accept Jenny's opinion and judge it by her own experience.

'Everybody has some kind of weakness,' she said.

'I know too much about his,' Jenny said, 'and it's
specially silly in a man. I like sensible people.'

'Poor Edwin! He was sensible about everything except you. Have you told Master Doubleday about him?'

'He knows I was in the shop.'

'And about Cyril Merriman?'

'Why should I?' Jenny said haughtily.

This time her cheeks took on a deeper colour and Dahlia realized that, dissimilar as she and Jenny were from each other and from their mother, all three of them had a memory or a sentiment to be treasured and protected. Loving him too well to marry him, their mother had run away from her young squire and kept her idyll perfect, and Jenny's was still beautiful though she had deceived her lover and found him not worth the pains. There must have been, for both of them, an unforgettable glamour in their loves, but the glamour Dahlia had created was already growing dim at the first breath of common sense; her web was losing shape under the light touch of Jenny's finger, and the sorrow she had cherished was changing to a dreary sense of emptiness. She had not expected this sort of thing from herself; it was humiliating; she wanted to be alone with it and look it fairly in the face and she was glad to free Jenny from the obligations of her good resolutions and to see her going across The Green with Reginald, but she felt rather desolate in a new, vague knowledge of the demands life made on one's integrity. She had spun her web out of too thin a substance and it would not last much longer. Was this the falseness she had suspected in herself, this effort to make a physical attraction, dying for want of response, first into a sorrow and then into a love great enough to resign Simon happily to Jenny? How stupid, how young and how natural and how little like her conception of herself! And, this was a searching question, would she give Jenny to Cecil if he wanted her? No, she would not willingly do that. She felt now, but more intensely, as she had felt when she agreed to marry him. She could not contemplate a future in which he was entirely absent; he need not be very near, but he had to be there, when she wanted him. And he might not always be there, for why should not he, as easily as she had done, discover that he had been living with an illusion? She was confused and flurried, in haste to build something solid and enduring against that danger, yet warned by an inner sense of rhythm to do her building slowly. And she saw the pathos in the dependence of human beings on each other and the perilous ease with which they could be wasted and life seemed like a scattering of broken pieces to be put together like a puzzle, though with less hope of fitting them without a gap. There must be gaps and jagged edges, but, in a spasm of rebellion, she felt she was learning this too soon. She ought to have had some perfect hours without a single doubt, before she adopted this puzzle-solving for her occupation. Her mother must have had such hours and had she not seen Jenny coming back, all bemused, from the fields and woods across the river? Dahlia had been nearest to that enchantment on the night of the bazaar; she remembered how lightly she had walked by Simon's side, with all her perceptions sharpened, but apparently it was possible to have them so much sharpened that they became untrustworthy, and it needed two people for the creation of an ecstasy she would never have. Cecil could not help to give it; he might give something better, but the physical charm which, for a time, seems to include all others and lays a spell on the intelligence, had never been his for her. But it was hers for him and she knew she would be cruelly hurt if his intelligence broke through the spell and revolted against his senses. Being proud, she would not submit to a smaller gift than he could give her; being loyal and pitiful, she wanted to make amends for her unkindness and, being thrifty, she knew she must not waste him or herself for the foolish potency of hands that pleased her and absurdly attractive little lines at the corners of the eyes, hands, moreover, that did not want to touch her and eyes that never looked her way. And that was very fortunate, she thought; it was easy to be good when no one wished to tempt her; it was harder to get on friendly terms with herself and acknowledge her debt to Jenny who could be so clear-sighted where she did not love, and now seemed determined to love only where she was not afraid to look frankly at everything with her lover. The examiners had cheated Jenny once and she was on the watch for their tricks. They had cheated Dahlia, too, but she would get the better of them, she would read between the lines of their cunning propositions, and again she remembered sadly how young she was to be so vigilant.

'But it's rather fun,' she thought. She found it made all the difference in the world to see the future as a mixture of a game of skill and a work of art, an attempt to make imperfection nearly perfect, and in that new and exciting discovery she finished her household tasks and went out to do some errands.

She took it as a good omen to see Cecil coming towards her in Beulah Mount and when they met, almost in front of the door of her old home, she was touched by the pleasure on his face.

'Do you remember when I threw the duster on your head?' she asked, glancing at the upper window whence she had taken her careful aim to remind the curate of the parish that here were people in need of lodgers.

'Yes, I remember. It was a good shot.'

'Are you sure of that?'

'Quite sure,' he said.

'Then, if you are not busy, come with me to the shops. I don't like men who go shopping with their wives, but it's different at Christmas time. No, I draw the line at your carrying the basket when it's empty.'

'Yes, rather like a retriever,' he said.

Her laughter was arrested by an unmistakable voice behind them and, glancing back, she saw Mrs. Doubleday on Miss Jewel's doorstep. Miss Jewel hastily shut the door on her visitor and after a few words with the Sproats, who could not well pretend not to have seen her, Mrs. Double-day turned to walk up the hill as they went down it.

'Is this,' Dahlia said, 'part of the Christmas treats for the parish? Does she go and see everybody? And we ought to have asked after her health. No, perhaps we oughtn't. And I don't like her going to see Miss Jewel. Miss Jewel and Mrs. Doubleday is a bad combination. But they can't hurt you and me, can they? And they can't hurt mother. Yes, it's a good thing I didn't ask after her health. Master Doubleday would have got into trouble. I don't suppose she knew he'd slipped out when she was in bed. Didn't you think she looked rather pleased just now?'

'I always look at her as little as possible,' Cecil said.

'Poor thing!' She was thoughtful for a moment. 'Could she have been trying to get some information against us? She'll want it if she thinks Master Doubleday likes Jenny. But Jenny's all right. She's cleverer than Mrs. Doubleday, only I wish we'd gone to the farm this morning. He's coming with us this afternoon. I knew he would, so, unless Mrs. Doubleday is very quick, she won't be able to tell him much that he doesn't know already.'

'I think this is rather a fantastic idea.'

'So is Mrs. Doubleday. I wonder who thought of making her. It couldn't have been God, could it? Poor thing! And I wonder why the vicar married her. And do you suppose I could ever get like that? Ah,' she said seriously, 'it's not nearly so impossible as you think.'

CHAPTER XXXVIII

AT dusk, on Christmas Eve, Dahlia went into the church and slipped into one of the back pews. She had done her share of decorating earlier in the day, and now all the parcels had been delivered, all the calls on the sick had been made, she could think of nothing she had left undone and she was very tired. To-morrow she had only to attend the service in the morning and eat Mrs. Bagshot's lavish dinner in the evening and that was more than she wished to do; she wanted to stay in bed and sleep for hours without a dream. It was almost dark where she sat, but there were lights at the other end of the long church and she could see figures moving near the pulpit and the chancel rails. They were far enough away to seem like figures thrown on to a screen and there was an unreality, a sort of futility, in their movements. Jenny was there, and Reginald, with the gleanings from the neighbourhood of the farm, and among the nondescript women, who, like rabbits at nightfall, popped out of their obscurity on such occasions as this, she could distinguish Miss Fairweather strolling here and there as she had done at the bazaar.

A great deal had happened since the bazaar, but most of it had merely occurred in Dahlia's mind. The events themselves were very simple though, when she looked back at the past half year, there had been too many of them for so short a time; they should have been spread more thinly over a future promising to be monotonous.

A year ago her father had been alive, and he and Jenny and Dahlia had gone to the Christmas service in Combe Friars Church. If he had not died, what would they have been doing now? She wondered whether he had made any plans for their future. They certainly would not have gone to Beulah Mount and let rooms to lodgers, Jenny might have met Cyril Merriman, but she would not have known Edwin Cummings or Reginald Doubleday and Dahlia would not have married Cecil Sproat. Their lives had been too early and too readily circumscribed by their encounters with these men and it was strange to think how easily accident might have turned them into different paths, and how this little world, in which they were living so intensely, might not have existed for them at all. Even so small a thing as the choice of a house in some other part of Upper Radstowe would have completely changed their circumstances. They had been like people wandering in an unknown city where the names of the streets and the signposts had no significance for strangers. It was all chance which road they took, yet they became responsible for results as intricate and far-reaching as the windings of the streets.

Dahlia drooped forward and laid her arms and head on the book-rest. The voices at the other end of the church reached her faintly, except when some freak of acoustics changed a discreet remark into a proclamation, but these sudden sounds disturbed her no more than the hooting of the motor horns outside. She was snatching a short rest in a sheltered part of that city where the names and the signposts took on meanings when it was too late to choose another way. Yes, they were malignant people, those examiners, with their attempts to puzzle poor candidates into gross mistakes, only a limited time allowed for the paper and no opportunity for answering the same questions at a later date. They did not even start with simple papers. At the age of twenty-one she was expected to make decisions only fit for the mature, and their one leniency was the permission to take help from a neighbour. That was not counted as cheating and, after all, she thought, it was a great concession, but first the right neighbour must be chosen.

She was already half asleep when a slight stir, some subtle change in the atmosphere, caused her to look up, and there, just inside the door, and looking towards the chancel, was Simon Tothill, the collar of his great coat turned up, his gauntleted gloves in his hand. That was how she always saw him in her mind. Tall and well made, with his head finely set, he seemed to her like a modern knight errant in the accoutrements suited to his time and habits and her heart began to beat with a sickening quickness. She had no more control over it than a sea-sick passenger has over his physical reactions and she was at a greater disadvantage for she could not get relief from this kind of discomfort in angry abhorrence of its cause.

He saw her and sat down beside her. 'I thought I might be able to help,' he said, sighing heavily, 'but I see I am not wanted.'

'How do you know?' she asked quickly. 'You haven't tried to find out, have you?'

'Yes, I've found out. I've been watching. I don't have much luck,' he said.

Dahlia leaned forward again and held her chin in her hands. With his very first words he had confirmed Jenny's criticism, yet, a few weeks, a few days ago, she would have heard real sadness in them.

'What a pity!' she said with a sigh. He had spoilt something and though it was fortunate for her, she wished, just for the sake of beauty and completeness, that he could have matched his looks.

'That', he said, 'is rather an inadequate way of putting it.'

'Oh, I think it does well enough. Pity, pity! That's what Mr. Doubleday would say. It doesn't mean anything, it's just a noise, but it does well enough.'

'I thought you were more sympathetic,' he said.

She turned and gave him her wide smile, but it was not quite steady. Now, close to him, she could see the little lines she liked. She knew she would always like his face. Thus, Jenny had thought of Cyril Merriman's, even when her mind had finished with him.

'I don't believe you really want what you want,' she said. She almost held her breath for this was a critical moment. If he laughed at himself he was going to make things very hard for her. He smiled, instead, without mirth. She recognized it as a bitter smile.

'No, I always want what I can't have.'

'But perhaps you don't want the same thing for very long. I'm thinking', she said, 'of the other lady, the one with the red lips.' She felt pity for a foolish Dahlia and gladness for a wiser one when she saw him repressing his surprise and struggling for a recollection. Yes, he had forgotten his confidences on the Downs, she had only been one among his listeners.

'That', he said solemnly, 'was a mistake.'

'It's so easy to make one,' she murmured.

She wished he would go. Her light mockery was all turned against herself and she understood the comfort of the confessional, but she did not feel in need of absolution from anyone but herself and she had no hesitation in giving it. Marrying for friendship and not for love which, in her narrow experience, had not proved successful, and finding the friendship incomplete, she had discovered the need for the romance she could not see in Cecil; she had learnt what passion was and she could feel none for him; she had seen this man who pleased her senses and attributed to him everything else she wanted, and now she thanked the God in Whom she did not much believe that the finger had not beckoned when she would have followed it. 'But I shall always like his face,' she thought

297

again, smiling at him very kindly when he said good-bye.

It was Miss Fairweather who drove him away. She came drifting up the aisle with a sprig of holly in her coat and there was no sign of the fanatical expression she wore at sewing meetings. She took Simon's place and sat there in silence.

'Peaceful here,' she said at last.

'Yes, I wish I could stay here all night.'

'Are you very religious?' Miss Fairweather inquired with interest.

'No. Only tired.'

'Oh, you'll get over that. I thought you might want to keep watch like the shepherds.'

'Where's the flock?' Dahlia asked.

'It's old enough to take care of itself. No lambs. Not one of us would attract the hungriest wolf. I was never a particularly tempting morsel myself,' she said after a pause, 'and I dodged the only wolf who showed any appetite for me. Silly, that. Much better to have been mauled. Even eaten,' she added. 'But how did I know a pleasanter wolf wouldn't come along? One likes to exercise some choice in the way one's mangled. Such a mistake! Well, I shall see you in the morning, harking to the Christian angels. It will be the first time for you, in this church, won't it? And I shall soon be in my third dozen.'

'Why do you come?' Dahlia asked.

'I don't know,' Miss Fairweather said slowly.

'And the sewing meeting?'

'Oh, I love the sewing meeting. It's my weekly treat. I enjoy that. It does me good. I'm not just stitching seams, you know. They think I am, but I'm not. They all have names. There's nearly always one for Mrs. Doubleday and somebody else is sure to irritate me and there's myself, once a week, at least. It's an exciting moment when I know there's another seam coming and

I haven't settled who it is. Sometimes it's just a thing, a puncture in my bicycle tyre or something of the kind, but that's not so amusing. When I've had a really successful afternoon I feel quite amiable till next Monday.'

'What a good idea,' Dahlia said.

'Yes, it works very well. It's a kind of game. One has to amuse oneself.'

She drifted away again leaving Dahlia to wonder what sort of person Miss Fairweather really was and what she would have been if she had not dodged the wolf, and she imagined her with a set of little wolves, plain, like herself, with pointed noses and perhaps not materially well cared for, but receiving odd fancies from their mother and snatching at them as actual cubs would snatch at the meat produced for them. On the other hand, the presence of the cubs might have eliminated the fancies and perhaps she was happier as she was. One had to be happier as one was, she thought, and when Cecil entered the church, a few minutes later, she watched him for a little while before he saw her. This was her particular wolf, a nice one, and she had chosen him for herself; she had not Miss Fairweather's right to dodge and she was losing her wish to do so, except playfully, for a little longer, but he was not very good at playing back. That was one of the things she missed in him, that response to absurdity of which he did occasionally show himself capable, and why should a grown man show it more than occasionally? All this time he might be missing his own gravity in her and she went to him and said a little wearily, 'Shall we go home? It's no use waiting for Jenny. I believe they are putting things up and pulling them down again, just to make it last a little longer.' And wistfully, she added, 'It must be fun.'

'I'm sorry you can't share in it,' he said stiffly.

There had to be a moment when his patience would give

out and this was the moment. They walked home in silence but as soon as they were inside the house, while they were still in the narrow hall, he gave vent to his anger in a cold stream of words far more devastating than a fiercer, less well directed torrent. Though it might undo the careful work of weeks, he could not help it. All the little wounds she had inflicted, though some of them had let out humours of which he was thankful to be rid, had started festering. She rarely spoke to him, he said, without some light gibe, some implied regret or complaint. To all the rest of the world she was kind and unselfish, he was the target for the shots she aimed at no one else. Did she imagine he was happy? She was so much concerned with her own emotions that she never considered his. Yes, in a material sense, she cared for him; she looked after his comfort as though he were some dumb animal for which she was responsible and, just as though he were a faithful dog who would not bite or snarl and could not understand the exact import of what she said, so she spoke to him, careless of how much or whether she hurt him. How would she have felt if the positions had been reversed, if she had not known her beauty always charmed him and a kind word or touch could always soften him? Surely her own unhappiness ought to instruct her in his. What would these months have been for her if, in nearly every word he uttered, she heard an implication of his disappointment? She had the advantage of him and she knew it, but it was one that could not last for ever. Already it was beginning to turn against herself because, in its essence, it was mean and cowardly.

These were only the headings of his discourse. Each one was amplified and illustrated and the words battered on Dahlia's ears until, at last, she heard noise without meaning, until she felt physically unable to stand against them, but actually they all reached her consciousness and they were all true; it was a little exaggerated, but it was all true; she had been lightly cruel and regardless. Under the coldness of his words she could hear an emotion which made a mock of her sentiment for Simon and again she realized that here was a human being in her keeping, a great responsibility. More humbly, she understood that she was in his and that neither of them could find happiness until each was willingly adjusted to the other. He had tried to do his share, but she had not. Yes, it was true. She had treated him like a faithful dog, to be petted sometimes, to be fed, to be turned out when she did not want him, a solace and a protection when she did. She had not been fair, she hated unfairness, and, at that moment, when she was ready to take a step towards him, the front door bell was rung. It was necessary to answer the ring, even at this crisis, and she took in two long boxes addressed to Jenny.

'Flowers for Jenny, flowers for Jenny,' she said, and then, for the first time, she heard her voice as he heard it, with its faint, half humorous regret. She dropped the boxes and went to him hurriedly and pressed her clasped hands against his breast. 'But I don't want them, I don't want them!' she cried, so earnest to make him believe her that she could only repeat the words.

'I don't know what you want. Do you know yourself?' he asked severely. And then he put the question he had determined not to ask. 'Are you in love with someone else?'

'No,' she said thoughtfully. 'No, I'm not, and what I want is to like you as much as you like me.'

He took a glance in the little mirror. 'You'll have a hard job,' he said grimly.

For once, she did not laugh. 'I think that's sad,' she said, 'and it isn't true and it's rather frightening for me, because it's not the real me you're loving. The real me is the one you've been telling me about. It never does,' she was admonishing herself, 'to trust just to a face.'

She ran down the stairs to get the supper and for a minute she stood still on the threshold of the dark kitchen. It was all true. Secretly, in a way that did not annoy people because it was not often apparent, but fundamentally, she was self-satisfied and conceited and just as she had been treating Cecil, so Mrs. Doubleday had probably started marriage with the vicar and poor Norman had never had the sense or courage to scold her.

CHAPTER XXXIX

'WHITE lilac,' Jenny said with satisfaction, when she opened one of her boxes.

'Of course. You practically asked for it the other night.'

'Did I? Well, I'm very glad. Let's guess what's in the other box.'

'Lilies of the valley,' Dahlia said.

'No, it's something with long stalks. It must be roses. Passionate, blood red roses,' Jenny said dramatically, 'and as nearly purple as possible.'

'Lilies,' Dahlia repeated, but she knew they were not quite right for Jenny. They were meek in their virginal modesty and Jenny was armoured in her little dignity, though she looked gayer to-night than Dahlia had ever seen her. 'And I think you're quite heartless,' she added.

'But I'm quite right, too. You see, very dark red and drooping a little. You can have them if you like.'

Dahlia drew back. 'No, thank you. I don't want them.'

'What shall we do with them, then?'

'Give them away to somebody who's ill. Do you think Master Doubleday has given white lilac to his mother, too?'

'No, I'm sure he hasn't. He couldn't do anything so inartistic.'

'What do you think she will give him?'

'I don't think about it at all.'

'I wish I needn't,' Dahlia said.

Not only was she concerned about Mrs. Doubleday's view of Reginald's friendship with Jenny, but she saw an unpleasant likeness to her own situation on the other side of The Green. The vicar there had a wife he was afraid of and here there was a curate who was quite capable of making his wife afraid of him and though she preferred this possibility to the other certainty, and liked Cecil all the better for having shown his mettle, she was half humorously afraid of his growing as harsh as Mrs. Doubleday while she might become as placatory as the vicar.

'And I wonder,' she persisted, 'what she'll give Mr. Doubleday.'

Mr. Doubleday could have told her. He knew exactly what his wife would give him. He could not remember a Christmas when she had not given him half a dozen linen handkerchiefs, monogrammed and of the finest quality. On his birthday he received a pair of gloves, also of good quality. She was not mean; these things could not have been better of their kind, but she lacked imagination and he was not of enough importance to create it. He was always a little sad when he beamed his thanks for these unvarying gifts. She saved herself a good deal of trouble; he suspected that orders had been given for the regular delivery of the handkerchiefs on Christmas Eve and the gloves on the first of June and he supposed that the orders would only be countermanded on the occasion of his death. She was very methodical and by these means two tiresome little details were taken off her mind, but he would have much appreciated a parcel of a different shape; he was tired of that neat rectangle. Naturally convivial, he liked the merriment proper to the season. He was childishly fond of surprises for himself and other people and, with any encouragement, he would have devised cunning hiding places for extra, unexpected little gifts, a small parcel tucked under the tea cosy, or handed to Mrs. Doubleday on a covered plate instead of her eggs and bacon. He would gladly have filled her stocking if she would have hung it up, but it was impossible to attempt such diversions with Flora. Nevertheless, he always took pains to find a suitable present for her and he was particularly solicitous this year. He had to show her that the change in their relationship had not made him neglectful and he felt sorry for her, too. It was sad to see her small, clumsy efforts at amiability; they were signs of distress and while he recognized their pathos he was not unduly moved by them. The distress was unreasonable; Mr. Doubleday could not sympathize with it; he knew its cause and he also knew that if, by any unlikely chance, it were removed, she would regret her slight approaches, she would behave as though she had not made them.

'Poor woman,' he thought, 'poor woman!' She had a most unfortunate nature. She could not make the best of things. She had married the wrong man and he was a sword in her side, while the wrong woman could be reduced to a pin prick for him who had the comfortable qualities of a cushion. Life offered him so many consolations, sunshine, a bright fire, a good story, the sight of a happy young face, these simple, easily won pleasures far outweighed his disadvantages. He did not dwell on the supreme consolations of religion, but it did occur to him that what Flora needed was an overwhelming spiritual experience, such as public confession at a revival meeting and, a little maliciously, he pictured her rising in her place, crying her sins aloud and tottering towards the platform where the revivalist begged or threatened and gathered in his trophies.

After weeks of abstinence, Mr. Doubleday began to hum, nervously but not unhappily, for suddenly, while he was thinking how salutary it would be for Flora to be emotionally turned and twisted by someone who was not herself, he remembered what he had never consciously noted, the comparative meekness of his wife under the

305

good-natured, loud masterfulness of Mrs. Tothill. This realization streamed like a great shaft of light in front of him. Mrs. Tothill had no hampering respect for Flora's position and no fear of her as a woman; she would criticize her freely and snub her suggestions like a steam roller going over pebbles, and though Flora made plenty of acid comments afterwards, her resentment was almost silent at the time. And how quickly she had responded to his own change of manner! She had not become more agreeable but she had been much less aggressive and he saw that his constitutional indolence, his refusal to face problems and his readiness to get through each day as pleasantly as possible and leave the rest to chance had been unfair to her, to himself and, worst of all, to Reginald. Nature had given her a formidable face, but those out-works were not impregnable. 'By no means,' he said. 'By no means.' The fortress looked strong, but it could be taken. 'Easily, easily,' he said. Yes, by assault. Why should she be allowed to starve herself in that garrison, try to keep Reginald inside it and see an enemy in anyone who approached? Fortunately, she could not control the boy, but she could worry him and so spoil that little idyll which made Mr. Doubleday very envious. Therefore, the only thing to do was to force and keep her out of her fortress and head her off when she attempted a retreat. He did not particularly want her company in the sur- rounding pastures but he saw how he had neglected his duty and this was one which could not be performed for him by Sproat, though probably, he thought, with a return to humour, no one would find more satisfaction in the task. The vicar shook his head at himself reproach- fully and spared a few minutes for the contemplation of his negligence.

Meanwhile, Mrs. Doubleday had her own plans, but there was a truce during the Christmas days and no one knew her painful efforts to thank Reginald for the tea-caddy, the very object at which he and Jenny might have been gazing when she saw them outside the shop. The shops were shut for these two days and Reginald had no excuse for his little excursions, nor did he make any. He went to church with her on Christmas morning and returned by her side; the whole of the day was devoted to his parents and, on the next, he was kind and attentive to the little group of forlorn ladies of the congregation who were their guests. In the relief from constant listening for the sound of his departure or return and agonies of specu-lation during his absences, she could almost believe in her own creation of her misery, but on the following day the first shots were fired after breakfast, when she produced the printed information she had gathered in sheaves from a travel agent's counter and thrust it before him.

'What's all this?' he said. 'Do you want spills made of it?'

'I want you to look at it. I got it on purpose.'

'Then,' said Reginald, glancing at the pile, 'I shouldn't think you left a leaflet in the shop. You've got duplicates here, you know,' he said, idly turning them over.

'Very likely. I was in a hurry,' she said and as he saw how she handled her knitting needles, he knew with what rough swiftness she must have pillaged the shop. 'Your father says we can have a holiday. I thought we might go abroad and I want you to look through the advertise-ments.'

'Well,' said Reginald, good-humoured but cautious, 'here's a pretty picture of a steamer in a Norwegian fiord. That's no good. Ice-bound, I should think, at this time of the year. Here's another of the same steamer, no, it's a different steamer but the same fiord. The Baltic Ports, that's no good either. Ah, now we're getting further south. Spain and Portugal. How would you like Spain and Portugal, or one without the other? You could go and see a bull-fight, you'd probably run into a revolution.'

'I wish you'd be serious, Reginald. We must get this settled.'

'There's no hurry, is there?'

'I want to go soon after the new year,' she said quickly.

'And leave me?'

'Of course not. I'm planning it for you. You said this air was enervating.'

'But I'm getting acclimatized. I've never felt better in my life.'

'I need a holiday myself. So does your father. Your father would come with us if you persuaded him.'

'Would he? But he likes his own armchair and foreign chairs are so uncomfortable.'

'It would do him good to get out of it.'

'I'm not so sure that people are any the better for doing what they dislike.'

'Well,' she said, plying her needles and getting motive power from her elbows, 'all I can say is that I've had to do a lot of it.'

'I know,' Reginald said quietly. He stared intently at the presentation of a young lady who sheltered under a parasol from the brilliance of a southern sun, and he tried not to see the confirmation of his theory in his mother's words.

'And now that there's something I really should enjoy, you are not at all encouraging,' she said.

'It needs thought,' said Reginald. 'Such a lot of places to choose from and something wrong with all of them. How would you like to amble down to the South of France with me and leave me at Marseilles when I'm due to sail?'

'We can't be away for months.'

'Oh no, we shouldn't start yet.'

'But the whole point of the plan is to go away now,' Mrs. Doubleday said with a jerk.

'I see. It's rather sudden and there are some engagements I should like to keep. There's the Tothills' dance.'

'That's not worth waiting for.'

'There's the play at the Mission.'

'The play at the Mission! What has that to do with you?'

'I'm stage manager,' Reginald said modestly.

Mrs. Doubleday dropped her knitting. 'It's your father's fault!' she cried. 'I tried to stop the play, but he had given his consent already, as of course, he would.'

'Why shouldn't he?'

She found this simple question highly irritating. She could not answer it truthfully; she could not explain, indeed she hardly knew, that she found pleasure in frustrating certain people, but there are few women who are not supplied with several equally forcible, though possibly divergent reasons for an objection or a persuasion, and Mrs. Doubleday was able to produce one.

'It's bad for the girls,' she said.

'But why?'

Here was another of these simple questions, but she controlled herself. 'Can't you trust me to be wiser than you in some matters?' she asked.

'I just wanted to know,' he said amiably. 'I shouldn't like to do them any harm.' He had a lift of the brows, a twist to his mouth which she found attractive and exasperating.

'And most unsuitable,' she went on, 'for you to be mixed up in it. How did you manage to get mixed up in it, Reginald?'

Her accents, quiet but firm, were those of an elder determined to get the truth from a child. She saw his hesitation and misinterpreted it. He was anxious to avoid mentioning Jenny's name. He had a great aversion from using it in his mother's presence and a greater one from hearing it on her lips with the disparagement which would make it almost impossible for him to behave with filial courtesy.

'We were talking about it at the Sproats',' he said.

'Now Reginald, just listen to your old mother for a minute,' she said and he was troubled by a manner altogether alien to her in this effort to be sympathetic and lightly wordly wise.

'I think you are making a mistake in seeing so much of the Sproats. Mrs. Sproat has married into a respectable family and she has to be treated as a member of it. She takes her husband's position and I sincerely hope,' Mrs. Doubleday said mendaciously, 'that she won't disgrace it, but that little person who is staying with them is quite another matter. It's all very well to be polite to her, but she's bound to misunderstand you and you'll only turn her head and make her unhappy. There are plenty of girls in Upper Radstowe in your own station in life. And with your own standards,' she added. It was now her turn to hesitate. She could not see his face, it was sheltered by his hands, and she decided to be cautious. 'I won't say anything else against her,' she said generously. 'After all, it doesn't concern us. I'm just warning you, for her sake.'

Reginald made a neat pile of the leaflets and he took a little time about it. His hands, like the rest of his body, were shaking with indignation. The vision of Jenny in her funny, friendly little dignity, the remembered sound of her low-pitched voice and the beautiful precision of her speech, made him long to throw the leaflets in his mother's face and, at the same time, restrained him from any expression of anger. He must try to keep this affair in harmony with all Jenny meant for him and he managed to smile at his mother who was not sure that she liked the way he did it.

He stood up. 'I promise you I won't turn her head,' he said.

'Reginald!' She called him back. She was very uneasy. 'I want a better promise than that. If you won't give it, you'll force me to say what I meant to keep to myself. I've told you her mother isn't respectable, and the girl takes after her. I've proof of it. What else could you expect, living in that house without a decent woman to keep an eye on her?' There was no response and when she saw that his face was white she asked plaintively, 'You're not going to break my heart, are you?'

'Your heart?' he said coldly, and he went away.

CHAPTER XL

SHE heard the banging of the front door, gave him
five minutes start and then went down the garden path at
a great pace.

Mr. Doubleday, who had already peered out of the
study window to watch Reginald's departure, and who
was now peering with greater caution, recognized something abnormal in his wife's gait. She seemed to be im-
pelling her feet faster than they could go at their usual
angle and the effect was peculiar. They looked as
though they might come off.

'Dear me! I hope she won't have a tumble,' he murmured.

Where and why was she going so fast? She was not
carrying her shopping basket, he feared she might be
going in pursuit of Reginald and Mr. Doubleday remained
thoughtful for some time before he put on his overcoat
and hat.

It was a lovely morning. The air, no longer enervating
to Reginald, was very soft, the sunshine had a pale brightness. The year had turned and the sun seemed to be
sending out long fingers towards the world it was approaching, renewing acquaintance with twigs eager to swell
responsively and lightly giving the earth, with all its
hidden stirrings, the promise of a steadier warmth.

Mrs. Doubleday did not notice the sunshine. She
knew where she was going, but pain and anger made her
insensitive to all else. She had been hurt — what had he
meant by those last cold words? – and she was being
thwarted and she could not remain inactive.

No woman had ever loved a son as she loved hers and

had so little in return; no other woman had meant so well and found so many obstacles in her way. She remembered, not without shrinking, that vision of herself in the long glass, the new hat she had bought, her wish to have a pleasanter expression under it, her concession to Norman in letting him choose Reginald's new chair; she had done her best, she had violated her instincts in her desire to make Reginald's holiday perfect but, from the very first evening, there had been trouble. It had started with the Sproats, it had continued with them, it looked as though everything would end with them and if Reginald would not save himself, she must do it for him. This was how she put it to herself, but her maternal love had always been a kind of self-glorification and it was her own downfall, not his, she was determined to prevent.

Even in ordinary circumstances she would have had no hesitation in making her way, on some pretext, into the Sproats' house. She had begun her training in this sort of invasion when she was a girl in her father's parish. To-day she did not trouble about a pretext; she had expended all her tact in her interview with Reginald; moreover, tact was not wanted now; but when she was half way across The Green and had her eyes on her destination, she saw that she need not enter the house. Reginald could not be within, for here was her other quarry at the gate and turning towards the hill above the river. What she would do if she found them up there together, she did not consider. Doggedly, like some slow and inescapable tracker, she followed the girl who was moving quickly, with a lightness Mrs. Doubleday could not emulate, and so age plodded after youth, prejudice after hope, a passion to grasp after a new desire to give.

The path was winding, Jenny was soon out of sight and when Mrs. Doubleday came up with her she was standing alone beside the railings, holding the top bar with both hands, her body at arms length from them. She turned and smiled a little shyly. 'I think spring's come already,' she said.

Mrs. Doubleday ought to have been touched by the sight of that happy face and she knew it, but the memory of Reginald's cold words only hardened the heart he had doubted, and she was exasperated by the complete absence of vulgarity in the girl's voice and manner, though, and this was comforting, she should certainly not have spoken until she was addressed.

Mrs. Doubleday had not hurried up the hill to talk about the weather and she only waited to recover her breath before she started on her mission. Its difficulties for her were inherent in the problem, not in any need for delicacy of approach. Dozens of times it had been her duty to reprimand young women, she had always gone straight to the point and she did so now.

'I followed you up here,' she said. 'I want to talk to you.'

She was pleased to see a little colour in Jenny's cheeks though her expression did not change as she said politely, 'If I'd known you were following me, I shouldn't have walked so fast.'

'Ah,' Mrs. Doubleday commented meaningly. 'I don't think you'll like what I have to say. You've been seeing a good deal of my son lately. Now, I want you to be a sensible young woman and put a stop to that. For your own sake.'

Jenny, who had been looking across the water at the woods where her first lover had caught her in his arms as she ran down the steep slope towards him, and all the leaves of the birches had clapped their hands, now turned to look at Mrs. Doubleday and asked quietly. 'What harm can he do me?' A tiny smile curved her straight mouth. 'I think he's very nice,' she said demurely.

Mrs. Doubleday moved, almost stamped, a foot impatiently. 'Of course he's nice. Do you think I came here to tell you he wasn't? He's too nice. That's the point. A nice man who realizes that he has been unwisely friendly with a girl is always in a difficulty. He doesn't know how to drop her. He blames himself and imagines he has a duty towards her, but a girl with any pride will know how to behave, she will relieve him of such feelings by doing what is necessary herself.'

Jenny nodded her head. She had released Cyril Merriman from any necessity for self-reproach. She had walked through the rain, across the bridge, over the familiar roads, and found him at the trysting-place under an umbrella. The umbrella had been very helpful. There was something definitely foolish in a man who took an umbrella to a serious, perhaps a tragic, interview.

Mrs. Doubleday, seeing that nod of assent, thought she was doing better than she had expected. 'I'm glad you're sensible,' she said. 'I was afraid you might think he was serious.'

'He is sometimes,' Jenny said, thoughtfully. 'One wouldn't like him not to be, but, on the whole, I think he's rather merry.'

This was not so good, this was insolence, and Mrs. Doubleday asked in a loud voice, 'Are you wilfully misunderstanding me?'

To her great surprise, Jenny looked her frankly in the face and said, 'Yes, Mrs. Doubleday.'

'Then you are a very rude girl!'

Mrs. Doubleday heard and hated the inadequacy of the statement, and Jenny explained patiently, 'It's just because I don't want to be rude.'

'It's because you don't mean to do as I ask. I might have known it. Of course you wouldn't!' She tried another line of attack. 'Give him up for his sake! Can't you see what a disaster it would be for him?'

'To give him up?'

'To marry him!' In despair, Mrs. Doubleday allowed the hateful words to pass her lips.

'He hasn't asked me to marry him.'

'But if he does!' She was pleading now.

'But you said yourself he wasn't serious,' Jenny said mildly.

'Pooh! You can make him think he ought to be.'

For an instant Jenny hid her face in her hands. 'This is dreadful!' she said in genuine horror.

'Yes, dreadful,' said Mrs. Doubleday. 'And it would be worse for him. Do you realize what it would mean for his family? He is extremely well connected – on my side.' She mentioned in detail the famous dignitaries of the Church. 'They would probably refuse to have anything more to do with him,' she said solemnly. 'You mustn't think that your sister's marriage has raised you to her position – such as it is. And how do you think my son would feel when he met your mother?'

Here was a question demanding an answer but, during the last part of her speech Mrs. Doubleday had been indignantly, incredulously, aware that Jenny was not attending to it. She was smiling a little, frowning a little, holding her head as though she listened to something else, far off, not quite distinguishable. What was it? A step? Mrs. Doubleday cast a glance behind her, but only a few children had come to play round the little tower at the top of the hill. Wisely, however, she had kept her most telling question in reserve.

'How', she demanded, 'would you like my son to know your own little history? Now, I'm not threatening, but I know more about you than you may imagine, and Reginald, and other people, shall know it too, unless I have your promise. Are you going to give it?'

'Oh please, just wait a minute,' Jenny said.

316

'Take your time,' said Mrs. Doubleday generously.

'I'm trying to remember something. This doesn't seem real to me, not a bit, but I know it has happened before.'

'I can well believe it,' said Mrs. Doubleday.

'But where?' Jenny said as though she desired assistance. Then a candid smile broke across her face. She would not be really rude to Master Doubleday's mother, but surely this might be allowed her. 'I knew someone else had said these things, nearly these things. It was Lady Catherine de Burgh.'

'I don't know her.'

'Don't you?' Jenny's surprise seemed to indicate some lack in Mrs. Doubleday, who condescended to inquire whether the lady lived in Herefordshire.

'Herefordshire?' It was strange that Mrs. Doubleday should mention Herefordshire and Jenny checked herself from any reference to her aunt Isabel. She would not claim a single advantage for herself. 'No.' She longed for Dahlia. 'Not Herefordshire. Kent.'

Mrs. Doubleday was puzzled. These girls were claiming important friends and relatives all over the country. 'Well,' she said doubtfully, 'I know nothing about her, but she must be a practical, straighforward woman and as you have had my own advice from her, I shall say no more.' She began to wonder whether she had said too much. 'Is she a friend of yours?'

'Not exactly,' Jenny owned.

'Ah,' said Mrs. Doubleday, 'I thought not. I shall say no more, but I shall keep my word. Good morning.'

She took one way round the hill and Jenny took the other, running very quickly, with happy leaps, almost forgetting Mrs. Doubleday's insults in her own amusement, and Mr. Doubleday, who had taken up a strategic position on The Green and sat patiently under a bare tree, saw her long before he saw his wife descending slowly by the other path. They must have met up there on the hill and what puzzled him was the liveliness of Jenny's motion. An interview with Flora would naturally produce melancholy and though the poor girl might be running home to cry, she did not give him that impression. Her movements were sprightly and, keeping time with them, the lifting and falling of her hands were the gestures of a happy child.

'Pretty, pretty,' he thought with a sigh and he watched his wife's ungainly approach.

She was astonished to find him sitting there on a hard seat, and displeased. 'What are you doing here?' she asked.

'It's a fine day, my dear,' he replied.

She glanced about her to verify his statement. 'But it doesn't look well for you to be sitting there, like a man out of work.'

'Too fat,' he said, 'I'm glad you've been having a little walk. Pleasant up there, I expect. Tide in?'

'I didn't notice.'

'Remarkable!' he said softly.

'Not at all. I had other things to think about. Norman,' he rose and tripped on beside her, 'I want you to talk to Reginald about the holiday. He doesn't seem very anxious for it, at present, but if he thought you wanted it, I believe he'd go at once.'

'But I don't want it.'

'What has that to do with it?' she said. 'I'm thinking of Reginald.'

'So am I, Flora. I'm thinking that he's a man of sense and character, not a child in leading strings.' He opened the gate for her. 'We shall soon be having the snowdrops up,' he said. 'There's nothing extraordinary about Reginald,' he went on. 'I've seen dozens of men like him. He's an English speciality. Pleasant, quiet, does his job well, says very little about it, but,' Mr. Doubleday turned his key in the lock and let his wife pass into the house, 'but,' he said again, smiling cheerfully, 'he's the very devil to drive on a road he doesn't want to take.'

She had no reproach for language which indeed seemed to her quite suitable, she waited while he hung up his hat and coat and she followed him into the study. 'Then,' she said, meekly enough, 'what are we to do?'

'Stay at home, stay at home,' he said. 'We're very comfortable here.'

She despised him for his blind ignorance, but she had to have help and, most reluctantly, she realized that he might know more about Reginald than she did, and she looked at this plump, rosy, lazy man and felt a small absurd fear of him.

'I've never had any trouble with Reginald before,' she muttered. Then her sorrow became vocal, her face distorted. 'We've been like one person, always,' she said, 'and now it's all spoilt. He won't do anything I ask him!'

'Why should he?'

'Because I'm his mother!' she cried.

Mr. Doubleday, now seated in his chair, tapping the finger tips of one hand against those of the other, pitying her stupidity, thought the time had come for clearer description of her difficulties. 'What, exactly, have you asked him to do?'

'I didn't ask him anything,' she said hurriedly, defiantly, 'until I'd made sure about the mother and about the girl herself. It's worse than I thought. That man she's married always in and out of the house and the girls left to do as they liked. And this little one went off with the lodger! Yes, she's been living with him in the country and back she comes when she tires of him and tries to settle herself, like her sister. And even Mrs. Sproat behaved very badly with the man who married one of the Dakin girls. Miss Jewel herself saw him kissing her through the window.'

'H'm, not a very satisfactory kind of kiss, I should think. However, I know what you mean. And do I understand,' he said suavely, 'that you have been interrogating Miss Jewel about these girls, a nasty, malicious old woman like that?'

'She's one of your own parishioners! She's a good, Christian woman!'

'I'm afraid she is,' Mr. Doubleday said, drily. 'You've behaved in a very undignified manner, to say the best of it, and you know you don't believe half the woman said.'

'And half is more than enough,' she ejaculated.

He shook his head. 'But you want to believe it. You are not pitiful. You haven't a kind heart, Flora. And if we are not kind-hearted at our age, we're in a sad case, a sad case.'

Through Mrs. Doubleday's seething, silent indignation, those words came with a familiar sound and as, like Jenny on the hill, she bent her head to catch the echo, she saw Miss Fairweather sailing down The Avenue, a witch on a broomstick. And Reginald had said 'Your heart?' doubting its existence. She thought of the weekly sewing meetings, the Christmas treats, the ceaseless, dutiful labours of a lifetime. It seemed to her that everybody was in a conspiracy against her.

'I've spent my life for other people,' she protested. 'I've lived to make Reginald happy!'

'Yes, in your way, it had to be your way.'

'Because it's the right way. Do you want him to marry into a family like that?'

Privately, Mr. Doubleday thought it would be very nice and comfortable for Reginald. There had been a time when his wife had talked often and much about her distinguished relatives, and always with reproach for his mediocrity and condescension for his humbler origin; he was glad to know that Reginald would be spared that

320

discomfort, but before he could frame a reply, Mrs. Doubleday made one for him.

'Of course you wouldn't! Well, I've done my best and I shall go on doing it. I spoke to the girl this morning.'

'Did you? That was helpful, Flora.'

'Helpful?'

'Yes, to Reginald. Yes, my dear, if she tells him what you said, he'll ask her to marry him at once. Bound to,' he said, tapping his fingers again. 'Bound to.'

'She'll be afraid to tell him. I made sure of that.'

'Threats?' Mr. Doubleday inquired.

'Reginald shall know all I know if she continues to run after him.'

'But she runs so nicely,' Mr. Doubleday said in gentle, appreciative tones. 'I saw her coming down the hill. Very nicely. I think you've left that out of your calculations, my dear.'

CHAPTER XLI

In the Vicarage the period of feminine ascendancy was coming to an end. For some little time it had been insecure and Mrs. Doubleday had been uneasy, but she had not foreseen the day when Norman would address her admonishingly, frankly, without embarrassment or the stave of a tune. Perhaps, under her anger, bewilderment and sense of general disruption, there was a secret satisfaction that the man she had been despising ever since she married him should dare to upbraid her and reveal an independence of thought which might be translated into action.

There was no secret about Mr. Doubleday's satisfaction, though he did not let her see it. His victory was not complete, but he knew it would be. The poor woman had not the ghost of a chance in this contest and because he really had the kind heart indispensable to the middle-aged, it was a comfort to know that his cruelty was necessary. He could not have enjoyed it, he would have had scruples about this self-indulgence, without the excuse Reginald's cause had given him.

In the thin slice of a house occupied by the Sproats, something of the same kind was going on, though the emotions creating it and resulting from it were very different. Since his outburst on Christmas Eve, Cecil had preserved an attitude towards Dahlia which almost amounted to indifference. No behaviour could have suited the situation better, but it was not calculated; it came of weariness and pride, successors to mental conflict and disappointment. He was not jubilant, like Mr. Doubleday, but he would have been very dull if gradually he had not become aware that he had stumbled on the right technique for the occasion. He saw that Dahlia watched him as once he had watched her and he was careful to sustain a manner which affected the whole atmosphere of the house. Jenny became a little wary of invading the study at odd hours and though Dahlia rushed about the house and wielded brooms and dusters with her usual energy, she did not talk so much and she was less inclined to laugh. She was not sure whether she were being punished or simply neglected because she was not wanted. It was strange not to feel Cecil's eyes on her when she was near him, to get no response to the little tricks of voice and manner which had always moved him and it at once became imperative that he should want her still, and natural that she should observe him with new attention and appreciation. She must not let him form a habit of doing without her; she had always known she could not spare him for very long, but it was plain that she could not have him on terms of her own making. She was glad of that. Mrs. Doubleday might see capitulation to Norman's views as a long-deferred justification of her marriage, but Dahlia was in search of happiness, and, unless she delayed too much, it was here, waiting for her, in the house, not with the perfection youth expects, but of the quality she had seen in Cecil from the first. And, in her mind, she went very cautiously, testing her approaches. This was not so much like a game as like a dance, like a minuet, gracious and witty whatever the secret troubles of the dancers, and she must learn the steps before her limbs were too stiff to let her down easily in a curtsy, and her partner wearied of waiting for her. Born in her, less evident than in Jenny but just as strong, was a feeling for beauty and seemliness which took the place for her of a moral code. Technical unfaithfulness to Cecil would not have afflicted her as a sin, if it afflicted

323

her at all, but in retrospect, as she grew older, she would have seen it as a false step in the dance, misleading and confusing other dancers. Her father's failure in marriage, her mother's affair with Thomas Grimshaw had been such errors, making difficulties for their children who, with good fortune added to their natural taste and skill, had the chance now of winding through the intricacies of life with grace and dignity and they must take it.

A direct statement or question about their feelings was very rare between these sisters, but Jenny was constrained at last to remark on the changed feeling in the house.

'You are different and so is Cecil. Well, I've written to Miss Headley.'

'Why must you always think everything has something to do with you?'

'I don't. But it seemed a good chance to tell you.'

'She won't get your letter for ages. She'll be away for the holidays.'

'I know, but I've written.'

The answer, Dahlia divined, was not of immediate importance, but Jenny was protecting herself at all points and Dahlia, knowing that her possible wishes and Cecil's had not much influenced her, said ingenuously, 'You mustn't think we want you to go. And have you kept Aunt Isabel's address?'

'Are you going to write to her?'

'Certainly not, but it might be useful.'

'Not to me!' Jenny cried.

'There you are again,' Dahlia said, but she knew very well what Jenny meant. She did not wish to reveal her possession of desirable relatives, and the precautions she took were for her own dignity, not for her advantage. But Dahlia, who had not been told of the interview with Mrs. Doubleday on the hill, for pride and a tendency to weep had soon overcome Jenny's mirth, might if necessary be able to do for her what she would not do for herself and discomfort Mrs. Doubleday at the same time.

She looked at the card Aunt Isabel had given Jenny in a sentimental moment, and she said, 'I wish she had a title', and wondered why Jenny looked rather sly, made ready to speak and then thought better of it. 'But I think it's what people call a very good address.'

Had Mrs. Doubleday forgotten about the living in the uncle's gift? And had she ever believed in it?

Mrs. Doubleday remembered it very well and she was preparing herself not only to believe in it but to advertise it, for she had reached the stage where, though determined to fight bitterly until the last moment, she had to plan the face she would show her neighbours in the probable case of surrender. She was no longer anxious to prove Dahlia's mendacity or to see Lady Catherine de Burgh as a fiction or the haughty patroness of this troublesome family and she wished she had not spoken of Dahlia in derogatory terms to Mrs. Tothill; she searched her memory for hints of dissatisfaction dropped to other people and, as though a tooth were being dragged from her head, she prepared to reverse her judgment about the manners of these girls, to admit that even the bishop might have been deceived by them. But all these plans, regrets and decisions were in a conveniently fluid condition; with a turn of fortune, they could be tipped away like waste water, and, as the days passed, she began to be hopeful, so tremulously hopeful that she did not try to discover where Reginald passed the hours for which she could not account, and as it did not occur to her that he could have any doubt about his fate and fear to risk a question, she could at will and with almost equal pleasure, decide cn Jenny's timely discretion or Reginald's lack of serious intentions.

The Christmas treats were over, two weeks of the new

year had passed before Reginald, with becoming seriousness, told his parents of his betrothal. To be out of the
range of his wife's eyes, Mr. Doubleday pushed back his
chair and with a series of double nods he approved his
son's choice and applauded his gravity. Marriage was a
serious thing, it could be a very serious thing, he thought,
glancing at his wife's ominously stiff figure, and he disliked the modern young person's light and jocular way of
announcing decisions of this kind. He was proud of his son
and he held out a plump hand and wished him happiness.

'Now, Flora!' he said remindfully, but with indulgence
for the mother whose claims had been superseded and who
now seemed to be turned to stone. He would give her
every chance to behave kindly and keep the day unspoilt
for Reginald but, in the unforgiving part of his mind, he
hoped a sudden miracle of generosity would not rob him of
his opportunity to tell her a few home truths.

He need have had no fear. Such a change of front
demanded a greater suppleness than hers.

'You'll have to get her mother's consent,' were her first
words and they were surprisingly cheerful.

'Yes, I've done that already,' Reginald said, looking at
his nails with interest.

'And she's given it, of course.'

'She didn't withhold it.'

'I should think not! Oh!' Mrs. Doubleday's cry was
piteous. 'To think that my son should ask anything of
that woman! You've been misled! You've been trapped!
If you'd seen her first, you wouldn't have made your offer!
It's no wonder you don't look happy!'

'Oh, my poor Flora,' Mr. Doubleday said and he shook
a warning finger at Reginald. He did not want the boy to
quarrel with his mother; that was his own task.

'It's all right,' Reginald said aloud and reassuringly.
He was not going to lose his temper. 'I should like you to

know that I met Mrs. Grimshaw before Christmas. I was taken to see her,' he said with emphasis.

'Excellent,' said Mr. Doubleday, nodding again. 'Excellent. I like that.'

'Very clever!' said Mrs. Doubleday. 'But did the girl tell you anything about her mother?'

'Why should she? I didn't tell her anything about mine.'

The outrageousness of being coupled with that woman stupefied her for a moment and when she recovered she was in the possession of a new thought. 'Ah, but the girl talked to you about me!' She turned to her husband. 'You were quite right,' she said and this was perhaps the first time he had received a word of praise from her. 'Why didn't you warn me before I spoke to her?'

'Why didn't you ask my advice?'

'Because I knew what it would be,' she replied with bitter inconsistency. 'You are always against me. And I'm too frank, too straightforward, I say what I think, and I couldn't imagine she would have the effrontery to repeat it.'

'No, my dear, you can't imagine anything that's likely to happen, only the things that haven't happened and won't.'

'Perhaps', Reginald said, with studied politeness, 'you will tell me what you are talking about.'

'Better not, better not,' said the vicar, but Mrs. Doubleday said loudly, 'You're not going to tell me she didn't repeat every word I said to her?'

Reginald smiled for the first time. There was pity for his mother and pride of Jenny in his expression. 'She is very fastidious,' he said quietly.

Once more Mr. Doubleday nodded, but he doubted whether Flora were not too stupid to take in the full meaning of that remark. Finesse, he decided, was merely wasted on her.

'Yes,' she said, 'much too fastidious to tell you about that young man she should have married. Should!' she laughed at her own moderation. 'She is married to him already in the sight of God!'

Mr. Doubleday had to postpone his pleasure in this remark, often heard from less orthodox lips, until a more leisurely occasion, for now Reginald had risen, he was very white, he was telling his mother he would not hear another word and, looking about him wearily, he said, 'How ugly all this is'. He addressed his father. 'I could have told you a week ago. We've been engaged for a week.'

'Ashamed to tell your mother,' Mrs. Doubleday mourned.

'Don't be silly, Flora. He wanted to enjoy his happiness. Quite right, quite right. He knew you would do your best to spoil it for him.'

'Well,' she called after Reginald as he went. 'I shan't receive her. You can tell her from me that I shan't receive her.'

A sympathetic ear could have heard in these words the last defiant cry of the vanquished who would become, who almost wished to become amenable under persuasion, but no such ear was at her command.

'This will interest the parish,' Mr. Doubleday said, after a long silence.

She raised her head. 'You know,' she said indignantly, 'that I shall try to keep up appearances – for your sake.'

'No. You've never done anything for my sake. You are a conscientious woman, Flora, when your feelings are not involved, and a hard worker, but don't deceive yourself into thinking you've been doing it for me. You've tried to prevent other people from sharing your opinion of me as a fool, but that was for your own sake. But it's you who are stupid. Yes,' he said slowly, 'you are a very

328

stupid woman. You've lost a husband, oh yes, my dear, some time ago. Not a very good one, I admit, but very ready for friendship and for a long time unwilling to admit that his marriage had been a great misfortune. Yes, a great misfortune, except for Reginald. Reginald was worth it, though I never claimed my fair share of him. Whether that was kindness or cowardice, I'm not quite sure. A little of both, perhaps. He was your son, so you thought, but whose son is he now? No, I won't be interrupted. You've handed him over to me, Flora, because he's in love with a charming, pretty young thing you ought to be thankful to have for a daughter. And, for your consolation, well connected, too, on the father's side. He married beneath him, as they call it, and so did you, not quite so far, perhaps, but I think you'll agree that it was definitely beneath. I've ascertained that the father of these girls comes of a better family than you do, in spite of the bishop and the other fellows. Mrs. Sproat . . .'

'Oh,' said Mrs. Doubleday, recovering some of her spirit, 'if your authority is Mrs. Sproat! Of course she's in the conspiracy.'

'I think,' Mr. Doubleday said, mildly, 'you put a higher value on Reginald's worldly position than they do. He has been engaged for a week, and I rather suspected it. I'm pretty observant, pretty observant, so I made my little investigations and proved the truth of them a few days ago. I didn't doubt Mrs. Sproat for a moment, but I knew you would.'

'Oh,' she said, 'you needn't have bothered. I heard of those Herefordshire people long ago. It's the moral aspect – and I heard of Lady de Burgh, too. I'm sure they took care to tell you about her. This girl of Reginald's says she lives in Kent.'

'Ah!' said Mr. Doubleday. He covered his mouth with his hands, he blinked in rapid thought. 'Ah!'

329

There were times, even now, when he neglected his detective novels and turned with relief to a literature which had some of its delight for him in the knowledge that his wife would not understand it if she tried to read it. And that little girl had taken her small, mischievous revenge. But there was need for care here, for Reginald's sake and hers.

'What else did you hear about her?' he asked.

'Not much,' Mrs. Doubleday said cautiously, sadly, knowing that things were now beyond her keeping.

'Then say nothing yourself,' Mr. Doubleday advised seriously. 'From what I know of her – No, Flora, don't introduce her into your conversation as a valuable acquaintance. However,' he went on, 'I don't think you'll have the opportunity.' There was a tramping to and fro above their heads and he pointed to the ceiling. He sighed. 'I believe Reginald is doing what I've often longed to do myself. He's packing his bag and leaving you. Yes, you have been very foolish. Do you think he will stay here and listen to your insults? And you are stubborn, you are just fighting for the sake of fighting. That's a bad habit, Flora.'

'I'm not,' she stammered. 'I'm not.'

Then, he leaned forward and patted her shoulder. 'Go and make your peace with him. Quick, before he leaves the house.'

He was really sorry for her now when he saw the difficult tears on her cheeks, and his resentment had gone with the expression of it. The fortress had been taken and he had nothing but mercy for the vanquished.

'You mustn't stay here and cry for him. Go upstairs and make sure of him for ever.'

'I'm not crying for Reginald,' Mrs. Doubleday sobbed. 'I'm crying because you want to leave me.'

He rose and, behind her back, he lifted his eyebrows

330

in comical dismay. He patted her shoulder again and let his hand rest on it. 'Not now,' he said, 'not now. That's all over. Just go up and cry on Reginald and you'll find you are perfectly happy, perfectly happy.'

He dropped into his chair feeling exhausted and rather old. The victory was complete but it was all for Reginald; it came too late to be of any other value.

CHAPTER XLII

DAHLIA stood at the study window and watched a little procession going across The Green for luncheon at the Vicarage, Mr. Doubleday bouncing lightly ahead. with Reginald, Mrs. Doubleday marching behind with Jenny. The men, with everything settled to their satisfaction, would not dwell, except with pleasure, on the situation; the women, much more foreseeing about details, were probably anticipating little vexations and disadvantages and difficulties.

'The baby elephant looks quite frolicsome,' Dahlia said, 'but even the pleasantest camel can't help looking indignant. Didn't I tell you Master Doubleday might be very important? And I was always afraid I might get fond of her, and I shall, if she's good to Jenny. Poor thing! Her smiles were very stiff, but you could see what they were meant to be. And she kissed me! I don't think that was necessary and it wasn't very nice, but she was doing her best for everybody. She kissed me, Cecil,' she turned to him as he sat at his desk, 'just here.' She indicated the spot and brought her face close to his, but he took a very casual glance at it.

'And the vicar? Did he kiss you, too?'

'No, but he wished he could and some day I shall let him, for a treat. Just imagine having no one to kiss except Mrs. Doubleday, all these years! I do hope he loved some one else before he married her. I hope he has a secret he likes to remember. Aren't you interested?' she inquired when there was no response.

'Yes, very much,' he said, but his interest was not for the vicar's improbable romance; it was all for this girl

332

who had missed her own and he did not know how to give it to her. As though her whole body had gone slack, she leaned against the window and the bright hair seemed too vivid, now, for the tired young face.

'Well,' she said, and he was able to guess some of the thoughts leading to her next words and the comparison she was making between her lot and Jenny's, 'well, I have a nicer mother-in-law than she has and I think you have, too.'

'Much nicer,' he agreed sincerely, but without the heartiness which might have sounded false.

'And both Jenny and I,' she went on, 'are rather like what our grandmothers must have been. We just get married. There was nothing else for them to do, nothing else for us. It was the right career for them; with us it's a sort of accident.'

'A makeshift,' he suggested.

'No, not that. I mean if we'd chosen to be doctors or nurses or schoolmistresses we should have been very serious about it because we'd chosen, not just happened on it. We shouldn't have expected it to be perfect. It's so easy to forget that marriage can be a career, too. I didn't think of it like that and I don't suppose Jenny does, but she'll be better than I am, she'll do all the things nobody would expect.'

'But then,' he said, 'she happens to be in love with Master Doubleday.'

'Yes, but loving's more important,' she said slowly.

He saw the quick beating of her eyelids and he asked himself whether these words were offered to him in avowal, in an invitation like the face brought close to his to show him the spot Mrs. Doubleday had kissed, but he was not in the mood to accept her long-deferred invitations, he was not altogether trustful of them. Moreover he would not resign the ascendancy he had gained, he would not wait for her pleasure; he would do without her or choose his own moment and, feeling very masculine and amused by his new assumption that men and women were essentially primitive, yet believing that it did actually fit this case, he decided to make Dahlia's words applicable only to Jenny.

'Doesn't she love him, then?' he asked.

'I don't suppose she knows. She can't tell yet. That's one of the tricks they play on you, that's why it has to be a career, not just the happiness you think it will be, or the unhappiness it may turn out. I suppose,' she said, her eyes grave, her mouth smiling, 'you wouldn't like to change into a missionary and go and convert the savages who live nearest to Master Doubleday?'

'No, I would not. I'm much more likely to turn into your greengrocer.'

'That would be nice for me, but not much use to her.'

He grunted and turned to the papers on his desk. She was ready to sacrifice him and herself to the savages for Jenny's sake, she was forgetting the obligations of her own career in this preoccupation with Jenny's and, still absorbed in it, she continued uttering her thoughts.

'But perhaps she won't need me,' she said sadly. 'She'll be very competent and devoted and unselfish, but I like her as she is. I believe she'll soon be able to look at Mrs. Doubleday's feet without remembering to feel ill. There's nothing more I can do for her. I feel rather lost. But,' she said, brightening a little, 'she will have children, lots, I expect, and they'll have to be left at home and I can take care of them.'

'No you can't,' he said. He was very matter-of-fact, gathering papers together, snapping rubber bands round the little bundles. 'You'll have your own to look after.'

Dahlia stepped back a few paces. 'Shall I?' she said in a

334

meek, puzzled tone, and as though only half his mind was on his answer, he said 'Yes'.

Like Mr. Doubleday, he had decided to storm his fortress. He was tired of waiting to see what she would do, he would not waste any time in parleying, and he found it was not necessary to fire a single shot. An ultimatum framed in words entirely free from sentiment and delivered at exactly the right moment had done the work for him. With her retreat and her question, Dahlia seemed to come running down from her place on the battlements and open the gates to him, and the instinct which had inspired him to this easy victory instructed him to refrain from a tender word or a caress.

'Come along,' he said, 'let's go out. It's a kind of holiday. Where shall we go?'

'For a walk in the country. Shall we – shall we go to the Monks' Pool again, to see if it's still there?'

'No, I don't think I want a walk in the country.' He knew he would kiss her in the first field. 'Let's go and buy something. Let's go and buy you a hat. Or a trinket.'

'A trinket!' The old-fashioned word from him who never thought of hats and trinkets, who had not known that women like them even when they do not want them, made her laugh rather tremulously.

He looked at the plain band on her finger. 'I'll get you a ring.'

'Oh,' she cried, 'you know we haven't any money for rings!'

'We'll go to the bank first and take out all we've got and then we'll have lunch somewhere and then we'll get the ring. Master Doubleday will get one for Jenny. Why shouldn't you have one? It's the day for a ring.'

'But . . .' Dahlia began. She had lost faith in herself, she was afraid to cheat him, afraid to believe in the permanence of this sudden happiness. 'There's such a long life before us,' she said. 'And I'm so stupid. It must not be counted as a sacred promise. How do I know what's going to happen?'

'We don't know. At this moment I don't care. You may fall in love with someone else hereafter, but I don't think you will, and so may I, but I don't think I could. We are in love with each other to-day,' he made the statement boldly, disdaining to look for its effect, 'and we're not concerned with the future. Let's throw that wedding ring into the river and get another one.'

Gravely, she gave him the ring and went upstairs to put on her hat.

Also of interest

THE LOVE CHILD
by Edith Olivier
New Introduction by Hermione Lee

At thirty-two, her mother dead, Agatha Bodenham finds herself quite alone. She summons back to life the only friend she ever knew, Clarissa, the dream companion of her childhood. At first Clarissa comes by night, and then by day, gathering substance in the warmth of Agatha's obsessive love until it seems that others too can see her. See, but not touch, for Agatha has made her love child for herself. No man may approach this creature of perfect beauty, and if he does, she who summoned her can spirit her away...

Edith Olivier (1879?-1948) was one of the youngest of a clergyman's family of ten children. Despite early ambitions to become an actress, she led a conventional life within twenty miles of her childhood home, the Rectory at Wilton, Wiltshire. But she wrote five highly original novels as well as works of non-fiction, and her 'circle' included Rex Whistler (who illustrated her books), David Cecil, Siegfried Sassoon and Osbert Sitwell. *The Love Child* (1927) was her first novel, acknowledged as a minor masterpiece: a perfectly imagined fable and a moving and perceptive portrayal of unfulfilled maternal love.

"This is wonderful..." — *Cecil Beaton*

"*The Love Child* seems to me to stand in a category of its own creating...the image it leaves is that of a tranquil star" — *Anne Douglas Sedgwick*

"Flawless — the best 'first' book I have ever read...perfect" — *Sir Henry Newbolt*

"A masterpiece of its kind" — *Lord David Cecil*

THE SHUTTER OF SNOW

by Emily Holmes Coleman
New Introduction by Carmen Callil and Mary Siepmann

After the birth of her child Marthe Gail spends two months
in an insane asylum with the fixed idea that she is God.
Marthe, something between Ophelia, Emily Dickinson
and Lucille Ball, transports us into that strange country of
terror and ecstasy we call madness. In this twilit country
the doctors, nurses, the other inmates and the mad vision of
her insane mind are revealed with piercing insight and
with immense verbal facility.

Emily Coleman (1899-1974) was born in California and, like
Marthe, went mad after the birth of her son in 1924. Witty,
eccentric and ebullient, she lived in Paris in the 1920s as
one of the *transition* writers, close friend of Peggy
Guggenheim and Djuna Barnes (who said Emily would be
marvellous company slightly stunned). In the 1930s she
lived in London (in the French, the Wheatsheaf, the
Fitzroy), where her friends numbered Dylan Thomas, T.S.
Eliot, Humphrey Jennings and George Barker. Emily
Coleman wrote poetry throughout her life — and this one
beautiful, poignant novel (first published in 1930), which
though constantly misunderstood, has always had a
passionate body of admirers — Edwin Muir, David
Gascoyne and Antonia White to name a few.

"A very striking triumph of imagination and technique...
The book is not only quite unique; it is also a work of
genuine literary inspiration" — *Edwin Muir*

"A work which has stirred me deeply...compelling" —
Harold Nicolson

"An extraordinary, visionary book, written out of those
edges where madness and poetry meet" — *Fay Weldon*

PLAGUED BY THE NIGHTINGALE

by Kay Boyle

New preface by the author

When the American girl Bridget marries the Frenchman Nicolas, she goes to live with his wealthy family in their Breton village. This close-knit family love each other to the exclusion of the outside world. But it is a love that festers, for the family is tainted with an inherited bone disease and Bridget discovers, as she faces the Old World with the courage of the New, that plague can also infect the soul...

Kay Boyle was born in Minnesota in 1902. The first of her three marriages was to a Frenchman and she moved to Paris in the 1920s where, as one of that legendary group of American expatriates and contributor to *transition*, she knew Joyce, Pound, Hemingway, the Fitzgeralds, Djuna Barnes and Gertrude Stein: a world she recorded in *Being Geniuses Together*. After a spell living in the bizarre commune run by Isadora Duncan's brother, she returned to America in 1941 where she still lives. A distinguished novelist, poet and short-story writer, she was acclaimed by Katherine Anne Porter for her "fighting spirit, freshness of feeling." *Plagued by the Nightingale* was first published in 1931. In subtle, rich and varied prose Kay Boyle echoes Henry James in a novel at once lyrical, delicate and shocking.

"A series of brilliant, light-laden pictures, lucid, delightful; highly original" — *Observer*

"In delicate, satirical vignettes Miss Boyle has enshrined a French middle-class family...The lines of the picture have an incisiveness and a bloom which suggest silverpoint"— *Guardian*

VIRAGO MODERN CLASSICS

The first Virago Modern Classic, *Frost in May* by Antonia White, was published in 1978. It launched a list dedicated to the celebration of women writers and to the rediscovery and reprinting of their works. Its aim was, and is, to demonstrate the existence of a female tradition in fiction which is both enriching and enjoyable. The Leavisite notion of the 'Great Tradition', and the narrow, academic definition of a 'classic', has meant the neglect of a large number of interesting secondary works of fiction. In calling the series 'Modern Classics' we do not necessarily mean 'great' — although this is often the case. Published with new critical and biographical introductions, books are chosen for many reasons: sometimes for their importance in literary history; sometimes because they illuminate particular aspects of womens' lives, both personal and public. They may be classics of comedy or storytelling; their interest can be historical, feminist, political or literary.

Initially the Virago Modern Classics concentrated on English novels and short stories published in the early decades of this century. As the series has grown it has broadened to include works of fiction from different centuries, different countries, cultures and literary traditions. In 1984 the Victorian Classics were launched; there are separate lists of Irish, Scottish, European, American, Australian and other English speaking countries; there are books written by Black women, by Catholic and Jewish women, and a few relevant novels by men. There is, too, a companion series of Non-Fiction Classics constituting biography, autobiography, travel, journalism, essays, poetry, letters and diaries.

By the end of 1986 over 250 titles will have been published in these two series, many of which have been suggested by our readers.